HARVEST IN TRANSLATION

I AM SNOWING

PAVEL KOHOUT

I AM SNOWING

The Confessions of a Woman of Prague

TRANSLATED BY NEIL BERMEL

A HARVEST BOOK
HARCOURT BRACE & COMPANY
SAN DIEGO NEW YORK LONDON

Library of Congress Cataloging-in-Publication Data
Kohout, Pavel.
[Sněžím. English]
I am snowing: the confessions of a woman of Prague/Pavel Kohout;
translated by Neil Bermel.—1st Harvest ed.
p. cm.—(Harvest in translation) (Harvest book)
Originally published: New York: Farrar, Straus, Giroux, 1994.
ISBN 0-15-600187-X
I. Bermel, Neil. II. Title. III. Series.
PG5038.K64S6413 1995
891.86'35—dc20 95-11761

Printed in the United States of America
First Harvest edition 1995
A B C D E

veritas vincit!
veritas vincit!
veritas vincit!
veritas vincit!
veritas vincit!
veritas vincit!
veritas vincit!
veritas vincit!
veritas vincit!
vincit veritas?

I AM SNOWING

1

MEA culpa. Mea maxima culpa!

But why so dignified? I'm an idiot—an idiot squared!

Except, except . . . could I really have anticipated this? When I began tremulously to explain to my Gábina over her fifteenth-birthday cake that she would soon start to bleed (I, the untutored child of timid Catholics and unfortunately the most mature in my class, had been at one point despairingly sure that I had sustained severe internal injuries), she informed me almost indignantly with a stolid bullish expression that she wasn't even a virgin any more.

This young guy stood over six feet tall and looked like the type who could satisfy a choosy woman. I had occasionally seen him in our company cafeteria (you couldn't overlook him) and with time I felt a pleasant flutter that meant he was well aware of me. It had certainly never occurred to me even in my dreams to get mixed up with a man a generation younger than me. When I spotted him on the riverboat (our firm had put the money allocated under the old regime for parade placards and banners toward this first-of-May excursion), out of nowhere I suddenly imagined how pleasant it would be if he embraced me. Immediately I was appalled at myself (a bit early for a first young buck!), so I turned my back to him and threw myself determinedly into a conversation with my colleagues from the classifieds. After two glasses of wine they were no less tedious, but more intrusive; my breasts again became the target of their tortured compliments. (For work I always laced them up tight, like a Prussian cavalry officer; for the boat ride I'd put on a relatively snug sweater.)

I was momentarily diverted by a crack at the expense of our lead correspondent. He had also flown to my side, unmistakably attracted by the "beacon of my bosom" (to quote Olin, formerly an outlawed sculptor, now an administrator or dean or something), but at least he tried to mask his lust in a civilized fashion with accounts of his journalistic activity, which had brought him the reputation of a Communist-hunter and brought the paper increased circulation. Except he bragged shamelessly, which irritated me.

"How long have you been working here?" I asked innocently.

"Seven years." He fell guilelessly into my trap.

"Shame you didn't write about this stuff earlier; till two years ago they had it pretty easy here."

"But . . . that just wasn't possible."

"Well, of course; now everything's allowed!"

He quickly threw back half a glass so he could head over to the bar. On the lee side of the captain's bridge I later undertook a task that could no longer be postponed: explaining to the deadly boring but likable editor of the personals column (the only one of all the official Catholics in the firm who went to church even before the revolution) that the main thing preventing me from accepting his offer of marriage was the existence of Julien. (My fictitious French fiancé from Amiens helped me to defend and cloak my privacy; his last name, Sorel, I revealed exclusively to suitors who I was sure had not read Stendhal.)

Later, when the little Vltava riverboat was turning around beyond the Vranovský floodgate and garlands of colored light bulbs flared up overhead in the dusk, I was bitten by remorse. It was the first of May—the time for love, as the poet Mácha said—but even today, after a month of silence, Viktor still hadn't called. According to popular belief, therefore, my next amorous kiss wouldn't come till the following May.

I returned to the buffet for another glass of wine. It made me long for a smoke, so I had to have a bit more to drink, to equalize the levels of alcohol and nicotine (otherwise, I'd face either a headache or heartburn). For a while I tolerated the drunken competition between my obese boss and the scrawny director of marketing. Both of them offered me a nightcap afterward in their offices, which were equipped with standard institutional couches (ugh, never again!), before I hypocritically put an end to the farce by reminding them that they were married men and now supposedly Christians, too.

I, who for over a year have been living in mortal sin!

Before we docked, I positioned myself to be the first one off the boat. Once ashore and past the Mánes artists' union building, I slowed down and dawdled wistfully toward the tram through the deserted embankment's evening moisture—as if I couldn't be assaulted immediately in post-revolutionary Prague—until a shadow looming from behind startled me. It was the tall kid, and he sealed my fate: he introduced himself quite civilly (Václav, teacher of something or other), and surmised quite correctly that maybe I'd be up for one last drink in a more congenial setting.

Of course, the little restaurant was far from it. The tablecloths were stained, and even a twenty up front didn't improve the waiter's mood. ("You want to become capitalists here overnight, and laze around like socialists until you die!" to quote Viktor. Oh, my darling, why isn't it you that's here with me? What do I want with this casual little Don Juan? But I do know: freedom. Freedom from you!)

I can't say he bored me; he had a certain amount of class (respected the difference in our ages but didn't play it up), had read and seen things, and even had opinions about them. Then it was my turn to excel: when the conversation turned to modern music, I unabashedly parroted what I half remembered from listening to Gábina and her underground rockers; what the hell! Now these banalities came in handy; the kid was amazed, you could see he was falling for me. Meanwhile, regret turned into my most dangerous mood: spite.

So, fine, my dearest, let it be as you have commanded! I'll cheat on you, and it'll all be over.

In spite of this I paid my share of the bill and ordered a taxi home. O Lord, can't You see that I'm leaving this in Your hands: if this course of events isn't to Your liking, do something to stop him from inviting me home! (On top of everything else, I'm a deplorable coward.) Between the bar door and the taxi he managed to ask quietly if he could invite me to his place—for some coffee and music, of course. He had a couple of incredible records by Joan Baez, whom I so greatly esteem (ha ha). He was a bit nervous during all this, which (in my befogged state) I liked; he respects his elders! I laughed to myself and said, Why not? Everything was hastening toward a historic deed . . .

Despite all my desires (ah, and as the years go by I'm more and more desirous!), I am to this day old-fashioned in my faithfulness. As God is my witness, I only slept with one man at a time, but when he let me down, he lost me altogether—whether it was my handsome young husband, or even you, Viktor . . . Today I'm deceiving someone for the first time, and once again, it's you.

This good-looking adolescent had no inkling of all this. I, too, was flying high: he has to think that for me this is as routine as daily bread. (Next time he says hello in the cafeteria, I'll cut him off. Let him think he dreamed it; he is the chimney sweep who will unwittingly deliver me from cruel love.)

Thanks to the wine, I didn't notice the street, building, floor, or apartment, only his room, which in its decoration and disorder resembled Gábina's (this, too, should have warned me). But I was resolved. He put on the record player (scratching the record in the process), turned off the overhead light (fortunately, he'd forgotten about the coffee), knelt down in front of my chair (in such a way that it would have been impossible not to kiss him), and bumped me on the nose.

I should have recognized my mistake, but it was too late; his awkwardness actually touched me, so I led him along, showing him how one kisses when one wants to. And then he confirmed my first impression when he unerringly found my key—he began gently to stroke my face. Only two of my lovers have ever figured that out by themselves. The rest, for some insane reason, immediately began to fondle me; it never ceases to irritate me.

Right after that came another useless warning, when he asked inappropriately, "May I?" Yes, I said, handicapped by my total loss of judgment. I slipped out of my black top to save us more awkward groping and fumbling, and it even pleased me, in a vain sort of way, to think how astonished he'd be at what he found.

Viktor, my dearest, who so adores the luxuriant terrain of my body:

you could have had it all to yourself, been its sole owner, if only you'd believed me one last time!

After my year of futile faithfulness to Viktor, this little Václav comes out of nowhere; he had a chicken's hairless chest, a slender waist and sides (like a mannequin from a store window). With a minimum of fuss, I drew him to myself. Quickly now, let's get this over with and put an end to my foolishly revived love!

Ow! A burning sensation between my breasts; what, did he bite me? He was in a trance and kept mumbling something, until I understood the sentence he was rhythmically beating into me: "You'll see—you'll still—dump me . . ." The naïveté of his despair revealed the extent of the mess I'd gotten into: I was in the hands of a love-crazed simpleton! And without any warning he reared up and the slender waist between my knees shook wildly. Fear deprived me of my strength; I couldn't pull away in time.

He came to his senses more quickly than I did. In a cold sweat, he let go and took his weight off me, stammering an apology. I was struck dumb. How could this happen to me? In the middle of my cycle! Oh no, oh God, this sort of hocus-pocus can't be what You had in mind. It already happened a couple of times last year and this year, and nothing ever came of it! (I had been concealing my cycle from Viktor in some wild hope.)

In spite of this, I immediately asked the way to the bathroom; the traces of him repulsed me. Crushed, he pointed the way, not daring to accompany me. I grabbed my top and skirt, so as not to return naked. I was shaking with rage and humiliation and at the same time I felt a strange satisfaction, as if something better had triumphed over my disgusting ego. (You deserved it!)

Clearly, no woman had set foot in this bathroom in a long time, but his private life couldn't have interested me less. There was no key in the lock, but I didn't believe he'd dare follow me; I took the towel that seemed cleanest (because it was brown) and got into the tub. In the mirror opposite I saw a pretty sight: just above my breasts was a splendid crimson blotch.

I knew from my wild summer with Josef that this would adorn me for at least two weeks, by turns purple, blue, and greenish-yellow. In my despair I hoped rebelliously that at least Viktor would appear in time to appreciate it. (It might just startle you, darling; you might realize what you're driving me and both of us to!)

The hot water wasn't running; I whipped myself like a flagellant with freezing water from the hand-held shower head, flooding my lap until it lost all feeling from the cold. When the door sprang open behind me I gave that excellent lecturer a lesson he'd long deserved.

"Get out, and fast!"

A gruff voice answered back: "I live here, little lady."

I almost sprayed him with the shower as I turned around. He was older, dark, and hairy, dressed only in boxers, over which a beer belly drooped; his neck was as thick as his head—a newt! I put down the shower head and covered myself with my hands, as much as I could.

"Who are you?"

At that moment I figured it out: the fool had let me promenade around naked in his parents' apartment!

"That's what I'd like to ask you," he said, leering at me with disgust. "And also where Váša gets the money for your type."

I saw red.

"You ought to be ashamed!" my accused lover shot back from the hallway. "Go back to bed!"

He led his father from the bathroom by the elbow. A fight was brewing, and what about me? There was no end to the absurdities. Fatty wilted and disappeared through the nearest door. Fortunately, the kid was dressed and conscious of his fuck-up.

"Please, don't be angry; I've liked you for so long . . ."

He grasped immediately that this was the last thing I was prepared to listen to, and left me to get dressed in solitude. He emerged only later, his eyes like a beaten puppy's.

"Can I go downstairs with you to let you out?"

Idiot! I fumed; you ask about bullshit and forget the important stuff!

"You'll have to," I said, cutting him short.

I didn't wait for him to call the elevator, and strode down the stairs so fast he could barely keep up with me. Before he unlocked the door, he wavered; probably he wanted to continue his repentance, but my furious expression dissuaded him. I went off into the night without saying goodbye, away from this shame! I didn't hear the door close, so he must have been watching. Let him rot there!

Heaven sent me a taxi driver who was heading home to bed in the opposite direction but took pity on me. God forgive me, I prayed as we drove; and you, Viktor, don't break up with me, darling! I repeated this all the way across Prague until I was a bit calmer.

My daughter, of course, was not home; I'd finished the wine yesterday and forgotten my cigarettes in that dive. Of all the possible forms of relief, only two remained: to take a bath and have a good cry. With one leg poised over the steaming tub, and on the verge of tears, I heard the phone ring. I went barefoot, expecting to hear the usual message that my idiotic daughter (why has the man who conceived her lost all interest in her again? why do I have to swallow all of this?) was happily drinking and fucking around somewhere (just like her mother; her father only ever whored around in politics).

"Am I disturbing you?"

Only Viktor asked that (and still did, after all these years).

❄ ❄ ❄

In the not quite three years since she turned fifteen, my daughter has gone through more lovers than I have in two decades, and I consider myself flighty. Not long ago I sat down at home over a glass of wine and counted them up (in and of itself a sign of failure).

The total: I married the first one immediately, divorced soon after on account of the second—my fateful love, from whom I obsessively escaped with various insignificant suitors, until he lost his nerve and emigrated (to escape me) overseas. I almost married one of them out of the indomitable needs of the flesh: he came my way after I'd lost my love, and called me My Final Bell (he was going on fifty-five). One long summer we rampaged like tigers. (Literally: we chased each other around his attic apartment. Josef would jump on me from the couch and I, on the rug, would fend him off with my hands and feet. He had scratches all over, and I couldn't go swimming because of all the bites.) Only that was when Gábina (a hypersensitive kid) obviously needed me most (and for the last time); she wanted me around constantly, but I left her at home with the TV. When I finally introduced her to Josef she decided to hate him as punishment. I took this as divine retribution and left him with a heavy heart. (But also with good reason: I already knew who he was, and didn't believe I could handle it.) I tried to put our shattered family back together, taking on the penitent role of a self-sacrificing mother; those were my best years, when men (at that age all married too long and ripe for their first divorce) courted me and rutted. But I held true to my mission (and to my Christian duty: I'd started to go to the closely watched church and was taking my daughter with me) so well that I only bestowed my favor on three of them (and that mostly out of fear that otherwise I'd soon be past my prime). I was with one a couple of times at his country house, with another twice at a hotel (in Socialist Prague, entailing the risk that they would again try to force me to collaborate with the secret police like some kind of whore), and with the third (even today I blush with shame) in the office on our adjoining desks, tipsy after a party where we had been celebrating (fortunately) his transfer to his native Ostrava. At the height of my "asceticism" I found out that Gábina hadn't been to school for a month.

It was the last time that a classic beating worked, allied with the threat of having my work-loathing daughter stuck in a reform school, which she knew "they" were capable of doing. She quickly figured out, the little beast (wily like her daddy), that nothing could threaten her as long as I kept signing her excuses. And I did, of course; what else could I do? The first time she didn't come home until morning, I let her have it good. With that, she vanished for the weekend, and when she deigned to return, I kissed her again and again, insane with happiness. (I must have been a shocking sight, my face distorted beyond recognition after hours of crying; she didn't stop roaming, but most of the time she at least called to wake me up and inform me, through the throbbing of bass guitars and the din of voices, that she was still alive.)

Alone and empty, I didn't say no to the lifeguard from Podolí, where I made daily pilgrimages one summer after work. He was naturally masculine, not unintelligent, the same age as me, and also divorced. Because his little cabin at the pool was squalid, and because his mother supposedly eavesdropped on him at home, I started taking him to our place early on; Gábina, enamored of some underground rock drummer at the time, hadn't turned up at all in a while. (All of Prague seemed to be a single huge underground, which was nonetheless content to leave the Communists at the helm.)

Jarek brought me back to life; he was quite skillful with me and one night I even had to scream, when suddenly there was a light and in the doorway my daughter saying "Mommy, what's wrong?" while her eyes popped out at Jarek's bare backside. Then this guy with no high school degree or upbringing turned to her: "She's quite alive, kid, you can go back to sleep." She didn't bug me about him; she even respected him, only it was too late. That fall the Bolshevik house of cards finally came crashing down even here, and in the spring Viktor Král came back; Viktor, whose surname means King, my True and Last King . . .

I expected his call from the November day when the revolution broke. In a flash I realized that I had been and always would remain his, and that it was the devil himself who had led me into temptation to spoil that which was purest in me. At once I knew with perfect certainty that this time he would find absolute security with me. I am Petra, I repeated to myself like a madwoman before going to sleep, and that means rock! Jarek sent me sad letters (to no avail; they sounded trite) and my unsuspecting Gábina announced with disbelief that I was a monster who didn't know how to respect love. Then Viktor appeared—but not until May!

First I asked my daughter not to come back for the night, and let her believe that she was helping me effect a reconciliation with Jarek. I hadn't thought of Viktor since he left; after the first shock, I'd suppressed all thoughts of him to preserve my own sanity. And all of a sudden here was this all-encompassing relationship spanning half a lifetime, nearly twenty years! (The ten years apart had metamorphosed into the tale of Odysseus and Penelope . . .)

I fixed his favorite stuffed eggs and bought two bottles of spiced wine, which we used to like so much, but no sooner had we wet our lips than we began obsessively recalling the past, which seemed to us like an endless holiday. (Do you remember? Do you ever think about it? Guess what else?) In barely an hour we covered the same path we'd traveled during our first years of acquaintance, and once again fell in love. All the bitterness was behind us; we found ourselves at the beginning, just as unaware, eager, agitated, and astonished as before, and just like then we journeyed from shame to affection, from affection to longing, and onwards to a passion that I had approached only with Josef.

This time, however, I was in love, and my exalted thoughts carried me past a boundary previously undiscovered.

I soon should have realized that it was also the boundary at which giddy happiness ends and limitless torment begins.

Viktor, my eternal loved one, couldn't hide the fact that our weightless nighttime flight had shaken him. It was not I but he, a Christian only on paper, who over morning coffee looked like the prisoner of mortal sin. He was pale and his voice faltered as he described to me (unemotionally, as if he were explaining the basics of monetary policy to his students) how after each of my provocative flights he had been more and more desperate (and up until Olin I can't even remember what any of their names were), until he could see no means of salvation other than emigration. In his first months in Canada he was tormented most by the knowledge that he would never see me again; for several years he wouldn't sleep with anyone (while not long after he left I had consoled myself with a friend of his, who turned out to be . . . better to forget about it). Until in his first year as a professor a young Slovak girl (ah! a passionate people!) enrolled in his lecture course, the daughter of Jewish doctors from Bratislava (ah! that illustrious race!) who left after 1968. After a short courtship he married her. (Was she that beautiful, smart, and gracious? Don't ask: 'tis better to dream false hopes than recognize horrid certainty . . . with apologies to Erben.) But they decided to wait to start a family until she'd finished her studies (while lazy me dropped out of correspondence school), so their daughter is only a year old (and I never gave you a son).

Upon hearing this I should, of course, have sent him packing, except in my sorrow I couldn't think of anything better to do than let the coffee grow cold, kneel in front of him, take both my encumbrances—which, like before, he couldn't kiss enough that night (as if maybe his wife didn't excel in this department?)—out of my nightgown

(I'd gotten dressed for breakfast) and lay them on his palms, like before. Immediately he blushed (I'd forgotten how light used to bother him, and the morning sun was shining into the room), but the offer was more powerful than his shame. He leaned toward me and laid his face on my heart, like old times, and clung to me like a child, I have no idea whether for a minute or an hour. At some point we began to make love again, and by the end we were both crying from delight, love, perfect happiness.

We parted in confusion; he forgot to give me his address or telephone number, we didn't make any plans, but it was clear that he would call me that day or the next, at the latest. After three days I was shattered by the realization that, true to his nature, he would not throw his new life to the wind but would remain a Canadian, a professor, a husband, and a father, and would never again be mine.

He called a month later, by which time I'd decided he must already be back overseas, asked as always if he was disturbing me or keeping me from something, and how I was doing. I wanted to scream, as I'd done years before, I'm freezing over! (We'd always conveyed emotions to each other by means of images that expressed them more closely than hackneyed formulas.) But unfortunately this was now, my dearest had a youthful, passionate (certainly) beauty, whom on top of everything else he adored (definitely) because she had borne him the Queen of Jews and Christians—and therefore, with my heart pounding, I said fine, thank you for asking. He was alone for a change, he informed me breathlessly; could he come by? (With any other suitor I would have slammed down the receiver.) But of course! he was told (Gábina had left a scribbled message that she'd gone somewhere with someone and would be back at some point), and in my agitation I set about changing the freshly changed sheets.

When, as always, he gave two short rings on the doorbell, my knees began to shake; in my confusion I offered him my hand (as one did before our common era) and I trimmed the three roses he'd brought in the kitchen so he wouldn't see my hands trembling. Would he like a coffee, I called out (my normal voice failed me); yes, he would. I managed to calm myself down, and in a while the spoons were tinkling in my old mugs. (Announcing what? Resurrection or burial?)

My beloved sat across from me in the small armchair, just like years ago: curly-haired and clean-shaven, with a hint of cologne, indistinguishable from the young student my handsome husband had smirkingly introduced me to. ("This is Vít'a, my astral twin, except unlike me he's seriousness itself!"—No, unfortunately, he wasn't lying; it's the reason I kept taking offense and fleeing from Viktor, and why now I'm madly in love with him.) I milled about randomly to avoid the devastating message that shone from those eyes so completely incapable of deception: that he adored his wife and her offspring and deeply regretted if he had given me the slightest false hope, last time, that we could revive what had long since died.

"Petra," I heard when I finally caught the thread of what he was saying, "I love you. I think of you constantly. I miss you so much that I'm losing my judgment and self-control. Even when I'm with her!"

In four sentences he opened heaven and hell before me. Once again, as befitted his temperament and profession, he painstakingly mapped out the space that was left for me. His wife had suffered through difficult times with him; it was unthinkable that he repay her by ignominiously abandoning her or publicly humiliating her with an extramarital affair. Besides—and I was the first to hear this, since Vanesa (oh, even her name is prettier, and they have the same first initial!) was still in their Bratislava apartment, which lacked a phone (thus I learned the reason for both the long wait and for this brief happy moment)—today he'd been appointed economic adviser to the vice-chairman of the government.

"But only, of course, if in spite of everything, you stay with me, Petra; otherwise I'm going back!"

In this way my sweetheart announced to me, along with his declaration of love, that he would not stop having conjugal relations with his lawfully wedded spouse, and what's more, would only have time for me once in a blue moon—but I was in seventh heaven. He loves me! He'll stay with me! I am the rock that moved a mountain, and if I patiently bear the humiliation of a secret relationship I will be paid back in full, because each time he rests his head on my heart he will be a little bit more mine, until . . .

If he was so bold as to want me when he could offer me so little, he continued agitatedly, I would have to help him. Oh darling, gladly, anything! He couldn't bear the thought that I might be hanging about waiting for him. He would give me absolute freedom and would never ask me about it: he thought it was the only possible solution. Petra, try to understand (sweetheart, I'd understand you even if you were speaking Portuguese!); I at least want to try to keep some equilibrium in our lives (your wish is my command and my penance).

After this implicit vow of unfaithfulness we made love fantastically until morning, and for three days afterward his presence rang and shone in me, until it hit me that he was certainly back with her by now. (My consolation: if he thinks of me when he's with her, like he said, he can't truly love her. My doubt: does it really work that way?) That's how the tortuous merry-go-round of heaven-hell-paradise began. After each fulfillment: emptiness, an agonizing longing growing for two, three, even an unendurable four weeks when he wouldn't call. But each time he came back he made love to me all the more ardently.

Alongside my amorous conflict a political one was also brewing. The country was swarming with innumerable doughty foes of Communism (which they had, until recently, lived off so adeptly), and because it had already been defeated, they were waging a surrogate war (mainly against the former dissidents, and mostly for the right to keep loafing and stealing). Gábina could forget about school; since the student strike never ended (her anarchistic slogans hid the fact that she was as lazy as a sloth), no one cared—except for me, who had to support her. But it was the only way to keep her in sight; she had a whole collection of lovers (if you could call them that) but still not a speck of common sense. (I watched her like a hawk so that at least she wouldn't take drugs.)

Viktor's name was seen more and more often in the papers; they appealed to him and cursed him as one of the apostles of privatization. He crisscrossed the republic by car and Europe by plane. (A ritual developed from this, at least: on the way from the airport he'd call and stop by, every time with a beautiful present and often for a quick embrace.) I took comfort in the fact (and was ashamed of it) that he didn't even have time to warm himself by the family hearth. From my moronic job at the classified ads, which I'd intended to jettison after the revolution but whose survival I now prayed for (the reforms were cutting out excess posts everywhere; where would I go?), I would rush home in case he called (I wasn't allowed to call him) so that at least thirteen out of fourteen evenings I would rummage through the house, washing and ironing everything I could find (mostly Gábina's dirty laundry) or watch hour upon hour of TV that was different than under the Bolsheviks but just as moronic. As time went on I opened my poetry notebook less and less, and solitary bottles of wine more and more.

Because his last visit at the end of March lasted an unbelievable sixty hours (from Friday evening to Monday morning: Gábina was fortunately off again somewhere with someone, and I was too proud to ask him the reason for this miracle), and because he was easygoing and happy in a way I'd never seen before, it occurred to me that maybe he had finally understood what we were depriving ourselves of when we weren't together. Leaving my house straight for the office (what a shock to see my naked lover turn into a gentleman in a double-breasted suit and bow tie), he caught me in the hallway as I was checking the stairwell through the peephole, his hands in the sleeves of my nightgown, and whispered despairingly, Soon!

My disappointment was all the worse thereafter. That young buck named Václav was supposed to drown it out and destroy my unbearable dependence. And I now wanted to cleanse myself of that, although it was past midnight and the rumble of the water was making the flaps in the air vent shudder when Viktor called—first time ever at night!

"Or am I keeping you?" he said, posing his second customary question.

"No"—to my surprise I was speaking quite normally—"I was just about to take a bath."

"I've been calling all evening, every fifteen minutes." Bitterness seized my throat. You're too late for the funeral; my horrid evening could have been our holiday! "Petra, are you there?"

"Yes . . ."

"I couldn't hear you."

"I didn't say anything."

From the telephone in the hall I surveyed, bedraggled, the tableau of a bungled life: from the bathroom the washing machine and ironing board greeted me; from the kitchen, the stove; from my room, my lonely bed. He must have sensed it; he sounded forlorn.

"Is something wrong?"

I couldn't muster the strength to play the heroine, and my raging spite gave way to self-pity.

"I'm raining a bit." He knew across the gulf of years what that meant.

"Oh, please don't! I'll come over, okay?" He astounded me.

"Now? Are you alone?"

"No, but that's no matter." What was up? "The car's right out front. Can you come down in twenty minutes and let me in?"

"But . . ."

"I have to talk to you. So stop raining now, okay? See you!"

I was left holding the receiver, and in the mirror under the coatrack I caught a glimpse of a well-proportioned nude with a blood-red splotch and a befuddled expression. Must I endure in the course of a single hour a cheap trick and a marriage proposal? What else could it mean when he calls in the middle of the night from home? Did he tell her about us? Did she realize that she didn't have a prayer and let him go? Or (since Slovak women know how to rage and Jewish women how to punish) did she set his suitcase outside the door?

I wanted to take a lightning-quick bath, scour myself of the feeling that there was someone else's sweat clinging to me, put on fresh underwear. (Throw the old pair in the garbage!) When I tried to get into the tub for the second time the phone rang again. I was dismayed. She wouldn't let him go? She threatened to jump out the window with the kid? (Slovak Jews must have a touch of hysteria!) To see or not to see? Better not! He won't leave me waiting out on the street, at least he'll come. What if he needs to tell me something?

I picked up the receiver and heard Boom! Boom! Boom! (my own heartbeat) before a voice came on.

"Mommyyyy . . . Mommyyy!"

Only after a couple of seconds did I recognize this howling as my daughter's voice.

"Gabby! Gábina! Is that you?"

"Mommyyy!" she wailed heart-wrenchingly, as I hadn't heard her do since her last childhood tantrum; ever since, she had just contemptuously clenched her teeth.

"Yes, Gabby, it's me, what's going on? What happened?"

The only answer was a howl. I pictured her curled up by a broken telephone (like in a recent made-for-TV film), a knife in her chest.

"Where are you? What's wrong? For God's sake, speak to me!"

"Ibe . . . ayyyyp . . ."

"You're what? I can't understand you! Calm down, you have to tell me where to go and what you need. An ambulance? Are you hurt?"

"Nooo . . . I've been raaaaped."

"Christ Almighty! Who . . . where . . ."

Suddenly, no doubt realizing my despair and powerlessness, she began to talk more coherently than I; she described comprehensibly where she was. Her weeping ended in snuffling, and the conversation ended in the confused explanation that some taxi driver had driven off, and she'd run as far as the main road. Not understanding a shred of it, I left the bath to its own devices, put back on those undergarments laden with the stench of fornication (God, did I really enrage You so?), and flew downstairs to the street (thank You for sending him in Your mercy; that proves that You haven't deserted me entirely!), which of course was empty and deserted. I gave him five minutes before I would set out on foot. I could probably flag someone down. He arrived exactly on time.

"Quick!" I squeezed in next to him. "They raped my Gábina; she's somewhere along Na Petřinách in a telephone booth!"

He didn't ask questions, just took off, offered me a strangely thin cigarette from the glove compartment (had to be his wife's, he never smoked, but I couldn't have cared less), pushed in the cigarette lighter, and repeated (like my father used to do), "Everything will be all right, you'll see!" And, systematically disregarding all traffic laws (him!), he careened like a race car driver through the fortunately deserted city.

Darling, darling, I said to myself in the moments when my fear abated; now he was, as I had always dreamed, Gábina's father and my husband.

❄ ❄ ❄

The long, wide avenue lined with prefab high rises looked, under the fluorescent streetlamps, like a post-apocalyptic scenario from Bradbury's *Martian Chronicles*. There were three telephone booths next to the department store, but they were empty. I began to tremble and couldn't do anything, but Viktor got out and found her immediately. She was cowering on the floor of the middle one, her head resting limply on her shoulder. I flew out of the car.

"Wait . . ." He held me back, before I myself started to howl like a wounded she-wolf. "She's sleeping."

My little lamb wasn't disheveled or bedraggled, as I'd expected her to be (the influence of films and literature); a childlike expression had settled on her face, which always disarmed me, encouraging the false impression that she was still my little girl. Viktor woke her very gently, but this still brought on her usual morning crankiness.

"Not yeeeet . . ."

Then she started, and pressed herself against me like . . . when had she last done so? Two years ago, when her father first didn't show up to celebrate Christmas with her (he had always come a day early anyway, so he could spend the real holiday with his new kids; now even those few moments irritated their mother, and he wanted to keep the peace, my once-courageous husband), she had hugged me like this next to the Christmas tree. I'm melting, I sang in my soul, but already she was telling me she was off to a friend's house; she was sure I'd rather listen to Ryba's Christmas Mass in peace.

"It's only Viktor," I said, trying to insinuate him into her confidences (I almost added, "my Viktor"). "Viktor Král, Víťa, remember?"

There was a lot to remember: the way he accompanied me with the baby carriage around Struhy and around Stromovka Park in place of her father (an assiduous devotee of Marx, for the sake of his future career) until there, under the chestnut tree during an April shower, I dared to kiss him (she glared at us balefully with her not-quite-one-year-old eyes, as if it went against her sense of decency). She was even there when I (a godless adulteress, whose lawful spouse was tarrying unawares at his parents' in Pardubice) seduced my sweetheart at our house. Yes! He himself (even today a more tepid Catholic than I was at the time) would never in his life have coveted his friend's wife—nor would I have coveted my husband's friend, if his suicidal plunge for that drowning cur hadn't kindled my warm sympathy into a burning love. Then for another six years my little girl (just raped!) slept, fortunately soundly, within earshot of our embraces, our breakups (I was always the one to raise hell when I couldn't bear his righteous reprimands), and our reconciliations, which led me inexorably to further flights, rousing him to anger and anguish, so he would once again love me more than his work. When, without warning, he punished me by emigrating (like an idiot, I had been arrogantly sure I was his Mount Everest), I started going out to my lovers' places for consolation (the bell had tolled for true love), so as not to despoil my newly flowering virgin (and in this way I lost her).

Astonishingly typical! I realized, on that Martian street when Viktor woke her in that filthy telephone booth, that we hadn't spoken of him in ten years. The unexpected blow had hit me with such force that I'd pushed him out of my memory, and hidden his return from my daughter, which in the given circumstances wasn't even really a return.

"Will you need to see a doctor?" he asked her when we were seated in back of him. (Why was he using the formal "you"?) "I have a friend who's a doctor."

"No," she decided with that innate practicality that stunned me every time. "He didn't do anything else to me."

Not even a trace of the fact that half an hour before she'd been bawling like a baby. A wild beast awoke in me, demanding the worst possible punishment for the violator of my daughter.

"Do you know who it was?"

"Yeah, some Gypsy."

"And where did you . . . did he . . ."

"In the taxi."

"And the driver didn't protect you?"

"Well, it was him. That Gypsy."

"Gábina, please try to explain things clearly so we can figure out what to do . . ."

She cast a glance at Viktor and said bluntly, "When we get home, okay?"

"I told you, Viktor's my"—careful!—"our old friend; that's why I asked him to drive me."

She looked him over as if she were x-raying him; he seemed to interest her more than her fleeing rapist. I knew those glances of hers, with which she marked people once and for life; one of them cost me Josef, and I wanted to prevent something similar here.

"He was in Canada for a long time, became a professor of economics there, and is working here as an adviser to the government."

It was his question, though, that got through to her first.

"You probably don't want to report it, do you?"

"No way."

I couldn't understand them. "They'll find that Gypsy driver at once!"

"Given the current state of the police and press in this country," he explained to me, "it is not impossible that they'd release her name, even though she's a minor. And if she goes to testify against that jerk in court, his whole family could come in and smear her. She ought to sleep on it and try to figure out tomorrow what she was doing with a guy she barely knew."

I was bristling all over, but the victim said appreciatively, "Good idea."

I had to be satisfied with the fact that she continued to let herself be hugged. (For a long time now she'd wriggled out of my grasp like a snake when my maternal tenderness got the better of me.) On the way back all three of us were silent, and it occurred to me that the male gender had sown its wild oats in both of us, mother and daughter, at the same time. And if I, seasoned as I was, reacted that way, wouldn't she be scarred for life? In my arms the tiny child whom I raised myself (poorly or not, from first pee through the complete collection of childhood illnesses up to puberty) lay dozing, and the thought of an unknown boy ripping cruelly into her horrified me.

In a couple of minutes we were in Bubeneč; I had to wake Gábina, but she said goodbye to him without a trace of surliness.

"Thanks!" she even said, which I almost never heard from her.

"See you!" I managed to add, "and I'm sorry."

The bathwater was still hot (my senses must have been dulled before; the two calls saved me from a scalding). I placed my darling Gabriela in it and lathered her with a washcloth just like I used to. She let herself enjoy this as well. Of course during it I looked her over for signs of violence, but there wasn't a single bruise (or even a hickey). Her eyes were closed; she'd always bathed that way, ever since she was a child (like her father when he was young; he had breakfast, read, and studied for his state exams in the tub, occasionally pulling me in fully dressed, one of his inspired little gags).

It had been a long time since I'd had a chance to look her over so thoroughly. My little child was turning into a woman: her chest had almost my curve to it ("Rodin's curve," to quote Olin), which must have been what drove that beanpole crazy tonight. Oh, my little girl, just don't turn out like me . . . no! How could she? From above the surface of the water an exact copy of her father's face gazed out at me: a man still successful even under the new regime, in which he convincingly pretended that he, too, was a (violated!) victim of the previous one. (But wait, wait a minute: where had that inherited craftiness of hers been tonight?)

"Gábina, are you sleeping?"

"No."

"Then tell me what happened!"

"I told you already."

"Oh, come on, is getting raped just like a trip to the store for you?" (The comparison, surprisingly enough, hit the mark.)

"No, but . . . it's painful."

"I'm your mother!"

"Whaddya want me to tell you? Me and Mikan took a taxi and he got out first, that's all."

Mikan, no doubt originally Milan or Michael, was her most recent find, as she called them, the son of architects and prior to the revolution an architecture student. At the moment he was a black marketeer ("I'm paying them back for stealing the revolution from us!"), but I believed in the lasting effects of a good pedigree.

"He let you go by yourself?"

"He lives in Motol, Mom. It was on the way."

"He certainly has the money to swing by Bubeneč first!"

"Why waste it?"

"Why? Maybe so you wouldn't get raped? My God!"

"You don't usually get raped in a taxi, you know."

"Jesus Christ"—I was so far gone that I was taking the Lord's name in vain in nearly every sentence—"what do you think just happened to you?"

"It never happened before to any girls I know, all right?"

"It should have been enough that there was a Gypsy driving. According to the statistics, it's mostly Gypsies who attack people in Prague!"

"But it's not taxi drivers."

"You know very well that there's such a thing as putting yourself at risk. A girl shouldn't be alone these days in a car with a Gypsy, even if he is a taxi driver; don't you at least realize that now?"

"Since when are you such a racist, Mom?"

"I'm not! That's just what the statistics say!"

"I don't even really know if he was a Gypsy."

"Mary, Mother of God, you were the one who said he was!"

"Well, he looked like one, but he could've been from Yugoslavia or something."

"Fine, it doesn't matter, how did it happen?"

"Well, he cut across Strahov Park, said he could save me fifty, 'cause Mikan gave me a hundred, see? And we were having this really excellent conversation."

"About what?" (I was looking for the key to this monstrosity.)

"About the new clubs. He was saying there's this amazing disco in some tent over at Bílá Hora, why don't we check it out?"

"And you . . ."

"Said why not."

"Were you out of your mind?"

"Mom, he was a normal guy! Anyway, before that Mikan got all out of joint at some guy and out of nowhere calls a cab home, so I was bumming, see?"

"Go on, what happened at the club?"

"It was closed. So he says, no prob, we'll go somewhere else! So he goes a little way farther and suddenly we're on some road above Košíře which just ends in this hillside in the bushes, and I say, 'Man, you're some cabbie, don't even know your way around.' " (I noticed she used the familiar form of "you.")

"Sounds like you were being pretty friendly."

"I told you, he was young, twenty-five max"—just like my little biter!—"and he was talking the same way to me."

"Go on!"

"Well, so he says, 'Who told you I don't know my way around? This is my dance club, and it's always open.' Then he puts on a tape and goes, 'C'mon, let's get on the dance floor.' "

"There was a dance floor there?"

"He meant the back seat. So he grabs my elbow, his fingers were strong, like a vise, so I go, 'C'mon, man, don't freak out, I won't take this,' and he goes, 'Yeah, you will, you'll see, I always get good reviews, maybe you shouldn't freak out or it might hurt instead.' So I crawled back there and he came after me."

"Why didn't you run away?"

"He was pretty clever; says, 'It's a safe bet you're underage,' and grins, 'and these here are childproof locks,' and then he, well . . ."

"How did he . . ." My question stuck in my throat, but then I managed to spit it out. "How did he undress you?"

"Well, he just pulled up my skirt and I took my slip off myself, it's this new one"—she pointed next to the tub—"he woulda just ripped it up."

"Did he hurt you?"

"No, but I was scared stiff he was some kinda weirdo, so I shut up, and he just wanted to make an impression, see, so he came right away."

I blurted out the question that had been torturing me the whole time.

"Were you careful, at least?"

"Like how?"

"I mean . . ." God, how do you say it? "Did he at least have protection?"

The eyes of my young husband looked out at me with a mixture of compassion and scorn.

"You haven't ever been raped, see?" I must have been pale; I felt my hands go cold as ice, and I saw an unusual fear in her eyes. "What's wrong, Mommy?"

"What if something happens, Gabby?"

"Like what?"

I was getting paid back for my cowardice in leaving the sexual education of my only daughter to—to whom? That's the question; I lacked not only the most basic vocabulary but, most important, her trust. Kneeling by the bathtub, I finally understood that I no longer had a child.

"At seventeen you surely know," I babbled, "that an incident like this can have consequences!"

"Yeah, that's why I've been on the pill for a while now."

At that moment it hit me: but I haven't!

2

THE telephone woke me.

From two onward, after I put Gábina to bed (she fell instantly into a sleep usually reserved for the just—but, after all, she had been, or could have been, an example for me of truthful morality and healthy reason), I tried in vain to escape my conscience. As awake as if it were noon, I wrote a couple of despairing verses in my diary ("Three blows / to the drum / of my soul / struck me dumb / O Master Timpanist / don't strike again / The fourth would be / the end") and then once again took stock of my life.

I couldn't find a single bright spot. Youth on its last legs, marriage long since buried (the one thing I don't regret), my daughter a cipher, talents neglected, diligence turned to apathy, job a hopeless mess (shamefully low pay and spiritual masturbation), and my sweetheart ("May, when the turtledove gives voice to love . . ." to quote Mácha) leaves me to the mercies of little boys and their bodily fluids in order to have time for his sacrosanct family . . . Wait! What could he have wanted from me at this time of night? I pulled him into our family maelstrom and sent him off with a "See you!" as thanks!

By daybreak I had thought over the half dozen possible reasons, from the most ideal, which had occurred to me after his call ("She knows everything; I'm coming back to you for good!"), to the catastrophic ("She knows everything; we must say farewell forever"). I wrote off getting any sleep and after two coffees the mixture of anxiety and exhaustion lifted me steadily into a state of weightlessness. Everything ran together; I knew with certainty only that I was not going to work that day.

I couldn't leave Gábina alone; maybe after this experience we'd find a common language and prevent a breach (which would be a cue for old age to descend on me). I didn't intend to risk running into my little Boy Scout lover until I'd figured out how to act: send him a withering glance (to extinguish his desire to get closer) or just overlook him like part of the scenery? Most of all, I wanted to stay by the phone—wary Viktor never called me at the classifieds, and it would certainly occur to him that I would remain at home with my daughter.

My boss didn't even dare suggest that I count today as a vacation day; he apparently decided that I was punishing him for his objectionable familiarity on the riverboat, and preferred it to another lecture on Catholic morals. He magnanimously announced that, after all, I usually arrived at work before him and left after him. (He had no idea that I was trying to offset inflationary pressures by writing my poetry and reading in the light and warmth of the office when Gábina was away.) Finally (on the third try since midnight), I crawled into the tub and immediately fell asleep.

This time the phone probably saved me from drowning.

Gábina's acquaintances slept in the morning; my few relatives knew that I was at work. It had to be him calling. I didn't think to dry myself off, leaving a watery trail and drenching the receiver.

"Yes?"

"Hello," said a woman's voice, "Is Mrs. Tarantová there, please?"

"You mean Miss Tarantová," I said. (I had long since abandoned my husband's wonderful name to my successor, who insisted on her right to it. Gábina had kept it in revenge: "Let my stepmom fume!") My heart sank at the thought (a reflex from the totalitarian era) that my little lazybones was finally being hounded for social parasitism.

"No, I mean her mother."

"That's me, but that's not my name."

"Is this Petra?" What an odd accent!

"Yes, who's calling?" Aha; she's speaking Slovak!

"This is Mrs. Králová." No! It's her! The First and Last Vanesa! "I'm the wife of Professor Král, you know, Viktor Král?" I know, but I don't know what you know and have no inkling what you want to know, so I have no idea what to say to you! But she didn't wait for an answer. "My husband urgently needed to talk to you yesterday, but he said you had other matters to attend to. This morning I realized he wouldn't dare try again, so I thought I'd try myself."

I looked around dully at the stain growing on the runner under my feet, saw the same sight in the mirror as when he'd called yesterday: bathtub, washing machine, untouched bed: is it all the same dream, isn't it over yet?

"Are you still there?" she asked, just like him.

"Yes."

"I didn't hear you."

"I didn't . . ." I tore myself out of that familiar routine. "I'm listening."

"I know it's unusual for someone you don't know to bother you like this, but this is such a serious matter, I'm sure you'll understand. I'm calling without Viktor's knowledge and I'd like to meet with you."

And here it is! She's going to appeal to me not to take away her husband and the papa of her little Lady Kunhuta (I never wanted to know the kid's name). You yourself know best of all, she'll say (assuming he filled her in on what happened to Gábina last night) what it will lead to . . .

"I won't keep you more than half an hour," she said earnestly, as if she were selling me life insurance. "Believe me, a lot depends on this; I know you and he used to be very close . . ."

The form of the verb (past tense, habitual) broke the spell that had sapped me of my strength; torpor gave way to resolution at the thought of her proposed meeting. Fine, if you want, I'll show you why I used to be close to him, and why I am and will be, until I decide otherwise of my own free will! It was almost eight-thirty, Gábina wouldn't be up before noon; I needed a good hour to rise like the phoenix from my own ashes.

"I can be at the Café Slavia at ten-thirty."

I resolved to make my entrance noticeably late, so she would experience how half the men would turn to watch me (a further sign of my degeneracy).

"Maybe we could meet somewhere in a park?" Before I could insist, she changed her mind. "Actually, why not? So where is it?" Doesn't she know Prague at all? However, she cut my explanation short. "I see, got it. How will we recognize each other?"

You'll know me, I felt like saying, because I'll hang his scalp from my belt!

"I'll be wearing a crimson sweater," I said, and deliberately didn't ask how I'd recognize her.

He had brought it back from London for me that winter, so thick and coarsely woven that it almost stood by itself on the table. "Yes," he said, "it reminded me of armor; I wanted to protect your jewels for myself!" He spoke so romantically, then caressed them so tenderly—while outside the taxi meter was ticking away to take him back to his wife. I was left alone with the sweater, and couldn't think of anything better to do than to slip that prickliness on over my naked body like a hair shirt and promise him—while he was undoubtedly at that very moment giving his wife a present (and a hug)—the eternal faithfulness that would finally bring him back for good.

Except, except: promises, promises; words, words, words. I didn't meet the laughable test of time, and now here I was, setting off in this ineffectual plate mail for a meeting with the wife of its freshly betrayed donor, so I could . . .

So I could what?

But, of course: so I could return him to the womb of his family, from which I had untimely ripped him. My brief torment would be allayed by the blissful knowledge that I had found the strength to wrestle with mortal sin and thus with the devil himself. At last the gates would open, the gates through which I had desired to pass as long as I could remember—except that the highest earthly powers had slammed them shut shortly before my birth. (Get thee to a nunnery, Ophelia! I will get myself thence, but I will not go crazy; quite the opposite, it will be my salvation . . .)

Those pious and useful orders, whose veins were drained so deeply, are once again open; they're waiting for new blood, and mine is still quite fresh. I've loved Christ since I was little, before Viktor and even before my handsome young husband. I wrote my first poem to Him: "O Virgin Mary, / Christ's love has snared me. / O Virgin blessed, / Let Him say yes! / Let the Lord of my life / Take me as His wife! /

O Father, once we're wed, / Let Christ take me in His bed . . ." It's high time I became His bride. To Him I'll be forever faithful, and He will shelter me from this crazy world and bring peace to his confused lamb Petra Márová.

I hung up the phone at peace and deeply satisfied, finished my bath at a relaxed pace, got dressed (I stuck with the provocative sweater; no need to give the impression that I'm some poor soul capitulating to her), and did my hair and makeup (I powdered the ruby-red bite mark, too, although it would stay covered) so that I'd seldom looked better. I strolled to the Hradčanská metro station at a leisurely pace, and then from the Staroměstská station proceeded to the café, where I made my entrance at exactly half past, devoid of both nervousness and ambition. (After my liberating decision, there was no sense in putting on a show.)

Rows of empty tables greeted me; only the booths by the window were taken and Czech was nowhere to be heard: the pensioners and students had been driven from their paradise by the flaming sword of pricing decontrol. (Was this also the work of my . . . was he already my former lover? Yes! He had been my lover only so long as I had remained unreformed.) I crossed the spacious expanse with my best step. ("Those knees straight out, at a slow cadence, make you terrifically sensual," to quote an official poet of the previous regime, who got me as far as a hotel, yuck! But in this instance he may have had a point.) The majority of male heads in the room did in fact obediently turn. Looking straight ahead (I do not seek, I am sought) I headed for the windows that face the river Vltava, intending to sit down, have a cigarette, and wait to see who showed up.

When a woman unexpectedly got up in front of me, I politely slowed down so she could get by, but instead she turned to address me.

"Mrs. Petra?"

Of the women her age sitting there I would never have picked her. My lover had been lured from me by a thin girl with short mouse-brown hair of doubtful quality. My mighty opponent, the specter of my lonely nights when I had jealously pictured Viktor in the embrace of a passionate daughter of Judea, had thick, oversized tortoiseshell glasses, which still didn't conceal the wrinkles around her eyes and mouth (I, more than ten years her senior, have miraculously few). Her whole face looked worn out (most likely she hadn't slept either, but unlike me hadn't managed to get herself all dolled up), which only underscored her casually elegant dress. (And expensive, too, you could see right away; from London or Paris . . .) As she stubbed out her most recent cigarette in the ashtray, she tried to smile at me.

"I still don't know what your last name is; Viktor has only Petra next to your number."

"Márová."

With that I sat down. Her appearance might disappoint; even in this guise she was still dangerous, and I didn't intend to say much to her. A young waiter appeared immediately to take our order.

"That's odd," she remarked (simplemindedness or irony?). "I couldn't get him over here before."

Once again she apologized for bothering me, and once again I let it go without comment. I'd foolishly stirred up the grounds in the coffee the waiter had brought us, so I waited, poised, to see how she'd start out. First she nervously took out another thin cigarette, and when I reached for my own, she offered me one of hers. I demurred, of course, but fortunately didn't refuse a light, and consequently learned that I must not display my lighter. (He had bought us identical ones. It hadn't occurred to him . . .)

"Viktor has very few friends here." Is this a surprise attack from out of nowhere? "I think he never had very many. He's such a closed person"—you should see how he opens up to me!—"but he always spoke of you with great fondness." No? What? "He respected you as a person and as . . ." Well? ". . . a Czech." What is that supposed to mean? "I mean, as they say, your political opinions." What kind of opinions could I have had at the time? The same as everyone else: the Bolsheviks are pigs, but they and the Russians will be here forever. So: fear and steal, let Daddy Masaryk turn over in his grave! "And he's convinced that you knew his sensibilities." Sure: I knew and know everything on him and in him . . . almost, almost! "That's why he was looking for you yesterday and why I want to speak with you now." Hold on: so this isn't about . . . "Mrs. Petra, I was born in Bratislava, but from age four until last year I lived in Vancouver, Canada, which is another planet, a planet with happy children who have never known war or despotism. I have little experience here, but maybe thanks to being a Jew—I'm Jewish, you know?" Yes! That mystical heritage has been giving me an inferiority complex for the past year; at least now it's abated so far as beauty is concerned. Petra, shame on you! "I have a nose for people who aren't okay; they're hiding some kind of guilt or inner turmoil, and cover it with radicalism. Believe me, two things always give them away: nationalism and racism." Did she call me here to lecture me? And why do I take such simpleminded pleasure in her lack of beauty? Doesn't it suggest that there are other wonderful qualities for which he married her? "Vic was always a black sheep among the emigrés." She calls him Vic, my Vít'a. "Ninety-nine out of a hundred of them strut about with a bravado that is proportionally worse the more they collaborated with the regime here, but he kept his objectivity, so much so that he opened himself up to the danger that they'd label him a crypto-Communist. It's lucky that his quiet respectability doesn't come across as weakness but as the opposite, as charisma. He must have been the same before, too, wasn't he?"

She fixed her eyes on me; even the thick glass couldn't disguise the expression I knew so well (but from where?); I didn't have time to think, because she was waiting for an answer. I blurted out an assent against my better judgment, which forbade even the appearance of conversation, especially about him. It encouraged her.

"See! Nobody who knows him would ever accuse him of falseness or lies." Tell me—I've been putting up with this for twenty years. Everything I'd ever done to him was an attempt to introduce him to the temptations of anger and passion, so that he wouldn't tower over me, a sinner, like an apostle, and would let himself be blackmailed. "It's odd that so many people like him, but he's still alone." The lot of saints, my dear woman; in the end they will no doubt crucify him. "Even I didn't catch the fact that he . . . that he wanted to get to know me." I know, I know. Starving little Gabriela had to help me; what did you use to catch him? "For a year he was just Professor Král, so proper that he only spoke English with me, but my illness changed that." A plea for sympathy? "It was nothing serious, I don't even remember what, but it cost me a few months. He noticed my absence, asked around and offered extra help catching up so I wouldn't lose a year. That was his declaration."

The eyes behind her glasses stuck placidly to me, but my distaste for listening to this was growing. In the year since he returned he had said barely ten sentences about Canada, and that was quite enough to be an inexhaustible source of sorrow and jealousy for me in those weeks of waiting. So it's only about the three of us? Has she decided with her innocent expression (oh, of course, it resembles his!) to lay mines in my field of consciousness that would never stop exploding? I couldn't stand it.

"Mrs. Králová"—how you wound me even with your name!—"I made time for you, as you requested, but half an hour is nearly up and I really can't stay. Would you tell me how I can help you?"

She reacted to my churlishness with a humility that put me to shame: nodded, took off her glasses, and wiped her eyes, which I could finally see without the distortion of the lenses. No! Green, like mine! Does my sweetheart think of me whenever he sees her? (Or of her when he looks into mine?) But enough about eyes for now; when will she begin the attack?

"Mrs. Petra, you are truly the only person who can help him with this!" Him? With what? "An unbelievable thing has happened!" What? "They want to do him a terrible injustice!" Who?

Because she was suddenly incapable of words, I gave up on my resolution and put my three questions to her out loud. She shook her head distractedly.

"It's so low . . . horrible! If it happened to me I'd die!"

"Can you explain?"

She stubbed out another cigarette, put her glasses back on, and pulled herself together so decisively that I was further confused. Isn't she the stronger of the pair? Didn't he find in her what he had failed to find in me? I plagued him so he would keep an eye on me; now I'd be so happy just to be his baby-sitter. Too late!

"I'd never be able to. Not in this short a time."

"I can stay a bit longer." She managed to hook me.

"No."

Her wrinkles suddenly didn't look careworn, but uncompromising; this bespectacled bug was no poor little girl! It made my blood boil. I won't be taken for a fool, especially not by her; does she want to play cat and mouse with me before she lashes out with her claws?

"In that case I don't understand why you asked me here!"

She answered as if confirming my senility.

"He wanted to speak to you alone. Last night he wasn't able to and this morning he began to doubt anything would help, but I know you're his only chance. That's why I resolved to talk to you personally: find the time for him! I'm doing this behind his back and don't dare to do more. I beg of you: meet with him!"

Her request so took my breath away that I must have sat there with my mouth hanging wide open. Was this some clever trap, to catch us together in flagrante, or was she asking for help—out of complete ignorance and need—from precisely the person who for a year has been slowly but surely estranging him from her? Instinctively I leaned toward the second version, but felt none the better for it. (The other part of my nature was meanwhile shamefully rejoicing that he must really long for me when he's with her.)

"I still don't understand, but of course I won't say no. So, when?"

"He's conferring all day with American economists and wanted to be home this evening with us." Ah, woe! "He so rarely can be these days"—I wait even longer!—"but this takes precedence; shall we say eight?"

"And where?"

"How about at our place, in Barrandov; we're renting part of a private house. We wouldn't want to disturb you with the little one."

No, never! To see my sweetheart among his loved ones (maybe even sit on the couch where they embrace), brr! She sensed my resistance.

"I know it's far, but considering the nature of the problem, privacy is advisable."

"So, how about my place?" I offered (and felt even more base when, within the limits of her abilities, she beamed radiantly at me).

"If you wouldn't mind, it would be easier that way, but your daughter's sick . . ." No, those eyes couldn't lie; my wonderful sweetheart had concealed Gábina's shame from her.

"Fortunately it was a false alarm. Anyway, she has her own room."

And would unfortunately be home, my poor little victim, so that Mr. Spouse would return virginally pure this time, unless . . . Unless he had thought up a story that would allow us to see each other more often! If that's the case, it's no problem with my daughter, she's been living her own life for a long time. She lived through Jarek the lifeguard's bouncing bare behind; let her find out about the love of my life. He made an impression on her last night; maybe he can stop her slide . . . Except my dear Viktor would die of shame, and most important: he isn't capable of deceit! I stood up.

She jumped to her feet, like a student when the teacher leaves the class.

"I'm so grateful to you!"

"For what?"

"I'm positive you'll help him." Oh, gladly, of course, if he wants help; but if he asks how I am, I'll scream: I'm burning! "Vic told me that you have always been a Catholic, and publicly, too." She gave me her small and unusually cold hand. "For me, there is only one God. I will pray to Him to reward you for your kindness."

I crept down to the metro in the fear that in doing so she would instead call down His righteous wrath.

❄ ❄ ❄

At home, instead of my daughter, I found a scrap of paper.

"Mikan was here, he apologizes to you, too. He invited me to Karlovy Vary for three days. See ya and thx. G."

From this I gathered that she had either kept quiet about her experience the night before or served it up in a more palatable fashion; otherwise I would have to concede that rape has nowhere near the stigma I'd always given it nor the meaning I'd attached to it. In the eyes of her admirer, her value had in any case appreciated; last time he only took her to Karlovy Vary for a day trip. I put it out of my head (what else could I do?) and decided to have lunch. Not that I was hungry or even felt like eating, but out of concern for my body, which I'd given nothing but hell since yesterday. However: the kids had cleaned out the refrigerator. (Her husbands—yes, she'll probably go through more than one—will hang me from the rafters because she won't even know how to shop, cook, wash, or iron, only . . . and she taught herself that.) All that was left was some rancid butter and (why did they leave it?) a stale hunk of bread. I poured myself another coffee, dug into my reserve of cigarettes cleverly hidden in the bookcase (where my little ignoramus never went) and tried to figure out what his wife was up to.

So many people like him! They want to do him a terrible injustice! I couldn't make rhyme or reason of it. Maybe (an idea which cast everything in a different light) she's a bit soft in the head? Bonkers? Blessed with a vivid imagination? It's true, I never asked him about her, but isn't it odd he never mentioned her on his own? (While I scrupulously recounted to him all my adventures under the old regime, just like I'd always done.) It was precisely from that silence that my vision of an Old Testament mistress was born, who in contrast to plebeian me would grant him Pharaonic pleasures. I had understood his unexpectedly and unprecedentedly passionate confession to mark my miraculous ascendance, but I still thought of her as my equal and my rival. Meeting her in person at once contradicted and confirmed it.

I don't often get people wrong. (My problems and losses have always stemmed from people getting me wrong.) I have always been an unerring judge especially of women's character. ("Márová, the barometer of teachers," to quote my grateful fellow students; "Petra, a radar on the boss," to quote my amazed pre-revolutionary colleagues.) I only foundered when it came to my own flesh and blood (the eternal story of youth). Vanesa Králová had disoriented me twice: first, she didn't look at all as I had imagined, and second, after half an hour of intensive surveillance of her, I was none the wiser.

Aside from the fact that she didn't seem Jewish (of course, what do I know about Jews? I respect them as one of the three pillars of Prague culture and condemn all persecution of them, but ascribe to them responsibility for the growing arrogance of the state of Israel) or at all pretty (but what does that prove? that ever since childhood people have praised my beauty; I've gotten used to measuring beauty against myself. For someone else, maybe she'd be beautiful and I'd be a heap of fat pillows . . .), I began to doubt her sensitivity and intellect.

If in fact her (my! so our?) loved one was seriously in danger, she wasn't able reliably to convey her fear to me, from whom she expected vital help. And she had simply failed in her attempt to tell me coherently what she wanted from me; basically (I don't mean to slander her, but why give her more credit than she's due?) she had just prattled senselessly.

Except: why did he marry her?

It was three in the afternoon when I realized that if I kept caffeinating and smoking, this evening he'd find—instead of the exact opposite of his spouse, as I fancied myself—a devastated human wreck. I set the alarm for seven, to give me time to make myself presentable, put one of the pillows over the telephone, covered my head with the other, and fell at last into unconsciousness.

The bell rang twice precisely at eight. My brain had reached full speed again, while my nerves were only now readjusting, so I could welcome him without shaking. (Sleep always gave me a necessary distance: school lessons, ideas for poems, joy and disappointment, everything that was basic I had to sleep on before it could appear in its undistorted form. It worked that way even today.) I had put back on this morning's clothes (my sweetheart liked to see me take off my armor). The morning's elation was gone; I trembled with tenderness and passion, a form of love that only he awakened in me.

As always, he hugged and kissed me, but immediately the routine was broken: he didn't cup my breasts in his palms. This had been the manual switch to the alternating current that, even after his return from Canada, held us in a force field from greeting to farewell; even in sleep we let go of each other only to change sides, so the one in back could again clasp firmly to the one in front. (In those weeks of waiting I had suffered most not from the image of him making passionate love to her, but of how he, as I put it in a despairing couplet, "joined with her in a catamaran / drifts softly sleeping onto morning's sands.")

By not sending this amorous signal he underscored the extraordinary nature of our meeting. He was taking us back (intentionally? unintentionally?) to the past, when we would start from square one to renew our relationship after my most recent escapade. (The astonishing difference was that today I was the steady partner, waiting for the return of the flighty one!) He filled the initial silence (what had caused it?) with questions about Gábina's condition. Meanwhile, I made two coffees (would my heart burst? that's one solution!) and genteelly sat down with him (as when he arrived a year before) in one of the armchairs by the small round table in my room, so I could finally find out what this was about.

"I was shocked that Vanesa spoke with you . . ." He began from out of nowhere.

"Me, too."

"I hope it wasn't too unpleasant for you."

"She said it was important."

"Well, yes, but I was afraid . . ."

"Don't be. She didn't find out anything she didn't already know from you."

My slowly awakening nervous system sought refuge in curtness, which always robbed him of speech. This wasn't desirable right now; I quickly collected myself.

"I figured out it's not about us. But would you please tell me . . ."

"Do you know what the Register of Contacts is?"

The radical change of topic confused me.

"No."

"It's a supposedly unfalsified directory of agents of the former State Security, the StB."

A television broadcast from Parliament sprang to mind. Six weeks before, it had split the country asunder when ten representatives who apparently were listed in the register resolutely and rather convincingly challenged its reliability.

"That's right, I remember."

Both my boss and my colleagues, whose sails always caught the prevailing political winds, had been overcome with emotion and cursed either the accused or the parliamentary commission in charge of the investigation. I was paralyzed by the fact that I alternately believed one side, then the other. None of them voluntarily resigned, and I, funnily enough, thought less about the representatives than about their wives. (Had they known the truth, or were they now experiencing the same sort of schizophrenia? Madness!)

"Well, I'm in it."

"In what?"

"In that guaranteed-to-be-accurate Register of Contacts."

"As what?"

"As an informer. The official term is secret collaborator."

From the time he called yesterday to this very moment, I had never in all my ruminations come even close to this absurd turn of events.

"Are you serious?"

"The investigative commission of the Council of Ministers certainly is."

"And what does . . . What do you . . ."

"They gave me a choice: either clear out quietly within two weeks and go back where I came from, or they'll release my name publicly."

In spite of my thoughts on the subject, I had followed the so-called lustration broadcasts from Parliament, mostly out of curiosity (the television screen reduced the tragedies of real people's lives into a sort of made-for-TV drama). But here was my sweetheart, curly-haired, clean-shaven, but without his usual attractive male musk; he was depressed and in pain.

"But that's . . ." I groped desperately for words . . . "nonsense!"

"Of course it is."

"I mean, you never . . ."

"Of course not."

"So how did you end up in it?"

"After those sadly notorious television lustration sessions, I thought everyone knew that there were two ways into the register: either you really did squeal, or they wrote you in to show their diligence."

"Diligence? What . . . oh, right!" The accused representatives claimed that agents had written in people without their knowledge in order to document their own activity and get further rewards. "That's disgusting!" A surge of anger swept over me. "Know what I would do if I were you? Pack my bags and so long!" Immediately I was struck by horror; I'd just advised him to leave me!

"That's as good as confessing! Everyone who was promised absolute discretion in return for leaving quietly bears the mark of Cain, because someone always makes it his business to spread rumors." He's right! So he'll stay with me . . . "Do you know how my famous university would react? Communist agents scare them more than sharks!"

"So defend yourself!"

"That's what I'm doing."

"What are you doing?" Relief had infused me with strength, which I longed to give him. "You're sitting here at my place? Go write a disclaimer or track down some witnesses or whatever; I don't know!"

"What should I disclaim? That my name was unmistakably entered in an infallible register? But I am looking for witnesses, which is why I'm here."

"Of course I'll testify that you were always against them!"

"Petra, that's childish. No real stool pigeon would ever announce that he was for them; he'd be a dissident, you know that as well as I do." I was stung.

"You mean Olin? Olin wasn't a nark!" (Petra, you idiot, why are you reminding him of the cause of your fall?)

"I'm sorry, I definitely didn't want to talk about that . . ."

Mea culpa; in this case only he could do the forgiving. Olin, Oldřich Luna—formerly a banned sculptor and signatory of the famed Charter 77, momentarily one of the notorious top brass in culture whom the revolution had swept into the Academy of Muses—was the last of those with whom I roused Viktor from his amorous lethargy (I probably also espied in this a patriotic act); my sweetheart didn't wait around for the next one. But what's over is over; we had a different worry now that had nothing to do with me.

"So you're the only one who can help me, Petra."

"Your wife already told me that, but how?"

"The worst thing is that they don't have the burden of proof. 'After all,' they insist, 'we don't make accusations; we only state which names are entered in the register.' Anyone who feels injured by this can lodge a complaint with the Interior Ministry and can even collect damages along with an apology if he can provide reliable proof."

"Like what?"

"The only chance I have is to find the so-called commanding officer who wrote me in and persuade him to admit that I had no idea what was going on."

"And how can I . . ." Before I finished I knew.

"When we were together for the second time after I came back, you honored me with another of your confessions. I've never understood why you brought me each of your lovers on a silver platter . . ."

"Aren't you flattered that you're the only one I've never wanted to deceive?" Vainly I tried to change the topic—which was inevitable—and on top of that I was hiding my real reasons.

"We might have gotten along better without truthfulness like that—it turned each of your escapades into a fateful affair—but that's behind us now; maybe fate wanted it that way. But last time you named one person who confessed to you that he worked for them."

"Josef Beneš . . ." Instinctively I defended myself. "You were the one who introduced us!" (Unfortunately, he'd introduced me to all of them, up to Olin . . .)

"Yes, but as far as I knew he was a business analyst who as my reserve officer helped me get vacation time so I could see you; that's why we came into contact with him."

"He didn't start seeing me until a long time after you left!"

"You said that. And that he was your only serious interest . . ."

"We broke up after he told me!"

"But not because of it, because of Gábina, right? According to you he was an honest man you could have lived with; you said he was trying to change things there."

"Víťa, I was terribly lonely back then, but more than likely I would have come to my senses in time!"

"Wait, listen; we can think what we want about their decency, but now he has the chance to show his. Would you be willing, or better, would you be able to meet with him?"

I was dismayed. I tried to talk him out of it.

"State Security was a full-fledged octopus! What makes you think he can put you on the trail of the person who falsified the register?"

Never before in any of our previous wars (and I had punished him for that odious moral superiority all the more) had he ever raised his voice so irritably.

"You still don't understand! It was him!"

❄ ❄ ❄

For the rest of that crazy evening we went around like a dog chasing its tail; we tried in vain to put together the pieces of a story that each of us in his own way had thought he knew. It always ended with one shocking fact.

A man by the name of Josef Beneš, first Viktor's acquaintance, then our mutual friend, finally my lover and almost my spouse, entered in that notorious Register of Contacts the claim that the economist Viktor Král became a secret collaborator of the State Security (the StB) on December 23, 1980, having previously proved himself as an informant. The lustration commission concluded from this that Víťa had staged his flight abroad to continue his work there as a foreign agent.

When I fully grasped it, I began to shake, until he was so afraid he almost called the doctor. A bit of rum, which I ferreted out from Gábina's night table, took care of it. "If it happened to me," the words echoed in my head, "I'd die." (Who said that? His wife?)

"How did you meet him?" I interrogated him so we could figure out the source of the betrayal. "When did you become close? What did you usually talk about? Did he ask you about anything in particular especially often? Anything that stands out? Did he ever want anything from you? How open were you with each other? Did he sense you wanted to emigrate?"

He searched his memory for precise answers.

"He was the only nice one among the top officers at the training camp. We were both interested in economics. We talked quite openly about what a mess things were here. He didn't know Western theories; he was mainly interested in monetarism . . . I was surprised that a guy like him didn't have a woman; I even figured he was probably gay, since he was one of the few who didn't go after you. This made me like him even more! We never talked about our private lives, neither of us were much into that; except once it must have occurred to him that things weren't going so well for me . . . After Mr. Luna, see? He gave me an odd lecture about the kind of women who were capable of anything when they didn't have enough love." Did he mean his Marie? Does that explain her horrible free-fall? "I had no idea I'd stay there, even when I was getting off the train in Vienna. Only there did it dawn on me that I had to get out before you left me for good."

Oh, my darling, you were right; you fled around the world and back to me, who now lies, reformed, at your feet.

"So now you tell me." He was now the interrogator. "How long after I left did he show up? Did he ever ask about me? Did he know anything about me? Why all of a sudden did he want you, when he hadn't before? Did you feel his interest in you was unusual in any way? Did you ever notice something not quite right about him? How come he accepted the breakup so easily, if it was on account of your daughter? Did he ever show up again? Have you seen each other since? Are you still on good enough terms to move him to tell the truth?"

I, too, tried hard to be precise.

"Not right away, maybe a year later; he was wondering what had happened to you. He heard you were gone, but your institute claimed you had a long-term visiting position. He asked me once, then never again; I thought he was being tactful . . . He said later that he'd wanted me from the start, but that you were his friend. Even so, it took a month; for a long time you were my chastity belt. I know what you're thinking, but I was completely off balance; I wanted only you!" Just like now! ". . . Interest? He was so . . . I've never experienced such concentrated interest. I'm sorry, but those women who are capable of anything carry on that way mostly to make sure their position is secure . . . He didn't seem at all suspicious to me, especially as a man; he had old-fashioned high moral standards, but when he fixed his eyes on you he was anything but gay." Petra, stop! "I'm sorry, I think we need to establish what kind of person he is! We never spoke about work, no one ever did in this country; you said once that he was a business manager, and I was aware of that. He explained his sudden confession about his work by saying that he didn't want to lie to his future wife. That meant more to me than his illusory belief that he could protect the sheep better from inside the wolves' den. When, on top of that, Gabby put up a fuss, it just couldn't go on any longer . . . He still sends one signal: every year in August I get roses; yes, in August, on the anniversary of our breakup . . . I don't know if he still lives where he did, but I know how to find him: through his family. Then I can ask him if he wrote me down, too!"

The idea so enraged me that he had to calm me down again with rum. Princesses have children, too (he was quoting the classics), and StB agents can fall head over heels in love, but I won't do any good if I flat out attack him.

"The absurdity of our times lies in the fact that the victims of government extortion are put through the meat grinder a second time, while the extortionists and the meat merchants open private detective agencies." His anger showed in the way he blew on his face to cool off, just like he did before a climax in lovemaking. "For him—and this, Petra, shows the perfidity of the situation—it makes no difference at all whether he admits his deception or not; it has nothing to do with him. The one hope is that you might awaken in him some better self, and he might want you to remember him kindly!"

By around 12:30 a.m. we'd finished. All the basic facts had been brought up, discussed, and evaluated several times; there was nothing to add. My eyes stung and watered, and only then did I notice that my sweetheart's were red as a rabbit's from my cigarette smoke. (But it's the same for him at home!) When I opened the window, a gray curtain seemed to billow up into the darkened sky. In an uncharacteristic need for fresh air, I leaned out over the windowsill. In all of Winter Street (a phenomenon: the writer Zikmund Winter had retained his street from the Hapsburgs through Beneš, Hitler, and Stalin all the way to Havel, a mark of unimportance rather than quality) only my window was lit; the liberated metropolis still behaved like an occupied village. After what I'd lived through in the last twenty-four hours I could understand why.

It quickly became brutally chilly, and right now I couldn't afford to catch cold. I reached out for the casement windows and at that moment, there was a sound, a movement: I caught sight of a shadow pressed into the entrance alcove of the old apartment building opposite mine. The picture I conjured of two lovers warming themselves reminded me of my daughter, who was no doubt living the high life (pharmaceutically protected) in the once-again world-famous spa town with her Mikan, while I? My usual desolation descended on me, from which I was suddenly roused by the realization that here, two steps behind me and two more from the bed, was my sweetheart!

In my excitement I slammed the window shut rather loudly and nearly pulled off the window shade. I turned around. He was looking at me. (I'm drizzling! I wanted to tell him, but he saw it himself.) I shut off the overhead light, turned on a small, dim lamp (he called it the "lovemaking" lamp; in its glow he'd learned to forget his embarrassment). I knelt down in front of him (my ritual) and placed both his hands on my heart.

"Stop torturing yourself. I'll do what I can. I love you!" Finally he grasped me, so hard that it hurt splendidly.

"And I love you! I love you!" Then he released his grip. "I'm sorry. I can't today."

"Don't worry about it!" I bravely banished my regret.

"Does it bother you?"

"Oh, come on!" Suddenly I was glad that today of all days he wouldn't spot the traces of another man's love on my skin; it was the worst timing imaginable.

"I want you so much and I can't even manage to . . ."

"What are you talking about? I feel as though I've been hit by a sledgehammer, so how must you feel?"

"You're my only love, Petruška!"

He used this nickname sparingly. Tears sprang to my eyes.

"And you're mine."

And you will be mine alone, because only I can cleanse you completely of this filth, even if I have to . . . (What? Well, say it! I will!) . . . kill Josef.

We went silently down the stairs, fingers intertwined, like when I used to see him out (the family friend who was helping me give my daughter a bath) while we were briefly deceiving my absent young husband. (When I confessed to Tarant, he simplified everything with the magnanimous suggestion that we "each go our own way." At this I placed our first suitcases full of his carefully washed and ironed clothes and underwear by the door for him with a light heart.) My body felt weak, like after lovemaking, except that there was no wonderfully liberated soul to rejoice in it. Fear added itself to the tension.

His Japanese car was standing right opposite my building. (Of course: he had permission from his wife.) We kissed tiredly, and he left for Barrandov and for her . . . (Woe is me!) I stared dully after him, when a cough from nearby startled me. Then *he* tottered out from the shadow of the alcove.

"Good evening."

At the intersection ahead the big brake lights of my sweetheart's car were still glowing; although he had the right of way he was still carefully checking the deserted street (must be a Canadian habit), and in front of me, in linen pants and a shirt (he must be freezing!), just the way I'd seen him in the canteen, stood my shameful fresh sin with a hypocritically apologetic expression.

"I can explain . . ."

All the rage I had been suppressing since yesterday, at the rapist, the secret police, their wives, finally found an appropriate target.

"Shame on you! Treating me like a whore and then spying on me like a cop! Just try to come near me again and I'll call the police!"

Like a fury I strode into the house, locked the door, but didn't turn on the hallway light; my legs gave notice they were about to quit, so I plunked down on the bottom step and asked myself where I would find the strength for all this.

3

AGAINST all expectations, I slept like a dead woman. I had exhausted my hopes along with my energy; but having slept on it, I now found my sweetheart's problem solvable, if I could exert the necessary pressure. ("Truth will prevail, but it will be one hell of a job," to quote Jan Masaryk, son of our first president.) Once again I called my boss to take the day off. Because it was Friday, he reacted as if I'd insulted his intelligence.

"Why didn't you just tell me straight off yesterday that you wanted to take a long weekend? I'm a reasonable guy!"

My boss had replaced his universally despised predecessor thanks only to a merciful coup. If she was six of one, then he was a half dozen of the other (despite being in the services of the supposedly Catholic press, they had denounced a Catholic petition drive for freedom of religion the year before last), but no one else wanted all that deadly paperwork, and he at least kissed up to us pleasantly enough.

"It's a family matter; I couldn't have known."

"Are you calling from your country house?" He tried ineptly to catch me.

"I haven't earned enough to buy one working for you; I'm calling from my apartment and I'll come right in if necessary."

My anger had the desired effect. He began to fawn.

"God, that was a joke, Jesus Christ, stay home, whatever you have to do, you're the only one who's on schedule."

"Thank you," I ended with a flourish, "and try not to take the Lord's name in vain so often!"

Josef Beneš had never been in the telephone directory (why had it never struck me as odd that an ordinary businessman had an unlisted number?), and he'd dropped out of my address book a long time ago. Because the infamous bouquet from him had arrived even last year, he must at least have survived the revolution. It seemed best to start with the address I knew.

It was too soon for Gábina to call and a while until I could start worrying; the conviction that I'd be able to help my sweetheart grew. My mood was improved by the discovery that the bite had turned purple overnight and in its own way looked quite attractive. I tried my best to imagine what a woman should wear to make an impression on her sometime lover years later that would move the secret agent in him to repentance. The window test showed that it was noticeably warmer and I could go forth in full spring regalia. (The lilac-colored silk suit had been another gift from my sweetheart: a barely fastenable cropped jacket that functioned as a corset went with billowing Turkish pantaloons. He dressed me with unanticipated fantasy, which must have been inspired by longing.)

The choice definitely helped me; on the way downstairs I carried myself as if I were going on a date, which psychologically was more advantageous than getting nervous at the thought that I could scarcely avoid a hostile conflict. I was almost surprised that there wasn't a sporty cabriolet waiting outside with a young dandy bowing to me. I admitted to myself reluctantly that I was a quite passionately but still only secretly adored woman, middle-aged and middle-income (eight hundred crowns a month over the minimum wage), and set off, as was my wont, for public transit.

His building stood above the hospital complex at the end of the street where little Gabriela first saw the light of day. (My still-doting husband hauled in so many gorgeous bouquets that the maternity ward staff proclaimed him model father of the year. Later he merrily confessed to me that in return for a bottle, one of his former classmates—who was on a work brigade disposing of used flower arrangements at a crematorium—had taken care of it.) All of "Josef's summer," I walked past the maternity ward with a bad conscience; I guess I knew beforehand what would happen between me and Gábina, and despite this I obsessively (today incomprehensibly, yes, groundlessly!) worked to turn a blind eye to it.

Even today, the simple 1930s apartment house seemed more modern than the low prefab buildings that had been built alongside it in my absence. The doors giving onto the corner terrace (where we went out naked in that doubly hot July to cool off) were different, with white curtains replacing the blinds. I assumed, of course, that he had changed his address after the overthrow of the old regime; instead of swallows, uncovered undercover agents were now swarming everywhere, but suddenly there were no warmer climes for them, so they fluttered nervously around their homeland.

Unfortunately for him, he had revealed his hideout to me once, which definitely wasn't a part of his cover. They must have known about him from the beginning; his whole family couldn't just have disappeared, and, most important, I had a good chance with his sister. ("Josef is the only honest one in the whole bunch!" she said back then; did she mean just the Communist Party or also his "company"?) Before leaving home I had miraculously managed to get through to the transit information hot line and had written down all the afternoon buses to Kladno.

Then, at the foot of the stairs, I spotted with disbelief a yellowed name card in the building's tenant directory: J. BENEŠ.

The elevator had been newly outfitted with a lock, so I walked slowly up to the top floor so as not to be gasping for breath, and rang the bell straightaway before trembling could overtake me. I had figured out—as best I could—that he was around sixty-three. Policemen were entitled to an early retirement and his sort got sent off pronto; I now believed he'd open the door for me. My ascent confirmed I was in good shape (despite a slight indisposition from the rum, I had exercised this morning the way he himself had taught me: "Graceful tits like yours deserve to be exercised; they have muscles, too!") but mostly I was driven by righteous wrath.

He wasn't home, but a relatively young woman looked out from the neighboring doorway (there'd been a deaf old woman living there before, so we hadn't had to restrain ourselves) and examined me in a fashion "natural to the lower classes" (to quote my late mother, referring to a very specific sort of primitive aversion). Because she didn't bother to say hello, I rang the bell again. She couldn't keep quiet any longer.

"Mr. Beneš is at work!"

"Hello." I acted as if she'd just appeared. "When does he usually get back?"

"Depends. Why do you want to know?"

If I didn't know his taste, which could hardly have sunk so low, I would have thought there was something between them. Still, I needed information.

"I was in the area for the first time in years and wanted to ask about something. He isn't retired yet?"

"Yeah, he is," she said, a shade more personably, "but he's still working for some firm."

That got my dander up. (As Viktor said, they throw us back into the meat grinder . . .)

"Did he open a detective agency?"

"Him? A detective?" Why be careful? Let her know the truth about him!

"Well, he was in the Interior Ministry!"

"Yeah, yeah, but he screwed them over, so then they fingered him, like they always did; he did time at the prison for political offenders in Bory until the revolution. So now they want him back, but he told 'em, 'over my dead body!' " She smiled vengefully while I reeled. "Some Australians come get him every morning; he's, like, an accountant for them. Comes back around six, can I give him a message?"

"No, I'll stop by."

I said goodbye and went downstairs as if in a dream, until the sun warned me I was out on the street again. Josef—a dissident? So he wasn't lying to me? And what does this mean for Viktor? It was noon; there'd be no answer to these questions for at least six hours. I had to do something; six hours of this tension would do me in. With that thought I began to yearn deeply for a church.

There was one quite nearby where I'd last been as a child, most likely with my father, who was known in my family as a storyteller. Only from him could I have such a vivid memory of the story of its builder, who made a pact with the devil on account of its audacious dome (just like the majority of creative souls during the recently ended occupation, except they had nothing to show for it). Even this dearly bought vault made no impression on me today (I thought of the one at Kutná Hora, which was certainly built by angels), so I averted my eyes and said my prayer in a whisper.

"Our Father, who art in heaven, hallowed be Thy name. Thy kingdom come . . . Forgive me my sins, even if I rarely know how to forgive those who trespass against me. Protect my daughter Gabriela, whom I raised so poorly. I tried at least to make a Christian of her; maybe that seed will grow. In the meanwhile, please look out for her, my stupid little lamb, for Jesus' sake. Send her Your guardian angels, don't let anyone hurt her. And especially protect my darling Viktor for me, I beg of You, for everything on this earth. I am a sinner, over and over I fall into temptation, but You have given me the gift of love, and with it I love him, o Lord! I pray, I want to be better and I'm trying at least not to cause anyone pain and to be especially nice to his wife. After all, in the end I'm protecting him for her sake. Deliver all of us in this wretched world from evil. Let this be Thy kingdom and Thy power and glory unto the ages. Amen."

I had barely finished when a lively old woman with a packed shopping bag came out of a nearby confessional; her face radiated contentment, as if she'd gotten an especially good buy on something. I grasped at the opportunity, and almost bowled over the clergyman emerging from the richly carved booth.

"Father, could I also . . ."

The heavyset man with the roundish face of a country boy looked at my Muhammadan pants.

"Is it urgent?"

Suddenly we both must have felt ashamed, I for my absolutely inappropriate attire, he for his reaction, which could seem like a refusal.

"I'm sorry, I'm just . . . if you could wait a moment, I have a meeting that can't be put off." Then he practically begged me. "You can contemplate in the meanwhile."

"Yes, I'd be glad to."

I had time, and more importantly I could put off meeting the new priest of "my" church. In vain, I urged myself to have some Christian humility. For me, churches were like theaters: in certain ones even the Spirit seemed to be lacking, and this absence was reflected in the person of the protagonist, in this case the spiritual leader. For years my main repentance had consisted in making confession to the old priest, who fortunately wasn't in the collaborationist group Pacem in Terris, although his questions (Lord have mercy on me) reminded me of my single (but sufficient!) interrogation at the StB headquarters on Bartolomejská. Nothing ever satisfied him; he grilled me in excruciating detail (with which immoral thought had I actually sinned; exactly how often had I fornicated), but as opposed to the police I had to answer him and wanted to. It was he who urged me—because I had deliberately forgotten something—to keep an erotic diary alongside my poetic one. He doubtless wanted me to be truly disgusted by my actions; how could he have guessed that he'd end up in it, too—I couldn't help myself! As a result I didn't dare take confession with him again, and therefore (God forgive me!) I was relieved when another priest replaced him due to illness. My hopes were dashed at the first Mass: his successor gesticulated wildly and exaggerated his pronunciation (like an operatic tenor). He seemed to me filled with worldly pride, so I put off meeting him in the confessional as long as I could.

At the moment I couldn't concentrate at all, let alone contemplate. The loud conversation in the sacristy disturbed me, and eventually, want to or not, I started to pay attention to it. It sounded to me like a political argument, inane and out of place in this setting: the priest was repeatedly disparaging the new system, saying the old one could easily have lasted years, which an unknown bass voice called playing with fire. It hurt me that such a worthless argument took precedence over my confession and I stood up to leave, when he emerged and hurried over to me.

"Please forgive me, the electricians are here; we're converting to

220-volt electricity but they're carrying on as if we're building a new church."

"I'm sorry, maybe another time?"

"No, no, please, if you don't mind, they're conferring among themselves now; after all, you're why I'm here."

He disappeared, only to reappear behind the thick grille of the confessional as a disembodied voice.

"When did you make your last confession?"

"Before Easter . . ."

"You can't have sinned too much in five weeks, can you?" Was he afraid the workmen would run off?

"I have consistently broken the seventh and ninth commandments!"

"Did you act in good faith, without selfish or base intentions or desire to injure others?"

"Yes."

"Then say ten prayers for the souls in purgatory and sin no more."

The glorious thrill that energized me during confession had not materialized, while my suspicion grew that, thanks to my stylish pants, he'd lumped me in with those pampered girls who fool around and then pester God just when He's busy dealing with the illumination of His tabernacle. (I'd expected a reprimand, explanation, consultation, and at least a full rosary!) He salvaged it with an unforeseen question.

"Do you genuinely desire to be free of your sins?"

"Yes! I want so much to live in God's grace, but every time I lose my strength again!"

"Keep wanting that, daughter. God is merciful to everyone who tries his hardest to want more than he is capable of. Often God rewards him with the realization that he is capable of more than he wanted. Avoid being led into temptation, and if it begins to lure you, pray until you can suppress it. I absolve you in the name of the Father, the Son, and the Holy Spirit. Go in peace."

He raced off to his electricians, but he had given me hope. Yes, it's that easy, all you have to do is obey. I will cleanse Viktor and then ask him in return to help cleanse me by not calling anymore. I prayed, and even felt it physically as my passion departed and grace coolly entered me from the beads of the old woman's rosary.

❄ ❄ ❄

I waited out the remaining time in an oasis I came upon when my unrelenting heartburn forced me to stop at what looked like an ordinary corner tavern. I expected the usual dive with a pitiful menu and surly service, but instead I was greeted by a fresh-smelling coat of white paint, a carefully preserved Thonet café furniture set, and most noticeably by a chubby little person who looked as if she'd stepped out of the illustrations from my favorite children's book, *Hýta and Batul.*

She apologized hastily for the fact that everything wasn't in tiptop shape just yet; her son in Germany had bought her the pub at auction a short time back, it had always been her dream. She had opened two weeks ago and some of the suppliers were late ("They didn't believe me," she said, beaming, "when I told them I always meet my deadlines!"), but they could surely accommodate me, what would I like?

I wanted something to ease my thirst, but not soda water—I can't stand bubbles—or cola, which I find revolting; I'd had one too many coffees already and it was too early for wine. "So tea, then!" she called out joyously; I objected that it's harder on the stomach than coffee, but she waved her little rolling-pin arms, saying she meant Chinese jasmine, which you can drink anytime, to calm you down and pick you up, to cool you off and warm your insides, because it knows how to adapt itself to the person and the environment.

She made me remember a melancholy short story by an until recently banned author. A frail customer in a run-down socialist beer hall orders jasmine tea over and over again in vain, until as a joke and with great difficulty they get hold of some, except it's too late; he never comes back. Now I understood his longing as I sat enchanted by that singularly delicate aroma and taste which prolonged my spiritual celebration.

The proprietress (her happiness completed a harmony unknown in Prague restaurants), lost in reverie, described how next to the ever-boiling samovar two dozen porcelain pots would be waiting, in which guests could brew their own tea chosen from a beautifully printed menu according to their needs and moods. She expected to have mostly men who could skip over from the café to the hospital to check how "their" delivery was going; of course smoking was permitted (I lit up immediately), and in the event of twins she'd serve nettle tea, which, she chuckled, would make even a horse fall fast asleep.

As if on cue, a nervous young man stepped in, obviously belonging to the target group, and she bustled off to him. On the way she carefully turned on the music, the kind that creates a strange sort of quiet and privacy in public places, and I sipped my pale tea slowly to the music of a Spanish guitar. All these pleasures couldn't prevent me from realizing after a while that my spiritual elevation had once again come to an end, and I was thinking anxiously about the meeting with Josef.

After years of knowing each other through my loved one, Josef and I met again as friends a year after Viktor left, only to fall for each other out of the blue. Up until then physical love for me had always been a phenomenon incidental to emotional arousal (almost a necessary evil; hence my infidelities never gave me any pleasure). Suddenly it was as if physicality had become independent of emotion. I was not in love, and yet a person who'd been almost a stranger to me had become more intimate than Viktor had ever been; for a while, making love with him ruled my life. From work (at the time I was still a custodian) I flew home to cook Gábina dinner, checked her homework (well, pretended to, and soon it showed up on her report card, for which I, in my deranged state, gave her a good hiding), promised her heaven and earth, put on the TV, and in half an hour was beginning another round in Josef's bed (the whole room had become an arena and like lunatics we boasted to each other about our collection of bites and scratches of all hues). He was a die-hard; we'd eat a little and then frolic around far past midnight (with cigarette breaks) and he remained aroused long after he fell asleep. Before six we'd greedily say goodbye (he called this brief moment of passion a strap: "That's how the soldiers used to do it to the servant girls in the entryways," he said, laughing, "they held them by the belt!"), and at seven I was already home, sending Gábina off to school.

The same cycle repeated itself for one week, two, six. The tension didn't let up even during the day; I'd scrub the last endless staircase and think about the coming night. Today I know it was a delayed hysterical reaction to a mortal loss (which I compensated for quickly enough with a similarly hysterical morality!) but at the time I was wild with lust, willing to make love unto the death. I got thinner than I'd ever been when I was single and loved more than anything how I looked in the mirror. Then the summer holiday was upon us and my obsession compelled me to break my promise that I'd go with my daughter as usual to a small hotel in Zvikovské Podhradí (all winter I had longed for water like a fish and suddenly I was alarmed at the thought of going three weeks without a man's embrace). For the last time I managed to persuade my former husband (no longer young and handsome, but all the more successful and proficient in his collaboration) to go with her if he didn't want to lose her entirely. A vacation with her father would have been her dream, except this summer she figured out that it was a pretext for me to abandon her, and resolved to pay me back for it.

No sooner had the door closed behind her than I put her out of my mind and moved over to Josef's. He took the back vacation time his firm owed him (I didn't care what kind of firm it was; I barely mentioned it to him myself when a job came up for me at the Catholic classifieds), so we gorged our bodies on into the daylight hours, but our appetites never slackened. More and more I came to understand the profound difference between what I'd thought for years physical love was (which precisely fit the term "sexual relations") and what I was undergoing just then: an unrelenting approach to the boundary of interpenetration (recalling the sensational American photo series depicting a sunbather, starting with the widest lens from the top of a Chicago skyscraper where he was an unrecognizable dot, up to a microscope's enlargement of one of his freckles) where that climactic joy almost never let up. (What luck that the first embrace of my newly rediscovered sweetheart a year ago immediately surpassed all those spurious climaxes; *amor vincit omnia*!)

Then came the night I was thinking about over jasmine tea. Three days before Gábina's return would put an end, for now, to our madness, we both simultaneously felt the need not to touch for a while. Even after midnight the heat didn't break; we dragged our mattresses out on the terrace, where no one could see. We were high up, and all around us was the hospital, where everyone was either asleep or dead. The radio was playing, we were smoking (he his strong Gauloises) and sipping our summer drink, "white bears" (a cold cocktail with Russian vodka, which cut the sweetness of Czech champagne), and we floated gently beneath the unmoving stars.

"I'd like to tell you something," Josef whispered.

It was strange that we mostly spoke to each other in whispers, although we weren't hiding from or disturbing anyone (and it was probably the only thing the old regime didn't have a law against: even dissidents were allowed to fuck).

"So let's hear it!" I encouraged him. I was expecting negotiations about our time "after."

"I love you and I'd like to marry you."

We had never professed to love each other. And it had never occurred to me that he intended to marry again. In the one photo hanging in the apartment he was hugging his beloved slender wife; parachutes adorned both their backs. Hers had at some point failed to open. He described it to me once, briefly. They were skydiving in an eight-person rosette; they'd completed it successfully and joined hands in a circle (the last time the two of them would ever touch). It does happen, he recounted with a bit too much detachment (and in this way betrayed to me how attached he still was to her), so you even train for it; in most cases you can brake with your arms and legs. He would have reached her and hooked her up to his chute, but she (he wouldn't even say her name) obviously went into shock and plummeted through the clear air, her palms clasped to her sides as if she were jumping into the water before him, until his instinct for self-preservation made him pull the parachute cord. ("She lay on her back in a meadow lightly frosted with snow, one hand under her head and her eyes closed, as if she were sunbathing; I sailed down toward her in that quiet, and howled with despair and shame . . .")

Years later (I hadn't found the slightest traces of a woman's presence at his place; was he a hermit returning to worldly life?), he confessed his love and proposed—to me. And I, the eternally fleeing weasel, who told her lawful husband, "Take everything but our daughter and get lost, I don't want you anymore!" Yes, I who fled even my beloved not only to make him love me more, but because I intrinsically valued freedom over everything else—I shivered with delight that at last I was in strong hands. (Today I know that for the first time I'd heard the tolling of old age.)

"Do you really love me?" I whispered with the intelligence of a sixteen-year-old girl who has just lost her virginity. (I couldn't rule out the possibility that I'd start bawling.)

"I really do love you, so much that it exhausts me. I love you so much that I'm going to ask you to get dressed and go for a walk with me."

This unusual request rang with unforeseen meaning. In a few minutes we left the house. He held me, as usual, firmly by his side, his right hand under my bosom ("My nest!" he would call it, and it didn't bother me that it sounded hackneyed; this was how our shift from friends to lovers had begun that spring), and led me with his decisive stride downhill to the square. (To Barbara? Barberina? Bibita? Which bar does he want for our celebratory drink?) Suddenly he broke stride.

"Let's have a smoke—to us!" He shook me out a cigarette from my pack of Spartas, which he'd carefully taken with him (his made me choke).

The park was of course deserted and under the Communist dictatorship safe and welcoming; Gypsies didn't attack people then, only policemen did. One was bound to surface any minute.

"Walls have ears, Petra, and this conversation isn't for them."

"You're trying to frighten me!"

He continued this odd courting ritual at his own pace and in his own way.

"It's precisely because I love you so much that I can't keep playing games with you."

True to the cliché, I took fright. "Is there someone else?"

"You can't be serious! How would I have the time for her?"

"So, what games?"

"Hold on a second. First promise me that tomorrow you'll definitely go to Kladno with me!"

"Why?"

"Because my parents and all my people are there. I want you to meet them."

"I'd love to!"

"Promise me!"

"I'm telling you: I'll go see them tomorrow."

"Say it: I swear on my daughter's health!"

"Josef . . ." I bristled. "Why all the . . ."

"I'm begging you! Please!"

"For me to . . ." In light of his offer, can't I at least indulge this whim of his? "I promise on Gabriela's health that I will go with you to Kladno to visit your family as your girlfriend; it goes without saying, there's no need to get dramatic. Satisfied?"

"Yes." It was evident that his thoughts were already elsewhere. "You never asked me what I do."

"Well, did you ever ask me?"

"But it's clear to you at least that I'm a Communist."

"It's always been clear to me that you're a decent person. As opposed to my ex-husband, who wasn't a Party member and grumbled constantly about the government while leeching off it shamelessly."

"Petra. I'm a major."

"I knew that ahead of time. Viktor met you in the service. But aside from that you're a business analyst, right?"

"It's my cover. I'm a major in the State Security." I was silent. "You're speechless."

"Yes."

He led me along, still in a tight grip, and spoke softly into my ear.

"I know how you feel about our organization and what your experience has been with it. When they picked you up at that painter's"—what a nightmare! Olin and I didn't even have time to get dressed; they broke down the door—"my man interrogated you. More precisely, he tried to, but couldn't, even when they brought you to headquarters." I was no longer capable of words. "He reported that you behaved arrogantly, refused to answer, and wrote into the transcript, 'I have nothing to be ashamed of.' " He quoted it exactly; so he really was one of them! That cop had made me out to be a whore. "I was so proud of you." Suddenly my bile rose.

"You? Why you?" It shocked me how fast my lover had turned into a secret policeman.

"Don't shout! We're here so I can tell you what you don't know. I'm committing a criminal act; it could cost me not only my rank and position but my freedom, too." Well, of course, but still . . . "I've known for a long time that I'd either have to break up with you or come clean. With Marie it took a lot longer." Who's Marie? Oh! The star-crossed sky diver. "I'm basically a loner, and most of all there was no woman I wanted to wake up next to every day. She was the first. And, until you, the last."

"Did she know, too, that you were . . ."

"At the time I wasn't yet. That's why I'm dragging you to Kladno, so you can decide for yourself. I have the right to have you know my roots and figure out on your own who I am and why I am what I am. You'll discover a dynasty of workers that was able to send its first son to school only after the Second World War and, soon after that, experienced how they betrayed us. I went to college from a trade school and as a lawyer deliberately joined the secret police—that was already under Khrushchev—so that that sort of garbage wouldn't happen again, but they used me as a paper pusher. The accident with Marie happened in January of '68. My nerves just went dead, but inside I never stopped screaming; I spent one year under treatment and another incapacitated. I came back untarnished by everything that had afflicted this country in the meanwhile. And I saw this as my chance . . . Watch out, you'll burn your fingers!"

I threw away the tiny cigarette butt, but was in critical need of more nicotine. He had to let go of me to give me a light, and afterward didn't return to his intimate grasp, which suited me fine.

"Marie was from the same background as me and had the same temperament, but what's more, she was incapable of deception; I'm sure she would have been one of the first to sign Charter 77. When they started to woo me for the StB, which only dim-witted Communist brats applied for—while my background was straight out of a first-grade primer: sports champion, clean reputation—I decided to become a Czech Paul Thümmel."

"Who?"

"Thümmel was a German agent who waged a secret war against Hitler; he spoiled his own side's work by leaking it to the Resistance. And that's what I do. Didn't they stop bothering you immediately? And didn't your friend Luna get out of it with his skin intact?"

It's the gospel truth; he had been absolutely sure they'd lock him up just like the other unemployed people whom they'd caught with fresh packets of hard currency coupons and the dissident journals *Svědectví* and *Listy* during their raids. My ingrained distrust of that organization (a truly physical aversion to it) overcame even my desire to believe the man I'd just lived through such a dizzying time with.

"How could you keep it up all these years?"

"A logical question. First I had to ask it of myself: how long can you play around with such a powerful organization? Fortunately it was a scale model of our society: it was swarming with deadbeats, and turned out shoddy products, but always managed to ferret out the vermin in its own henhouse. I learned to be thinking every instant about what I could not do."

"Such as?"

"Such as biting off more than I could chew. Or letting my emotions get the better of me. I kept my fingers out of everything another agent had covered, as we say. Meanwhile, I took full advantage of situations offered to me by the law of conspiracy: only one person can handle a risky case. When it was necessary, I dropped the ball. A couple of times, so that my quota of successful cases wouldn't be lowered suspiciously—on the contrary, so that it would legitimize me for further solo cases—I was the first to reveal things that were bound to come out anyway, or I shunted the blame onto those who wouldn't be hurt by it in any event." He noticed my deep skepticism. "Yes, that's a cost you'll have to judge for yourself, Petra. I'm trying to replace blind righteousness with a righteousness that's well thought out; I see this as my service to my country. And my contribution to our marriage is that I put myself at your mercy. You're sensitive—after all, you write poetry; I think there's a chance you'll believe me."

A tram went by, somewhere a tower clock struck the hour, and I was incapable of rational thought (dramatically ragged wisps of the dark clouds rolling beneath the moon imprinted themselves indelibly upon my retina); we walked and walked wordlessly around the endless oval of the park's path as the short distance between us widened into an endless no-man's-land.

"Do you want to sleep at home?" he asked at some point. "I'll take you back in a taxi."

I shook my head (it would have only made things horribly awkward). He was visibly relieved, grasped me lightly by the arm as he'd done until that spring, brought me back to his place, and went to take a shower, so I would have time to fall asleep. Surprisingly enough (was it a surprise? the soul gets exhausted along with the body), I succeeded immediately.

I woke up at ten. In the kitchenette there was a note leaning against a thermos of coffee. *I'll be back at noon. If you're still here we'll go to Kladno.*

I heard a faraway voice. The plump queen of the teahouse was standing at my table. With great effort I returned to the present.

"Yes . . ."

"I was asking if you needed anything else."

"No, thanks, I'm fine."

"Because we're closing now."

"Oh, no!"

Six-thirty. Did I miss him? Hurriedly I collected myself. My three beloved jasmines (when did I order them?) cost more than an opulent dinner; I had only a hundred crowns left till next payday. My sweetheart brought me expensive clothes, but on Monday I'd have to borrow money for cigarettes, coffee, and bread, too.

❄ ❄ ❄

"So, it is you!" he welcomed me. "You're the only one who fit the description." He opened the door when I had three steps left to go; he must have been watching for me.

I stepped back into time. Virtually nothing had changed here, especially not him. His still-thick hair had already been an interesting salt-and-pepper shade (I'd pay my hairdresser anything, I used to laugh, to get that color) and at the beginning of May he was already tanned. (Of course: he was an avid skier! He had promised to teach me, but too late now . . .) The only difference was that he didn't kiss me (why not? it's a common greeting these days), but instead put out his pleasantly large hand (which had carried my right "jewel"—Olin's term—when we used to walk) and led me into his single room.

"Have a seat. You look great."

He didn't hide at all what he loved most about me. That straightforwardness was catching; there was a tension, as if we were continuing a conversation interrupted only yesterday.

"You can't complain, either."

"You're right," he laughed, "and I've got no one to complain to."

In which way he informed me that he was still single. And immediately changed the subject.

"Do you want tea?"

"No thanks, I just drank a whole sea of jasmine."

"In our new teahouse? Today, for a change, I didn't stop in. What a shame; I would have met you an hour earlier!" Was he always such a charmer? I'd forgotten.

"Weren't you a coffee drinker?"

"Heart and soul. But when my doctor informed me that I could only keep one vice, I chose alcohol."

White bears? I wanted to ask. But I didn't dare remind him in any way of that summer.

"I heard you're working for the Australians."

He tilted his head toward the apartment next door and grinned.

"She's confused by the A on the car. I'm helping the general consul of Austrian industry find his way through the local tax laws, which even our own finance minister doesn't understand."

"Don't you need foreign languages for that?"

"I speak German and, in a pinch, English." So, you hid that from me too? was on the tip of my tongue. "In the last few years I studied a lot, I had more free time." Without me, he must have meant? That odd bit of news floated before my eyes.

"She said that they locked you up."

"Yes. My bosses were furious, so they cooked up a Soviet-style shortfall in the office's foreign currency account."

"But why were they furious?" I was trying to get at something that might have influenced Viktor's case. "Did you confess?"

"The only way to get out of that job is through the crematorium. I headed them off by signing the human rights document Charter 77."

"You? But Charter 77 was much earlier!"

"They kept collecting signatures. In '87 the StB was evidently already after me; my days were numbered, anyway. I didn't want to end up in a mass grave in Siberia, so I chose to give up my anonymity. I was the only secret policeman to sign the Charter, and I did so on its tenth anniversary. First the StB bundled me off to Bohnice among the crazies; I'd had a nervous breakdown at one time." Josef, did you forget I knew? From the corner of my eye I could see the photo of two parachutists, and who was the woman next to them? No! Me . . . "Except the doctors overturned that for them, as luck would have it, so I got hit with the full twelve years. Then I had a piece of amazing luck and only did two and a half."

I must have been shaking my head in disbelief, because he added reproachfully, "You're the only one who shouldn't be surprised; you knew my intentions. Obviously you didn't even believe me at the time."

"That's not true! I didn't think it made much sense, but I didn't doubt what you believed. Otherwise I wouldn't have stayed with you for a minute!"

"You didn't stay with me at all . . ."

"You know very well why! My daughter was ready to jump out the window because I'd deprived her of her favorite father figure and intended to get hitched to my boyfriend. You saw how upset I was; I couldn't have been less interested in your secret police work. And you didn't stop me! 'I don't want to be a secret lover on top of everything else,' quote: Beneš."

"I'm sorry . . ." He sagged and pointed to the wall. "And I'm sorry about the photograph; I took it from your file."

His professional perspicacity was still working. I sensed the appropriate moment.

"Anyway, you could show some decency today."

"How?"

"Is it true that you entered our mutual friend Viktor Král into a certain black book officially called the Register of Contacts?"

He looked me straight in the eyes, and didn't bat an eyelash. (Was he ready for it?)

"Yes, it's true."

Upon which my heart began to thump at the horror of it.

"And were you really his . . . commanding officer?"

My God, what if he says yes? The heightened pressure made my ears ring; I heard him as if from afar, but clearly.

"No."

There was a burst in my eardrum, painful but relieving, as if I was swimming up from the depths. Fear gave way to indignation.

"How could you do such a cruel thing?"

It seemed to me that his lips whitened, but he answered normally.

"I'll remind you that I also confided to you how I managed things there. I wrote him in without his knowledge when I found out that he'd stay abroad at the first opportunity. So I arranged for him to get there. I pretended to my bosses that we'd keep him on over there, an ace in the hole for us."

"You, you . . ." I couldn't get my brain around it. "You knew he wanted to get out?"

"I'm continually amazed that you didn't know."

"I never had the slightest, not the slightest idea!" I was shouting. "I would have talked him out of it!"

"It was you he fled from. You made him unhappy."

That one hit home. I wanted to slam the door and keep going until I got to the metro, but now of all times I couldn't do that. He was the one to get up and light us cigarettes.

"Petra, Viktor was my friend and I knew more about your escapade with Luna than he did. No! I never suggested anything to him, but I got the distinct impression that a guy couldn't depend on you, because precisely when he needed you you'd bolt."

With each drag on my cigarette I tried to swallow my tears inconspicuously. He was right. He'd experienced it himself. Mea culpa, mea maxima. But why the high drama? I've always been a rotten person, and now I'm a leaky watering can . . .

"Don't think that I had secret designs on you; you know it took another year before I dared, actually, until you suggested it yourself." He's letting me have it, he's really letting me have it. "Thanks to his background and his behavior, Viktor would never have gotten to go abroad. When it hit me that he saw it as the only way to save himself from you—I'm sorry, but he was on the brink of suicide, did you know that?—I jumped into action. It goes without saying he had no idea. The logic of the times told me that he was never coming back; no register could hurt him over there. And on his credit I was able to protect a couple of people."

Tactfully, he didn't name me. I looked in vain for my handkerchief, until he offered me his. I blew into it unhesitatingly so I'd be able to speak.

"Except history tossed that logic out the window, and your entry prompted the government chair's commission to give him an ultimatum: either get lost quietly or run the gauntlet of shame."

"I didn't know he was back. I'd forgotten about that incident."

"You forgot?"

"I was in that mill almost twenty years!" He wants to play the victim!

"You ground him up in it!"

"You're not being fair! I was throwing sand in the works. Did he send you?"

"That's not the issue! Only what you will do about it! Are you"—I took a deep breath, because this was the crux of the matter—"willing to clarify how it really was?"

"But of course I am!"

"And how?" I perceived that he was irritated, and in the interest of the cause decided to back off. "I don't mean to impose on you, I'd just like to tell him what he can expect from you."

"First he has to tell me who is intending to act on this, and when and where." Right! "Is he willing to meet with me?" That hadn't occurred to me.

"I don't know. But you have a phone, don't you?"

I was quite excited at the thought that I could call Viktor first myself;

she had given me their number! Josef Beneš looked at me as if he was hearing that word for the first time.

"A telephone?"

"I'll ask him right away."

"You think he'll be glad to? That's why he sent you, isn't it? So as not to create the impression that he's muddying his tracks with my help."

"You mean they still tap phones?" I was aghast.

"It's probably just a hazard of the profession, but experience is experience. I'll be waiting tomorrow evening at eight on the sidewalk in front of the church on Resslová Street, the one where they hid the parachutists after the assassination attempt on the Nazi leader Heydrich—you know where! Either he'll stop and we can go on together, or at five after I'll continue on alone."

It depressed me that, of all places to conduct an illegal rendezvous, he'd chosen a monument to a previous occupation, with the succeeding one so recently over.

4

AT two I still couldn't sleep a wink, despite having tried: watching TV, studying English (meeting his wife had reassured me I could measure up to her if I raised my level of education considerably), continuing with my diary, and finally finishing off the awful rum. When even that didn't do the trick, I ferreted out some sleeping pills from Gábina's room. (She's like a magpie; while looking I found my missing gold ankle bracelet, the last of the lifeguard Jarek's vain attempts.) Given the circumstances, I refused to acknowledge the doorbell when it woke me at seven-thirty, and buried myself under the pillow until suddenly it hit me.

Gabby! I'd left the key in the lock!

I flew out and opened the door unwashed and uncombed in a short nightshirt which undoubtedly clung to me like cellophane, unnerving the unfamiliar elderly postman, who seemed quite shaken by the sight.

"Whoops, excuse me, miss, I have express mail for you."

"What? Yes, thanks, goodbye, hold on"—the tip!—"wait a second . . ."

He took off, vanishing around the turn in the staircase as if he feared for his own innocence.

The letter was written in an unknown hand and on the back, instead of a return address, it carried the mysterious initials V.D. Some new mess of Gabby's? I tore it open and realized instantly: a mess of mine!

"Most respected Mrs. Márová," wrote the impudent boy I'd just threatened with the police, "I beg of you, read this letter through before you tear it up." He hasn't the foggiest idea about women; doesn't even know that as a matter of principle they only tear things up once they've read them. "You undoubtedly think I'm a heel," an accurate self-portrait, "and it's true, believe me, that I'm horribly ashamed." Thank goodness for small favors. "I had no idea that my father was home, and I was terribly excited." That's an accurate statement. "You're mistaken, Mrs. Márová, if you think I behave that way with every woman." As a matter of fact, I don't think that anymore. "I'm not some kind of Don Juan!" Lord knows, little boy—forgive me, God, I lose self-control when I think about what I got myself into!

"You won my heart before I'd ever even seen you." No! How? "I liked one poem in our Saturday feature section so much that I remembered the name of the author: Petra Márová." Surely he doesn't think . . . "Such inventive verses!" A drunken bet that makes me blush even today. Those vermin printed it while they keep putting off my real poetry, supposedly until there's a full page for it; how did it go? *Missing numbers / missing numbs / Something's missing / from my sums / I count you in / You count me out / Countless countings / Counsel doubt / Are we twosome / or merely lonesome / What's the final amount / Adding rows / of your dreary / zeroes / in my / quiet / account.*

"And such an interesting name," the letter continued. "Right away I figured out an anagram for you and was amazed again at how well it fit you." Why didn't he write it down? "In addition I found out that you worked at our paper, and finally they even pointed you out to me." He'd been spying on me for a while, then, the sneak! "Don't worry, I only asked casually." Where was your discretion on Wednesday night? "I knew immediately that this was a real woman." What a compliment.

"When I met up with you after the boat ride, dear Mrs. Márová"—the more he writes the more intimate he gets . . . Well, after all, I did sleep with him; I should be happy that he doesn't call me Petra—"it was no coincidence, but it wasn't really my style." Which is quite uninhibited! "I'd never forced myself on a mature woman like that before." Mature! Disgusting! That word ought to be banned! "I wanted to express my admiration for your poems and in general. Except then I lost all judgment; I have no idea what I was babbling about, all I could think about was that I wanted just once to kiss you."

And inside of an hour you also got to . . . "I couldn't believe my ears when you accepted my invitation"—I don't want to believe my memory!—"and I can't even remember what I did afterwards." You acted, my child, as if I belonged to you; let's hope the impossible doesn't happen. Calm down, Petra, you've tried it with Viktor at high noon, so to speak, and nothing! Old age has its benefits, too. "I will never be able to apologize enough, as much as you deserve, but if you should ever need something and no one else is there for you, remember that I am forever at your disposal." It sounds like a joke, something neo-baroque; where did he crib it from? "That's what I wanted to tell you yesterday outside your house, because your address was in the telephone book; I was just waiting there until you got home, and hadn't thought that you might come out with someone." Aha, he didn't know I was off that day, so he stood there all afternoon and evening. At least now he knows that I'm not available! "Once again I beg your forgiveness and remain respectfully"—for the life of me I don't know why—"your devoted *Václav David.*"

My irritation dissipated as I read; by the end I was confusedly scratching my hair, which had been itching since last night. What now? Tear it up and throw it out, of course, but first maybe I should reread it without the ironical commentary. I did so and felt even more at a loss. What next? He got more than he expected from me, and wants an encore? That I would understand. Has he realized that he not only made a colossal fool of me, but upset me greatly as well, and is truly sorry? Oh, please! But to offer himself as a servant? Or does he fancy himself a gallant musketeer? How should I react? I thought I could safely ignore him; is that still possible? Won't he conclude just as rightfully that I'm the one acting pigheaded (sow-headed)?

In the meanwhile I woke up sufficiently to calculate that I had two days to decide how to react. (That's why it wasn't our usual postman: he sent his letter overnight delivery so it would get here before Sunday!) Today an incomparably more important task awaited me.

I had already called my sweetheart yesterday evening. Josef Beneš (my Czech centaur: half cop, half stallion) had so infected me that I called from a telephone booth. No one picked up and a jealous bitterness welled up in me (was I running around for them while they made good use of the time together?) until I figured out that I was reading a 7 instead of a 1. (You should wear glasses, you vain old woman!) A quiet voice answered immediately.

"Yes, can I help you?"

(Don't always ask questions! I suggested to him years ago; men should call the shots! And now he was; he was the one who defined our relationship.) I indicated to him (the way years under Bolshevism had taught me) that I had a good feeling about our venture, which he would have to follow up on himself. He should come see me tomorrow, Saturday, at seven in the evening; I'd be waiting out front. He was surprised we were to meet at my place, but was careful not to show it (he evidently wasn't there alone); I sensed that he longed for me as I did for him. Of course I had in mind to propose that he come by afterward to tell me about the meeting; she could hardly object to that. And in the meanwhile . . . oh!

I had the whole rest of the day to wait.

The morning went by mercifully quickly, thanks to price liberalization. Market economics had replaced standing in line with running from store to store pricing a single item. Just finding the cheapest butter took me more than an hour. (A five-crown price difference for a quarter-kilo meant five more menthols, which the ads said were healthier than not smoking at all.) I got hold of a liter of red wine for only thirty crowns, and with it spied a chance to pull through Sunday evening in a more humane fashion. (I'd planned to go out rollerskating during the day; I have to watch my figure for my sweetheart!)

By the time I'd fried some eggs and had a beer (I'll go skating tomorrow) it was two. A mound of laundry loomed in the bathroom, but I was already imagining how he would hold me this evening, and didn't want to present myself for love with the soul of a washerwoman. (So, tomorrow, and consequently the Sabbath is broken; once again I wanted more than I was capable of, and He still hasn't granted me the strength to change.)

From the drawer I pulled out my abortions, as I call my unfinished opuses, and looked for anything that might have matured since the last time. I paged through poems, begun in every conceivable mood, which would burst forth—until my toiling foundered on some particular phrase (poetry demands continuous brilliance; "Pegasus is no good as a hobby-horse, he'll fatten into a brewery nag!" to quote the Party poet, ugh! but he hit the nail on the head) at which point my originally promising verses would seem like a dilettante's nursery rhymes. (As if I were anything different. "How do you bring spirituality into art?" I once asked Olin. "You can't flirt with art, you must suffer through it!" he responded. But love was the only thing I knew how to suffer through.) My poetry was a sort of high-quality classified ad, which I edited in my free time.

I raked through my poetic salad with a growing aversion, and then something came to mind: "Right away I figured out an anagram for you and was amazed again at how well it fit you." So said the youthful V.D., my lover number . . . thirteen! (That explains the bad luck.) At one time I'd been interested in the etymology of my last name ("What do you expect? Your name means funeral bier, so your ancestor was a sexton!" to quote my cheerful husband when I introduced him to my parents) but never in its anagrams. I took out a clean sheet of paper and wrote out several times, once to a line, like a school punishment:

PETRA MÁROVÁ
PETRA MÁROVÁ
PETRA MÁROVÁ
PETRA MÁROVÁ
PETRA MÁROVÁ

Then I started to underline and cross out the letters I used. After an hour I took the kid for even more of an operator; there was no way to make an anagram out of my name that made any sense at all. Even the most meaningful combination, which had a Czecho-Slovak federative ring to it, was pretty farfetched.

ROTA PREMÁVÁ

"The company is on the move." My alert brain cells rendered up a memory of the famous sign in the Tatra ski resorts in Slovakia: "Lanovka nepremáva," meaning "the ski lift isn't working"—which hadn't bothered us on our honeymoon, since my smooth little husband and I were busy trying to conceive Gabriela, our now violated (apparently to her own advantage) child. Second place went to an utter absurdity:

TRAPEM ORÁVÁ

"He usually plows at a trot." And that was a gem compared to the garbage that made no sense at all:

MORAVA PARTE
ATRAPA ROVEM
TRVÁ RÁM POEA
MÁTE PRÁVO AR
RAPORT MÁVÁ E

The fragments that followed were even sorrier. With one stroke that greenhorn made me suddenly seem like a spiritual cripple. Then a light went on in my brain and an absolutely first-rate anagram shone forth on the page:

METROVÁ PÁRA

"A meter of steam"? If this was what he had in mind, then on top of everything he was vulgar beyond comparison.

* * *

Desire chased me out onto the street fifteen minutes early. (If he comes early, we'll have at least half an hour upstairs at my place for a hug; who knows how much time he'll have later on, and I desperately need some tenderness after all this.) However, he was late (as always), and my expression must have betrayed me, as I had eyes only for him and didn't even notice his wife through the reflection of the car window. ("Watch out around their wives; you eat your men up with your eyes!" to quote my own daughter commenting on my short-lived platonic romance with her homeroom teacher, whose wife worked at the school.) I struggled not to faint, but she was upset (or her glasses were too weak?), so apparently she didn't catch it. She got out first to squeeze my hand and thank me. I hurriedly suggested that we get in the car. (I won't let her upstairs!) From the back seat I told them about yesterday's conversation (censoring the personal parts). Although her mood seemed to improve, he was unusually peevish.

"Why doesn't he simply arrange for a notarized declaration?"

"He wanted to know precisely for whom and what."

"For the commission, of course! And the truth, what else? This way there could be a suspicion of conspiracy."

At that instant I realized I'd done him a disservice. (And my fury at Beneš rose sharply.) I tried to correct my gaping failure of intellect.

"No problem, drop me off there on the corner and I'll explain it to him myself . . ."

At that moment she pitched in.

"But Vic, go talk with him directly, then there won't be any mistakes. You can't want Mrs. Márová"—ow!—"to act for you; it's enough that she did what she did, how can you expect her to do more?" Oh! "The man's ready to help, don't risk a misunderstanding!"

I decidedly did not want to be his agent, and so I hastened to support her.

"The type of meeting he proposed guarantees its confidentiality. And how long it lasts and how it goes depends on you."

He visibly did not want to go. But it was two against one.

"So, where is it?" his wife asked me, his lover, and when her husband and my sweetheart nodded that he knew, she urged him, "So, let's go, there isn't much time. Are you going with us?" She turned to me.

"Me? No!"

Once he had brought her in, it ceased to involve me. (Maybe she brought him in, Petra. Be fair!) He didn't even regret the lost opportunity. (Does she have to keep an eye on you or what?) On the contrary, it was his wife who seemed troubled.

"You ought to find out how it turns out"—aha, now I see why—"in case . . . your presence is necessary . . ." And, of course, I won't say no! "But if you can't spare the time, we can stop by here later; we have a baby-sitter with the little one." And I'll wait out on the street again, because I don't want them to go upstairs . . . this is getting stupid. I gave in.

"I'll go."

"It's awfully nice of you," she gushed earnestly; all of a sudden her face relaxed and she looked much better. (So this is how he sees her all the time . . .) "Vic, drop us off somewhere close by, where we can walk around for a bit before you pick us up!" (Both of your women . . .)

I suggested the shipping locks under Jirásek Bridge. When he stopped to let us out near the artists' union, she kissed him on the cheek.

"Break a leg!"

He certainly knew how I felt (before important exams and lectures I had always made the sign of the cross on his forehead) and this time, riskily, he looked me in the eyes.

"For now, thanks, Petra. Thanks so much."

I crossed him with my eyes and then once again followed the red taillights of the Japanese car as it blazed across the intersection by the bridge, while the mother of his child and I slowly descended along the ramp to the Vltava. She was childishly charmed by it.

"Oooh, look at the little steamboats."

Looking at the idling river fleet I counted: seventy-four hours ago a certain V.D. caught up to me here. The turtledove had squawked to its love; in my desolation I had suddenly desperately needed a lover, only he turned out to be an anagrammatic nitwit. At the same time my whole private life began to collapse (like the old timbering in that Kladno mine where I'd learned what fear means), and I was hard pressed to put it all back together. And put what back together? Neither

Gabby nor Viktor would ever again belong to me the way they once had. And for that I had only me, myself, and I to thank.

"You can't begin to imagine," began the one who instead of me shared his bed, table, bath, and toilet—yes! I can remember even now how in the quiet of the night I would hear him peeing; if we truly love a person, we love even his bodily secretions. I know what I'm talking about; I nursed both my miserable parents at home over the objections of my tidy little husband, whose scent had begun to sicken me—"what it means to be brought up practically in the antipodes, in the language of a people and the traditions of a country which for you must seem like the light of burned-out stars. In Vancouver we didn't know any other Slovaks; I didn't understand why until later, so I was always wondering why my parents were teaching me this comic language which only the two of them spoke. Then I came down clear out of the heavens to the Danube and there were old people, young people, everyone was speaking it! Except I was also raised on the concept of a Czechoslovak state, and here because of it an ice-cold malice met me everywhere I went. At the beginning Vic wanted to work in Bratislava"—Oh! Was he afraid to be near me?—"but I gave up first. Everywhere, the first question I got was on my attitude toward the Czechoslovak federation, and no one bothered to ask further. When I saw the words 'ŽIDIA NIE SÚ L'UDIA'—'Jews Aren't People'—on a wall, I said, 'To Prague!' " Thank God; but on the other hand, if they lived in Bratislava he could stay at my place. "It isn't so different here; a couple of people have already asked him if there were really so few Czech women in Canada. And on top of it this mess . . ."

A monologue? I didn't object. I won't have to force a conversation, cover things up, or lie; I won't blab anything by mistake and I might find something out! Her green irises wandered across the patricians' houses in Smíchov on the opposite shore (which had just been returned to their former owners, who thus in one lifetime went from being millionaires to being beggars and then to being millionaires again), along the river, the bridges, and the river's edge where life stopped. They seemed to imprint the details on her memory, as if she were a painter saving them for some future canvas. (Were we alike in that way? I often caught myself playing back across my retina a film of a landscape or a trip which my brain had mysteriously recorded years before; but I certainly wasn't going to ask.)

"The worst thing is that for me it seems like the continuation of a bad dream. My father is from Bardejov, in eastern Slovakia, and of his whole family, all sixty of them, only he was left alive; the rest were all killed in one way or another. Dad is a rarity; he was in absolutely every concentration camp. He traveled with a group of Jewish children from Majdanek to Bergen-Belsen to Auschwitz and on from there until he was the only one left. He was fifteen years old and weighed twelve kilograms when they rescued him. They fattened him up in Sweden and sent him to Canada, where he thrived and went on to medical school, and even married a Slovak woman, one of the second-generation immigrants, who wasn't bothered by his being Jewish. He was an excellent doctor and could have gotten rich quickly, could have been the proud owner of a hydroplane like everyone else in British Columbia and flown out to go salmon fishing on the weekends, except he was obsessed by two ideas: being a Slovak in Czechoslovakia and finding his remaining relatives.

"Mom loved him, so in 1960 she went back with him. The fact that he gave up his Canadian citizenship only made things worse for him; they took him for a madman at best and for an imperialist spy at worst. Finally, instead of his native Bardejov, where he wanted to live, they assigned him to Bratislava—the place everyone except him was trying in vain to go!—apparently so they could keep him in sight. He didn't find any relatives, only lots of the old Nazi Guard members who had the murder of his family on their consciences; now they were Communists. Of course, all their little bosses had dispersed themselves around the globe, where my father was once again forbidden to go. So the one thing he actually accomplished there was the delayed fruit of his love: me."

She turned to me with a laugh and suddenly she was decidedly charming (yes, my sweetheart had had good taste his whole life; after all, he always returned to me!), and I already knew that it had been her primal fear for him that had tormented her and distorted her features in the café, and I realized that it is I, that it is my sacrifice that restores her equilibrium and her joy, that makes her prettier and more attractive (for him); but I was acting without blame, explanation, or persuasion in the spirit of my repentance, and as it turned out, I was capable from the first of more than I had wanted.

"On that August night in '68 when the Russian tanks came, I'm told a friend of my father's woke us up; he was also a Jew who'd had the privilege of sampling our own concentration camps after the German ones, and had no desire to try the Russian ones as well. He insisted that a pogrom was starting, simply stuffed us into his car and took us to Vienna; in the confusion my parents took almost nothing with them. Of course, they applied to Canada for asylum, but they had to wait a year for it and ten more years for citizenship, because they pegged my father for a spy from Moscow for a change. If it hadn't been for the Jewish lobby, which understood that he was simply meshuggah with his patriotism, they might have expelled us from Canada instead of the real criminals who had in the meantime firmly ensconced themselves, usually right on top of an oil well.

"One day in the mid-eighties, my appalled father got a letter on Slovak state letterhead. 'Brother Horňanský,' the computer addressed him intimately in his native tongue—my father had Slovacized his name before I was born for my sake; it doesn't bother me any more"—Of course not! Not when my sweetheart's made you a queen!—"but back then I always longed to be a Gurfajn!—'we call on you as a true-blooded Slovak to contribute to the erection of a monument to the Slovak martyr and our one real president, Josef Tiso, unjustly executed after the war by the Czechs, signed for this or that society, Ján Bartolomej Kolodaj.' My father turned white and began to wheeze, until we were afraid he was having a heart attack, before he said: either it's a morbid coincidence with the name, or I've found our murderer. He hung up a sign that he wasn't seeing patients, and flew east, where he was able to shed some light on the matter. This Kolodaj was the head of the Slovak community there and an elder of the church, father of an honored family and dedicated Canadian citizen, successful businessman, member of a number of societies and organizations, holder of diplomas, friend of politicians, and was in fact from Bardejov! A young local by that name had personally put sixty Gurfajns onto the cattle wagon and sealed it for the journey from which only my father returned."

Behind the Prague castle the sky still glowed, but as this girl (careful, she is after all his wife . . .) spoke without pathos, with disarming simplicity, the postcard kitsch transformed itself into the twilight of the crematorium ovens, which were the earthly version of hell.

"When my father had returned and calmed down, he wrote to Simon Wiesenthal in Vienna, the greatest authority on the hangmen of the Jews, because he has evidence against almost all of them. My father's tile fit exactly into the mosaic of the young militant's criminal past; he'd evaporated after the war just in time and, with the help of a mafia similar to the one that's protecting the old Bolshevik murderers now, he built a new existence for himself in an honorable land where the greatest measure of inhumanity is if pigs hunting truffles don't get some to eat after the search to sharpen their sense of smell. The crimes of the Kolodajs are beyond all normal comprehension and thus are assigned to the realm of Freudian dreams or political slander. Wiesenthal confided to my father that his only chance—and it was an absurd one—was if he could manage to get the annihilator of his kin to publicly confess; then, under pressure from appropriate representatives, the Canadian government might feel itself justified—oh no, don't get me wrong, no chance of initiating criminal prosecution for genocide—in initiating government proceedings due to concealment of information, as a result of which Canadian citizenship had been improperly procured. The worst punishment would be entering the guilty party on the 'watch list,' a registry of individuals who were not permitted to enter Canada. He was in Canada, and therefore he could stay there; however, he'd be under house arrest. At first glance this seems humorous, but there it's just about the worst thing that can happen to you: the loss of your honor, societal ostracism.

"For the first time in years my father went to confer with the rabbi. No one had ever said anything about it, but he had been ashamed of changing his name, he couldn't face his fellow believers. Now, however, he came to realize how his new name would help him lay a trap to punish the murderer of fifty-nine Gurfajns. The rabbi agreed that it was good, that the plan might work, and, furthermore, he connected him with the right man, a journalist with a major television company, who was shocked by the case. Up until then it had never occurred to this young Canadian that his native land, of which he was so proud, had become the home port for the worst Nazis of all, who used a simple trick: they substantiated each other's claims to be democrats who had dedicated their lives to the struggle against Bolshevism and therefore had to taste the bitter fruit of emigration at an early age.

"My father's strategy was just as straightforward, and what's more, the journalist said, very telegenic. It sounded quite horrible, but guaranteed an effective revenge. The television crew first filmed my father in the camps he'd been through; for this purpose Poland and even East Germany gave him visas. Then, without my father, they visited Bardejov with precise instructions about what, where, and whom to film. Even Communist Czechoslovakia under Husák had no qualms about this; the fight against Fascism distracted their attention from the imperatives of the fight against Communism. In the recollections of the witnesses one name was heard over and over: Ján Bartolomej Kolodaj. In the local museum they even found photos: Ján Bartolomej saluting on the tribunal under the imperial eagle; Ján Bartolomej with a whip, watching over the Jews as they scrubbed the cobblestones in the street; and Ján Bartolomej stuffing them into that cattle car. You could even make out my father in the picture!

"The Canadian journalist returned home determined to rid his land of at least one attested villain, as an example. In those few weeks he had grown from a coddled child of freedom into an adult citizen of the world. With the cold-bloodedness of the hunter he wrote to Kolodaj's society that he was investigating the lives of minority communities in Canada, and that apparently interesting things were happening in the Slovak one. In return he got a pile of publications printed on glossy paper and the assurance that Ján Bartolomej Kolodaj himself could offer Canadian television a good picture of how indebted he remained to their viewing public after all these years. He was even happy to take on the role of subject of the proposed documentary: opening their meetings with prayers, honoring worthy sons of Slovakia, dedicating memorial plaques, growing prouder with each moment that his every move was being recorded on film. So, finally my father's day arrived . . ."

When she paused to breathe I seized the opportunity; it had gotten dark, and neither the streetlamps from the embankment nor their reflection in the water sufficed to light the deserted riverbank.

"Vanesa . . ." What am I doing, calling her by first name? Of course: it wounds me to call her Králová! But no further intimacies! "We should turn around and wait up above; Prague is catching up to the West in lots of ways, such as its crime rate."

"Yes. How is your daughter doing these days?"

"Fine, thank you." So he let it slip, her train of thought makes that clear enough; I'm disappointed in you, sweetheart! "Things are just fine, she's back in school." Forgive me, o Lord, such a lie to another mother!

Everything in me wanted to speed up, but she was caught up in the rhythm of her tale, which even determined the rate of her stride. I could either leave her behind or rein myself in.

"One last scene remained, which would be the culmination of the program Kolodaj had long dreamed of, celebrating Tiso's government (by the grace of Hitler) as a tragically flooded Atlantis of true democracy, and of course celebrating the chairman of the largest Slovak community in Canada, the apostle of Atlantis's resurrection. Ján Bartolomej believed firmly in this cause and got the drums of propaganda rolling ahead of time. The camera was located in front of a supermarket where the conscientious head of the family would go that day with his grandchildren to personally conduct his holiday shopping. The journalist would stop him and ask him the last question, to which the civil servant would reply with an Easter greeting in which he would wish his old countrymen and new fellow citizens peace and goodwill. This is how it happened: Kolodaj, in a half-circle of his descendants, dressed in evening wear even for shopping, his white mane combed straight back, giving him an air of grandeur, with great feeling and without a single mistake pronounces the speech he's learned so carefully.

"Then the journalist says unexpectedly that he has a little surprise for Kolodaj for his pains and exemplary cooperation: an old neighbor from the town where he was born, whom he hasn't seen in forty-five years. My father steps into view, and only my mother and I know how agitated he is, because he has a completely alien expression on his face; his eyes are like a blind man's. The main subject lights up immediately like a Western statesman and declares that he will always have a special place in his heart for Bardejov, that lost paradise. 'Do you recognize him?' the journalist says, luring him into the depths of the trap. 'Ah!' jokes Kolodaj, 'back then we were young and handsome, now we're only handsome! I'm a Kolodaj from the town square, these are my Canadian grandsons, and who are you?' Father ceremoniously nods and answers in a steely voice that we've never heard before, 'I'm a Gurfajn from the Jewish street, and the last of that name, since you locked up, starved, and packed my whole family, fifty-nine souls, into a cattle car like dumb brutes and sent them off to perish in the gas chambers.'

"What happened next, Petra, defies description. Kolodaj was still beaming away thanks to inertia, and at the same time he somehow collapsed inside; it reminded me of pictures of bombed-out buildings where only the outside walls were left standing. He couldn't run away or even burst into tears, I guess, let alone apologize; he started to blurt out things that made you sick. 'It was a confusing time, mistakes were made . . .' as if he were bungling his way through some essay he'd written for school! 'They betrayed us, they let us down, they hid things from us! We should thank the Good Lord each and every day that together he led us out of the valley of the shadow of death into this promised land, where we can live together in one big happy family.' As if those fifty-nine Gurfajns were standing there next to my father!

"Then Kolodaj heaved himself at my father and grabbed him by the shoulders. 'We are both Slovaks!' he cried out like he'd lost his senses. 'Let us be brothers forever more! It's Easter! Let us forgive each other, let bygones be bygones!' He let go of my father's shoulders and with both hands began to shake Father's right hand. 'Roll 'em!' he screamed hysterically at the cameras. 'Get this on film and broadcast it so all Canada can witness our reconciliation!' Only then—but suddenly, as if he'd gotten an electric shock—did he let go and stagger out of the picture, where his stupefied progeny and my motionless father remained. With that the film ended.

"That very evening after the shoot the young journalist had a full-fledged tempest on his hands. Pleas, protests, and threats exploded at him from all sides, so on top of it all he realized what a mighty swamp he had waded into. This is one of the wonderful things about Canada, though, and why she's my true homeland; she wants to listen to every opinion and then judge for herself. When the film was broadcast, edited to perfection—with alternating shots of the shouting people's tribune and the eternal Jew silently wandering through the fields of bones that sweat to this day—the whole country screamed out in revulsion. The journalist got a national award, Kolodaj was put on the watch list, and my father enjoyed a sensational success: he didn't get even a single threatening letter, so the hangman's henchmen must have been momentarily afraid. The only person who went wild with rage when my father presented him with the videotape of it last year in Vienna was Simon Wiesenthal."

"There he is!"

Captivated by the story, I hadn't immediately recognized the person approaching us to be Viktor. The storyteller eagerly jumped into the present.

"Well, so?"

"Scotch!" He noticed that I didn't understand the English word. "I need a whisky badly."

I'd rarely seen him drink. And I couldn't remember him ever craving alcohol this way. Of course, she was the one who should urge him on, but I couldn't stop myself.

"At least tell us . . ."

"If I don't have a drink first I'll be afraid to."

All three of us had a cadaverous tinge from the fluorescent street-lamps, but he looked like death itself, as if in that single hour (how long had he been with Josef?) he'd gotten frostbite.

"First of all you have to have something to eat!" his Jewish wife decided. (Uh-uh, Petra, after that story maybe it's time to stop the name-calling!) "You haven't eaten since yesterday morning!" (My sweetheart had truly suffered from the suspicion!)

He turned to me.

"Is there a decent place nearby?"

Without me, I wanted (in a more civilized fashion) to say, but my stomach intervened first (I had last eaten hot food three days before on the riverboat), and presently another thought weighed in: taking the time to hear his story and having a meal meant I could mix business and pleasure, and to boot I could enjoy my sweetheart in public for once. Yes, it was practically the only time since his return that I had seen him outside my cramped birdcage of an apartment. Even in the old days we'd spent the great majority of our time together alone at home, whether at my place or his. Hour after hour we'd read or study together (mostly in bed); his enthusiasm for English was infectious and I started to study it seriously. (When he left, I stopped out of sorrow, or was it just a pretext for my laziness?) He was definitely a domestic sort, just like me; we loved and tortured each other, broke up and got back together without spectators. In time we created an artificial world for ourselves, which then shattered when confronted with the real one.

His fata morgana was the study of all accessible descriptions of and works (especially outlawed ones) about market economics, which he swore by, although paradoxically it was the so-called socialist economics he disdained that supported him. Poetry became my optical illusion: whatever I longed for and dreamed of I put into verse, and I placed my trust in those chimeras in much the same way the great poets of mid-century did in the star of Communism. After our reunion what distressed me most was that he and I couldn't leave those four walls and go out in public. (For secret love you get house arrest, constantly reminding you of its impropriety.) Now he himself had requested it.

God, once again I am capable of less than I would like. How I long to be faithful to Your commandments, but stronger is the sinful desire to be with him! Even if she is present, too!

It turned out that the cafés and restaurants had also taken a long weekend off—naturally when they were most needed. ("Many of you have up till now confused free markets and freeloading, but your free ride will end in free-fall!"—a frequently cited quote from a television appearance by the government adviser Professor Viktor Král.) Finally I (unhappily) suggested Wednesday's fateful restaurant, and it was like a dream: this time the tablecloths were sparkling clean and it was as if they'd changed the waiter along with them; he brought three kinds of whiskey to choose from (I ordered the same kind of bourbon Viktor did; I only know our domestic brand, King. His Jewish—whoops!—his wife asked for a cola, ugh . . . "Drink up, Vic, I'll drive"—oh, well, one more thing I don't know how to do) and recommended the marinated steak, "our specialty!"

I watched him as he ordered and for the first time that whole year of our love I could see objectively how much he'd changed for the better in Canada. His self-conscious pride, which captivated me but also could drive me crazy, had often been the cause of absurd situations. At one dinner in a restaurant, when he was served an uncuttable cutlet, he had put down his utensils and waited for someone to ask him why. They simply took away his food, but charged him for it; in anger I let him pay and go hungry. Now I bore astonished witness to the way he quietly and yet self-confidently put the waiter through his paces.

"Cheerio!" Viktor tiredly raised his glass, not looking at either of us, and absentmindedly drained it. He didn't even wince; before it would have knocked him flat. Who taught him? Couldn't have been her . . .

"So don't keep us in suspense!" She joined my refrain.

A good swig pulled him together. His color started to return; he even smiled.

"There's nothing to tell. Petra arranged the whole thing."

I could have purred for joy. ("For your praise I would walk the world over," to quote I don't know whom.) She wasn't satisfied.

"But what actually happened?"

"What actually happened was that he let me read the paper he's taking to our commission tomorrow. He wrote that he saw me on television"—clever idea!—"knows that lustration is being carried out in the governmental organs, and considers it his moral obligation to forestall any possible wrongdoing. He is willing to testify to it in person."

"Excellent! Exactly what you'll need," she comforted him. "So why are you upset?"

"Why would you think that?" he cut her off and shot her a glance as if she'd betrayed some secret to me. (Why? I'm yours, too, your lover, your second woman, actually your first one, chronologically!)

"I'm asking," said his first-second woman, showing herself to be a surprisingly vigorous personage, "because I can see it in the way you act." (I would never argue with you, sweetheart, I'd attend to your every whim unto death!)

"Look, Vanesa, even if it were a hundred times what I need, and even if he behaved like an English lord, my stomach still turns at the thought that this guy pretended to be my friend and didn't tell me he was one of them. I'm revolted by the idea that I got out of here thanks to him—anyway, I hope he was just making that up, too; I'm sure they burned those records in time. I have to trust in the good judgment of people who had more experience with the cops than I did. And I don't want to hear or say another word about this today!"

What nice little horns and claws he was growing! (He's decidedly not under her thumb; good, good.) The waiter had already correctly served us one steak "well done" (for her, so she's not a real predator), one medium (at my sweetheart's request, half mine and half hers), and a third for me, barbarously bloody. (Yum yum! Since the triumph of capitalism men had invited me out for a glass of wine at most; for someone in my salary bracket, a real steak was as exorbitant as a diamond.) The sumptuous feast continued with a real Beaujolais, so the only thing I needed to complete my happiness was for her to vanish into thin air.

However, she was all the more present, because from the moment when he yelled at her, she was silent. Odd. If I were his wife (if only) and that happened to me, I would have tried to cover up the damage with an earnest conversation in which it would quickly be forgotten. She, on the contrary, was making a show of publicly disagreeing with him, which was unwise, since it evidently pushed him over to my side. (She, of course, had no idea that she was strengthening the lovers' bonds.)

I was thrilled by the idea that out of nowhere he might explode and reveal the hypocritical game he was playing here with her and with me, that he might on the spot leave that life of lies, which otherwise would require him to lie down with the wrong woman an hour from now. How would she take it? Would she kick up a scene out of jealousy? Would she blackmail him with tears? In my mind's eye I saw her father nod to the cameras and tell a powerful man: You wiped out my entire family. If she had inherited his steeliness, she was dangerous.

Even so, I was indescribably happy that he could devote himself exclusively to me. (Should I feel remorseful? He was amusing me instead of her because she was deliberately sulking. She's the one who keeps dragging me places!) He calmed down and explained to me quite humanly for the first time what was meant by coupon privatization of state property, which was causing huge arguments in the media. (In the past year at my place we'd gotten around to his field maybe twice.)

I soon had to confess that once again I'd lost my concentration, because their quiet domestic war distracted me. I thanked them for the invitation and he quickly (a bit too quickly) called for the check. The waiter served up the punch line when he brought a receipt with an astronomical sum on it. He anticipated my horrified objection with an explanation.

"As of today we're privately owned. Quality has its price, doesn't it?"

Arms extended, he seemed to caress the bar where just last Wednesday filth and surliness had flourished. My sweetheart (the victim of his own economic theories) paid without a word of protest (given the exchange rate it was a trifle for him, anyway) and the waiter once again reminded us what country we were living in when he helpfully announced to me: "And at any rate I let you off for the last two glasses of wine from when you were here with your son."

"You have a son, too?" Viktor was aghast and in this way got it out of me.

"No, I was here with a friend . . . from work!" What's with my cheeks? Am I blushing? How awful . . .

And here I realized that something good had come of this: she noticeably brightened, as if only now I had stopped being a threat to her. And he? Yes, my sweetheart, it was one thing to impose an obligatory freedom on me, so your conscience wouldn't trouble you, but it was another thing to find out after that blue moon, when you must have been longing for me, that I truly was not waiting day and night for your call! The unguarded expression in his eyes betrayed to me exactly what he was thinking: that in his absence an unknown young lover was embracing me. My sweetheart was suffering and I was surprisingly glad.

❄ ❄ ❄

Hosanna! I wasn't mistaken!

When she'd driven me home (she wouldn't have it any other way, and continued to behave amicably toward me, even with that certain trust which had most likely prompted her confession down by the river's edge), she warmly wished me all the best. Viktor got out and walked me up to the door of the building, where he thanked me again and as he wished me a good night squeezed my hand so powerfully I almost yelped. I had managed to get undressed, take my makeup off, and wash up—ruminating on why it hadn't occurred to him to whisper even one tender word to me (past forty has he become less daring, less resourceful, or does he love me so little?)—when the telephone rang. Gabby! Finally! (I pined for him unceasingly, but her silence crushed me more and more the longer it went on.)

"Yes?" I called out.

"My love . . ." someone whispered, the way deranged murderers used to do in films.

"Who is this?"

"It's me . . . I can't talk out loud or for long, but I want to tell you you're always with me!"

What's happening? Has she left him? If so, he wouldn't be whispering. Aha, she's somewhere else in the house, also getting undressed and washing up before they go to bed . . .

"Víťa! I want you!" I couldn't control myself any longer. "I want you now!"

"I want you, too! I'd like to . . ." An incomprehensible whisper.

"I can't understand you!"

"I'd like to make you ring"—What?—"to ring your bells." Never in his life had he talked this way!

"Yes! Come on over and ring me! Quick!"

"I can't. But Tuesday, at five, okay? I'll stay over. Can you wait till Tuesday?"

"Yes, yes! I wish it were here already!"

"Ah . . . ah . . ." Why is he stuttering? "Will you really wait?" He's so direct . . . "All of a sudden I'm jealous, see?" That's good! That's very good! "Do you still love me, even a little?"

"Yes! And how about you?"

"Yes, yes! Like mad!" He began to whisper quickly. "I can't get you out of my mind. Tuesday!"

End of call. Now I should really have started to say my rosary until I overcame sinful temptation, except I just stood there with the receiver in my hand and stared as if drunk at that passable naked figure with the outstanding hickey (it'll make it clear to him what he's driving me to), who would be adored so wonderfully just two days from now. Bathtub, washer, stove, and especially you, o empty bed: the curse has ended, King Král is mine!

5

I WOKE up still in a kingly mood. I made myself coffee to drink in bed (oh, if only someone would occasionally bring it to me, ideally of course my sweetheart, except he was waiting on someone else) and hedonistically enjoyed two cigarettes as well, while the radio informed me about foreign fortunes and misfortunes. The Americans were leaving Iraq, where the war had ended, while around the corner in Yugoslavia things seemed to be just starting up. (Luckily, shooting was out of the question between the Czechs and the Slovaks; we just hurl dung at one another.) One curiosity was the item about a student who had painted the gigantic Soviet tank in the Smíchov district (a memorial to the liberators in 1945, which became a monument to a new occupation) a bright shade of pink. Under the law this qualified as an insult to one of our allies. It fascinated me that I was actually living in one of those in-between times known to me only from historical literature, where the laws of the defeated mix with the laws of the victors to make a bizarre cocktail. (Or an explosive mixture? Wasn't my new-old love with Viktor brewing into one, too?)

On a whim I flipped on the television and they were broadcasting a Mass! I set my mug and ashtray aside on the rug, stuffed some pillows behind my back, and so took part in a service in the House of the Lord. (God, this isn't blasphemy, is it? I felt You so strongly!) In my elation I knelt over and, palms clasped, leaned my elbows against the footboard. I believed that it was correct to accept divine love in the place where I accept earthly love, too.

With my thoughts in the heavens, I set out to roller-skate along the planned route from Struhy to Stromovka Park; but right at the start I came crashing down to earth. I tripped on a clod of dirt; what a clod I am! I'd given myself a nasty bump on the right knee, but worse than the pain was the panic, the fear that come Tuesday at five I'd be in a cast. I limped my way home and of course couldn't find the acetate, not even in Gabby's lair. (Where is my little duck, anyway? Should I think about calling the police?) So I kept the bruise cold with ice wrapped in a cloth and meanwhile sinned out of necessity as (obviously chastised by pain) I did my washing and ironing on the Lord's Day.

Then, for the first time in a long while, I started a poem, which I was quite pleased with by later that evening:

There you were
near enough for touching
hearing feeling
for in my blood you were
coursing through my heart

Here you are
far past weeping
your body tracing
soulless circles
round a foreign star

I said a rosary and added an imploring request for my daughter to return to me safe and sound and for me to be able to make love on Tuesday without a plaster cast (of course I didn't dare ask Him so shamelessly). Before going to sleep I was buoyed by the blissful hope that my sweetheart was also slumbering alone and that I would be the first to embrace him.

By morning my knee had turned blue (forming an intriguing counterpoint to my hickey, which was in its lavender stage), but the pain had noticeably lessened, so there was hope. My luck even held in the metro, where I bought a ticket and shortly thereafter was able to present it proudly to the inspector. (I hadn't had enough money this quarter for a transit pass, ergo: four crowns a ticket—four trips a day, including transfers—means sixteen crowns a day, sheer insanity! But on the other hand, Thou shalt not steal! Mass transit in Prague is on the honor system, so the compromise I worked out resembled roulette: I would buy one ticket in each direction, instead of two, and be prepared to accept a fine as divine punishment.)

The escalator brought me out into the park, where in some other life I had sworn to my suitor on my daughter's health that I would go with him to Kladno. I really should go thank him for Viktor. (Why? Because! Good behavior deserves encouragement.) Maybe he could give me some advice, anyway, about how to find a missing child . . . Petra, look out!

Passersby must have thought I was a pickpocket shuffling frantically back into the bowels of the subway. I hoped that V.D. hadn't spotted me during this little maneuver (it would have been the worst possible moment). Fortunately his head stuck out in any crowd (a real human giraffe). This near miss was a warning: sooner or later I would inevitably meet him at the office. (What does he do? On International Workers' Day we had other things to do than talk about work.) And I should know exactly how to behave toward him! (The best way would be no way, but how to arrange it?) With the eyes of a hawk I spied another flight path to my workplace; I couldn't think of anything to say to him and quickly forgot about it.

Everyone was already making their first cups of coffee and exchanging glum remarks about the state of their country houses, marriages, and the Czecho-Slovak federation. As always on Mondays, our boss was making the rounds, during which he would agree with everyone about everything. At my office he jovially seated himself on the table, asked how I managed to keep looking better and better (his bug-eyes were no doubt meant to convey affection), and tried a new trick on me: he raised my salary three hundred crowns. He dampened my happiness (three hundred wouldn't compensate for inflation, but would slow my fall) with the condition that I finally learn to use the computer, a child's toy that even he, a technological idiot (only technological?), had mastered. A course was starting today that was to be included in my work schedule.

Want to or not, I agreed, and in return I brazenly borrowed a hundred crowns from him as an advance. It did me good (like all of the sansculottes) to see this moron, for whom I had been a suspicious insect until two years ago, almost rip the button off his back pocket as he pulled out his wallet. Because I didn't want to risk a meeting with V.D. in the firm's cafeteria, I went out for a sandwich.

An hour before the end of the workday I sent off the last pile of answers to a classified ("Gdlookng widower, form. prof. sportsmn., 50 yrs./180 cm./75 kg., seeks long-dist. runner to share final stretch, age no mtr., funds to start bus. nec."; we received fifty-five offers) and set off, accompanied by the envious glances of my colleagues, for a small, bracingly cold conference room where a dozen financially motivated employees waited watchfully. On the hour, the teacher came in and I flushed red-hot.

It was V.D. with a pile of textbooks. He ducked to avoid bashing his head on the hanging light fixture, greeted us, and looked as if despite the near-miss he'd suffered a slight concussion upon noticing me. A pair of equally flabbergasted eyes met his. We must have simultaneously realized that we couldn't both vanish at the same time, and because we couldn't decide who should, we both stayed. Anyway, we each had other problems to attend to: he how to present mankind's cleverest invention to its dullest members, and I how to conceal my stupidity from my admirer (and also my lover, what an awful thought!).

His short introductory lecture granted us both a moment's respite. There are people, he informed us, for whom computers are the be-all and end-all. For him, although he believes in them and computers are his love (hey, look, I've got competition), he sees them only as a means to help mankind free itself from the corsets of its up-to-now limited possibilities. (Where did he have the sense to borrow that from?) It's not about bending ourselves to the whip of Karel Čapek's robots (aha, that's where), so that soon they can make decisions for us and about us, but about having a perfect assistant in our daily lives, one we would have absolute control over, like our ancestors had with horses. With that he distributed flat exercise panels and keyboards to us, and we were transformed into first-graders.

Against my will I sent a couple of despairing glances his way, and each time he halted his explanation and repeated the last portion of it. No one noticed; we were all too busy tumbling from the saddles of our electronic steeds. The last five minutes of class I didn't even try to pay attention to the material as I racked my brain: what next? Shoot out of here first? (Adolescent behavior!) Leave casually, without saying goodbye? (Too stuck up.) Stride out with a general "bye" directed at everyone? (No imagination, no spark.) He decided it for me. Before I could pull myself together, he adjourned the class until Wednesday and headed straight for me.

"Hello. You really gave me a fright!"

Fearing a scene, I glanced around to see who was watching us, but the future computer-tamers all gave the impression that for the moment they didn't even know their own names. The conference room emptied out immediately except for the two of us.

"I gave you a . . . ?" Yes, I did, unfortunately!

"I was afraid I was in the wrong class."

"Like what?"

"Maybe poetry, but that probably isn't here, is it?"

"Of course not. But you've probably figured out I'm not up to it." An attack is the best defense. He was horrified at the thought.

"No, not at all! Women get it much faster. And for you it'll be a piece of cake after a couple of lessons." You'll be surprised.

"I had no idea you taught here."

"Only since March. This is the second cycle."

"It seems to me I've seen you here before. In the cafeteria." Why do I keep on talking to him?

"I worked around the corner in the printshop."

"As what?"

"Well . . . as an apprentice." Isn't he too old for that? He noticed that I was counting. "I needed a job. In the fall I'm starting college. In math."

"You have a high-school degree, then . . ."

"Sure. From a while back."

"I see . . ." Is he seriously expecting me to ask him to please explain? To hell with that! He's approached me again in spite of my warning; let's get it all out in the open at once. "Mr. David, you sent me a letter."

"Yes."

He looked at me from upon high the way a scolded high-school kid in detention watches Comrade Teacher.

"Leaving aside the fact that on the one morning when I can sleep in I was woken up by the mailman"—Hang your head in shame! I'm not going to let you off for any of it!—"I read things which I didn't understand"—Careful! He's taking a breath!—"and which I don't want to understand! I propose a bilateral agreement: I won't get angry at you, you stop paying attention to me, and the rest of it we'll just forget, okay? Because otherwise you've seen me in your class for the last time." That hit home!

"No, please, don't . . . as you wish. It'd be a shame about the course . . ." And his eyes clearly said why: because he wouldn't see me. Am I stuck up? Probably, but it's plain as can be!

"Good." I won't punish someone for liking me; nota bene *post festum*. "So then, let's say goodbye until Wednesday."

"Sure!" he rejoiced and added (clumsily or cunningly?), "I'm also leaving."

With a complete lack of fanfare he accompanied me to the elevator. What now? Will I have to announce dramatically, "I won't ride in the same cab with you!" I could just hear his reaction: after knowing me for an hour she went to bed with me and now she's too shy to stand next to me in the elevator?

The situation resolved itself; our elevator was already at rest. V.D. went down the stairs a step behind me and on the correct side; at the door he let me go first. (So he has some kind of breeding; surely not from his newt-father?) I remained quiet on principle and he didn't dare make a peep.

The difficulty began when a thought started to buzz around in my head, and being the way I am ("curious as a goat," to quote Mom), I couldn't bear the thought that it might stick there. I was intelligent enough not to raise the recently lowered floodgates of his interest with an overly pressing question. At the front desk I added to my goodbye nod (don't shake his hand! no more physical contact!) a surly remark: "And there's no way to make a meaningful anagram out of my name!"

"What do you mean?"

"Just that. I was trying to figure out what it takes to amaze you. Apparently not much."

He reacted as if, of all the pills I'd given him since Wednesday, that one was the bitterest to swallow.

"Your name forms an anagram that reveals your character!"

"What?" So it is 'a meter of steam'?

"You have a vegetable nature."

"Excuse me?" What was he blathering about?

"One of the Indian philosophers divides human character into groups by animal, vegetable, and mineral." Him? Indian philosophy? Spare me! "A friend of mine lent me a book at one point"—so that's it—"and we used it to classify our teachers, fellow students, and jailers. When you're right about someone, it can help you out."

You silly goat! On account of that stupid anagram you've gotten yourself tangled in more of his snares. Wait a second, on the other hand: with that piece of news the ball was in my court.

"You said jailers. You did time?"

"Yeah . . . twice." Some Indian philosopher! I'd gotten mixed up with a criminal on top of everything else.

"For what?"

"For the fact that I stuck out."

"Do you always speak in riddles, Mr. David?"

"I . . . I'm pretty tall, see?"

"Yes, it is somewhat apparent." Even now he loomed like a bean-pole; it hadn't escaped me how many passersby were surprisedly or appreciatively measuring him. "But what does that have . . ."

"So, during the demonstrations I was visible on all the police photos, because I stuck way out."

"Demonstrations?"

"Yeah, the ones the year before last in August, and then during the Jan Palach protests; they came for me twice at home." I could shoot myself . . . "From the school they found out that I'd been a troublemaker there, too. The first time around they hassled me and the next time they tacked on two years' probation. If it hadn't been for the revolution I would definitely have been back in there already." Why did I ask!

I was loitering with this curious dissident right in front of our building as if on a first date, and I couldn't think how to put an end to it. He gave me another lesson when he elegantly demonstrated how.

"Well, goodbye," he said, politely and simply.

"Goodbye," I was working so hard on my nonchalance that I stepped into the flow of traffic like a small child into deep water. Through the wild clanging and honking of the tram and car drivers I somehow reached the park, alive but conscious of the fact that the term I'd seen on the lips of those furious gentlemen behind their vehicles' windshields had probably occurred to V.D., too.

When I stopped shaking, I found I was striding (my knee had stopped hurting) up toward the hospital, and it was clear where I was heading. I put my recent disgrace out of my mind; that kid brought me nothing but bad luck, but so? He was only a bit player in my fate. Which certainly couldn't be said of the man I'd just set out to see again. Beside the fact that I was carrying in my bag his washed and ironed handkerchief and that I needed professional advice, it seemed imperative to bring this chapter of my history to a certain close, after which I would have only my sweetheart unto the death.

❄ ❄ ❄

My victim wasn't in the tea oasis at the moment, and I was seized by temptation, causing me (put a hundred crowns in my pocket and I'm a grande dame again) to order a jasmine tea. The roly-poly hostess was providing moral support to a hysterical fifty-plus man who was experiencing the tortures of childbirth for the first time; from the ceiling wafted feeble strains of the Carmina Burana (in my opinion a number from a heavenly discotheque). From my bag I took the last of my notebooks, in which since childhood I have occasionally inscribed events, thoughts, verses, and, when necessary, other messages. (The most recent: buy potat.!) On a clean page I wrote once more in big letters:

PETRA MÁROVÁ

and let my intellect sparkle, reviewing in my memory the botany I'd had in school. None of the flowers, even the exotic ones, fit into an anagram. The trees likewise failed. No, he's not a clumsy bumbler, just a pipsqueak who's trying out a new ruse on me. (Convicted of sticking out, he made that one up out of thin air! Although . . . they were capable of that, too.)

My hand with its fragrant cup remained suspended beneath my chin; the plant I'd been hunting for in vain jumped straight out at me from the last two syllables.

TRÁVA

So I'm grass to him! (The best and most appropriate rhyme for which is ass.) Wait a second, we're not finished. What's left?

PE and MÁRO

No! How could I have been so blind? When cracked, my etymologically senseless name yielded a poetic image that really did have something to it.

TRÁVA MÁ PERO

"The grass has a pen"; it writes. So for him I'm some sort of writing grass, and it remains only to hope that grass has a positive connotation in Indian philosophy. (No choice but to ask him again.) At any rate, for the moment he was imbued with a somewhat less negative quality in my eyes than before.

"Writing poetry?" asked a familiar deep voice.

Josef Beneš stood there in a dark suit with a tie. I took fright.

"What's happened?" I thought of his family in Kladno.

"What was supposed to happen?"

"Are you coming from a funeral?"

"No." He understood and laughed. "These are my work clothes; my Austrian masters are sticklers for propriety."

His well-tailored jacket showed off his muscles; even today he must be a fantastic lover. (Hey! Don't complain! Your lover is wonderful, and what's more, you love him. And he wasn't a secret policeman!) I squelched the inappropriate sentiment with small talk.

"How's your family?"

"Thanks for asking. My dad died soon after your visit"—Oh, no, now I've reminded him of it—"and my mother three years ago."

"I'm sorry to hear that."

"I think she died at the right time." He's right: she would have been grieved by the tragic end of her dream and also for his sake, although what happened to him? He fell on his feet . . . landed on velvet!

"What about that little girl? Léna was her name? The one who wanted to teach the truth?"

"You mean Fína? At the time they wouldn't let her, understandably, so she had children . . ."

"Mr. Beneš!" chirped the coffeehouse (or rather teahouse?) owner, scurrying over to him from the hidden kitchenette, "what'll it be today?"

"I've just run into an old friend," he confided to her, "so something on the strong side, Mrs. Rézi."

"We'll brew up some Earl Grey, then"—her eyes drank him in—"because it smells of fire!" I, on the other hand, might just as well have been empty air.

"No!" He stopped her. "I'll have my brick instead."

"What sort of code was that?" I asked once her back was turned.

"Some British lord named Grey, whose tea warehouse in China burned down a hundred years ago, tried to sell the bales he saved at a deep discount. The smoky flavor drove the price way up and it stayed in fashion. Want to try it?"

"No!" No friendly gestures! Pass on the message and go. "I have my own."

"I can smell it. The drink of kings." Such a primitive allusion!

Should I call him on it? "I got hold of a tea breviary, and found out that I was reading world history. I just ordered the tea that Napoleon drank at Waterloo and that Lenin drank on Stalin's advice."

"The same?"

"The emperor's supply lines weren't working, so his aide-de-camp offered him his souvenir from the Russian campaign, a little brick of pressed tea from Georgia."

"What a shame we had to wait seventy years for the Bolsheviks' Waterloo." To business, Petra! "Are you surprised I'm here?"

"Did he send you again?" What must he think of me?

"Of course not. You lent me something." I presented him with the handsomely folded square of material.

"You are and will remain the only woman in my life"—he confused me a bit with his tragic tone—"to whom I can lend a handkerchief."

We laughed. Just as on Friday, the tension fell away. He reciprocated with one of the strong black cigarettes that had caught my eye last time.

"What is that?"

"It's Russian." He gave me a light and was amused when after the first draw I stubbed it out and gasped for breath.

"How can you . . ."

"Necessity is the mother of invention. I can't afford Gauloises any more. Listen, what's your daughter up to?"

Typical of him to bring up the reason for our breakup. And typical that she was actually the reason for this meeting, which was otherwise superfluous.

"She'll be an adult soon. Except at the moment she's run off somewhere, and I also wanted to ask you how one looks for a child these days."

"Run off with whom?" he asked, businesslike.

"With a guy, of course." My doubts grew that this was the right person to tell my troubles with Gabby to, but who else was there? "She's been going with him for a while"—well, a month—"he's from a good family"—so good I don't know them—"and he invited her to Karlovy Vary for three days." After letting her be raped.

"How long has she been gone?"

"Today's the fifth day . . ."

"Isn't it a bit early to start worrying?"

"She usually calls me."

"Why don't you call the boy's parents?" And here we are!

"I don't have their address . . ."

"All you need is the last name. As long as it isn't something common like Novák." He's caught me.

"I must be going senile." Better than being such an awfully bad mother. "All I can remember is Mikan."

"There can't be that many Mikans." He's playing with me like a cat with a mouse.

"It's his first name and some kind of weird nickname to boot."

"Did he make a good impression on you?" There's no sense playing games!

"I've never met him. Things are different these days, you know? In spite of it I rely on her judgment. Maybe he plays the man of the world a bit, kids do that now, but he was pretty attached to her. She bragged about how jealous he got."

"How old?"

"Twenty-two, about . . ."

"A student?"

"Of architecture. But he dropped out or something . . ."

"What does he do for a living?"

"Well . . ." How to describe it? "He's in the travel industry."

"Trades on the black market?" There's the secret policeman in him.

"Probably . . ." Well, out with it, already.

"Did he go there to do some smuggling, too?"

"I don't know." And you already know enough.

"He could get into a lot of trouble there."

"Oh, come on! The police look the other way, that's why they dare to do it!"

"After every revolution the police have enough problems of their own to keep them busy. I was thinking about the local gangs protecting their own turf."

"How . . . ?"

"Violence."

"Please, don't frighten me!"

"You asked, I'm telling you the answer. Her name is Gábina, right?" He was thinking about something.

"Her full name is Gabriela."

"Does she have a passport?"

"No. I wanted to celebrate her seventeenth birthday with her with her first trip abroad"—and so I sold the gold-plated coffee-set I got from my grandmother—"but she couldn't manage to get out and get one"—before household expenses ate up the money. "She's a bit of a lazybones." She certainly didn't get it from her dad . . .

"Did she leave the country with that kid on this trip?"

"No, she couldn't have, she still doesn't have a passport!"

"Petra, it's no problem today, even without one."

"What do you mean?"

"Barbed wire, barriers, ditches, the whole iron curtain is gone." So it had its good side, after all . . . "The guard towers serve as perches for hunters and the few soldiers we can afford can't watch all of it. Unless you hit bad luck, you can breeze right over." Just what I needed to hear!

"What should I do?"

"If you want, I can ask after her for you."

"Where?"

"You know my history. I'm not the only one who was monkeying around in State Security; a couple of my friends are still there. I have a good friend in the criminal division." What?

"What does Gábina have in common with . . ."

"The criminal unit does searches; don't you know that TV program?"

"You can't mean showing her on television!"

"That's the last resort. But you can fax photos to the local offices."

"And what if . . . they get picked up for something?"

"Like what?" How should I know what he's gotten her mixed up in?

"I don't know . . ."

His admirer hurried over with a steaming pot, from which a bitter aroma wafted forth, and presented him almost significantly with a small oil-painted mug. (Is there something between them? And why do I care? Tomorrow I'll have my sweetheart!) I quickly finished my tea, except I had just remembered about paying when another customer called her away. It was time enough for Josef Beneš to make his point.

"At the very least you must have some idea what you can expect from the daughter for whom you sacrificed your own life."

He left out "and not only your own life!" I hadn't expected an ironic reprimand from him, and it was worse for the fact that it was well deserved. Out of here on the double, I'll pay on the way!

"It's nice of you to offer to help, but I'll work it out myself." How? That's beside the point now! "I wouldn't have bothered you on Friday, either, except Viktor Král's case gave me no choice."

I threw all my things into my handbag; he didn't move.

"Are you seeing him again?" Who does he think he is?

"You should know I didn't come here to be interrogated! I wanted to let you know that I recognize that at least after the fact you behaved decently, that's all!"

"What do you mean, after the fact?"

"I suppose you think garbage like entering him in the register"—I had lost control of myself—"was also 'behaving decently'?"

He was still looking me straight in the eyes. (Where is all this going? I've seen those pupils dance with passion; now they're cold, foreign.)

"Otherwise you wouldn't have come?"

"Why should I have?"

"Maybe because you were interested in what happened to me. Have there been so many men since then who asked for your hand?"

"You know full well why it wasn't to be had."

"And are you sure it was worth it?" Are you asking for it!

"I'm sure that being the wife of an StB officer wouldn't have been my cup of tea." There you have it!

"It seemed to bother you less at the time, at least that was my impression after Kladno."

"Let Kladno be. I saw how honorable your family was, but you still belonged to the people who deprived us of our rights. I'm not saying I wasn't willing to believe in the sincerity of your messianic behavior, but soon I would have ended up in an irreconcilable conflict with my own self. How much damage did that disgusting regime inflict on us before they brought it down; how could I have simply sat there, knowing that my husband was mixed up in it? Sooner or later I would have started to fear you; I'm afraid of the Communists to this day, when I see what they're capable of!" Ouch! Will he object?

His only reaction was to tear his eyes away from me and start to sip his steaming tea. In spite of my sudden flare of disgust, even now, years later, it scared me: the tea was scalding hot. ("I have asbestos in there!" he used to laugh.) For the final scene I took a gentler tone.

"But no, that's all in the past. Why stir it up again? Check, please!"

He kept on taking steaming swigs and staring at the dark surface of the tea.

"Except it's not over, Petra, that's the awful thing."

"What's not over?"

"The garbage you accused me of is unfortunately much older than forty years of Communism and is far from just the work of a few Communists."

"Who, then?"

"Czechoslovakia could never have turned out the way it did if after the war a whole huge class of people hadn't flooded into the Party like a swamp into a ravine, the same class that earlier served the Nazis and probably sold out the parachutists . . ."

"And you're proud of this?"

". . . and which is now pouring uncontrollably into your Civic Forum."

"Ha! Even if it's true, they must be ancient by now."

"Wrong. That class is immortal, it multiplies as you divide it. Now it's made up of people who for years served us, but now jangle their keys with the protesters as loud as the bells of Saint Vitus's."

"You asked for the check," said his Rézi as she hurried up with the bill (she kept an eye on him from every corner; my attempt at a hasty departure had given her hope) and backed off in alarm when he shook his head wildly. "Oh, excuse me, then . . ."

"You called me a messiah." What does he want with me? Should I be pleased? "But my messianic tendencies have their limits. Once I betrayed my identity to you out of love, so I wouldn't have to deceive you. Now I'll fill it in for you on the grounds of self-preservation. I won't stand for you, of all people, to think that I'm some crook who got out just in time. You asked me on Friday if I was Viktor's commanding officer, didn't you?"

"Well, yes . . ."

"And I told you correctly that I wasn't."

"And, so?"

"You didn't ask anything further."

"And what should I have . . ."

"How about whether he had a different commanding officer." No!

"What do you mean?"

"What I'm saying."

"And he did have one?" Say no! Don't torture me!

"Of course."

"Viktor Král?" I must have yelped, a couple of heads turned.

"Don't shout."

"Viktor . . . worked for you?" Jesus Christ!

"More like he got snared in a trap." I don't understand.

"And all the same you're certifying . . ." There's some other dirty trick in this!

"Only that I entered him into the Register of Contacts without his knowledge. Aside from that he belonged in it." Lunacy. Sheer lunacy. "Do you want to know the story?" Unwillingly, I nodded. "Do you remember his car accident?" At a loss for words, I shook my head. "He left your place upset. You might remember, you'd just broken up." He was always breaking up with me, my poor dear, only to return all the more mine. "It was over your painter." He means Olin! Yes! The last and greatest scene! "On the way back Viktor banged up his car."

"It's starting to come back to me . . ." The car was an old Škoda; I christened her Viktorka.

"He probably told you it wasn't anything much. It was more than that."

"What?"

"He hit an old lady on a poorly lit street."

"And drove off?"

"No. Took her to the hospital."

"What happened to her?"

"Nothing much, really. She came through it with a little shock. He didn't find that out immediately, though, because the police did a blood test on him. They found out he was loaded." Oh! The one time he drank with me; he was gulping right from the bottle in a self-destructive rage and I, drunken beast, let him get behind the wheel! "That by itself was nearly enough to cost him his driver's license. They probably would have given him probation because he helped her, but unfortunately his name was already in our computer." V.D. floated momentarily before my eyes. "It was our first one, and the first thing they did was input all the dissidents."

"But Viktor wasn't a . . ."

"He was like a rat following the Pied Piper, thanks to you."

"But I wasn't either . . ."

"You met regularly with the painter Oldřich Luna, a signatory of Charter 77 and a member of the Committee for the Defense of the Illegally Prosecuted."

"But not for that reason!" He was still sculpting his "Still Life with Tits."

"The computer couldn't know that. Recording all contacts is part of the routine, and Viktor was unlucky enough that my best StB man was there. He took care of the whole job: skipped across the street in person to the traffic division, where our friend was sitting, devastated by his fight with you, the alcohol, and the accident. My man informed him—a primitive trick!—that the old lady was at death's door, and that he could get up to seven years. Our unfortunate collapsed and was ready for anything."

"What's anything?"

"The guy promised him help if Viktor would help him in return."

"With what?"

"Information about Luna."

"What a foul thing to do!" I wanted to scream it out.

"But it was Král's weak point, Petra. He didn't object; he promised, and was caught." Sweetheart, darling, why? "When he soon found out that the supposedly badly wounded woman was long since home and unharmed, he made a further mistake: he repressed the agreement in his consciousness. Or did he mention it to you?"

"No . . ."

"Too bad. You would certainly have given him good advice."

"What?"

"To tell Luna, of course. It was his only way out of the jam."

"He wasn't fond of him . . ." Because of me! Why had I doggedly kept showing Viktor that everyone wanted me? Olin the Pooh would have been friends with me even without going to bed; after all, he wasn't much good in it . . .

"I know. That's how my man got to him so easily. He threatened that he'd play a recording of Viktor's collaboration promise for the Chartists. Viktor decided instead to do it in the hope that it would end there." Horrors without end!

"How?"

"With your contribution." So it's all a lie; I can vouch for myself! "He saw a couple of underground publications at your place, which you'd taken from Luna to distribute." Yes, and only when I got them home did I realize that I had no one I dared give them to. "So he informed us where they were stored. He didn't have any idea that you'd be there when the investigators broke in."

My strength deserted me, and I stared dully at this man calmly sipping his tea and revealing to me, as heavenly choruses sang, that I was in love with yet another stool pigeon.

"As you know, Luna had a stockpile there, and the victorious hunter came to me to boast about it. Before then I'd helped people who I'd never even laid eyes on; how could I leave friends in the lurch? I'd liked Viktor when we served together, but next to you he was just some guy; this was how I learned—and your differing reactions to interrogation confirmed—that the person of true character in your pair was you." Praise me, go on, what does it all mean now? "I could already feel how attracted to you I was, but one of my ironclad rules was and is that a woman in the home isn't for me, especially not a friend's girlfriend." Girlfriend, yes, I was Viktor's girlfriend, until I deprived him of reason. Why did I refuse to marry him back then, when he wanted to have Gabby as his daughter and a son with me? Maybe the haughty delusion that I would reward him with my hand only when he finally granted me priority over his beloved work? Or the subconscious fear that honoring the sacredness of marriage was beyond my abilities?

"After this second failure," Josef went on, "Viktor broke down. He confided to me that he wanted out, because of you. And I started to play a dangerous game behind his back. I chewed out my successful agent like a stray dog. 'You almost blew my best mole's cover; he's supposed to be planted outside.' He defended himself, saying Král had acted like a regular chickenshit and why hadn't he just asked for me directly? 'He was drunk!' I yelled at him. 'He had .2 percent blood alcohol, hit some old crone, and you start trying to blackmail him into singing as if he were some guttersnipe!' So why hadn't he defended himself even the second time, my man logically asked. 'Because he was trying to see whether or not we were in fact a collection of amateurs! Now he's itching to back down, and I forbid you to show your face to him before he leaves. Squelch this business with Luna immediately; didn't it strike you that Král set up his lover on purpose?' " Did he see the naked photos as well? Well, that's the least of my problems now.

"Everything went like clockwork," he continued. "Luna was let out, you were erased from the computer, and when Viktor got his travel documents, I wrote him into the register, with no idea of what would happen. I knew, of course, why he wouldn't be coming back." So he didn't leave on account of me? Yes! All the more so! He couldn't look me in the eyes.

Mea culpa, mea maxima culpa . . . but why not say it simply and plainly? I've fucked up my life, and his, too.

Oh, my undercover lover, what will become of us now?

❄ ❄ ❄

With that sentence stuck in my head like a phonograph needle in the record groove, I must have somehow said goodbye to Josef Beneš (or maybe I didn't? did I even pay?) and wandered halfway across Prague in a daze until I reached the Charles Bridge. I was still repeating it to myself as I leaned against the stone plinth of my revered Saint John of Nepomuk. "Nepomuk didn't give in!" was the first logical connection that I made; he let himself be tortured and drowned rather than betray his queen. And not even I, a weak woman . . . (The first one to get to Olin's couch had been the photographer; the head bandit, grinning repulsively, later threatened me, 'Would you rather see something like this in the newspapers?' 'Yes,' I seethed, 'anything would be better than going along with you!' And I had no way of knowing that behind me there loomed a powerful protector.) So, why Viktor? How could he? What inside him broke? (What did I break inside him?) Who will explain it to me?

Oh, who else beside him!

And who else beside me has the right to call him from the nearest booth? I know everything, come over and confide in me. You're my love, I'll understand all the more because I share the blame; after all, I blundered so far into the snowdrifts that I should have expected the avalanche. Come, confess everything to me, I can stand it. Who else can help you find the beginning of this tangled skein? With whom, other than me, can you find a solution?

And what kind of solution?

What is there to solve here, anyway? He made a pact with the devil, but his only service was a trifling matter with no serious consequences. The man who coveted his soul (the modern equivalent of a signature in blood was the audio tape) is dead! (That had somehow registered in my conscience back in the teahouse: also an auto accident, divine punishment?) And this morning the former major, Beneš, retracted his treacherous entry, which was in fact truly false. ("There are other things, Petra, which I am no longer willing to talk with anyone about ever again, only I owed it to you." And damn him!) Professor Král can thus continue in that deserved (and socially redeeming) career, which his talent, education, and clean honor (except for that one little speck) entitle him to.

And what about me?

Am I supposed to think, as in my heart I recommend to V.D. the Beanpole, that I dreamed all this? Should I forget Josef's baritone, with its undercurrent of children's voices, laced through with the sweet, bitter smell of tea, and rejoice that I helped my sweetheart avert a catastrophe? But: hasn't it happened already? Isn't the first failure of an honest person like the deflowering which precedes both motherhood and prostitution? In this land of constant subversion, thousands were fucked over that way for no reason at all!

And what about him?

After all, it was Josef himself (my mind felt like it was recovering after being bludgeoned; it would suddenly cough up information I'd blocked) who stressed that everything ended with Viktor's emigration; he gave him the status of "sleeping agent." But, but: did he avoid the depths only because they couldn't manage to wake him?

It's absurd that the reputation of a man who once in his life let fear get the better of him was hanging by a thread, while a high-level StB agent is the confidant of Western democrats and gives out certificates of good behavior to his own victims!

But, but, but: is a victim who to this day lives a lie still a victim? And is that victim the one I still insistently call my sweetheart?

As I stood there paralyzed, he came to me: the one who couldn't stay away. He was so arrogant that he didn't even attempt a disguise: he had horns, a tail, and a hoof, stank of brimstone, and spoke in the mocking tones of Gabby's peers.

"Petra Márová, metrová pára, I got my eye on you! This fucked-up world is full of assholes, everything you cared about has gone to shit, there's no fuckin' point hangin' round here no more. Just jump off this big old famous bridge and you're history, you can be with that Jesus guy of yours you're so crazy about, in that paradise everyone's dyin' to get into like some fuckin' Disneyland!"

With my last bit of strength I said to him, "Avaunt, Satan! I won't let you have him!"

6

I LOST my last girlfriends in ninth grade. All the boys in the class were after me even before that—because I always let people copy and was the best at whispering answers—but once I developed breasts I had the older kids running after me, too. Already in despair over losing my slender figure, I was forced to realize that my bosom would become not only a magnet attracting mostly undesirable men, but also a lightning rod for the hatred of other women.

Slowly but surely a rumor spread through the school that Márová was intentionally using her charms to steal the thunder from all her female classmates and friends. (The fact is that other girls' admirers were soon sending out unmistakable signals to me.) I'm afraid I have on my conscience more than one classmate's premature loss of virginity; they threw their virtues into competition with me as their last resort. (No one had the faintest idea that I was probably the only one who graduated a virgin!)

Our Comrade Teachers were the first to show me what life had in store for me from other women—once they noticed (long before I did) after summer vacation the effect I had on the male half of the teachers' lounge. I don't believe they were conspiring against me, but something like a "telephone game" of insulted womanhood must have kicked in, because, one after another, they all gave me hell when they called on me in class. (Except they all foundered when confronted with my elephant's memory; I didn't even have to exert myself.)

The withering of my girlhood friendships crushed me far more than the vengeful crusades of our sour pedagogues. I'd known a few of the girls since I was little, and all of them gradually grew cold; yes, they progressed from frostiness to hatred, not hesitating to abuse every private confession. That was the end of female confidantes for me, and I arranged my life around it: I trained myself so that during every meeting with a member of my own sex I switched on a complete set of defensive mechanisms. (That's why our horrid former boss had never had a chance to get at me and why Vanesa wouldn't, either.)

These mechanisms, of course, worked as well against men. This (and probably also my inborn decency!) explains why, in spite of all my supposed attractions, I had had only as many lovers as there were apostles. (At the thirteenth all the saints abandoned me.) With the passing of my onetime provocations and later flights from emptiness (until Josef and Jarek they had an ephemeral life and ended in hangovers), anyone whose eyes betrayed a desire for my breasts was stopped short.

I found them bearable only when my sweetheart was paying homage to them; otherwise they depressed me. ("Why marry, it's silly / I live in distress / with a heel of Achilles / upon my chest," from the diary of Petra M., age seventeen.) It was mostly their fault that I lacked even one friend who through her participation and detachment could help me figure things out during personal crises (for that's when closest life partners as a class become, instead, the worst opponents).

When I realized that evening on the Charles Bridge that I would remain alone with this piece of information for twenty-four hours (I'd overcome the hysterical notion of subjecting Viktor to a nighttime interrogation), I took precautions. I found an all-night pharmacy on the first try and was lucky that a young pharmacist opened the window. He didn't hide the fact that he would willingly treat my insomnia in a more organic fashion, but he gave me a barbiturate without a prescription.

Gabby was not home and there wasn't even the slightest sign of her existence, but I had reached the stage at which merciful God dulls our woes. I alternately burned and froze myself in the shower, swallowed two and a half tablets (two certainly wouldn't be enough, three seemed risky), and the divine mercy continued: I fell asleep that instant, slept like a log, and next opened my eyes at ten in the morning.

Nothing at all had improved since the day before, but after the pills I was pleasantly numbed and thus less sensitive.

I made myself a deliberately weak coffee so as not to lose this state unnecessarily quickly, and during my first cigarette resolved that I wouldn't go to work at all. The classifieds, which used to amuse me with their bizarre idiocies, repulsed me more and more, and my colleagues, who suddenly defended their faith with a bigotry proportional to their previous laxness, repulsed me no less. I longed least of all for the puppy eyes of that beanpole V.D. From experience I didn't call in, but waited it out until my absence unnerved the boss. When it happened and he called, I answered in a weak voice (I didn't even have to pretend).

"Mrs. Márová"—until last year "Comrade Márová"—"what's wrong? I'm trembling with worry!" He played right into my hands.

"Me, too."

"What do you mean?"

"I've had a fever and chills fighting over me since last night"—from my scotch and sodas—"and now I'm as weak as a rag doll."

"Have you called the doctor?"

"I probably just caught something in that class; it was drafty there." Trump!

"You poor thing! I'm so sorry . . ."

"Don't worry, these things only last a day with me. You know I have practically no absences." And two in the last week.

"Yes, you've always been an exemplary employee!" Since the revolution I've even gotten bonuses!

"Should I take a taxi to the firm's doctor for an excuse?"

"I wouldn't hear of it!" I could practically see him eagerly smiling into the receiver, anxious to make up for the traditional boss's scowl. "Just wait it out until you're better; let me take the rap for it." ("Hero of the Golden Bracken!" to quote Dad when I braved the wooded darkness behind our rented country house to take a pee.)

"Thanks," I said, rewarding him. "Tomorrow I'll be fine."

"Don't rush yourself, I don't want to lose you!" People don't usually die from colds. "If you don't feel okay, just call; I'll say I gave you work to take home." Like knitting him a sweater?

There was still a string of hours left until evening and my lack of self-confidence threatened to overwhelm my newly revived mind. To exhaust my body and self-esteem I decided to strap on my skates again, this time for a pilgrimage to one of our special places. My knee was a brilliant sky-blue, but didn't hurt at all. (I'd diligently powdered the rainbow-colored love-bite on my chest, and intended to cover it with a bandage for the evening, as if it were a boil; my dearest shouldn't be frustrated by anything right now!)

Even at noon Bubeneč was utterly deserted; without hesitation I scooted right off from the house. The venerable park, however, was surprisingly full of passersby whom I'd never seen there before. Unshaven individuals snored on the benches in spite of the fact that the sun beat heavily down on them (the empty bottles underneath them indicated the dose of soporific). As I went past, I startled a knot of people entranced by some illegal game with paper cups, who then returned to it like pigeons to seeds. Over by the small lake a colorfully equipped foursome of foreign hikers were packing up their sleeping bags. (And where were the ducks? Had someone eaten them, or had they fled to the Vltava? Everything was eclipsed by the memory of a rescued dog, fleeing, tail between his legs, from the icy trap . . .) Fortunately, the old bench under the chestnut tree was free.

I leaned my outstretched legs against the back wheels of the skates and lit up. Through my closed eyelids the sunbeams filtered in an orangish color, and tiny dark fishes swam across my retina (recalling the screens of machines in intensive care units that measure one's remaining life force). Stubbornly I tried to return from the miserable present to the wonderful past. A tangle of live images jumped forth from the flickering.

My young husband bends over his lecture notes, eyes on the next goal, and I, in love, circle around him like a bee, anticipating his every desire. One is that little Gabriela's vital energy—from the beginning indomitable—should not disturb him. Day after day I therefore run out for formula and cigarettes (after Gabby's birth I start to smoke like a chimney: a sign of my impending spiritual confusion?) and drag the carriage across Struhy to Stromovka Park, at first in undying bliss that in the evening we will both return to his embrace.

But it is an ever more grudging one (my sturdy little husband, worn out by his studies, quickly falls asleep and is generally reluctant to squander his energy on me), and everything is soon made worse by the illness of my parents.

We shared with them the apartment in which I grew up, and the only possibility I saw was to let them stay with us. Soon I found out, and cried in limitless despair, that even the very best care would prolong their lives by no more than a week at the price of even greater suffering. They had lung cancer (my father smoked moderately, my mother never had; apparently it was an inborn disposition, Lord have mercy on me!) and the doctor, with my consent, persuaded them they had viral bronchitis. My parents touchingly outdid each other in using the inhalers and for show I bossed them around, so that they wouldn't guess I was saying farewell to them forever.

A different thought had unfortunately taken root in my wary husband's brain. He claimed to have read somewhere (but more likely the possibility just occurred to him) that lung cancer was infectious, and he was constantly making a scene about my endangering our child. (His scenes were no more peaceful for the fact that he accused me in a whisper, and my unvoiced protest grew into revulsion.) He pleaded for us to move out for a while (I understood: until they die) to his parents' in Pardubice, a hundred kilometers away; he was willing to commute in every day to school. "You're afraid for yourself!" I hissed; "you move!" At the height of our marital crisis the heavens punished him: he was put in isolation for suspected infectious jaundice.

My walks in the park thus became my only liberating sorties from those four walls, which more and more were populated by death. I would look in at my gaunt old folks (just last year hale and hearty fifty-five-year-olds), admonish them not to cheat on their saltwater inhalers (or you'll risk a summer with no swimming!), and drag the carriage and Gabby downstairs from the fifth floor without an elevator. As I walked along Winter Street and across the triangular square I would be swallowing tears, and only once in the park would I start to notice the life around me. At a certain point Viktor Král began to help me with this.

My husband's close friend from his Pardubice childhood was temperamentally his exact opposite. Tarant had captured me on the run ("I came to the Winter Stadium to skate, saw her, married her!" to quote his beloved line) and nipped my doubts in the bud when he refused even to acknowledge them. It seemed to me that he was a true lion of the big city, while I was a country bumpkin. He was sure of himself, cheerful, sociable (but not spontaneously so, as I found out later; he was consciously laying the groundwork for his future triumphs), and, most important, smart: before I got over my bedazzlement he had become the first to possess my "honeydews" (I'm appalled that I tolerated that nickname; how much more human "boobs" sounds!) and with them my family's apartment, too, so he could leave the dormitory.

When he introduced me to his "astral twin" (who was his witness at the wedding; mine was my father, since I didn't know any other men), Viktor Král made a painfully bad impression on me. Curly-haired, his hair funnily cut behind the ears, and doused in cheap aftershave, Král was so small-town that it simply escaped me how much more interesting (and even better-looking) he was than the handsome Tarant. The whole wedding day all I heard from him was a quiet "Congratulations." ("What is he doing in Prague, anyway?" I asked my superb husband the next day. "Studying economics at the university." "Can he do figures?" "Excuse me, what's with you?" "I don't understand, how is he your twin?" "Don't let him fool you; he's deadly serious, but I've known Vít'a since we were babies. Still water runs deep but rises high!")

That summer we went on a second honeymoon to Yugoslavia; the older Tarants' political connections (like father, like son) opened a crack for us—for the last time after the Soviet invasion—in our homeland's cage, where once more it had begun to seem that a risky one-way escape was the only way out. At the time not even Viktor breathed a word about it, and surprisingly, he went with us alone. ("Is he seeing anyone?" "You know, I don't know!" "You're his close friend!" "I'm telling you: still water; he probably hopes the sea will wash someone ashore for him.") But on the beach, where he displayed a slender, well-built body, he stuck with us and his scientific literature.

From the sea we would return to our second-rate lodgings, angrily learning how low our once rich and mighty homeland had fallen. Zadar was firmly in the hands of the Germans, who, thanks to the black-market value of the deutsche mark, behaved like maharajas, although in turn the postmen and butchers among them were the worst. Once in a while one of them would address me, sounding like a white slave merchant, but would disappear in a panic when my two defenders instantly took off after him.

The Czech tour group shook off its humility at night on the floor of the primitive indigenous discotheque, which broadcast a wail of Western hits to the starry firmament. My dance-loving husband was once again excluded from the battle (not long after our arrival he had stepped on a sea urchin). Viktor wasn't much for dancing, and I wasn't anxious to be pawed at by wild Yugoslavs from the chain; my countrymen and I rejected them all indiscriminately. So I sipped a heavy Burgundy and savored the humid, fishy heat and the white lace of water-spume spread across the sand by the tide, all of which before long would become a mirage for us, maybe forever.

My future sweetheart had already impressed me with several terribly clever and dryly witty comments, which he divulged to the noisy company at most twice during the evening, but his remarks were the only things that stuck with me from the general hubbub. It didn't escape me that others (women, too!) had the same opinion, and it bothered me for my (up-till-now adored) husband: why wasn't he number one at the table? I paid attention and discovered, to my amazement and fright, that for the most part he prattled banalities.

When on the last evening everyone got drunk and a couple of ugly women announced under the banner of emancipation that tonight ladies had asking privileges, Viktor Král was passed from hand to hand and danced well (to my surprise, both of these facts bothered me). Later he was visibly suffering (and I in my heart with him) from the ministrations of a nimble fatty, who was trying to consume him right on the dance floor. His friend (my husband) logically asked me if I would chase her off. Rescued, Viktor called me his "liberating armada" and for a while it was innocent fun—until, fatefully, my favorite tango wove itself into the sounds of hard rock, and I felt an unfamiliar arousal. (I was experiencing everything except kissing for the first time with my young husband, and I was more wide-eyed than greedy.)

My dance partner didn't allow himself the slightest familiarity; it was I who (in all decency, but a tango is a tango!) drew him close to me, as the steps demanded, while he, having executed a step perfectly, would always return to a discreet distance. During the dance a dogged—although to the outside imperceptible—struggle ensued. How could I have known that twenty years later it still wouldn't be over? (And that to draw him more strongly back to me, I would begin to take others in my embrace . . .)

After our return I forgot about him completely; my whole field of vision was taken up by impending motherhood. (Gabriela was certainly conceived on that night in Zadar which the tango so languorously ushered in.) Král was rarely mentioned: he still went for beer with the father of my offspring and their old crowd, events at which women —and especially wives—were not welcome. At the beginning of spring he appeared at our house a couple of times; despite their being in different fields, he and Tarant had the same enemy: Marx. For a while they studied together for their exam on that most scientific of all theories, and I discovered a further difference casting doubt on their twinhood: my purposeful husband had decided to take the study of the revolutionary classics seriously.

"Any intelligent person knows," he reasoned over coffee, which I prepared for them in reserve before I went for a walk with the baby (no carriage, no bottle, and especially no cigarettes; at the time she was still a fetus), "that the Russians will stay here at the very least fifty, if not a hundred, years. Lifelong schizophrenia makes a person a spiritual cripple. I'll outwit the Bolsheviks if, like the good soldier Švejk, I identify myself with everything that enables me to succeed in my profession, so that I can shit on them from on high!"

Viktor Král, on the other hand, judged that an intelligent person could go quite far in his rejection of the system without noticeably injuring himself or suffering a moral breakdown. Only, he insisted, if he remained critical of everything that was tearing apart this society, would he protect it and himself against an even greater fall and retain the moral option of another choice under a luckier set of stars! In concrete terms, he wasn't willing to pretend his allegiance to a pseudoscience stripped of everything revolutionary and turned into reactionary dogma. Although memorizing bullshit was no problem for him (he was blessed with a memory like mine), he refused to pass the test with better than a C.

The argument resulted in my firmly resolved husband continuing his devotion to Marx alone, while his friend once again vanished from my life. The slight feeling of loss was soon driven out by happiness at the birth of our daughter and shortly thereafter by misfortune, when the doctor confirmed that both my parents had simultaneously (the probability: one in a million) been struck by the same incurable disease. During one of my escapes with the carriage into the world of the healthy, I happened upon Viktor Král in front of our apartment door. He'd come to ask why his friend no longer went with them for beer. Tarant's honor was still mine at the time; I didn't mention the sad state of our marriage.

His astral non-twin accompanied me all the way through the park. It was the first time we'd spoken together alone. I found out that he didn't have to save up his thoughts for two punch lines an evening; he had enough of them for hours. When I timidly interrupted him in the middle of a description (to this day I remember: it was about the mysterious giant statues on Easter Island and how an expert in České Budějovice had astonished the scientific world by demonstrating with concrete models how the Polynesian aborigines had moved the stones miles from the quarry without any technology—proof, Petra, that Communism hasn't made total imbeciles of us yet!) to say that I had to go home to nurse, he turned red, stammered an apology and would probably have disappeared forever (I didn't know his address or phone number) if I hadn't wheedled him into finishing the story the next day.

After a week I felt like Scheherazade backward (the sultan was telling the stories). It intrigued me that affection radiated from him, and yet at no time did he seem to be showing off or forcing himself on me. (Much less making a pass!) I finally figured out that I was pushing him to speak with incessant questioning. I tried deliberately not asking and the result was startling: he was silent. He was content to walk wordlessly at my side, until I couldn't stand it and thought up another question. In the same way, I came to feel, he would not have showed up again without a direct invitation.

In this way a highly unbalanced relationship, which was to be fateful for both of us, was formed and strengthened.

Although Viktor studied economics, he followed politics keenly and was interested in art. When in connection with something or other I recited a couple of verses (I still remember them)—*Which is true reality? / I in the world / Or the world in me? / This world of mine / was born just recently / and through my dreams / can turn out better / than it could be / and than am I / in a world dream-free*—and he wanted to know the author, he was amazed and persuaded me to bring a couple of my poems to Stromovka Park. There he let me read them to him, read them himself, and threw me into dismay when he wanted me to explain the images (as a result I became aware of their frequent impreciseness). I would have suspected anyone else of making a particularly artful move on me—except: he tortuously avoided all intimacies, which slowly but surely began to depress me. In the end it was I who took the first leap.

A storm rolled in, like in the movies. Black clouds flooded like ink across the blue patch of sky, lightening flashed and thunder roared (little Gabby woke up), and a downpour cascaded over us; someone upstairs must have tipped the bathtub right over. (The carriage had a plastic hood; my little one rolled her eyes as if in a glass submarine.) A man's jacket was cast over my shoulders—pointlessly; in a second it was soaked through. There was no sense in running. As far as the eye could see there was no cover, and the rain was pouring right through all the trees, including our chestnut. It was noticeably chillier, and so naturally it occurred to us to warm each other up with our body heat. In a close embrace we remained sitting on the bench by the carriage. (Noah with Noette and the Noahlet.)

The rain ceased the same way it began; only the puddles that the sand on the paths couldn't soak up, and the myriad of quivering droplets trickling from leaf to leaf, testified to its passage. I was afraid my partner would get up and the enchantment of the moment would be gone forever. So instead I kissed him myself. (I forced myself at least to make it seem like a friendly thanks for a chivalric gesture.) He reacted in a way I had never experienced before. (I had been until recently a virgin, and virgins are, it goes without saying, champions at kissing; for them it has to replace the remaining pleasures.) Everyone else had at that point immediately tried to squeeze my breasts (where I'd stop being kissy and start being prissy), but he left his right hand behind my back and his left on his lap. Even his lips barely moved; it occurred to me that he was offering them like fruit, indifferently, for the tasting. Right then I decided that I would never kiss him again unless I wanted to be horribly humiliated.

Now I leaned against my skate wheels on the very same bench beneath the very same tree, except between me and my sweetheart—whom I had long since fallen for—lay all of Prague (the least of the barriers), the gulf of years (which made him even more desirable), and most of all that horrifying, unbelievable, incomprehensible piece of news equivalent to an accusation despite the absence of a plaintiff or even (thank God!) a judge. My dearest, how could this happen to you?

Starting with his polite but firm rejection of my capable (of anything) husband's craftily justified ass-licking, I didn't once notice in Viktor any sign of willingness to collaborate with a regime he disdained. ("It is the moral right of the weak to deceive the powers that be with pretended approval!" to quote Tarant. "If power is founded on appearances, then appearing to approve it immorally strengthens it!" to quote Král.) Even after his studies, he was always able to apply the brakes at the boundary where his honorable profession ended (he called it service to the community) and where lucrative benefits began for which people paid with their souls.

While my ex-husband (how could I have married something like that? and as if that were all: how could I have had a child with him? what sort of shallow person must I have been?) would whisper his latest gripe about the Bolsheviks to his tennis partners, so that he could later sign the protest against Charter 77 without the slightest shame ("They would have fired me," he insisted to me; "they would have put some towering prick in there, whereas I can still salvage what's left!") and fuck with the intent of the laws far worse than an intelligent

Communist would have dared—meanwhile, his supposed twin had turned into his opposite: he managed to rise relatively high without libations to the repulsive demigods. It's true, he never got citations or awards, and wasn't permitted to attend scientific conferences beyond the confines of the socialist camp (except that once!), but these losses were made up for by the respect of others (and mine, of course) and the knowledge that he was at peace with himself.

As for the dreaded Anticharter, he simply didn't sign it. ("How did you arrange that?" "I didn't; when they shoved it at me with the pay sheet I just shoved it back. It sounds like a fairy tale, but it worked; they must have figured 'who cares about a humble peon like him?' and, in their own best interests, let it lie!") Dissidents infuriated people of Tarant's sort by reminding them of their own cowardice, but Viktor bristled at them only once, during our last argument, which ended so badly, mea culpa . . . ("You play at being martyrs and live like pigs!" He meant Olin and me—and I, so justly described, was driven into an unjust fury.)

My activities in the ranks of human rights defenders ended soon after the clash with the StB, although I passed the test with distinction (vanity, thy name is Márová). In my wildest dreams I never would have imagined why: Mrs. Dissident Lunová, in a vain attempt to obscure what her hubby had been looking for in me, spread the rumor that State Security had set me on him to scope out the samizdat storehouse, the beast . . .

Beast? In the end didn't they pick up Olin because of me? And my dearest sent them there!

With my eyes closed I gripped the worn seat of our love with all my fingers, as if I could squeeze a more favorable explanation out of the bench. Inside I rebelled against confessing the obvious to myself: that I provoked him to insane jealousy, and why? Because I was not capable of obtaining his love otherwise, when I was already pathologically convinced that he saved his passion for his work.

Let it also be confessed that I adored Luna's tenderly robust figures (he achieved a paradoxical result when he let a delicately worked torso emerge from the roughly hewn rock) and I, too, longed to be immortalized this way. While he was carving me (and measuring my breasts gently with his rough hands), I sipped sweet champagne, so that at the end of the session (two and a half times, all told) I embraced him in a pleasant stupor. (His strength as a sculptor equaled his weakness as a lover.)

When, a week after the raid (I went to him again to spite Viktor and the police, but also so he'd stay my friend even out of bed), he served up his wife's slander like an excellent joke, I slammed the door on him forever (it also closed on my inglorious dissidenthood). My sweetheart returned a few days later and once again adored me, so I simply repressed my infidelity, the raid, and the accident as water under the bridge. And no doubt I would shortly have started looking around again for someone else to provoke him with the next time I needed to bring him back under my thumb—except the heavens could no longer look upon my profligacy (whether it was the instrument of true and eternal love or not) and punished me as I deserved.

And they punish me still, as I reap the delayed fruit of evil: my victim is precisely the man I yearned only to care for unto death.

I tried to imagine what course our meeting today would take. His pained whisper on the phone Saturday assured that he was not coming to confess, but to testify to his feelings for me, which were all the more ardent for having been saved and hidden so long. And what about me? How to deal with the hellish summons served by Major Beneš?

Should I push away the arms that long for me (and I for them!) and confess to him without delay what has ailed me since yesterday? (I'm raining, my love, I'm simply pouring; stop this flood before the dams burst!) Should I swear to him that I'm his partner for better or worse and, what's more, his humble fellow culprit, ready to carry this cross with him? But what then?

Comfort him? With what? (That nothing will happen, because where there's no plaintiff?) Give him advice? What advice? (To confess to the lustration commission? Or to tithe anonymously to the impoverished victims of totalitarianism until the day he dies?) But most of all: who has ordered me to become the instrument of such a tardy and doubtful justice? An anguished feeling grew within me that I was appropriating something I had no right to.

If the Viktor Král of old, at the time the little-known friend of my young and completely unknown husband, was extraordinary in some way, then it was in his capacity for critical self-reflection. Didn't he examine his own soul like hypochondriacs do their bodies, so as to recognize right from the start what was threatening it? Hadn't I watched him torture himself over every supposed mistake (most of which struck me as funny) and analyze my awkward rebellions in order to locate in them the traces of his own complicity? (Which had suited me fine.) Wasn't it he himself who suffered longest and most deeply from this unhappy incident?

I tried to define how Viktor II differed from Viktor I. (Before now it hadn't even occurred to me!) The man who returned to me was ten calendar years older, the tensions of emigration had left a noticeable stamp on his face (I belong to the minority who are convinced that emigration was not an escape to something better, and that exiles had to push themselves to a degree that the slackers back home could never imagine), but was that really it? In the course of the last year, hadn't I caught him in mysterious funks at times when he should have been completely happy?

What was it that took place in Viktor I, if Beneš's story is true (why is it that I don't doubt it?), when he had an eclipse of the brain and caught a glimpse of himself hanging in their trap? How did he feel that whole time abroad, whenever he remembered it? Given his nature, he must have suffered and been ashamed. Yes! How could it have escaped me that this unfortunate failure had included a plaintiff and a judge from the very beginning: they were, they must have been, they couldn't have been anyone other than Viktor himself! And the punishment he meted out was the abandonment of his comfortable security (he, too, could have taken his hydroplane and flown out to go salmon fishing!) and a return to this loony bin of ours, so that here, through his own personal sacrifice, he could hasten the end of the old times.

If he had bravely chosen the hardest path of active repentance (what had he gone through after his return to the scene of the crime, what must he have gone through in the last few days?), do I have the right to wave his ancient guilt before his eyes only to nobly help him wipe it clean? Isn't he doing enough of his own accord? Am I playing at being the Salvation Army? And all this on the basis of an accusation, yes, an accusation!—could there be a truer word for it?—from one of the real architects of our national and human tragedy, who managed to supply himself with an alibi in time.

I opened my eyes. Above me the pink lamps of the chestnut flowers glowed, and suddenly it dawned on me: Josef Beneš had wreaked a deplorable revenge for his spurned affection!

The friendly park extended its green draperies, screens, blinds, and fans so that from the memorial bench I couldn't see the people and things sucking the lifeblood from our immature democracy (which certainly was consoling for the Benešes, if not their direct doing). I was surrounded by a majestic chorus of trees which had already been old and wise in that long-ago April when our first kiss rained down. Love him, our chestnut commanded me for them; if he wishes to, he will tell you himself, and if he doesn't dare, then forgive him, as those against whom we have trespassed forgive us.

❄ ❄ ❄

Around four Bubeneč changed into a human anthill; I carried my skates in a bag so the little boys who always made fun of them wouldn't laugh at me. I was almost inside the building when something stopped me. I took a step back and saw at the opposite curb a dirty and battered taxi, of which there are hundreds in Prague—except: a young man was lolling behind the wheel, at first glance a Gypsy. I continued on my way with the nagging feeling that I'd neglected something. (But what? Should I have said, "Hello, you didn't by any chance rape my daughter on May first?")

I immediately forgot about him and as usual scolded myself for not exercising enough when by the hundredth step I was puffing like a mountain local. Finally I shakily stuck my key into the lock and—it wouldn't turn. Panic hit me. (The lock had already broken on me once—although, it's true, that was when my dearest daughter left her key in it on the inside.) He'd be here inside of an hour; finally he could stay until morning again. Where would we go? (That Party poet ruined hotels for me until death!) With difficulty I extracted my key, but what now? Somewhere there must be a service for this. (We supposedly have capitalism now!) I was about to run downstairs (that taxi!) when our door opened and on the threshold was Gábina.

"Hey, hi," she said, unusually flustered. "It's you!"

"Who else? I couldn't open the door. Did you break the lock?"

"No, why? But I had my key in it." Once again!

"Oh, really, and why did you lock it?"

"I didn't lock it. But I stuck the key in it, see?"

"So you're back?" A brilliant question.

"Yeah."

"So?"

"So, what?"

"So, how was it, I'd just like to know." Slowly I calmed down.

"Oh, it was fine."

"How's Mikan?"

"Which Mikan?"

"Which Mikan! Your Mikan! You act as though you haven't seen him in a year!"

"Almost. I haven't seen him since Saturday."

"What do you mean?"

"Just that. He's a bonehead." My expression—at least she has something from me!

"Why?"

"He got jealous again. Packed up and was out of there."

"But why?"

"Some friend of mine came to say hi."

"Who?"

"You don't know him." I don't know any of them!

"When someone invites me somewhere, I don't invite anyone else, okay?" (Márová—the eternal goody two shoes.)

"I didn't invite him." Why am I bickering with her? I'm happy she's here, true? Except, except: in a little while my sweetheart will be here! What are her plans?

"So, what are your plans?"

"Like what?"

Her eyes shot off toward her room; she still didn't know how to lie

(I used to be like that) and was the incarnation of a bad conscience. I marched over there. There was an empty suitcase on the bed; to the left was a pile of dirty laundry (wash it, Mom!) and on the right a heap of clean clothes.

"What's going on in here?"

"Well, I'm unpacking . . ."

"And packing again, no?"

"Well, yeah . . ."

This got rid of one problem and immediately created another.

"Where are you going?"

"Just to look around a little . . . ."

"Where?"

"Like . . . to Germany." I was evidently looking at her as if I'd lost my senses. "What's wrong, Mom?" Beneš summons up evil spirits!

"Gabriela"—her full name was pronounced only in the greatest of need—"you don't even have a passport!"

"But Mom, they couldn't care less these days."

"What do you mean, they couldn't care less? A border is still a border! If they catch you, you'll never get out of it!" (Nonsense! "Unless you hit bad luck, you can breeze right over," to quote the cursed Beneš, and she certainly doesn't have bad luck. Don't shout!) "Please, go apply for one, these days there's almost no wait! What harm would it do you to put it off; you've got loads of time. Learn a little German; you don't know a word of it yet!"

She just about wilted under my beseeching gaze. (She wasn't evil; to the extent she could, she didn't torture me.) But on the other end of the rope someone stronger was pulling.

"Mommypleasedon'tworry," she mumbled, as she always did when she wanted something badly, "youknowit'ssuchanopportunitynothing's goingtohappenandI'llbebacktomorrowpromisepleaseMommy!"

"And who . . . with whom . . ." I'll lose, of course, but first I have to get some guarantee from her that will reassure me.

"It's, like, that guy who came to see me. He brought me back, too, so I could tell you." Liar! You needed clean pants; at least there's that!

"What kind of guy is he?" She desperately wanted not to go into it. "If you won't tell me, I'll lock you in; you're not even eighteen yet!" And what about Viktor? He'll wait, or he'll come another time; this is my only child, and I've done wrong by her too often. Speak, or else we'll both pay!

"He's, like, a taxi driver . . ." Kaboom! It hit me.

"That Gypsy downstairs!"

"He's not a Gypsy, he's a Greek orphan!"

"What . . ."

"Greek. He said you'd know." Wait a second . . . yes! I went with one up till ninth grade; they sent the orphans to us sometime during the Greek civil war, but . . .

"Come off it, he'd have to be my age!"

"He's, like, a Greek grandorphan. The Greek orphan was his old man, see?" Now a new demon attacked me.

"But he's the one who raped you!" Why is she looking as if this is news to her? "You wailed into the telephone, you were as white as a sheet!"

"Yeah, but . . ." I saw red.

"Did you make the whole thing up?"

"No, no way, Mom, please"—she's about to eat humble pie—"let me speak!"

"I'm waiting!"

"He . . . I . . . we . . . when Mikan got out that time, we were, like . . ."

"Like, what?"

"Like, making passes at each other, a bit. And I was probably coming on to him too hard." What a vocabulary!

"How?"

"I guess I kind of turned him on."

"So what was all the theater about? Why did you act so seductive and wild?"

"I was mad."

"Fine, but how can you a couple of days later . . ."

"No, you don't understand me! I was mad at myself. That I f—" Like a well-brought-up girl she stopped herself. "He's a totally great guy." Now I got angry, too.

"Call him up!"

"What?"

"Bring him up here, I want to talk with him." She was at a loss for words.

"He . . . he can't, Mom."

"Why in the world not?"

"He's working . . ."

"But he could follow you to Karlovy Vary."

" 'Cause it was Saturday, see. C'mon, Mom, he's taking some panels or something to Munich for an exhibition, he's got to be there by midnight; we're back tomorrow and I'll bring him up, Mom, lemme go!"

It was almost five, and I was trapped. But once before for a similar reason I'd placed my own interests over hers and almost lost her as a result! I turned to the palliative of all mankind: compromise.

"Gabby, listen closely. There'll be no arguing with what I say. You're not going to Munich!" She yelped in despair.

"Mommy!"

"Quiet and listen. You're not going to Munich or anywhere else out of the country until you get a passport, but you and your . . . what's his name?"

"Gavros . . ."

"You and your Havroš can go just this once. The condition is that he find you a place to stay somewhere on this side of the border. I know from the classifieds that there are loads of private guesthouses, and he can pick you up on the way back. That's my final word. Take it, or leave it and stay here!" No risk, I knew how she would decide.

"Okay!"

"Wait a second! Give me your word of honor!"

"On what?"

"That you'll obey me to the letter and also that you'll bring him here tomorrow evening. From now on I want to know your suitors personally, like they always do in good families!"

"Okay."

"I want to hear it!"

"Scout's honor."

"Don't pull that, you never went!" (My pride: I wouldn't let her join the Communists' Pioneer Scouts. "She never even went to nursery school!" I repeated ad nauseam to the functionaries, "She'll catch all kinds of illnesses, and it's enough that she has to go to school.")

"Word of honor."

I discarded the notion of having her follow the pattern and swear on her mother's health . . .

"In that case you don't need a suitcase. Put your nightshirt, pants, and socks in a bag and be off."

"What about my toothbrush?" she asked, fawningly.

That submissiveness should have warned me. But one weight had been lifted from my soul and I was already thinking about the other one.

* * *

She had barely left when the bell rang, precisely at five, but it was only the telephone. In a strange nasal voice ("Please excuse the bad connection, I'm calling from my car") he apologized that he'd be about an hour late. He'd gotten held up in Brno; could we wait for him? Yes, I promised, we would wait, we'd all made enough time. I hung up disturbed. I wasn't an Achilles, after all, just a normal, woundable woman, who had had quite enough of this for today.

I put myself and the apartment in order, so the hour passed like no time at all, although the second one was unendurable. My artificial equilibrium disintegrated into growing fear. Did something happen to him? Was she onto him (into him)? Or did some sixth sense warn him what awaited him here? Like a caged animal I paced from the door of the apartment to the window, until by the law of watched pots I missed him. When the bell rang I got the shakes.

He looked as if he'd stormed up the four flights of stairs without stopping, and scarcely had he closed the door than he drew me to his chest unusually wildly, as if he'd lost his senses, and he hugged and kissed me. Wild noises escaped from the corners of his mouth, which I understood anyway. ("I love you, you're my love, I want you madly, I want you, I want you right now!") He pushed me in front of him across the entranceway and over the threshold of my room to the couch; it was just like a "strap."

Yesterday at this time I would have given a year of my life for this. Only this was today, and his fingers and lips only caused me pain (and not just physical pain!); the command of the glowing pink chestnut tree had been drowned out by the argument with my daughter and then trampled underfoot as I paced from window to door; the long-desired scent of love (a mixture of my perfume, his cologne, and our sweat) stank from a carefully laid StB fart. I realized that if I didn't bring it up now, that stench would remain forever. I braced my calves on the edge of the couch and grabbed his wrists.

"Wait . . . I have to tell you something!"

He still wouldn't let go of me and started in just as woefully as Gabby had when I put Munich off limits.

"You mean today of all days you're having . . ."

"No, no, but, please, let me go!"

He kept holding me, although he eased the pressure. Disappointment gave way to irritation.

"What's going on?"

"Can we sit down for a while?" My knees were trembling.

He drew his hands back as if he were removing the supports from a shaky vaulted ceiling, until he'd cleared the way for me. I struck the match three times before I could light up with my horribly trembling fingers. He took fright.

"What's wrong?"

"You sit, too!"

He obeyed and didn't let his eyes off me, apparently ready to rush to my aid. I wasn't far from fainting. Because I hadn't counted on having this conversation, I hadn't prepared for it; a welter of disconnected words whirled around my mind.

"Vít'a . . . I love you! Do you know that?"

"Yes . . ." He sounded somewhat worried; he was still on guard.

"I love you with all of me, always, the way you are and the way you were, see?" (The illiterate little affirmative word my daughter uses when she knows she hasn't convinced you.)

He only nodded.

"I simply love everything about you! Even . . . your weaknesses, you know?" He didn't even nod anymore. Didn't he understand, or didn't he want to?

Instinct (chestnut or no chestnut) commanded me to jump headfirst into the putrid waters. (Close attention to his first reaction!)

"I spoke with Josef Beneš."

"I know that." Normal surprise.

"I spoke with him again yesterday afternoon!"

"I see . . . what else did he want?" Normal curiosity.

"Nothing. I wanted to thank him."

"That probably wasn't necessary, all he did was clean up his own mess!" The same revulsion as on Saturday. "The only person to thank is you." He leaned far over to pick up my clasped hands from my lap and kiss the tips of my fingers. "Let it be, Petra."

"He repeated that he wrote you in without your knowledge."

"Yes." He perked up. "They came from the commission today at noon with an apology."

"And then he announced to me that you'd worked for them, anyway."

"Excuse me . . . ?" Without emotion, as if he'd misheard.

"That they tricked you into it. That in the despair that I drove you to, you squealed on Oldřich Luna. And that you emigrated mainly because of it."

My heart was pounding in my throat; he was looking at me as if I were ill.

"So that's what he said."

"Withawholebunchofdetails." I was mumbling like my wheedling Gabby. "Doyouwantmetorepeatthemforyou?"

"And you?"

"What about me?"

"What did you say to him about it?" Yes, of course, why hadn't I foreseen this question? The blood rushed to my cheeks.

"I was in such shock that I didn't even say goodbye to him! I wanted to call you, but I didn't dare! Because of Vanesa!" In a pinch even a wife is fair game! "She should never know!" Only I, your true wife!

"Vít'a, I've been thinking about you almost every second since yesterday; I understand how it must have happened to you. These newborn inquisitors make me want to throw up; they're burning witches here because they themselves weren't worth the devil's effort! You managed to come back, to serve the cause of good, you show me your honor even in your relationship with your family, which I respect for that reason, even though I love you so much; I dared to talk about this weak moment only because I was the one who caused it all, and you're the one person I've never lied to."

"But I have?"

This new question completely derailed me.

"What do you mean?"

"But I've lied to you?"

"You're the only one who hasn't!"

"And did you tell him that?"

"I'm telling you, I didn't even . . ."

". . . say goodbye to him. But why didn't you tell him that lying wasn't part of my equipment? Why didn't you tell your Mr. Beneš that as an informer I would hardly have dared look you in the eyes without blushing in shame?" I couldn't think of anything to say. "We were together again a couple of Fridays after your affair with Mr. Luna." He always called them "Mister." "Do you really want to believe I was deceiving you so masterfully? I was cramming English and mentioned exile to you a couple of times; you refused it not only for your daughter's sake, but also for a principle which seemed to me, if you remember, funny." (Yes, I had not stinted to recite from Dyk's poem "The Homeland Speaks": "If you leave me, I will not perish; if you leave me, you will perish!") "But most of all: I told you after your penultimate escapade, the one with Mr. Stříbrný"—With whom? Oh! My gynecologist; I'd already blotted him out on the way back from the Tatras!—"that I could hardly bear another one. In spite of this you brought me Mr. Luna, on your silver platter, to boot." Yes, yes! "And now you think I'm a liar, and one of yesterday's grand masters of disinformation is speaking the truth?"

My reason refused to admit such a monstrosity.

"Is it all really a lie?"

"If you think it's true, then it isn't a lie." What does he mean . . .

"What do you mean . . ."

"If Petra Márová decides that Viktor Král is a repulsive stool pigeon, so be it."

He stood up. (Why is he standing up?) I grasped at fresher straws.

"What did you talk about on Saturday?"

"You know what. What he should write and who he should give it to."

"He didn't even mention . . . any of this?"

"If he had mentioned it, he would have been the first person I ever slapped in the face, the way you should have done, at least symbolically, when he played such a primitive trick on you! Yes!" He was screaming! "A ruse, a scam, an utter fiction, with which he finally paid you back for giving him the shaft!"

He strode out to the hallway, and I, in my total stupefaction, thought he was headed for the bathroom, except he didn't turn right, but the other way (to get a drink of water in the kitchen? wishful thinking), and then a shot echoed forth.

My sweetheart had with all his might slammed the apartment door behind him.

7

WHEN I managed to look at my watch it was eleven p.m. That's how long the numbness in my body and soul had lasted. (A fixation had gripped me: if I don't move, he'll come back, whether from the bathroom, the kitchen, or the street, or most likely he'll suddenly be sitting here again and I'll realize with relief that I had been afflicted by a fleeting bad dream.) My returning sense of time roused my thoughts and my muscles. My stomach growled. (Since morning not a thing to eat or drink.) I rose and went to make myself at least a coffee.

In the course of the night I drank half a dozen of them and incinerated a pack and a half of menthols; I'd had plenty of sleep earlier —all these things combined maintained me in a state of vigilance until the early morning hours. The second part of the night I spent in the armchair, where he had sat since time immemorial, as I tried to summon up his spirit; after all, it was on this little piece of furniture that it all started in earnest.

What followed our water-logged kiss was a mutual moral hangover. For me it was unthinkable either to deprive my baby of her father or to live an incessant lie, and Viktor in his way felt something analogous. Distance meant safety, and we probably would have estranged each other for good, if not for the incident with the dog. Once again (that winter: my husband was merrymaking at some family celebration in Pardubice; I had already lost interest) we had taken a short, moral walk around Stromovka and I (at the time firmly convinced that I was the poetic heir to Marjory Fleming's mantle) was tiring him out with my freshly written poems, after which we parted with our usual (security is security) handshake and went our separate ways. Soon I noticed that Gabby's rattle (a gift of my mother-in-law, who routinely took inventory of our possessions) was missing and retraced my steps looking for it.

The small lake we had always circled was freshly covered with ice, and onto it had artlessly stepped a dachshund–St. Bernard cross that we'd remarked on several times in astonishment. In spite of his monstrosity (a powerful body on wobbly little legs) he was an inexperienced puppy; he broke through the ice, and the shock of the cold nearly finished him off. It was clear that he couldn't save himself. Just when I reached the shore someone in a winter coat hurled himself into the freezing water, fell in up to his chest, but kept struggling (smashing through the icy covering with his elbows like an icebreaker) until he reached the despairingly thrashing animal and, despite its panicked struggling, dragged it onto solid ground. I sensed before I knew for a fact that it was Vít'a, and what touched me most about the whole scene was that it was not intended for spectators. (I was the only one, and he had no idea I was there.) I raced over to him (the dog shook itself off and galloped away, tail between its legs) and made him trot in his soaking coat alongside the carriage all the way to our house (I was gasping for breath and Gábina burst into tears out of fear and hunger) so he wouldn't get chilled through.

At home I turned on the bath, made a hot rum toddy, and rubbed his bluish body; only when he sat down in the hot water did it hit me that he was naked. I was already all aflame and longed to finally hold him. Since even now I couldn't expect him to take the initiative, I fell back on my feminine wiles: with the same distractedness with which he'd taken off his drenched underclothes, I began to nurse my wailing Gabby in front of him. In the meanwhile he warmed up, sat in my bathrobe in the little armchair across from me, and stared at this like a miracle; nothing will ever erase that image of his face, in which shyness battled with longing. Sated and exhausted, Gabby fell asleep on my chest and in a moment of sheer insanity I asked him if he wouldn't like to try it himself after all those years; he leaned over and actually suckled, giving me an indescribable delight, which, as soon as I had put Gabby in her crib, I tried to repay: I drew apart the folds of my bathrobe on him and kissed the tips of his comical male nipples which remind us of our secret common ancestry. (Then there was nothing left to do but sleep together, figuratively and truly, until the next morning.) I had never caressed anyone like that before, and those tender touches became a signal of all our overtures and also a symbol of our whole relationship.

Except on this painful May night even the metaphysics of my most beautiful memories couldn't help; his aura had departed with him, leaving no trace.

That chilly look (yes! downright furious) when he posed the question of whether he'd ever lied to me (the truth fanatic asks a notorious liar!) wouldn't stop frightening me. And I was still paralyzed by despair. (I felt it physically, like a straitjacket.) After all, under the chestnut tree I'd already realized what he flung at me as he left! In spite of it, I'd never doubted Major Beneš's truthfulness, and had swallowed his lie hook, line, and sinker.

It was now as clear to me that my sweetheart was innocent as it was that he would never again come by or call. Further proof of it was my deep tranquillity. (I am normally a peerless hysteric.) I sat here this way when, in quick succession, my parents died. (The tears came, my sorrow met its limits, and a cataleptic torpor overwhelmed me, from which only my daughter's vital needs and Viktor's calls could tear me forth; his mere presence at the graveyard was a source of support.) I didn't sit here, surprisingly enough, when his colleagues finally betrayed to me that he had fled; my heart insisted at the time that he would return. Now he, too, was dead.

I had no idea how to apologize to him. (It would be too difficult to manage over the telephone, a letter was inadequate and, what's more, might end up in the wrong hands; stalking him was too risky and also impossible.) Only heaven could help me now. But even if all the saints were with me, and if he forgave me and returned to my embrace, it still wouldn't ever be like it could have been. Taken together, all of my knives in his back couldn't have hurt him like the one I mindlessly accepted from the hand of a sevenfold liar.

Unbelievable, incomprehensible, that I lent Beneš my ear, permitted him to overwhelm me with that slander (till he'd vomited up the last bit of it), as if he was some sort of moral authority in the country he'd helped corrupt. How had he charmed me into believing him as I had ten years ago and—despite the new state of affairs—falling for a worn-out old police trick? The explanation: to this day I was still reeling from his masterstroke, the trip to Kladno.

Of course I had accompanied him there at the time, and not only because I had sworn on my daughter's health. (Just as in childhood I had kept the index and middle fingers of my left hand crossed behind my back during the oath, which meant it didn't count.) At the time I'd liked Josef Beneš, yes—quite a lot! (Ardent lovemaking with him wasn't just a form of remedial exercise for me; it changed friendship into a relationship not unlike love.) So naturally I was curious to see the home of the man who had asked for my hand (which naturally had pleased me greatly) and who presented me with, instead of an engagement ring, the admission that he was a secret billy club of the regime (which appropriately shocked me).

He didn't have a car, supposedly on principle. (They'd driven him in a "company" car, I realized today—except not right from home like the Austrians.) A bus took us there from Florenc Station. He was the only man on the bus (not counting the driver); otherwise they were all women of various ages, mostly in pants and every last one laden with bulging shopping bags. No sooner had they clambered up the steps than they broke right into conversation with no initial pleasantries, as if they'd stepped from the sidewalk into the sitting room. I relinquished my seat to one old woman, and she gave a toothless laugh at my guide instead of at me.

"You've got a nice daughter, Josef."

Others addressed him (as Józa, Pepíček, even Pepánek) and the compliments to his "daughter" multiplied (young, pretty, fabulous), until finally I whispered in his ear (the vehicle was rattling and clattering toward Bílá Hora), asking where they all knew him so well from and why then did they take me for his daughter. He held me by the shoulders and explained just as closely that in old Kladno there had arisen through the crisscrossing of miners' dynasties a sort of giant family, and that "daughter" referred to a girl of any kind, insofar as she was nice.

He held me closely on the way from the last stop and talked with them about unfamiliar people as if I weren't there, except the fingers of his right hand secretly stroked his beloved "nest" (today I burn with shame). I expected him to head toward the high rises (symbols of socialist luxury, although they continuously shed bits of damp plaster, and drying underwear and bras fluttered from all sides), but he turned into a block of low-built houses, and soon we broke away from the thinning clump of women in front of one of the row-house duplexes, which could surely remember back to the last Austrian monarch.

In a tiny garden wild roses were blooming; in their midst a large dwarf with watery eyes stood watch and a second one sat oddly on a bench by an arbor that only a very stooped Snow White could have walked through.

"Zat you, Josef?" he asked.

"Yes," said my intended (I hadn't told him no and that was already half a yes). "I've brought a guest, Mrs. Márová. Petra, this is my father."

The old man stood up. He didn't reach his son's chin, couldn't have weighed half as much, and had completely different, childlike, sky-blue eyes. I immediately held out my hand to him.

"I'm very glad to meet you." He didn't move.

"You have to take his hand, he's blind."

"I'm sorry." I pumped it awkwardly. "I didn't . . ."

"Realize?" He beamed, and immediately I saw it. "Gave me blue pupils. My wife always preferred blue-eyed men, now she got one."

"We're going inside, Dad," Josef announced. "Want to come with us?"

" 'Course I do!" The blind man nimbly headed off. (My helping hand extended itself too late.)

"Dad runs all around the neighborhood on his own."

"Used to be I had the run of the whole town, 'cept now everything's changed. Least the neighborhood's still the same."

"He'll be eighty"—instead of him, Josef was now leading me again in his way—"and it happened to him soon after I was born."

"What . . . ?"

"The explosives manager miscalculated. One patrol left while they were still loading up the store."

"But I worked even after that!" his father bragged.

"He worked the winch until retirement," Josef interjected, downright proudly.

What patrol left where? What's a store? A winch? I felt stupid asking, as if I were on an excursion.

"Where is everyone!" the old man yodeled in the narrow corridor with its steep staircase. "Josef is here!"

The living room was connected to the kitchen by glass doors with etched (evidently original) art deco designs. The furniture was on the old side, the appliances good quality: next to the gas stove an electric cooker, a tall icebox, and also (wouldn't it fit anywhere else?) a washing machine. A potbellied television, undoubtedly of Russian manufacture (a screen like a postage stamp encased in heavy wooden beams). Central heating piped in from the outside, so a later improvement. A cuckoo clock, underneath it a rather modern radio, and on the wall in the corner—no! A statue of a saint! (Which one?) I caught Josef's amused expression.

"Barbara. Patron saint of tunnelers. Almost like in normal people's homes, isn't it?" (I had evidently been gawking as if on safari.)

And the family was already here. The room filled up at once; I couldn't understand where they came from, and had no idea who they were until Josef introduced them to me like characters in a play. His brother had come right off his shift (he was forty at most; thus his begetter had known that he would never see his offspring with his own eyes); Josef's brother-in-law and his two sons, their sister from school; Josef's mother from the ground floor ("I made up the bed in case you two want to stay the night"); and her daughter, Josef's sister, from the cellar ("I was picking fresh mushrooms"), the mother of both tubby boys and the slender schoolgirl. There were eight people talking to me (or at least amiably grinning, like the two little boys) all at once, but surprisingly it wasn't unpleasant; after a little while the confusion smoothed itself out and the conversation was head and shoulders above the daily blathering of my new colleagues at the classifieds of the Catholic paper (by the grace of the Party and the government), where

I had just miraculously found a job. (A horrid thought from 1991: had he used his influence back then to get me the position? Will they find a record that I, too, am a "little bird" from the Interior Ministry?)

The men took turns in the single bathroom (by age?) without crowding, and then stretched out their arms and legs in the armchairs and on the couch (even the old man hadn't abandoned this heavy manual laborer's habit), while the women flitted around the stove top and the dining table. I of course offered to help, but readily acknowledged that I would only be a hindrance; things ran as smoothly as in the fairy tale: "Table, be set!" and "Cook, little pot!" In a quarter of an hour we were seated around the steaming plates (porkdumplingscabbage) and the youngest girl had even managed to run out (as I had done thirty years ago) for a jug of beer on tap. ("Because we have guests!" Josef let slip; "otherwise we drink bottled beer like down in the mountain . . . the mine, that is.")

The meal was at first glance fatty and quite awkwardly served (over my protests the mother served me five huge dumplings the size of dinner rolls and, in the pit in the middle of the plate, a hunk of meat, covering the mound with a large ladleful of cabbage with caraway), but it was surprisingly tasty and even light, probably also the work of the little glass of rye whiskey that the blind father unerringly placed nearly into my hand. It noticeably lowered my defenses; soon I experienced, in my pleasantly muffled state, what meteorologists call the calm at the eye of the hurricane. The family was arguing about politics.

Raised in and accustomed to the company of intellectuals (the more wonderful they were before revolutions, the poorer they were after them!), who from morning to evening watched their every word until the gunpowder of their defiance was trampled into mud (my parents taught me at home not to believe what they themselves were teaching me in school!), I was amazed by the wildness of an argument I wouldn't have expected from these Red Cadres (right-angled in their righteousness).

It became evident that a trench divided the family. Funnily enough, it ran precisely along the table; had they deliberately taken seats facing each other like two armies? It stretched from the head, where the father presided (like a blind version of the one-eyed Hussite general Žižka), and included, to his right, the sister and her three children. From the other end of the table the mother directed her troops, supported on her right by her son-in-law and younger son. Their numerical inferiority was balanced out by the fact that all three of them participated, whereas the youngest generation on the other side only murmured in the affirmative or negative.

The father and sister rejected the Russians as occupiers, President Husák as a collaborator, and "realistic socialism" as a loathsome deception and a mockery of the working classes. The mother and her ranks saw it, under the given circumstances, as the only sure way of waiting out the crisis in the movement and of not permitting the old ways to return. ("Why'd you lose your eyes, Dad? 'Cause the owners were looting the mines!" In response, from the pudgiest of the grandsons: "An' they're still looting 'em, Gramma; Dad can tell you how many injuries there are!" "Bullshit!" Josef's brother-in-law snapped at his son. "You're bunglers, morons, you're only crippling yourselves.")

The reasoning behind their positions unfolded gradually. The father, a founding member of the Communist Party of Czechoslovakia, resigned after the signing of the Moscow Protocols, in which his party approved the August 1968 occupation of its native land by foreign armies; his daughters (one had since gotten married and moved to Ostrava) joined him. The mother and the three men decided to stay in the Party. I knew Josef's reason; his mother's, brother's, and in-law's sounded honorable, too, but the other side (their own flesh and blood) accused them of colossal naïveté.

The brother-in-law was a mining engineer and the brother held some high blue-collar post (mines inspector?); they were united by their mother's conviction that their activities (for which Party membership was a requirement) guaranteed hundreds of people work and security. ("As best we can, in that hellhole," the brother-in-law insisted to his rebellious juniors.) The head of the family shouted that they were prolonging our society's agony by patching up the mine like tinkers. ("If you didn't coddle people and served it to them straight up, they'd take to the streets tomorrow and Husák would be out on his ass!") Both the youngest miners nodded, but their father's authority evidently prevented them from supporting their grandfather more visibly.

Josef's mother took up the defense with a frontal attack, accusing her husband of giving up the chance to put the Party back on the right track when he gave up his membership. ("You're a deserter! You made it easy on yourself; all you do is watch and criticize . . . !" A curious reprimand to a blind man.) The bristling old man now struck like the blind king John at Crécy, even holding his daughter's arm with his right hand while his left gesticulated with a fork. ("Bullshit! You're opportunists! You're letting them turn Communism into a poorhouse with a reform school attached, until the young miners want to puke from it!") Both the young ones grunted with assent, and dug into their roast pork.

Although I enjoyed sports as a kid, I'd never been interested in the competitions that the majority of the nation sat glued to open-mouthed for evenings on end. I must look just like that, I realized fearfully when I noticed Josef was noticeably smirking. Emboldened by the general openness (how infectious it is! no wonder they were so fanatical about censorship!), I retaliated with an unexpected sarcastic attack on him.

"Whose side are you on?"

The fact that no one from either camp had spoken to me could have been politeness, or more likely lack of interest in the opinion of a being from another world, who knew pitifully little (the family expression: "bullshit") about their life. It surprised me, though, that they skipped right over the first son as if he were thin air, especially when he reached right into the center of power. (Do they have any idea what he does?) So I asked the provocative question myself. In his place, his sister answered immediately. (I couldn't tear my sight from her hands with the web of blue veins like tattoos.)

"Josef stayed in that company, but he's the last honest one there."

The whole family laughed, each in his own way and in a mood affected by the quarrel, but together it sounded almost endearing. Unarguably, respect and affection for everyone reigned, regardless of differences. (Did they know, then, about his evangelical mission at the StB? Had that confession been my initiation into his family?) As if they'd switched channels, they were now suddenly and harmoniously exchanging pleasantries, mostly who was spending the upcoming vacation doing what. I was once again surprised that the best-paid citizens of this country, whose work in the mines often doubled the length of their nights, didn't head off to the seacoast as the greengrocers and waiters did, but instead went fishing, mushroom collecting; the women even looked forward to spending time in the humble garden in front of the house.

As they cleared the table I finally insisted on helping and was even permitted to dry dishes (nervously: the earthenware service with colorful decorations had come into the family when the blind man's father married!) as the sister washed. Meanwhile the men in the living room argued about sports for a change. The sister caught me looking at her hands and smirked (so that she resembled Josef).

"Bolsheviks, even former ones, have blood on their hands. So they say."

"What happened to you?"

"I worked in the coal sorting room so the kids could go to school. Except the boys figured out how much harder their dad works for less money, and they get on his case for belonging to the pigs up above. After high school they went back to the mines and I have these as a memento. Yes, Petra (without mentioning it she slipped into the familiar, and it flattered me), don't think that we're bigger pricks than the rest; you see our home, that's all that we've acquired since the revolution. Of course, as the ruling class we bear more of the guilt for the endless crucifixion of this country; Dad is right. And Josef knows it, too."

That was the extent of her recommendation on his behalf—insofar as that's what she had in mind. I watched through the doors the way he sat down next to his mother and hugged her; their heads touched in an intimate conversation.

"A long time ago she consoled him," his sister added (even that glance hadn't escaped her), "and since then he's been her baby."

No explanation was forthcoming; she devoted herself entirely to tearing apart the hot sweet rolls on the baking tray. When I brought them to the table and his sister carried in a pot of coffee with milk, the men gallantly changed the topic and they—especially the father—began to ask about my native Prague, as if it were not a stone's throw away but on another continent. The impression grew in me (Josef confirmed it that evening) that they were subjecting me to a test.

"Do you like the coffee?" Josef's mother asked unexpectedly (up till now no one had asked my opinion about the food).

"And how!" I blurted out, "This is real java!" (Its indescribable taste had died for me along with my mother.)

They rejoiced as if they'd heard an alien speak their language. Their reserve vanished, replaced by a heartfelt directness.

"We haven't even asked," his father confided, "what you think of all this."

"Of what?"

"What we're arguing about. You're not a stalwart, are you?"

"A stalwart what?"

"Communist."

"No!" It sounded harsher than I'd intended it to, but so what? Let them know! "No one from my family has ever been in the Party. And I was raised a Christian."

In return, they looked me over as if I were an exotic animal. The mother probed further.

"What do your parents do?"

"They're not alive, but they both taught."

"Oh." She was genuinely surprised. "And they were allowed to?"

"They were probably among the last who actually taught something!" her daughter said sharply. "And your granddaughter, I hope, will be among the first to do so again. Fína"—she pointed to the skinny girl with glasses who had wordlessly but passionately sided with the blind father's opinions—"is also going to be a teacher and has decided to tell children the truth at any price."

"What truth?" stormed the presiding foremother of the tribe. "Like, for instance, that the First Republic was an earthly paradise and the coal barons were the benefactors of Kladno? That's what young people think, even here, and who can convince them it wasn't like that except a well-educated teacher and those of us who lived through it? Didn't I cook that same soup from rotten cabbage day in and day out for five mouths? Didn't our neighbor Vincek hang himself at fifty when the foreman told him to turn in his miner's togs on the first of the month, 'cause he was too old? Didn't the tax collectors take even our little wagon, so that little Josef had to tote greens for the rabbits on his back?" She didn't shout, she just sat calmly at the table, but her fingernail dug a deep furrow in the holiday tablecloth with each accusation. "Didn't they send out the mounted police and armed troops against us during the strike, and after it didn't they fire anyone who so much as said a word? Will you teach them that, Fína?"

"Yes, Grandma. But also that today it's no better, that they've stuffed you full of 'I am a miner and no one is better' and now they have you over a barrel! I'll teach them that you happily put up with the Communist barons, who didn't even have to send their hired men out because you kept better watch over one another than any pigs could manage!" And Josef didn't even blink. "What do you have to thank them for, Grandma? That we can serve pork with our cabbage? But your grandsons sweat over practically the same 'miracles of Soviet technology' as Grandpa used, and on television the blacks in Africa are now the servants of their mining combines—and you celebrate this as a victory of socialism? I'm going to tell my students that they have a choice between the truth or the lie, nothing more. And that you can live decently off the lie, but only with truth can you have a decent life, and die honorably, too, so that you don't have to be ashamed that you were on this earth in the first place!"

The scolding from this young person, who was farther than any of us from the grave (God grant!), touched me, but also shook me up: she let me know in no uncertain terms that I was the addressee. I returned her gaze and showed my colors, guest or no guest.

"You asked where I stand in your argument. Nowhere! Or, more accurately, somewhere else completely. Ever since I can remember, Communism has seemed as suspicious to me as it did to my parents and even to theirs. They didn't have varicose veins, but they certainly didn't belong to the ruling class. They didn't sweat as much as you did, but for it they were far poorer. Their experience was called education, you might find it laughable in comparison with . . ." How to describe burned eyes delicately? ". . . with wounds on your body, but knowledge of history is the only thing that can warn us the way a match warns a child when it burns him for the first time—as long as we're willing to feel ourselves in the skins of those who have burned themselves before us." The girl was listening rapturously, and, buoyed by it, I continued my sermon. "Anyone who wanted to could figure out that, of all the types of coexistence that mankind has thought up, the only ones to have proved themselves are freedom of thought and freedom of the market—in a word, democracy—within the bounds of human abilities, of course, and they're limited by our baser qualities. History is swarming with betrayed revolutions; in none of them were the people victorious for long, only their rulers changed. That's why, forgive me, but I'm skeptical that any of you, one side or the other, can save our poor country until you stop thinking like Communists, which probably won't happen!" Where did that come from in me? I was spoiling for a fight.

It got them. Finally they looked to Josef with their eyes for advice. (A nice little fiancée you brought us!)

"She's right," my almost-spouse decided. "It's our tough luck that we won't have the chance to set things right again. Fína, Jirka, Jarka, it's up to you; maybe Petra would agree with you." He unexpectedly stood up. "Thanks, Mom; thanks, Marie, we couldn't have had a better time; I hope that next time we"—a significant look in my direction—"can do as well for you."

"You won't be staying over?" His mother seemed as disappointed as if, even in me, she were losing her own child.

"We've got something in Prague this evening," he explained. (More rigorous lovemaking!) "And before we go Ruda wants to show us around a bit." (Who? Where?)

His brother-in-law stood up, too, and nodded eagerly. The family said goodbye as if we had just spent an afternoon of splendid good humor together. The father made his way to me to affix a kiss on my lips, the sister pressed paper bags into each of my hands ("Half a Bundt cake for each of you; next time we'll leave it whole, all right?"), and the mother made a cross on my forehead! ("She was always a believer," Josef explained to me afterward, "except she doesn't talk about it; every miner's mother adds a bit of insurance upstairs for her sons!") The aforementioned tried not to crush my hand, and the future teacher also kissed me. ("You're sensational!")

"Where are we going?" I said surprisedly, when on leaving the garden we didn't turn toward the city.

"It occurred to my brother-in-law that, once in your life, you should take a peek at what we do. You'll get to know the place I spent my youth."

He didn't ask, he decided for me (how wonderful to have a man who knows how to!), and I took the hint. My unease was shouted boldly down by my curiosity and trust in these two stalwarts (who certainly knew their way around down there like rangers in the forest). The tall iron structure with a huge wheel that we were headed toward grew rapidly until it was towering threateningly over us. Josef (who held me close once again on the way over) began to let go of me until he was walking properly alongside me.

"Do you have ID?"

"My state ID . . ."

"Your work ID would be better."

He studied it and, satisfied, showed his brother-in-law the publishing house's stamp.

"Glory to labor, Comrade Engineer!" the incredibly portly guard (how does he reach his pistol?) called out deferentially. "Hey, Josef, hello!" He lit up like the sun in a children's book. "I see we've got company!"

"How are you, Mr. Kolmistr?" Josef held out his hand.

"As well as my thyroid permits. But it's still more fun than pushing up daisies."

"We're showing our comrade journalist from Prague around." The brother-in-law waved before his eyes proof that I was the smallest wheel in the classifieds department.

"Great," the guard beamed. "The last few years everyone shat all over us, but wait till nuclear power comes along; then they'll miss us!" As he wrote out the passes, the tip of his tongue moved in time with the pen.

We came out into a room as large as a school gym and I almost yelped when I looked up. (From the ceiling were suspended dozens upon dozens of hanged men.) The brother-in-law lowered one of the hooks, letting down a pair of clean overalls and a helmet with lamp.

"Miners' clothes for the next apprentices."

He chose me a pair of boots; he and Josef took only helmets with their street clothes.

"Why do I have this costume and you . . ."

"We won't get dirty." Well, well! Don't show off!

The outfit was big on me; its proportions were wrong. In the tremendous lamp room we picked up safety lamps and had a good laugh. (The lamp man to me: "You need a haircut, you hippie!" After an explanation: "Jesus, Comrade Editor, you're a dead ringer for a boy!") Josef chortled while he led me to the "elevator," as he called the two cages on top of each other. The three of us stepped into the top one and when a bell rang we simply dropped into the depths. My stomach remained somewhere up top (otherwise I would definitely have lost my lunch) and I dug my fingers into Josef's elbow as I stared, horrified, at the glisteningly wet black wall whizzing upward beyond the grille of the cage. Then we lurched gently and stopped. The bell rang again. Ruda pushed open the door.

"Second floor, everybody off! Six hundred meters'll be enough for us." (That's two Eiffel Towers, or ten of the miniature ones on Prague's Petřín Hill!)

The time that followed seemed to me despairingly long, even though it was actually (I am the chicken of all chickens) shamefully short. If at first I was comforted by the arched and sharply lit tunnel, reminiscent, with its solid vaulting and tracks, of the metro, I began to tremble after a hundred meters when we turned off at a shunting switch into a dark side hallway. It was possible to walk upright in it (I only occasionally stubbed my big toe in the rubber boots), although here the concrete framework was replaced by mere beams. (They seemed to be matches that had to hold up more than half a kilometer of earth.) The cone of the lamp in my helmet revealed droplets of water; here and there one would fall, as if the earth were sweating. I myself was swimming in sweat. In front of me, Ruda stretched his long legs; behind, Josef marched with the same step; I stumbled on the crossties, between the crossties, and against the crossties, but neither of them noticed; the light in my hands was heavy, I kept switching it to the other hand, but even that didn't get their attention. (Where are they running to? Why so far? What if behind us . . .) Immediately thereafter I saw a beam which had snapped into a V-shape beneath that unimaginable weight and held aloft the bulging mass of the ceiling like a strong man with the clenched joints of his fingers. I expected the brother-in-law to come to a halt on the spot, balk, and order a retreat (at a trot? will I make it again?), but they pushed forward with Josef breathing down my neck. (Have they gone crazy? Yes!) Broken timbers sprouted everywhere, the head in front of me slowly ducked lower, until it vanished below his shoulders; then the brother-in-law kept ducking, until suddenly he wasn't there. A hole no more than a meter high led straight into the wall; the wood stopped completely. In a panic I glanced at Josef.

"Go on," he smiled (or smirked?), "crouch down and don't be afraid, this is hard rock!"

At first I wriggled along squatting, then pitifully on all fours (the beanpole in front kept walking normally, even when bent double, as did Josef) and muttered in horror, Omyguardianangel watchovermysoul, so that they must have heard it. Suddenly I saw legs without a body, but before I could manage to pee in fright I, too, was out of the crawl space and dazedly straightened myself up in some sort of grotto like an underground vault, whose ceiling vanished in the darkness. Behind me towered Josef. Ruda looked jubilant.

"Here!"

"Yes!" my lover (momentarily a complete stranger!) rejoiced, "although you could easily bring tour groups here now."

"We're leaving the floor as is, in case they find a vein in the area."

Josef's light moved away, and with it his voice.

"Was it this corner?"

"Sure was!" The brother-in-law now shone in my eyes as he confided, "Here's where Josef and I spent our longest shift as trainees." Judging by their laughter it must have been fun. Had they gotten drunk? "We were digging over in this corner here when it fell in on this side." I must have jumped as if I'd been shot. "Don't be afraid, this area was worked out years ago."

"But how . . ."

He led me over to Josef by the elbow.

"Fortunately we'd just put in the conveyor in the main corridor, and underneath the belt were the tubes for the pneumatic drills, so we had something to breathe."

"And how many . . ." I turned my neck to Josef in the hope that he'd finally shout April Fool's! ". . . hours were you . . ."

"Five days, wasn't it?" offered the brother-in-law.

"Not even. Something like a hundred hours. Stuff kept sifting down in the tunnel."

"And what did you . . . all that time . . ."

"Good question," said Josef, as if it had occurred to him for the first time. "What did we do here, anyway?"

"I think I mainly breathed," said the brother-in-law and kept laughing.

"I probably was thinking about something."

"I know!"

"Well?"

"You told me all the places where you can always find mushrooms!"

"Yes! And after that you always beat me to them!"

Both of them chuckled. From out of the darkness a small stone fell and simultaneously an unfamiliar sound alarmed me, as if the mountain's stomach was rumbling. I couldn't restrain myself.

"I'd like to go back now . . ."

I don't remember much of the way back. My brain began to function again only in the bus. There were three of us, including the driver. (A real taxi-bus.)

"I have two questions," I said. "Weren't you ever afraid?"

"For years and years. Each and every time. That's also why I took college-prep courses and did law instead of mining. Because of it I went in for skydiving, a reaction to claustrophobia. Except after Marie's death I began to be afraid of the air, too. Second question?"

"Have you told your family that you're in . . ."

"I've never even hinted."

"And what do they think you do?"

"Exactly that."

"Your father and sister, too?"

"Almost definitely."

"And in spite of it they still like you?" Why the surprise? I, too . . .

"They know me," he said simply.

That night I (as if already at City Hall) was breathing yes, yes, yes.

Three days later Gabriela announced: him or me!

And even after years had passed in which he did who knows what (had he caught the Charter as he was drowning?), my memory of Kladno proved that I had given him more weight than my greatest love.

My sweetheart must be cleansed and revenged.

Only how?

* * *

I finally had to go back to work, but by then I even wanted to. Before Gábina dragged her . . . what was he, anyway? (despoiler? boyfriend? chauffeur? cross out the terms that do not apply!) home this evening I would have become a wild woman. (Nothing could do me in faster than idle considerations going round and round.) I needed to think about something else, whatever the price.

It didn't cost me much, after all. I sat out a couple of hours with the proof sheets, and a few times momentarily forgot my distress thanks to the bizarre texts that topped even the Dadaists. (The winner of the day: "One-legged man seeks one-legged woman for a mut. life journ. Attn: Lefty for righty." All that was missing was "Let's save on crutches!") My stomach was still resisting all thought of food; instead,

I demonstrated a compensatory diligence, and my boss was so rapturously thankful that I borrowed another hundred from him against my paycheck to put some decent wine on the table that evening. (I'll have to sell something else . . .) Just before three he tactfully reminded me that I had a class.

If there was someone I hadn't missed, then it was V.D., but I'd withstood the worst of it, so why avoid him? I also remembered that I'd gotten an A on my homework-slash-IQ-test. (I'll ask him what grass means . . . ugh! Don't ask him anything, Márová, educate yourself on the computer and homeward!) He entered the conference room and searched for me with such concentration that he finally banged his head into the light fixture. In the general merriment he flushed, caught it in mid-swing, and for a couple of seconds held it next to his ear like a basketball player. Then he began to lecture, staring possessively at me. (What a silly boy!)

I bent my head over my textbooks (there's nobody here) and left it there for the whole lesson (but us chickens). In this state I couldn't signal to him to slow down or repeat; after a short time I lost the thread. Stubbornly I scribbled in my notebook whatever my brain caught, living in fear that he would start to walk around the class. (What would I do if he wanted to look over our notes? Scream "Fire!" and snap my notebook shut under his nose? Oh, who cares anyway? This is peanuts compared to my other mishaps!)

Lost in thought, I missed the opportunity for a timely getaway while someone else was asking him for something. Before I could get my things together, he shook off the busybody and flung himself at me, slinging over his shoulder on the way his squarish bag, which he'd placed behind the teacher's desk at the start of the lesson.

"Are you clear on everything?" Did I look like such an imbecile?

"Are all your students usually geniuses? I'll be an exception; I'm dense. Maybe I should just drop it right now?" He almost shook his head right off.

"Jesus, no, why didn't you give me a signal like last time, I would have explained it again!" If you keep gawking at me nonstop I won't even look your way!

"Thanks, I don't want special treatment. If the others can follow you . . ."

"I think they can't, but I didn't want to hold you back on their account!" Kid, you could drive a person up the wall!

"Test us next time, all right? And then either break us up or find a way to work with us."

"Yes!" Once again he was standing almost at attention. Petra, don't take it out on an innocent!

"So I'm grass for you?"

His shyness went poof! He lit up. (Like a child.)

"You solved it! You know, grass is number one with the gurus!"

"Oh. And why?"

"Because it's indispensible and yet so humble." A pretty piece of flattery.

"That's not much."

"What do you mean?"

"Being good cow fodder?" He looks helpless; did I hit the mark?

"I understood it differently . . . The uniqueness of grass is that it's beautiful in the simplest possible way; its simple form and single color suffice. Like a person who doesn't dissemble or pretty things up. Like you!" What should I say to this? "And your usefulness is in your writing. You were grass for me even before I found your anagram. That's why I . . . why I . . ."

"Well, what?"

"You ordered me not to talk about . . . a week ago." Of course!

"Yes, let's drop it. So, goodbye until . . . when?"

"Friday at twelve."

"You're making that up!" Why is he looking at me like that again?

"So you could go right home afterwards. Your colleagues requested it!"

"Oh! Of course!" A short circuit in the brain. "So, see you then."

"I'm leaving, too."

We followed our usual route, and I was curious to see what subject he'd bring up. (I'm not going to entertain him!) As the silence grew and the remaining distance shrank it was harder and harder for him to start. (A task like in a fairy tale: prince, say something stupid and I'll vanish!) We passed the front desk (after the revolution they'd rejected recording arrivals and departures as a Bolshevik deformation, and then reintroduced it as an obvious necessity of capitalism, ha ha) and went out onto the square. He stopped and from his lofty perch began to talk seriously (like a real adult).

"Mrs. Márová, don't think so poorly of me. I'm only an oaf when you're around!"

"What do you mean by that?"

"That maybe I'm not as big an idiot as I look. It's only in your presence that I behave like a kid in special ed." Am I supposed to convince him otherwise? "I'm conscious of it, but I still can't help myself; the moment I see you it's almost like I'm a teenager again." You've surprised me, but you still don't get on my nerves any less.

"That's a simple problem to solve, isn't it?"

"I know that I get on your nerves"—He has antennae!—"but if you would have a bit of patience with me, it'll pass, you'll see!"

"But why?"

"Because I'm in constant fear that I'll botch something, and that fear makes me awkward."

"I mean, why should I take the time?"

"I attempted to explain that to you in the letter. You inspired my admiration and trust; I tried my hardest to at least get you to take me seriously, but I apparently overestimated my abilities. Please excuse me once more, and for the last time."

After a speech like that, it was clear his only option was to walk away for good. That's what I wanted, wasn't it? Nonetheless, I heard myself say: "No, it's you who should excuse me, Mr. David. I didn't mean to hurt your feelings, because I do take you seriously." What's wrong with me? "Our first meeting didn't go terribly well, I haven't been having the best week, and then the circumstances . . ." Your daddy was the second one, after those cops, to make me into a whore. "In the end I was impressed with how you dealt with it. No, there's no question of your seriousness!" He relaxed and visibly loosened up. "Of course I'm flattered by your interest—I'm a normal woman—but what of it?" Where had we ended up? By the hospital. Why did I go for a walk with him? Well, so that we wouldn't be lingering under the eyes of everyone in the firm! "Don't you realize . . ." Should I say it? Out with it, maybe he'll leave you alone! ". . . that I could be your mother?"

"You couldn't be."

"Do you have any idea"—Let's get this over with!—"how many years older than you I am?"

"Twelve years, eleven months, and thirty days." I gaped. "You're the first day of Leo and I'm the last of Cancer. So we're both crab-lions, the children of prudence and courage." I was furious.

"Where did you get that?" This snooping of his has got to end immediately!

"Well, from the list of students . . ." Whoops. The bastard here was my boss.

"The basic problem here is that you belong to the next generation." What am I going on about, it's not like he's asking to marry me! "Why aren't you interested in younger women; you might have more in common with them."

"Because I don't understand them, and they don't understand me."

"Why not?"

"They don't know squat about life. Which is even less than I do." So I'm to be his teacher?

"A relationship between two people isn't a school, though." Meanwhile, here I am teaching him. "And if they're young, they discover life together." Whom did I discover it with? Most of all with my StB agent, who was a quarter-century my senior, the devil take him!

"Except that I would rather do it with you, you see?" No! He's made me an offer! "And for good!" A real serious one!

"Václav . . ." And it must have me flying high or something. Why all of a sudden am I calling him by his Christian name? "Stop fantasizing and figure it out. You don't need a computer for this: when you're fifty, you'll be in the prime of life"—I'm prophesying like our

Czech foremother Libuše—"and me? I'll be an old biddy!" So old it chilled me. "Haven't you read or heard how marriages like that end?"

"I've experienced it. My mother was fifteen years older than my father."

"And how did things turn out?"

"Badly." Well, there. Even a tubby like him left her!

"So, you see."

"Except she left him. The next one was ten years her junior, and is crazy with jealousy to this day. That's why he did everything he could to see I stayed with my father, and just to make sure he provided her with two replacement children right away."

In an instant I softened. The case of V.D. began to appear to me in a new light. (A real classic.)

"Are you looking for a mother in all your women?"

He seemed to understand me as well as I understood computers.

"No, not in you!" It's true, Petra, you couldn't ask a more brilliant question of a recent lover, all honor aside!

"I'll prove to you"—Off the thin ice!—"that you have my trust by leveling with you. I'm not available. I have a lifelong"—What? Lover? Boyfriend?—"partner"—let him figure it out—"whom I'm faithful to. Unfortunately, you found me in a crisis; a vile lie shook our relationship. Normally I don't talk about my private life with anyone; I made this exception to prove to you that my *no* isn't intended to insult you." Finish the job, Petra, once and for all! "It's simple and straightforward: I have only ever loved one man. Before the First of May, and after it."

He took the blow like a man. And finally his nervousness and awkwardness left him.

"I thank you very much, Mrs. Petra." How proud he sounds. "Uncertainty bothers me most of all; I can deal better with certainties. And you won't regret your directness; people say that I can be a good friend. Do you have anyone to help you out?"

"With what?"

"Well, with this intrigue of yours. Could you use my help?"

The unexpected offer had a powerful impact. I understood at that moment several things in a chain reaction: that he was toting a camera in that squarish bag, and that heaven itself had sent him to me, so that he might make up for his offense with a special mission, for I urgently required a portrait of the very man to whose abode my subconscious was once again leading me.

From the time of my visit at his place, something about Josef Beneš's dissident past didn't fit the picture. Now I knew! And also how (don't shout it!) with a little luck to prove him guilty of a deception that would lend a motive to his actions and give satisfaction to my sweetheart.

"Do you develop your pictures yourself? I mean enlargements and so forth."

"Sure!"

"Do you have a driver's license?"

"Sure!"

He was looking forward to this so eagerly that he reminded me of a dog waiting for a ball to be thrown. Encouraged by this, I made my decision.

"I'd need you to take me somewhere on Saturday afternoon." Maybe he has a car?

"If a motorcycle would work . . ."

"Excellent!" It fits the task better, in fact. Wait a second! "Despite your kindness, I'd have to impose a condition."

"I accept it in advance."

"That you won't ask me to explain what I want and why."

"Well, sure. It's your business. I'm Panza."

"You're what?"

"Sancho Panza. Your servant."

"Except I'm not Donna Quixote. I'm not jousting with windmills but"—Should I tell him?—"with the former State Security."

"My lips are sealed."

We ended up where my legs had taken me for the third time in six days. We could start right away.

"I'm going over to that teahouse, the little pub across the way; it doesn't have a proper sign yet. You walk around for a quarter hour . . . Do you have time?"

"Sure!" Sheer joy had impoverished his vocabulary.

"Then go in and order whatever you'd like; it's on me, of course," I cut off his objection by raising my voice. "There's no use arguing! You'll see who I'm sitting with, and then go back out as if to take pictures outside. I need a perfect picture of him—even better, two pictures, front and profile—without him knowing."

"Sure! Like they were from a police file!"

Only inside did I scold myself for being such an amateur; we hadn't agreed on any other contingencies and one occurred immediately: our subject was not at hand. Chubs treated me like a regular, serving me a boiling hot jasmine without fuss, but when I asked after him, she turned cold and barely knew him. (Do my senses deceive me? Hardly! More likely she's on the prowl for him.) I waited until closing time (my employee modestly ordered a Turkish coffee with my money) and laid my trap for the liar.

At six I thought I had it, and knew how to act so as not to alarm him. After paying (what am I going to sell to fix this hole in my cashbox?), I looked around as I left to see Panza (more accurately Dr. Watson) intently studying an English instruction booklet for a telephoto lens. Quite unerringly he arrived shortly at the corner where I was waiting (beyond the sight lines of Beneš's terrace). I pointed it out to him.

"Do you have a zoom lens with you?" Shop teacher: lover number nine, with a country house; I admired him when he immortalized all kinds of meadow creatures perfectly with lenses as thick as a man's arm, and left him after a beauty of a fight when he disclosed that he had photographed me sleeping.

"Up to three hundred."

"Great. I'll see if he's at home and somehow I'll get him out on the terrace; do you think it'll work?"

"Sure!"

For the third time and with revulsion I trudged up the steps where at one time the thought of the embraces to come had carried me upward better than any elevator could. (Significant, that after an even longer endlessness I fell for Viktor as if only a day had passed, while here not a single nerve is aglow!) The door opened as I rang, except once again it was the neighbor's. A familiar personage greeted me with an even chillier look than the teahouse lady's.

"He's not home!" It sounded like: We don't give money to beggars!

I rang once again just to be sure.

"And he's not coming back!"

"Thank you." I won't stoop to your level! "Goodbye, then."

"He went to Vienna," she announced to my back, surprisingly enough. "He'll be back on Friday, can I pass on a message?"

"It's not necessary."

"You won't leave your number?"

"He knows it." Go burst from curiosity.

"But who should I say was looking for him?"

Already on the floor below, I answered the face hanging over the railing, my mind fixed on his yearly floral message.

"Rosa." Let him rack his brains for once.

V.D. was intently snapping pictures of pigeons around the corner. On the way to the tram I described the missing person as best I could. He assured me he couldn't miss on Friday.

"With that description you could paint his picture!"

"If he comes back, he could go first for tea or straight home; supposedly they drive him back, so pay close attention to the cars." I decided on a further show of trust. "And his name is Beneš, Josef Beneš, a former major in the StB, now a consultant to the Austrian trade consul."

"So he's a smooth operator, too!"

"That's what I want to find out. Meanwhile, thank you, and now I really have to say goodbye for today."

"Can I invite you for dinner? In return for that coffee!"

I very nearly lost my temper, but restrained myself. In considering whether he was naïve or bold, I decided to presume innocence.

"I'm meeting my daughter." And if it were my lover, what's it to him? "Listen, I also take you seriously when you say you want to help me without ulterior motives."

"Sure," he said unhappily.

* * *

On the way back, I found the shop gratings were down everywhere in the center, but around the corner from us a private store had opened just that day, with evening hours right from the start. (A hazy picture from my childhood: there had been a source of multicolored lollipops here. A Communist propaganda office drove it out.) I spent the remainder of my loan on fresh (in the evening!) bread, butter, cheese, and two bottles of Vavřinec wine. (Long live capitalism with a human face under the leadership of the reforming anti-Communists!) The Greek orphan's taxi hadn't weighed anchor yet; I could lay the table in peace.

I selected my grandmother's fancy china, which we'd used only on holidays and birthdays (let even my own child gawk) and then it occurred to me that I could easily and profitably jettison the spare silver. Solving the problem of V.D. (and his involvement in my mission) had put me in a favorable mood; the catastrophe temporarily receded into the background, and it pleased me to think how taken my dear Gabby would be with my waiting hand and foot on her rapist like a suitor. (I was beginning to feel a bit sorry for him.)

At eight I couldn't help eating a thick heel of bread with a hunk of cheese. At nine I opened the first of the two bottles and did my best not to be down with exhaustion (last night was weighing on me) when the pair of them deigned to arrive. The telephone rang at nine-thirty.

"Yes! Where the hell are you?"

"Is this Mrs. Márová?" an unfamiliar voice inquired.

"Yes . . ." Disappointment and suddenly fear, that they were probably calling from the hospital. "Has something happened?"

"No. I just wanted to touch base."

"Who's calling?"

"Excuse me, it's Vanesa Králová." Another awkward situation.

"Oh, no, it's you should excuse me, it's just my daughter's late." Why am I telling her this? Now she'll really think my daughter's a whore!

"I understand. I'll call another time." I heard disappointment in her voice and didn't want her to inform Viktor that I'd refused to speak to her.

"No, wait! Nothing's happening; it's just the way she is!" A rape every now and again, but otherwise a good kid. "Did you want to tell me something?" Did he tell her what I told him?

"Yes, I thought I'd try to repeat my invitation." What invitation? "I'd like to make you dinner." She doesn't know anything. "I haven't even finished my story." What story? "I mean my dad's story. And I'd just like you to . . . Viktor is in Moscow with the prime minister, as you probably know from the papers." No, I haven't known anything for a week already, except that I am in love with your husband, I suffer with him, and I want to clear him and avenge him. "I don't want to disturb you; he told me you write poetry"—That, too? Well, okay, at least in her eyes I'm not some *hey, you* from the stupid classifieds—"and I realize you have your own private life, but just this once perhaps you can find the time. I'll pick you up and drop you off!" Service for his lover? My skin began to crawl.

"But you've got the baby . . ."

"She'll come along, she's used to it. How's tomorrow?"

Aversion gave way to the sudden realization that it would definitely strengthen me for the battle with the enemy if I could find out more about the time my sweetheart spent abroad.

"Can I call you in the morning?"

"Of course. I don't need to go shopping; I'll make you authentic sheep-cheese pasta with ham and buttermilk." Ugh! "Have you ever tried it?"

"I don't know." And would rather not.

"So far everyone's liked it. Viktor insists that he married me for it." That would reassure me . . .

"I'm looking forward to it. But you'll have to excuse me, my daughter may be waiting." What kind of nonsense is that? Vanesa knows that I'm the one waiting!

"We'll call it a date. Good night."

" 'Night."

I hung up and kept my hand on the receiver, as if I could urge Gábina from a distance to call me right now. In this position I woke up, stiff as a board, at midnight, wearily cast off my clothes, slumped onto the bed, and fell asleep again (dried out, hollow, empty, nothing times nothing makes nothing) as if I would never wake up.

8

FEAR woke me. Soaked with sweat, I gradually recovered from the dream which had plagued me now for a good number of years and each time terrified me to death. (Another souvenir from Major Beneš.) It always began with the rattling of little stones and a fearful rumbling in the earth; then a massive cliff shattered around me and left me in a tiny, insignificant cave to my wretched death.

Relief at recognizing my own room had hardly flooded into me (behind the opposite roof the rising sun announced a good seven-thirty) when a new fear seized me, the worse for the fact that I hadn't dreamed it. What was with Gabby? Had she failed to show up on purpose when she knew full well I was expecting her? I rarely asked her for promises; as a result, in spite of her inborn oafishness (from me), she always tried to keep them. Sometimes her good intentions went awry; now that was my consolation . . .

Over my first coffee and cigarette I woke up enough to reject the half-baked idea of staying home in case she was in trouble and needed me. (She'd have to be soft in the head not to call me at work; the telephone number is on every issue of our paper!) I recalled her other returns, ending with the one where she described to me, who was half-dead from worry, how she had been so horribly bored at some moronic party that she fell asleep. ("You couldn't have called me?" "Mommy, how can you call when you're asleep?")

I roused myself with an alternating hot-cold shower and got lucky on the way to work (I beat the fare)—which further ruffled my conscience, but soothed my damaged sense of security a bit. The knowledge that I had to continue in my anti-Beneš crusade helped. However,

I decided to turn Vanesa's dinner invitation down. (I wouldn't be able to sit still; the entire time I'd be thinking about whether Gabby was looking for me!) Before I could find their number in my notebook, my phone rang.

"Márová . . ."

"Hi!"

"Gabby!" My world lit up. "What's wrong?"

"What should be wrong?"

"Are you okay?"

"Well, yeah."

"Why didn't you call?"

"Well, I'm calling, see?" Certainly. No reprimands, praise!

"I was dying of fear!" There's no helping me.

"Why?"

"You promised to come last night. With that boy."

"Well, yeah. He couldn't make it."

"I was mostly waiting for you!"

"But, like, I don't have a car."

"Where are you, anyway?"

"With this guy."

"Did he find you a hotel?"

"Yeah."

"So, you see?"

"Yeah, in um . . . what's it called . . . in Munich." She'll drive me crazy!

"You're in Munich?"

"Well, yeah."

"Didn't you give me your word of honor?"

"Yeah, I did . . ." If she were here I'd slap her!

"So, why did you break it?"

"But I didn't." Too late for slaps.

"So, then, who did?"

"No one." I should have given her a drubbing before.

"You're a bald-faced liar!"

"Mommy, let me explain!"

"You want to lead me along by the nose some more?"

"We looked, Mom, I swear, but there was nothing free. He'd have had to go back to Plzeň and he didn't have time, it's the truth!" Wait a second, how did they even . . .

"How did you get there?"

"Where?"

"Where! To Germany! I suppose you had time for that, to sneak through the forest like a couple of smugglers?"

"What forest?"

"You just walked right over the border, then?"

"No, I didn't." No, she'll give me a heart attack!

"So you flew over, or what?"

"No . . ." The most horrible thing of all was that when she was fifteen she had already learned to speak to me in the same voice I used on her when she was five. "I crossed in a trunk, see?"

"In a trunk?"

"No, not like a storage trunk. A car trunk."

"Wait a second, you got into the trunk of the car and he took you across the border in it?"

"Yeah. It only takes a second." I was close to fainting.

"What if they'd opened the trunk?"

"I was under a blanket and the panels with the photos were lying across me, too, see."

"And what if they'd found you anyway?" You goat! You know what she'll say!

"But they didn't find me, Mom." There I have it.

"But how will you get back?"

"Well, the same way." Lord Almighty!

"Gabby, I forbid you, do you hear me?" I'm talking nonsense already. "I forbid you to come back in the trunk!" Nonsense squared.

"So, how should I come back?"

"Well, I mean . . ." How? Beneš! He has to give me some advice, he owes it to me! "When are you coming back?"

"I dunno."

"Yesterday you said right away!"

"Gav has some work to do. These guys at the exhibition want him to drive them here; it'll be cheaper for them."

"By when?"

"Sunday."

"Fine." Beneš gets back on Friday! "On Saturday I'll tell you how and why. What's your number there?"

"What number?" It's not denseness, it's a method!

"The telephone you're calling from."

"There's no number on it."

"Where are you?"

"In some hotel."

"There has to be a telephone number somewhere!"

"I don't see one." She sensed that I was on the verge of tears. "I'll call you back, Mommy."

"I can't sit by the telephone day and night!"

"I'll call you on Saturday, okay?"

"Fine! Call me at twelve, but at home, not here, do you understand? And at noon, not at midnight! Write it down!"

"I can remember that, I think."

"Write it down!"

My boss stepped into my cubbyhole and visibly started. I must have been shouting.

"I don't have a pencil, see?" I had to rein myself in in his presence.

"So, Saturday at noon on the dot; I have to leave after that. I'll see what can be done. Be careful!" So they don't ship you back! I couldn't make myself say it aloud.

"Yeah, okay. 'Bye."

She hung up, no doubt with a clear conscience. What if that little Greek prick was listening in?

"Your daughter?" my boss interjected with a honeyed smile, the new emblem of the old order.

"Yes, she's . . ." Shut your mouth, silly goose! ". . . not in Prague."

"Well, feel free to call her." You're not paying for it, Mr. Generous!

"She called me!"

"Yes, of course, of course." He glanced at me conspiratorially; what nerve! "She can call you whenever you like, the firm is always in your debt." Should I . . . Oh, blow it off! "Here's why I'm disturbing you." You're the boss, aren't you? "I was telling my wife about you"—How you made a pass at me on the boat?—"and she'd like to meet you." She likes a ménage à trois? "I was assigned to invite you over for dinner"—All of a sudden I'm the lioness of the salons, whatever for?—"and to ask when would suit you."

At that moment I was struck by a peculiar realization: before the revolution, I hadn't rated his attention (he seemed afraid of women, anyway); why out of the blue, in a single week, had he offered me both his bed and his table? What was behind it? I was least of all inclined to believe that this was an outburst of Christian love for me as a fellow human.

"That's nice of you, except I've got a lot of obligations and, what's more, I'm not single." Just in case you had any ideas.

"We reckoned with that. You could bring your whole family; my wife loves to cook and we can put another leaf in the table!"

"I'll ask them, then." He puts up with my absences, lends me money with no questions asked; why not make him happy! I'll force Gabby over there as punishment, give her public manners a workout. "In the meantime, thanks for the offer."

I soon found a likely reason for this fit of generosity on the bottom of page three in our newspaper.

"Antonín Mára was yesterday named director of the newly founded joint stock company that includes this publishing house, printing press, and associated operations. Mr. Mára was until recently president of the British press concern Holy Cross."

In spite of the surprising frequency of my last name (twenty-seven times in the Prague phone book!) I'd never found a related Mára; my father was also an only child. The Briton (Anthony?) Mára wasn't hurting my reputation, in any case; if anything, the opposite. Acting on an unclear impulse (curiosity? or rather bald self-interest, Petra?) I decided to adopt him—passively! That day a couple more colleagues made insinuations. I answered with a vague and thus probably affirmative bon mot: "I'd rather not have an uncle in the house!" (An echo of a certain Josef Beneš's words . . .)

I went to the cafeteria to amuse myself with this notion (and affably returned V.D.'s wooden nod across three tables) and to momentarily escape the new worries my daughter had burdened me with. (I promised her a way out of this and I haven't the slightest idea what!) It went against my grain to go cap in hand to the person I was simultaneously trying to nail to the wall. Having first called my sweetheart's gratified wife to say she could have me this evening instead of him, I painstakingly continued my mission after lunch in my cramped (and therefore not shared) lair.

Oldřich Luna, at one time Olin, wasn't actually the provost himself, but the provost's right and left hand. His group of individualistic artists, banned their whole lives and constantly being arrested for "happenings," abstraction, and drunkenness (during which they alternately insulted one another, the barmen, the policemen, the governing party, and our fraternal superpower), suddenly in its dotage coalesced into storm troopers to tumble that bastion of artistic collaborationists, the state school for the arts. They were met with applause, laughter, and anger. (The main objection: enforced conventionality gave way to unconventionality that was also enforced and thus unbearable, merely in a different way.)

His secretary (does she have proper attractions? but we know Olin) was arrogant on the telephone (so she does!); she connected me only when I pulled out the heavy artillery (I was in prison with him!). The admirer of my attractions, however, didn't disappoint. He bellowed into the receiver until it hurt my eardrum.

"No! Marjoram!" His invention. "My sweet, spicy Marjoram! Where are you? Why aren't you with me?"

"Because they forbade me!" I wounded him. (To the quick!)

"You mean that old cow of mine? Piss on her, I did a long time ago! Are you in Prague?"

"Where else?"

"I would've guessed you'd sold your export-quality tits to some sheik by now."

"I saved them for my fellow countrymen."

"I'm one, too; roll 'em on down here!"

"Where?"

"To my office, at school; I'll make a death mask of them!"

"You have at least three."

"My old cow smashed 'em way back when. I'll make you new ones—in bronze!"

"They probably aren't what they used to be."

"That Rodin's curve could never disappear. Don't torture me, hop a cab down here—on me, I'll open some real champagne!"

"You've certainly done well for yourself." A glance at my watch: only one-thirty.

"It's part of my entertainment expenses. Why should some foreign cretin get shitfaced on it?" But a relative of Anthony Mára's can!

"I'll come, but on one condition."

"Yes, yes! I agree! Come on already, I'm sweating all over!"

"The condition is that you won't lay a finger on me!"

I realized that recently I'd been setting this condition for meetings (even with my sweetheart) like a confused elderly virgin. Olin flat out groaned.

"And why not?"

"As punishment for squandering six of my breasts."

❄ ❄ ❄

"I didn't choose her!" Olin defended himself resignedly. (His secretary was, on top of everything else, ugly.) "We can't afford bonus pay for good figures, and I wouldn't be able to fuck her, anyway. You don't know how they breathe down our necks here; now we're even on the president's shitlist."

"No! How?"

"We were his sweethearts; he protected us and showed us off like rare wild animals. So then he sent us here to chase out those shit-eating pigs. And now that we did it, he's mad that we still act like wild animals he can't show off anymore and doesn't even need to protect."

There was a reason why his righteous anger struck a false note, and it amused me in the extreme.

"You have a tie."

"What?"

"A cravat. A necktie!"

"Oh, yeah, I know. The dean is in America and at five I have to kiss ass to some lowlife from Vršovice; she was a dancer in the cabaret at U Fleků, got hitched to a drunken English lord, who died from it soon after. Now she's playing patroness of the arts."

"Why are you talking to her? In a tie, no less?"

"Because she wants to start a foundation here and is waving a hundred thousand pounds around. Right now I'm looking for a volunteer from the students to screw her so she'll give two hundred."

"Why not take it upon yourself?"

"Because I've been spoiled to death by my Marjoram, the most perfect spice in the whole wide world . . ."

He sat down longingly next to me on the couch, where he had cleverly placed me, but before I could voice an objection one of the telephones rang (he had three on his desk).

"Shit, excuse me." He stomped across the office; a bear of a man, amazing he never crushed me! "This is Luna . . . No, the provost already left two messages for the mayor that we're pissed at him . . . No, we're just not going to clear out . . . He doesn't give a flying fuck what's going to be there . . . The minister of culture can kiss my ass . . . What, how are you supposed to tell him? Exactly the way I said it, they all understand Czech!" He slammed down the receiver and came over to me again.

"So that's your officialese?" I demonstrated my desire to restrict us to conversation.

"Well, yeah, I mean, it's enough to make you shit. They keep wanting to steal this little building from us." What? "We have this work area with a garden shed. So now they're screaming that we appropriated it illegally."

"And you didn't . . ."

"We did, but it's in our complex and this is a revolution, isn't it? They can't see farther than the end of their nose, it's always 'we shouldn't provoke the public,' but they're trying to steal the only spot where we can put together a first-rate happening, out of the public eye." He was already pressing against me again.

"Olin"—an attempt at a friendly appeal—"remember, you're not at home or in your studio."

"Jesus, girl, what happened to the old days, when they arrested us in our finest hour? I'll never forget how you ripped the blanket away from that letch and roared 'Turn around, you bastard; I'll make sure your wife finds out about this!' He was as red as a beet!" He sniggered and tried to embrace me.

"Stop it, Olin." An attempt at a friendly defense: it met with stiff opposition.

"Why are you treating me like this?"

"Come on, for eleven years you didn't miss me."

"You know how it was. The cow and me had little kids, no money at all, and I was just waiting for them to snag me!" You needn't have; my lover was protecting you. "It was chaos. But I never forgot about you, swear to God, I mean, it was on account of you I got divorced!" He ought to be ashamed!

"Surely not!"

"Well . . . there was one more woman involved, but you were absolutely number one. Did you forget you were the one who left me? I kept waiting and looking in the underground press for something from you." I had forced him to listen to my poems; it amused me the way he didn't understand a single one of the images.

"I was published in the official press."

"You're putting me on." But suspicion flickered in his eyes.

"They allowed me to because I ratted on you."

"Marj, what are you talking about?" I had reached the goal of my visit.

"I didn't come to start another round with you, Olin, but to put an end to the first one. I spent time with you because I respected you as an artist and as a person. You didn't just grumble about the Bolsheviks over beer, you did something about it. I wanted to, too, and that was why I let you sleep with me." He looked hurt. But let him know; I owe Viktor that much. "Yes! If women can get into the theater through someone's bed, then why not into the dissidents? That crass bit of slander was amusing for you, but it turned my life upside down; otherwise my last ten years would have been entirely different! And certainly better!" Without Beneš!

"I'm sorry . . ." He quickly backed down, assuming the expression of a beaten dog. "I had no idea . . ."

"It's already happened and there's no way to undo it. But I wanted to hear one thing: did you ever think I actually did inform on you?"

"Are you crazy?"

"And what did you think? What did your gut tell you?"

"Well, that someone wanted to teach us a lesson—actually, wanted to teach me a lesson because of you." Here it was! I searched for a moment's respite.

"You? Because of me?"

"Out of stupid jealousy. It hadn't occurred to you?"

"No."

"I had a feeling even at the time. And now I know for sure." Oh! "Lots of people from the old underground are in the Interior Ministry now after the revolution; I had them look into it. Any ideas? Just one guess." And what then?

"I don't dare." Yes, I'm a coward! "Tell me . . ."

"You must have suspected it ever since."

"Why . . . ?"

"Because you paid for it the most. It was that cow! My old lady! Yes! And she had no idea, the stupid cow, that I had any stuff stored there!" A miracle . . .

"She . . ."

"Squealed on me, plain and simple. That was their hobby, talking to the wives and letting it slip who their man was fooling around with at the moment."

"She didn't even ask you?"

"Of course she did."

"And you?"

"Well, I told her we loved each other."

"But why? That was out of the question!" Feel insulted, if you like!

"Because she pissed me off. Then she went off the deep end and wanted to punish me, so she dreamed up this story that we were covering for the Charter's spokespeople." Revolting, but at the same time miraculous! "They were supposed to surprise us, so I'd shit in my pants and drop you. So, forgive me!"

He was in a sentimental mood. But I wanted to be one hundred percent sure.

"And you believe it?"

"Well, she confessed!" Lord God, thank You! "But I just said fuck it; in the end she changed her mind and nothing came of it"—Not for you!—"I still got divorced and she's raising my boys. They already think I'm a prick; how would they turn out if they grew up thinking their mother was a swine, too?"

Josef Beneš, you're the swine! Sweetheart, forgive me and come back!

❄ ❄ ❄

Such definitive proof of innocence (further ones were hardly necessary) buoyed and depressed me. If I'd visited Olin two days earlier instead of going for a sentimental skate ride to the bench under the chestnut tree, I wouldn't have let that horrid (and suspicious! how could it not have struck me?) slander past my lips. When my beloved rushed up to me and grasped me like a starving sailor, I would have let him roll barbarously all over me and everything would have been different! On the way home my chest began to hurt from the thought of it, and the burning pressure wouldn't let up. (Around now my woe-laden period should be looming on the horizon; there hadn't even been time to glance at the calendar!)

I had gotten an important promise from Olin (he was so ashamed he would have done my every bidding) before leaving.

"Listen, I'd like to find out, pronto, what information your all-knowing friends have about a guy named Josef Beneš. He signed the Charter in 1987 and had one distinguishing feature: he was a secret policeman."

"Yeah, wait a sec, I do remember that Commie!"

In return I promised him, without a second thought, that we'd meet in his studio as soon as we could find a free evening. (I counted on him forgetting about it.) He pulled out his diary (Olin with a schedule!) and looked for a slot.

"Tonight dinner with the tart from U Fleků, tomorrow Bratislava, Saturday . . ." (he avoided mention of it, like a schoolkid) "m-hm, busy that day, Sunday lunch at the presidential retreat in Lány, and with the president things always run long. Hey, listen, I'll give you a call, okay?"

For my sake he even untied and grandly flung off his tie (into the wastepaper basket) but even without it he wasn't Olin anymore, just one more anarchist subdued by the true queen, Power, and even the most seductive curves couldn't tear him away from her. (He most likely pulled his tie out of the trash as soon as I left.) He was finished sculpting, finished painting, finished loving, requiescat Olin.

At home I thoroughly aired out the apartment: I hadn't opened the windows since Tuesday evening, in the foolish belief that some traces of the spirit and probably the scent (he used a masculinely bitter brand) of my sweetheart might remain. I then sat down in "his" armchair with a coffee and a menthol to think through what was next and what after that. Step by step, word by word, I retraced in slow motion that unfortunate final evening so I could realistically evaluate my hope that it hadn't been the very last one.

During life crises I wrote scenarios in addition to my diary entries in order to get an overview and not end up like Olin: "It was chaos." Oftentimes I managed to foresee the possibilities in such a way that I could concentrate and exert my strength on behalf of the best option (or at least pray for it). Most of the time it even worked. From its hiding place (so my daughter wouldn't take undue advantage of her mother's weaknesses) I brought out my latest notebook (in the front, a diary swelling almost into a novel; in the back, verses) and drew two diagrams.

I continue to live in mortal sin
loves me and forgives me
as repentance I give him up
doesn't refuse to meet me
No longer loves me and won't forgive me
Sweetheart
refuses to meet me
I accept this as my punishment

apologizes to sweetheart
I forgive him, just as we...
confesses his lie
won't apologize
I punish him (how?)
Major
I prove him guilty (see above)
won't confess his lie
I can't prove him guilty (what then?)

The flow chart calmed me with its comprehensiveness. I tried to concoct a logical sequence of events from it.

Scene 1. Visit Vanesa K. (at her own pers. invit.) during which (a) I will get to know unkn. side of my swthrt., which will help me predict his fut. behavior so that (b) I can give him signal that I'm sorry + long to apol. as best I know how.

Scene 2. In meanwh. full steam ahd. with reconnaissance mission begun yest. To renew contact w/Major—'he'd frittered away the right to a civilian name with his baseness; let him have a code name, like any other jerk!'—use concern abt. daught.

ment. earlier—and simult. get her home safe + sound w/ his intervent.

Scene 3. Indep. of prev. actions begin search for witnesses. To this end charge V.D. (Wait a second, rather, ask him!) not to miss first opportunity to take phot. that would make ident. of Mjr. easy even for feebleminded. Conduct conclus. invest. in Kladno.

Scene 4. Deepen contact w/Mjr. (of course: within reason!) so that in case of need will be poss. to appeal to his human side in name of our form. relat. (and its event. renewal, so long as motive for lie is truly belat. jealousy?)

Scene 5. Busy as a bee, prep. finale in which T & L prevail over H & L—truth and love over hate and lies, to quote our president.

The outlines of a final scene emerged (a modern catharsis) in which my sweetheart could witness the Major exposed and morally chastised. (And maybe even delivered to the Law?)

Note to 1 through 5: Don't allow rash or indiscr. behav. and most of all conceal perfectly all susp. (which at the moment fit too perfectly and aren't concrete enough), limit V.D.'s knowl. to abs. min. ("I'm trying to intimidate a once high-ranking cop, whose disinformation is wreaking havoc.")

I read the scenario through and added to it with insertions and parentheses over and over, but it held. The fact that I had a plan encompassing nearly every possibility calmed me. I put it away in my hiding place and rapidly (I was fifteen minutes late, as always) polished my exterior to its highest gloss, as I rarely did before meeting him. (He always drew me close without delay and his passion soon destroyed my work; our closeness itself made it unnecessary, anyway. His spouse, on the other hand, would be uncharitably measuring, weighing, and studying me in detail from a distance the whole evening.)

The Japanese car was waiting in front of the house. (A pang: finally he had a partner who didn't multiply his chronic lateness . . .) It relieved me that our greetings were perfunctory (I outside, she in the car), since my sweetheart's daughter was sleeping in her safety seat in the back. I praised the child appropriately (fortunately she didn't resemble him in the least; with a pair of horn-rimmed glasses she could have been her mother) and was permitted to sit alongside the driver.

Worth noting: while I felt and apparently radiated calm (guided by the scenario), Vanesa K., regardless of the precious cargo in back, drove quite poorly and more and more nervously as we went on; she started late at intersections and once stopped at a green light, which elicited an orgy of honking. Her distraction mostly came from her uninterrupted descriptions—which were unnecessary, not to mention secondhand—of Slovak-Czech catfights in the Cabinet. I therefore (for reasons of self-preservation) steered the topic toward her little girl.

"What's she called?"

"Like you." She turned her head toward me and I doubtless turned red again.

"Petra?"

"No, Márka. That's almost Márová." What should I say to that?

"I didn't know that there was a feminine form of Marek . . ."

"She's christened Marie. But Viktor calls her Márka." Thank you, sweetheart! "It's a nickname from the Slovak name Mara."

And she unleashed a lecture about her child, accompanied by a new series of traffic violations. (Near the National House in Smíchov she even overlooked a red light; a guardian angel must have been directing the cross-traffic.) She was without a doubt highly agitated, but why today, when last week under dire siege she had been the picture of composure? I gave up on my vain attempts to calm her and concentrated fully (see *Scene 1* of scenario) on collecting observations that could be significant for the success of my venture. Luckily we missed by a hair's breadth the pillar of the pedestrian bridge across the highway entrance ramp and even negotiated the curves approaching Barrandov.

The little family from Canada had found lodging in one of the new rental villas below the film studios; whether deliberately or not (Vanesa: "Viktor would have taken even an old storeroom in the Old Town, but they were all gone and I breathed a sigh of relief") they were living the high life. All four units had an upstairs; each had a side facing the garden and a door into it. The general tastefulness of the structure did not extend to its vulgar furnishings. ("They lent us furniture from the government warehouses; most of it goes back to Gottwald in '48!") The apartment was rendered tolerable by a few items—modern pictures, an old clock, and vases—that they had "for now" brought over from some main home, whose existence aroused in me a growing sorrow, yes, outright envy.

I looked in vain here for traces of my sweetheart. None at all in the hallway; I didn't even find any in the child's room, where with my mysterious aperitif (pineapple juice and a drop of a burning mixture) I watched as Little Miss Márka was put to sleep. (Vanesa K. displayed tact in not showing me the master bedroom.) Later I found a curious sign of his existence in the bathroom: an open Czech detective novel placed on the windowsill with its spine face up. (He'd had troubles in the bathroom since he was a kid; in our days he spent many an hour there, which he passed with thrillers continued in installments.)

Before that I assisted in the sensationally equipped kitchen (all kinds of robots) with the making of the pasta, and further witnessed how out of sorts the lady of the house was; she babbled with forced animation about whatever came into her head. She had two more aperitifs; I, of course, gave sentimental preference to the flavored wine, obviously his purchase. (He remained true to our tastes!) The only result was that, on top of everything else, she tried to speak Czech (badly); my assurances that I was quite fond of Slovak made no impression on her.

Dinner, however, confirmed her talents in the kitchen (and the right of Slovaks to self-determination). I nostalgically remembered how Viktor had raved about my culinary gifts: "I adore elementary foods, and your potato dumplings are as simply ingenious as a wheelbarrow!" So now he was transported by her pasta . . . Nonetheless I was able to praise her sincerely, and as a result (how comical: she was an economist, after all!) she regained her balance. When we sat down in the ungainly leather armchairs, she once again seemed normal to me.

I lit up (she herself invited me to: "It'll air out!") and braced myself for a conversation on some other abstract subject (like the end of her father's story), resigned to the fact that my research expedition would fall short of its desired goal. However, out of nowhere my lover's wife suddenly looked me straight in the eye.

"Mrs. Petra, I'm afraid I deceived you a little bit. I claimed I wanted to show off my abilities as a cook, but that was only a pretext for luring you here." No questions! Keep looking at her! "I know more than you probably think." The cover's blown! "I understood even in Vancouver that Vic had a fateful relationship behind him; he never talked about it, but I felt it." What's she got up her sleeve? "It was worth it for me. I wanted him so much, I'm sure you understand why, so I took the risk of replacing his great, unknown love. I'd say I was doing pretty well"—No details! It hurts!—"until finally I was sure I could have a child with him." So it wasn't your studies?

"Except out of the blue your revolution came along," she continued, "and from the moment I saw the Te Deum for the new president on the TV screen, it was clear as day to me that I wouldn't be able to keep Vic there. So instead I myself suggested that we move here, at least for a while. I flew across the ocean with fear in my heart; I held Márka on my lap, and while he slept I whispered to her, 'You're all I'll have left once he goes back to her.' Yes, I already knew that it was you." Does she want to kill me or something, and then herself and the child? "The evening before our departure, when we had our suitcases packed and the renters were sleeping in the other room, he asked me to have patience with him once his past caught up with him; yes, exactly those words. First he named you. 'So that it's me and not someone else, he said; 'plenty of people in Prague know that I was attached to her for years, that's another reason I'd rather be in Bratislava.'

"Today I have the courage to admit that those first weeks I lived in terror that one day he'd return from Prague and inform me that he'd been with you and that it was as alive as ever. Vic, you know, has one frightening quality: he never lies." Yes, yes! How could I have forgotten? "I wouldn't want to be seriously ill around him; he couldn't even manage to lie for mercy's sake." And even for that I punished him with the heads of my freshly caught lovers! "He was in Prague a couple of times, and nothing." Nothing with me, either. "In Slovakia, meanwhile, storms were brewing on the horizon, and one day he returned with a preliminary offer from the deputy chairman of the federal government in Prague. That evening I was just as incompetent as today, when I drove like my head was screwed on backwards; I remember it also took me a couple of drinks before I could pull myself together. 'Have you been with her?' I asked him directly after dinner. 'No,' he said, 'and I won't be, because I'm afraid.' 'Then go to her,' I begged him, 'so you'll know if there's any reason to be; I'd rather be scared once and have it over with than have the fear never let up.'

"Only then—I think it was exactly a year ago—did he visit you." So only thanks to her! "And when he came back, he informed me that he could safely go to Prague. 'She accepted me as a good friend,' he said; 'of course she has a steady boyfriend, and anyway it became clear to me that time had taken care of everything.' " He said that to her! My sweetheart told a lie for the first time, out of love for me! "I have to confess I felt like that day was our second wedding." And did you celebrate the same way . . . "When we moved here, I suggested to him maybe three times that he invite you and your daughter over; he wanted to, but didn't get around to it. By and by he was glad even to see the two of us at all. It was only last week, when he was sitting here tortured by the ultimatum from the lustration commission, that he suddenly remembered that his supposed commanding officer was not only his friend, but yours, too. So I convinced him to call you."

The gradually increasing discrepancy between her perception and naked reality distressed me (my Christian morality was turning to mud) but there was no escape (was this the beginning of my divine punishment?); I could only keep listening, aghast at where this canal of lies (what is it I want to punish the Major for?) would empty out. Vanesa K. continued to fix me with her mirror-green gaze, to which only my dreadfully bad conscience could ascribe murderous lust (it probably expressed sincere thanks).

"I didn't keep doggedly inviting you here, Petra—can I call you that?" Smile and nod, what else is left? ". . . to bore you with stories that haven't concerned you for a long time now"—If you had any idea!—"but I have no one here aside from you." And I have only him . . . "He's mentioned one other old friend"—Who?—"but that person's caught in a merry-go-round similar to his, and Vic is, on top of everything, awfully proud." I didn't take even that into account! "He couldn't bear to have his private troubles aired in government circles like a juicy morsel for opportunists. So, please, put up with me a little longer! After your intervention it was as though Vic had been born again; Saturday night he even sang in the bathroom"—Yes, he did sometimes sing when shaving, or rather hummed tunelessly; I'd completely forgotten—"and hatched all sorts of plans." The most amazing of which he whispered to me over the telephone, evidently while you were washing up. "On Monday he was still—as we say in Canada—high; I had to get a baby-sitter so he could take me out to dinner." What I'd give. "At the same time we said goodbye; he went to Brno that night and from there was supposed to fly directly to Moscow." With a stopover in my arms, which I turned into a disaster.

"Instead," she continued, "he appeared at home on Tuesday morning"—Oh—"in a ghastly state of mind"—Mea culpa!—"and poured himself whiskey"—Again? Already!—"like I'd never seen him do before." I, however . . . ! And that night spawned a monstrous legend! " 'For God's sake,' I implored him, horrified, 'what's happened?' 'Nothing new,' he said finally, 'but it just hit me: we have to leave.' 'But why? The lie fizzled, they apologized to you!' 'Yes, but before that they were willing to believe it, it was the luck of the devil that I got off! After the explanation, a person who cares about his honor should pack his bags and so long!' " He was quoting me. " 'Vic!' I admonished him, 'you have a task here, one you dreamed of for so long; don't punish yourself instead of the swindlers and fools' "—among whom I belong—" 'bite the bullet and hold out until the summer. We'll take a real vacation by the sea, after a month with Márka and me you'll get your second wind' "—Suffer, Petra, you deserve it!—" 'and in a year we'll be laughing about it.' Finally he promised to let things lie, and with this he flew off yesterday at noon, but he looked to me like a sleepwalker who doesn't know what he's doing.

"In the evening I couldn't stand it and called you, ready to descend on you today at home if the trip here wouldn't fit your plans. Petra! I don't know what to do if he holds to his decision. I know that it's bad form to put the burden on you again, but you were once fond of him." I might just scream that I love him! "Help him get past this, too; I can't do it alone!"

The most absurd thing about this utterly theatrical scene was that she was behaving naturally; I wouldn't have (if I knew as little) acted a whit differently. Even in her youthful perplexity she didn't lose her dignity, while shame poured over me that even my simple participation and help amounted to committing rank deception. (But what to do?)

"How do you see it . . ." At least I'll leave the method to her.

"I was thinking . . ." she wavered, "that . . ."—once again nervousness overcame her—"I would . . ." Well, what? ". . . keep quiet about this meeting, and you could call him at work, so he could tell you how things are." An old poem of mine: *I lie, you lie, he lie . . .* "You could agree on a dinner date!" I was astonished.

"Without you?"

"With me, but I could excuse myself at the last moment, on account of the little one!" *We lies, you lies, they lies / and he to whom the truth falls / tells fibs of twice the size!*

"What do you expect from it?"

"Vic's pride operates at home, too." I know, I battled with it . . . "I'll tell you an anecdote. Once, when we were already close, all of a sudden he had terribly little time for me." I know that, too! " 'I have to work,' he'd insist, but then more and more often he wouldn't show up at school or at home, and I panicked that there was someone else." So in fact . . . ? "You can think what you want, Petra, but I couldn't stand it; I kept watch outside his apartment in my friend's car, and took off into the twilight after him. An Italian, I despaired, when he parked in Little Italy next to a modern apartment building, and I sobbed half the night away there"—Felix victor, we're all pathologically jealous over you—"when a couple returned who had left right as I'd begun my vigil. In a little while he appeared, and I just couldn't stand it and blocked his escape"—An act of character!—"like the very incarnation of reproach, and he blushed like a schoolboy caught red-handed, and why? The shame. Mine. He was working secretly, incognito, for a well-heeled family as a baby-sitter and a tutor for their twins, so that given his debts at the time he could permit himself to invite and properly entertain his mother from Pardubice." Oh, yes, his mother certainly hadn't lost out with his exile; on the contrary, after it he again belonged more to her than to me!

"You have to realize," she continued, "if it had gotten around, he would have been a social outcast. I'm so much younger than he is" —yes: almost like V.D.—"maybe he's afraid that he would let me down if he entrusted me with his fears. He might open up to a friend who helped him without a second thought. And then you could advise me what to do."

Her woman's intuition, which failed her when it came to her husband's relationship with me, was otherwise unerring; I would have extracted (almost) every secret from his soul, the way I used to, if only it hadn't been me personally who plunged him into despair when I brutally confirmed that the foul stain could hardly disappear. How to suggest to her that he would most likely refuse to speak to me?

"Vanesa." I can't bring myself to say Mrs. Králová again! "I think you're counting your chickens before they've hatched. Viktor had already done more than he was comfortable with when he came to visit that time in the night and ended up taking care of my idiotic daughter, and the next day had to ask me to play the middleman in such an awkward situation. Don't rule out one outcome that's clear as day: the most intolerable thing of all for a person of his sensitivity is having witnesses to his humiliation."

"In your case I can't believe that's true. He respects you even more than me!"

It was indicative of the situation that she obviously didn't mean it as a jealous reproach but rather as an argument which obliged me to do it. I managed to challenge her credibly.

"What do you base that on?"

"After three days of moping around here, he came back from your place on Thursday evening like a changed man. 'She'll pull it off!' he repeated like a slogan, and when you gave him the good news on Friday he had tears in his eyes. 'She's wonderful,' he cried"—Oh! That warms me!—"and in spite of that I didn't feel distressed like last year; I was deeply grateful to you." Oh! That chills me. "And on Saturday in that restaurant he talked to you so fervidly about things he's silent about with me; it's also that I know a fair amount about them, but mostly because he senses a kindred soul in you. Just as I used to fear you, now I beg of you: go out with him." A mad request against the background of that physical and emotional kinship she knows nothing about! "You have the right to find out if that Beneš did what he promised and how it turned out." But your husband did come to thank me with his love, only I put him in the penalty box! "Ask him!"

"I can't . . ."

"I understand that you, too, have your pride"—You don't understand anything—"to do so much and then have to beg for silly details, but you went into the lion's den for him; you're entitled to ask him not to take your sacrifice for granted!"

No! raged everything in me; out of this sinful game, in which I unwittingly rejected him, and she unknowingly chases him back into my embrace.

"I wouldn't dare . . ."

"Petra! There isn't one person far and wide who could get through to him like you!" Hands clasped, eyes tormented, the picture of despair.

"You mentioned another friend . . ." Surely not my former husband? He was already swimming successfully again in the warm waters of the new order.

"They haven't had time to get together yet."

"Who is it?"

"Olin someone-or-other."

"Oldřich Luna?"

"Yes! I hear he's a famous sculptor; I wouldn't know. Before he was banned, and now he's a dean or something like that. You must know him."

"Of course . . ." But Viktor only knows him as the last head from my silver platter!

"They apparently had some kind of risky escapade together. Vic wouldn't spread it around, you know how modest he is, he would only say, 'I collaborated somewhat less than was the generally expected norm for Czechs who claimed not to hold with the Bolsheviks.' It was with Luna that he went farther than that, concealed some emigré publications for him or something, you'd know better than I." I do. And I'm astonished. "It must have ended with a house search, you two were supposedly at the inquiry, which, I got the feeling, was the straw that broke the camel's back and made him decide to emigrate. And now, Petra, I'm going to admit something to you—because I like you—that one woman should probably never say to another: Vic—I'm sure of it!—suffered a long time, even when I knew him, because you refused to emigrate with him. While I owe my happiness to that fact alone."

9

ALL of a sudden I felt sick. My soul was fed up, but it was my stomach that heaved. My horrified host wanted to call an ambulance (and even to give them the remains of the pasta to inspect!); I rushed to assure her that my period ordinarily began that way, with a bang. Evidently it went along with the state of my nerves.

Vanesa K. hurriedly drove me home (the sleeping baby came along: "Soon there will be kidnapping here, too!"), and solicitously led me as far as the door of my building, but her icy hand gave me the chills. I managed to forestall an escort upstairs only by mentioning the child.

"I'll call you," she said awkwardly in parting. "I have to finish telling you my father's story about Simon Wiesenthal."

It seemed to me that we both had other worries at hand. I climbed the stairs as far as the landing while she turned around outside, and then I went back down. As I walked the nausea receded. Outside I managed to catch a glimpse of the big red taillights on the receding car. It wasn't even eleven—the night was young—so I set off aimlessly through sleeping Bubeneč to get some oxygen.

Before the awkward turn of events at her place laid me low, I had succeeded in convincing her not to conceal my visit, just to leave out her confession and of course her call for help. On the other hand, she was to emphasize my sudden indisposition. ("Yes, of course, Petra, he can't not call you!" It chilled me that in this net of lies I moved like a clever carp that knows every hole . . .) I recommended definitively leaving Olin out of the whole thing (I protected myself by remarking that this had briefly been a sort of triangle), because I wanted to figure out the puzzle first on my own.

Oldřich Luna was an exception among my lovers (they didn't deserve such a lofty title; they were more or less instruments in an amorous war with my one true one!): Viktor hadn't introduced me to him, because they had never met. (Belatedly I suspect that with each affair I had also estranged him from one of his friends, so that he would remain at my mercy and mine only.) My one mitigating feature (for Judgment Day) will remain that I was ironclad in my faithfulness to him so long as he loved me as I loved him. My flights (or rather dodges, followed by powerful leaps back) were a manifestation of my instinct for self-preservation—no, no excuses; for years I suspected that he was intending to flee from me (and finally he did). What's more, I never dared wound him when he was doing poorly. Each of my infidelities was a slash at his newly expanding arrogance.

For, yes, my sweetheart was, for all his self-effacement, arrogant when he refused to understand that I was his center of gravity and the foundation of his security! In his scale of values I continually had to battle for first place with success in his career. To be fair, I should emphasize: not success at any price (which my ex-spouse pursued by all possible means); for Viktor only success achieved without the support of the repulsive regime would count—yes, success achieved distinctly against the regime's rules and practices, through intellectual force, education, and diligence, in the service of a secret mission (he'd break open a window from that red tunnel of theirs into real economics).

The struggle with the Moloch of the party and government sometimes so preoccupied him that I became a burden. He was never able to handle it the way I expected him to (and as he always promised anew to do on all that was holy), couldn't learn to give his work what it required and love what it deserved; he would simply begin to slip away from me. When his desertion got out of hand, I would defend myself (defend both of us!) with the one method that worked on him: I would ostentatiously find myself a stand-in (most of the time someone he knew).

The move never disappointed, and each time the shock had a miraculous reverberation: my sweetheart at once postponed his until-then-unpostponable projects and tasks in order to have time for me alone. He would confess to me again exhaustively, in his own peculiar fashion: his far from fiery tirades were akin to complete reports on the state of our love, more reminiscent of government budget announcements than anything else. He would tick off, point after point, the things in his life that were less important than I, which was absolutely everything. Then he would kneel down, press his eyes, nose, and his mouth once again into my skin, and hold that position without moving for an hour; I wouldn't feel either his breath or his pulse and would be horrified at the suffering of his knees, but otherwise I held blessedly still. I won't mention the most loving of our reposes!

Of course he'd loved me duly, admittedly far less passionately than after his return. (Had she taught him how? I can't see that! More likely he's matured, and was like a believer after the Lenten fast.) But even at the time it evoked in me a delight that made the efforts of his replacements pale by comparison. (Of course, I didn't yet know what two bodies unsuffused by any great love were capable of, and for me the heights of passion were replaced by the tenderness of which he was King.)

The truth is that my second-to-last flight—probably the least meaningful one (a gynecologist who, although we'd known him well, in the course of a day in the car and a night in Tatranská Lomnice turned out to be a total jerk; during breakfast in the hotel I got up and, filled with disgust for myself, instead of going to the bathroom marched right to the tram. He sent the mountain police out looking for me and when he got my message from Poprad, he left my suitcase at the hotel out of anger)—hit my sweetheart exceptionally hard. Without wooing me less intensely than before (on the contrary, his renewed striving for me knew no bounds), he proclaimed all of a sudden something I'd never before heard pass his lips: "If you leave me once more, I'll leave you forever!" That sentence stuck with me and became a temptation akin to Lot ordering his wife not to look back (*così fan tutte*).

Even in the humiliation of self-discovery brought on by those May days in the Year Two after the flood, in which both protagonists of my life fatefully crossed paths, I nevertheless continue to hold that it was still Viktor who, in spite of his experience, was so far gone that my subsequent estrangement created an unbridgeable divide.

With his refusal to sign the Anticharter, he achieved a renown that attracted young people who were revolted by the venality of their physical and spiritual fathers. His seminars were overenrolled despite the fact that he didn't deviate much from the state religion; a side effect of the psychosis of the time was that even the accents and pauses of those proclaimed (usually incorrectly) to be nonconformists were interpreted as daring criticisms of the powers that be. He came under fire from the envious cowards among his colleagues, and countered it with an increased wariness, which was reflected in an especially painstaking preparation of his lectures. I hadn't seen him for two weeks, and he hadn't held me in a good month (I raged indiscriminately at the collegiate daughters of the elite, who undoubtedly intended to snatch him from me), when Olin came my way.

At the time, I was earning my daily bread in one of the professions reserved for third-class citizens (I was no less civic-minded than my sweetheart; I took up the political cross of my religious parents and followed it) as a building custodian. The regime displayed its innate ignorance when it entrusted to its least dependable subjects not only a brush for scrubbing floors, but also the keys to its apartments and offices; these subjects didn't photograph correspondence for the news services, but they did they brew up an abundance of government coffee and did telephone for free all over the world (where I didn't yet know anyone).

Around then the Prague tom-toms announced an underground (basement) exhibition by a sculptor whose name meant nothing to me, because he had been eliminated in Orwellian fashion. On August 21, 1968, the *Unknown Crucified* by Oldřich Luna had been carried out of his studio in his native city and mounted on a pedestal freshly liberated from the statue of the Soviet Liberator. Its creator later moved to Prague, so his presence wouldn't offend the local higher-ups who had taken it upon themselves to improve the town. Of course he never set foot there again, although his reputation blossomed in spite of it.

I called Viktor and begged him to go with me (I never enjoyed going out alone; even hanging around the house was preferable), but he excused himself (or made excuses) again. That day, for no reason at all, the biggest moron from the Housing Department bawled me out, and Gabby was out of control, too; I was on the verge of tears. When she fell asleep I got myself ready and set off for the exhibit alone. Luna's stone female torsos enchanted me with their delicacy; I tried to guess who in those crowded passageways was fit to be their creator. It turned out to be, surprisingly, a giant of a man, reminiscent of a Russian peasant, who was lounging on a heap of pressed-coal briquettes, drinking champagne by himself. (I found out in the meanwhile that the world-renowned Chartist elite were present; they were living hand to mouth, as I was, with jobs as stokers, security guards, and window washers.) I was the only person to whom he offered any of the champagne. ("Would you like to drink with me?" "Why me, of all people?" "There's champagne sparkling in your eyes!")

In reality he stared at my chest and after the third glass (originally a mustard jar) he asked if I'd like to model for him. I said (esteemed again at last!) "Why not?" and the next day became his model. In all decency (almost insultingly so) on the first and second visits he only sketched my face and showed me his older works; we had wonderful conversations and I continued to pine for my sweetheart. But when Viktor didn't call even over the weekend, that familiar demon entered me. As punishment, I loosened myself up with the bubbly at the next sitting and unexpectedly (for me, too) took off my sweater and shirt. It brought out the artist in him (he walked around me with reverent delight as if around an antique statue protected by armored glass) and he immediately began a cycle of headless busts. Until the third one (official name: *Curves 3*; working name: *Tits III*) he didn't touch me. My sweetheart didn't show up; the champagne and chagrin took their course.

The sculptor certainly wasn't a detestable sort; as a result of the sharp disparity between his creative and physical potency, he came across instead as pitiful (light-years away from that cosmopolitan artist who would send mayors and presidents you-know-where . . .), and so I would close my eyes and instead anticipate how his rough palms would gently transfer my "Rodin's curve" to clay and thence to stone itself. I waited out this diversion determinedly without blemish to my body or soul.

When I penitently informed my sweetheart with the usual reproach about what he had driven me to, he reacted differently than before. He flew into an uncharacteristic rage (until I loved him as never before!) and flung appalling words in my face. (I'm ashamed to recall them!) But he hurt me most of all when he announced that I had given him the right to fulfill his threat. In a sorrowful fury I took a long draft of King whiskey and, wielding that classic line as a cudgel, I shouted at him, "If you leave me, I will not perish; if you leave me, you will perish!"; he ripped the bottle from me and drank deeply from it twice, which seemed to me (idiocy upon idiocy) like an especially bad bit of theater. So I let him (woe upon woe) drive off . . .

He didn't call. I had no idea about the mess he was in and was mortally wounded (an absolute loss of judgment and feeling) that he wasn't playing by the rules; in defiance I visited Olin again. (Normally my flights came to a sudden halt with the ritual of informing and forgiving; my replacement paramours would whimper vainly outside the door.) Lot's wife's glance backward was accompanied even in the modern era by God's punishment: the police, whom He in His mercy preferred over fire and brimstone, broke open the door—while ringing the bell—at a most inopportune time. Instead of a pillar of salt, I metamorphosed into a raging Fury even they were afraid of. (The bizarre idea of threatening them with their wives occurred to me when they took off their shoes at the door of the studio like trained animals!)

That was how I ended things with Olin (I came once more for a forgotten makeup bag, and used his wife's accusation as an excellent pretext), and then did what I should have done long before: I wrote my sweetheart an apology poem, into which I poured my soul. *I'm here / without fail / your wife / ringless for life / No siren of betrayal / just an echo of our strife / Hear my pleas / for I'm your water / which you turn to steam or ice / Oh warm me / I'll be sorry if I freeze / Make me one last / sacrifice.*

In response to my letter he rang my doorbell, looking green and sunken, which I attributed to suffering brought on by our endangered love. (And still do; begone, Satan, you shall poison me no longer with your deadly myths!) Later he seemed (deceptively!) to return to normal; he rested his face on my heart. It was part of the ritual that the past was instantly erased without a trace; thus, I didn't even tell him about the attack on the studio, and only as he was leaving did he mention that in his whiskey-fogged state he'd given Viktorka a light scratch, but escaped with just a fine.

That was the whole story about me and Oldřich Luna, and thus my bewilderment that, to his wife, my truthful sweetheart had labeled Olin a friend. Why had he even mentioned him in Canada? Had Olin made such an impression on Viktor, thanks to the extraordinary role he'd played in our relationship? But why did Viktor name him as a possible ally here, too? Only one explanation offered itself: they did in fact know each other.

There had been a few weeks left before Viktor's departure during which I didn't see the sculptor; his little flatworm's denunciations deprived me of the desire and the courage (especially the latter; I was afraid the cops would take revenge on Gábina) to join openly with the only people in the country I had respected. Viktor therefore could have met his last rival without my knowledge.

I was even beginning to understand why he might have. In the ten years we'd known each other (of which we battled for five) Viktor had never ceased to be a gentleman, not even once attempting to find out the truth about me behind my back. The Czech habit of snooping and pumping friends for information was one he found repulsive. Friends who betrayed him (I always ratted on them in my confessions) he wrote off without a word.

In time he must have figured out this was probably a mistake he paid a price for. (I took advantage of his good manners!) Or maybe he told himself that a detailed knowledge of at least one of my infidelities might cure him of a deadly illness: his dependence on me, which strengthened itself with each return. Vanesa's surprising mention of Luna recalled to mind that hidden riddle: what actually gave (if I reject the spurious police version) my sweetheart a direct motive to flee me?

Wanting to hold to his threat was a weak explanation; over the years we'd regaled each other (more precisely: I regaled him) with threats that sounded as dangerous as they were concrete. (I, many times: "I'll throw your lecture in the fireplace!" He, once, in desperation: "I'll cut off your hair!") I hadn't reckoned with such a cruel punishment, on a par with a lifelong curse, especially because he forgave me so wonderfully even that time. I had been reassured most of all by the fact that our tender system of "tummy-to-back" was once again in order (even in deepest sleep we turned over at the same time and only changed our close embrace).

All of which minimalized—apparently at the time into utter insignificance—the fact that he stopped sleeping with me; he explained it as a run-of-the-mill infection, and, as always in the good times, I was simply basking in the delight of his tenderness. In retrospect that time before his departure (obviously a trial separation) became the thirteenth chamber that concealed the answer. The Major had deceived me into thinking that Viktor's guilt lay therein. When linked to Olin, it seemed, on the contrary, to conceal the key to his innocence.

What could it be? It appeared indisputable that my sweetheart had had an experience after our reconciliation that transformed his vague thoughts of emigrating (it occurred to most of our citizens once in a while) into the only possible means of escape. Except (the outline became clearer and clearer) it wasn't prompted by a weak moment in which he supposedly signed a cooperation agreement with them, but rather by the shock of his first detailed description of my infidelity—from the mouth of a coarse bohemian, who, in his simplemindedness, had no idea that his actions could cause such hellish suffering.

I imagine my sweetheart as he crosses the threshold into the studio (and out of his area of competence) to declaim like a Russian nobleman that he demands satisfaction. (First of all he inquires: "Do you love her?" I see the Russian peasant confused as a wet hen, because he doesn't understand what the lord means.) Then my sweetheart's eye falls on the three pairs of fresh bosoms labeled *Tits I*, *II*, and *III*, unerringly recognizing that exceptional form. Crushed, he sits down on the (make-out) bed, suffers to be offered a coffee, and listlessly takes in the womanizer's description (and a jolly aside about how I, naked, had threatened the bastards with their old ladies) together with a jovial clarification that there was no question of love (so his guest shouldn't worry!), just exclusively sex, and of course he'd been careful.

I began to shake, but the reason was an honest chill. After midnight the Ice Saints stalked Prague in May. I fled from them and from the whole world into my bed. The blanket warmed my outside, but not my innards. I felt I was getting close to the truth, but I still didn't know what to do with it.

❄ ❄ ❄

Sometime in the night an alarm in my gullet woke me. The remainder of my dinner ended up in the toilet; despite my strenuous gargling the stench of fermented pineapple lingered in my mouth and upset my poor stomach further. Fortunately I was able to sleep until morning. No chance of morning calisthenics; I was a shadow of myself. (I have to at least go to the firm's doctor for a calcium shot; I need my strength this week, then come what may!) A successful ticketless metro ride raised my spirits, because during it an effective repentance occurred to me: after payday I'll buy twenty tickets and punch them all at once! But my body remained undoped; our medicine man was out "due to sickness" (read: is skiing; the guilty party announced on the boat ride that this year he could go to Arlberg for the first time, since he had, with a heavy heart, evicted the day-care center from his recently repatriated house—originally his parents'—and rented the rooms out to a sex club) and we could be seen by someone somewhere else. So I reached right for the telephone.

Three times I breathed deeply in and out (my poor tormented stomach, this too!) and dialed the number of my once desirable (in what way, really?) husband. When they connected me, it became clear to me how far things had gone: I call Tarant when beyond him only the torturer and the hangman are left (a quote from my older diary).

"No, Petra! This is a surprise! Is something wrong?" He could safely bet there was; I always wanted something. "Let's hear it; now's as good a time as any!"

He was evidently compensating for the inhumanity with which he'd rejected my request before Easter to have a serious talk with Gábina.

("She needs a man to talk to!" "But you did decide, my dear respected Petra, to raise her without a father, didn't you?")

"I'm worried about Gábina."

"Again? Already?"

"She's going through a crisis."

"She should read *Principles of Crisis Development in 1968*, ha ha." I could imitate that moronic laugh to good effect. It wasn't the most appropriate time.

"You can have fun at my expense"—Go for him hammer and tongs—"but not at hers. You have a growing daughter, who will grow up to be your lifelong admirer or your enemy. To use a similar bon mot: Every parent writes his own job review." He wilted.

"I'm sorry . . . You used to have more of a sense of humor." Onward, so we can sidle up to my point!

"I need your advice; you have connections." It surely pleased him that it wasn't about money; still, he remained on guard.

"Don't be too sure. I'm the old order."

"But wily. And competent, if they left you there."

"Not only that." Instead of showing some pro forma guilt, he bragged. "I'm even quitting of my own free will."

"Were you lustrated?" Maybe I should watch my mouth . . .

"No. And I won't be. I like my head too much to leave it lying on the chopping block; I haven't come into contact with StB agents"—You must be wrinkling up your nose now!—"but I won't let myself be axed by the clever guys who fucked things up worse than I did"—unwitting self-criticism—"yet play at being the new officers all the more fervently. I'm starting my own business."

"What kind?" Politeness and curiosity got the better of me.

"A legal and consulting service for domestic and foreign firms. Contracts, taxes, assessments, amortizations . . . but that's not your field."

"No."

"You, I hope, have a literary stipend and at least two collections in print?"

"Not even."

"Instead?"

"Instead I'm still sitting at the classifieds and hoping that some consulting service doesn't eliminate my position."

"What do you mean?"

"Surely it can't have escaped you that there are layoffs everywhere and the cost of living is exploding?"

"I would have thought that for your abiding faith you'd be on the Vatican's payroll, ha ha." I boiled over.

"How do you manage it; you never had any taste, but you keep on losing it!" He backed off.

"God, I didn't mean to be nasty! But since you brought it up: I've been wanting for a while to offer to raise Gábina's child support. Shall we say, by a hundred? Except I'd rather send the thousand for this year"—Doesn't that make twelve hundred a year?—"all at once by money order; I'm sure it's better for you that way." Aha, Mrs. Spouse, the one Gábina called The Tarantula.

"Yes, thanks." Better a hundred than a slap in the face.

"Good. Then we're agreed. Thanks for calling."

"Wait!"

"Yes . . . ?" It sounded like: what else?

"I didn't even get a chance to explain."

"I'm sorry. Senility. What's she up to?"

"She's in Germany. In Munich."

"Great. Studying German?"

"How would I pay for it?" Once again the stench of money.

"I'm sure there are various free courses for foreigners there!"

"It's not about courses. I need advice on how she can get back without a passport."

"Why without a passport?"

"Because she went there without one."

"But why, for God's sake? These days she has the right to a passport automatically!"

I laid it out for him, in the revised version for an unloving father's ear: Gabby's attacker had become her boyfriend, a serious affair, of course. Our daughter recognized her rashness and bitterly regretted it, but that wouldn't help her get back.

"So, what's the problem? I mean, what are we talking about?"

"Whether you know a way she could get back without a passport." I repeated myself like a simpleton and he answered me in the same spirit.

"Well, in the trunk again, I guess, how else?"

"And if they catch her?"

"Then she'll get a fine, and because she's underage, you'll pay it for her. Or, you know what? March her over here with the ticket, I'll pay it for her as a birthday present." There was no hope for him.

"Fine." But quickly now to the heart of the matter! "I also wanted to ask Viktor Král for help."

"Oh. And why him?" The name didn't surprise him, so . . .

"He's in the cabinet, I read."

"Well, yes."

"I thought he might arrange things at the Interior Ministry."

"Come on, it's not worth the trouble! You wanted advice, here it is: let things take their course. As the Americans say: take it easy!"

"If you mean . . ." Go for it! "Have you spoken with Viktor?"

"Of course. You haven't?" Careful!

"I ran into him last year. But you know: ten years."

"In the meanwhile he's climbed his way up to the captain's bridge. I gave him some advice: once you see an iceberg, don't wait for the impact, just lower the lifeboats; the guilty ones are always those at the helm. Row to me and be my partner." Notice, Petra, he treats his rival in love as the architect of his success . . .

"And he?"

"Chuckled."

"Listen." I felt myself blushing again; I thanked the phone that I wasn't visible, and horrified myself with the thought that my boss might walk in. "Did you meet with him before he left?"

"Once in a while for beer with our old crowd. But he never confided to me that he was about to split; he must've to you, though?"

"No . . . Did you know that he had an accident just before that?"

"What kind of . . ."

"A car accident. He hit a pedestrian after he'd had a bit too . . ."

"I remember vaguely . . ."

"In spite of it they let him go to Vienna." How awful, I'm blackening my sweetheart's reputation! But otherwise I can't act in his interests. "Others had their travel papers revoked for that. Do you think he made an agreement with them?"

"What kind of . . ." He said just as uncomprehendingly as before.

"To collaborate . . ."

"Viktor?" It got through to him. "With them? Never! Wait, I'm remembering: it was a woman, but nothing happened to her. They slapped him with a hefty fine!"

"So what I heard is just slander?"

"I never heard it, and it's a mouthful. His leaving was like a bomb. But, after all"—Is he onto me?—"you were with him then, weren't you?" Off the thin ice, pronto!

"Of course! And that's how I remembered it. I think it's horrible how those things spread."

"The StB agents do it themselves, the bastards; they muddle their own tracks by lobbing stink bombs. Tell Gabby if they make me into a nark, too, that I played just as big a hoax on them."

"If they don't lock her up in the meantime." I covered my tracks.

"Count on it, they won't. And know what? When she gets back, I'm inviting you for an opulent dinner." What! No!

"Your wife isn't home?"

"What . . . ?" He gulped and tried for a casual tone. "No, she's at a spa."

"Good. I'll ask Gabby if she has time." That surprised him.

"Come on, she can't have that much work!"

"Mainly I'll ask her if she wants to." He took offense.

"Excuse me?" Let's add some spice to the conversation, so the Viktor theme gets lost.

"And what do you think? That she waits with bated breath until your wife goes away once a year? Invite her alone, and do it so she'll want to go!"

"Fine!" Used to be, he spoke jovially when taunted; soon he'll be a manager of the much-desired American variety. "Well, thanks and 'bye, Petra!" Kiss my behind!

I worked through a Friday-length portion of the both common and exceedingly stupid classified ads, and even found a daily winner with a variation on our fateful couplet ("Form. emigré, 60, widower, no kids, Eng. pens., seeks form. emigrée to 50 yrs. for mut. 2nd departure from homeland. Attn: Unless we leave it, we will perish!") just in time to stuff my colored pencils in a drawer and, two floors up, open my notebooks for a third lesson in computerese. I intended (my stomach, after tea, was behaving placidly) finally to penetrate the mysteries of the previous lesson, which our teacher had promised to repeat for my sake (although there were doubtless bigger numbskulls than I sitting here!), and in return I was to supply his assignments. But he was the one who didn't show.

Instead of him someone else came in to inform us regretfully that Comrade, excuse me (an understanding smile all around), Mr. David was feeling poorly and would see us at a make-up lesson on Monday. My colleagues enthusiastically scattered (by no means, of course, to their desks); only I traipsed back to the office like a scab. (What now? Will V.D. contact me? Why didn't he earlier?) My boss, who before leaving was conscientiously checking over the territory in his charge, couldn't believe his eyes.

"My dear Mrs. Márová! What are you doing here?" And when he found out, "But you could just have gone home!"

"I thought I'd get a few hours ahead on my work"—cleverer than "Working off a leave in advance," although it was exactly that—"in case I need to take more time off at some point."

"You have the right to it automatically; you're our most diligent employee"—he repeated his song—"and you never miss a typo." And shifted his weight from one leg to the other. Out with it, I'm waiting! "If only you could find time for that dinner at our place!" And could bring Anthony Mára along to pin on you the Order of the Garter for the Preservation of the Catholic Press against Bolshevism.

"I'll speak to my family this Sunday." Let's leave him at least the illusion.

The door closed ever so quietly, as if he didn't want to wake me. I racked my brains: what now? I hadn't even considered the possibility that V.D. might leave me in the lurch; according to Murphy's Law he must not have been able to call. I tried to mobilize my visual memory and: next to his bed (forget about that!) I recalled a telephone.

Nimbly I paged through the telephone directory, but confound it! It listed more than 130 Davids; of those, twelve Václavs—in addition to which the line might be registered under the newt-father's name.

After half an hour of waiting I spent a further half-hour puttering around before calling information and finding out the schedule of Saturday buses to Kladno. No insignificant cold should protect the Major from exposure. (I hoped that the cold's possessor would at least call me at home to apologize. If not, and if he hadn't at the very least broken a leg, he was finished with me; he'd never see me in the course again. My boss wouldn't force a relative of the British executive to go, let alone dare to check whether I was actually attending!)

Despite the never-ending complications I was in a good mood as I left. My inner voice convinced me that the upcoming weekend would bring a denouement, and that it would be favorable to Viktor.

❄ ❄ ❄

On the way home an endless series of catastrophes began. With the knowledge that I would do penance for my sin immediately after payday, I once again didn't buy a ticket and the conductor caught me again, this time in the act. This was my fine-paying debut traveling in this direction and I hadn't been morally on guard; I felt like I was in the pillory—and to crown my shame I dug out of my wallet my last twenty, which wasn't enough. He led me onto the platform in disgrace and wrote out a ticket with my ID number.

A fairly attractive man of my age got off with us, evidently on impulse, and offered to lend me money for the fine. V.D. had taught me that lesson once and for all; I chased the white knight away like a fly (I actually waved my hands!), so that even the male conductor's honor was hurt. (You defraud the government and insult decent people, too; you could have saved me from writing this out!)

Wearily I dragged myself home and ate up the leftovers from the day before yesterday. (Do all smokers here eat stale bread with sour wine to have enough left over for cigarettes?) In the midst of this it occurred to me that I didn't even have money for the bus. (Nothing for it but to dig into the reserves in the belief that things can't get worse!) I'd intended in turn to pass on a few nice things from my grandmother and my parents to Gábina (a golden treasure; there'd have to be a war before I'd sell it), but I had the silverware too, a joint wedding present from my in-laws. (When we got divorced, my thrifty little husband forgot it here by mistake; he'd taken everything else, even the pearls he gave me—"I'll save them for Gábina, so you don't pawn them!" Undoubtedly his better daughter would get them, the one they already knew at age ten would be a world champion figure skater.)

It was high time the silverware disappeared as the last reminder of his presence, and went to serve a good cause; I only hoped that tomorrow I'd quickly find a private antique dealer who would offer me a decent amount. I had moved the table aside to climb up to the upper doors of the credenza when the bell interrupted me. My one personal visitor this year had been my sweetheart (so this is how the much-courted Márová ended up!); the bell as a rule announced all sorts of suspicious types visiting Gabby (girls with wild tresses covering one eye like a pirate's patch, boys with earrings that deflected attention from their adolescent pimples). If she was home, they disappeared for hours into her room; if she wasn't, I threw them out indiscriminately, as I planned to do now.

On the threshold stood V.D. with his square bag, offering one of his most idiotic smiles.

"GoodeveningI'msosorry"—he was mumbling like my daughter—"butIcouldn'tmakeitearlierifIwantedtogetitdoneforyoutoday . . ."

My nerves weren't strong enough to deal with him on the staircase; my neighbor (she's certainly in the Register of Contacts!) must have recognized through the peephole (did she have a microphone before?) that this young buck wanted me.

"Come in, no, please, don't take your shoes off!" I was inordinately sensitive on this point—that's why I'd chewed out the StB agents at Olin's—mainly because a few times I had refused to cross the threshold when people had wanted me, a guest, to spoil my only and prettiest evening dress by wearing hideous bedroom slippers. "I can't tolerate people walking around in their socks!"

"Mine are clean . . ."

"It's the culture of muddy Communist tract housing, where they forgot to build sidewalks; I resist such barbarism in an honorable old neighborhood from the First Republic"—meanwhile I was leading him into the kitchen, to rule out the slightest danger of our confidences—"but why aren't you in bed?"

"In bed . . . ?" he repeated mechanically, and his eyes wandered from the refrigerator across the stove to the credenza. (What is he looking for?)

"Your class was canceled today on account of illness!"

"Well, sure . . ." I realized that he was eagerly acquainting himself with the abode of his idol, ha ha.

"So what happened to you?" He collected himself.

"You gave me an assignment, didn't you? I stood guard there since morning instead. So he wouldn't slip by me, you know?"

"Aha . . . and did anyone like that arrive?"

"Yes. A taxi brought him."

"And? Did you manage . . . ?"

"He got out practically right at the building; I couldn't even tell if the description fit, I just saw him from the back."

"So it didn't come off!"

"I had counted on that and thought it through beforehand." He grinned like a street urchin. "I whistled on my fingers, like this."

He demonstrated so that my ears rang. My neighbor undoubtedly flew to the window. He himself cringed.

"Sorry . . ."

"Don't worry about it. And what did he do?"

"Turned toward me. Like probably everyone on the block, except he was the only one in my viewfinder."

"So he saw you!" Bad news! The offender is warned; V.D. will no longer be of use.

"No! I found myself a hidden vantage point. I got the shot kneeling between the trash cans." So you have a knack for this!

"No one noticed?"

"Earlier I wandered up and down the street with all kinds of different lenses and took pictures of children, guards, and garbagemen, so they'd get used to me. Used to be they'd have thought I was a cop, now they most likely just saw a wacky tourist."

"Of course I'll pay for your films." With what?

"I was shooting on metal."

"Is that some new technology?" A more expensive one?

"No"—once again he bared his teeth—"that's what we call shooting without film. That way when someone's bugging you to take their picture, you just say you've got an empty camera." Why the idle talk?

"And did the picture come out?"

"Sure!"

He opened his bag, pulled out a cardboard box of photo paper and from it a sheaf of glossy black-and-white enlargements. The Major's face stared right out at me, snared by the whistle. It was obviously him and at the same time someone unfamiliar; I had never seen that watchful look before. (V.D. had masterfully exposed the soul of a secret agent.) The second shot caught him (just like in police pictures) in profile (the Major heading toward the house). I kept going. All copies of the same two pictures.

"In case you want to distribute them."

"What . . . ?"

"Um, to people who might recognize him." Smart boy!

"Yes, thanks. You've been a tremendous help." I still have to find the delivery receipts from the flower shop; every year I'd put them in my diary. "Are you hungry, by any chance?" I asked a fraction of a second before I realized that I didn't have anything to offer him.

"A little . . ."

"When did you eat last?"

"Well, this morning . . ."

"Oh, no!"

"I was afraid he might . . ."

"Wait here a moment!"

I did a thorough search of the house and the result reflected it. (Gabby would of course have grimaced and gone to bed hungry instead.) The hunk of bread and the remnants of the cheese were joined by a pickle from the icebox, a kohlrabi from the pantry, and, most importantly: the second bottle of Vavřinec. (I know all too well that he likes to drink . . .) I poured him a full glass and myself a careful half.

"So, once again: thank you."

"It was nothing. So here's to it."

"To what?"

"To the success of your venture. Even though I don't know what it is."

He drank deeply; I wet my tongue (although my stomach didn't say no). In the meanwhile I watched with amazement the way he ate. In contrast to the young man who in the restaurant had displayed good manners, this starving creature was packing it away. With the last morsel of bread he wiped the plate clean (no trace of the kohlrabi or pickle) and only then did he say with boyish horror: "I didn't leave any for you!"

"I've eaten. Can I pour you some more?"

"If I'm not keeping you . . ."

"Absolutely not!" I filled his glass to the rim. "I'd like to make plans for tomorrow. If you're still available."

"Sure. When and where are we going?"

"To Kladno. I'll have to call you about the time; I have something before then." I'll trade in my silverware for the gas, so to speak. "Will you give me your number?"

"Sure . . ." He took a slip of paper out of his bag and wrote down the number. "My father is in the directory, you know?" I know that I don't know his first name and neither do I want to. "Early tomorrow morning I'll just drop by here for the motorcycle and then I'll wait at home."

"Where did you say you'd be dropping by?"

"Here . . . for the motorcycle . . ." He must have recognized my dumbfounded expression from class, because he spelled it out in the same way. "Um, I'll be leaving it here, because I've been drinking."

As proof he pointed to his glass, half-empty for the second time already. He's right! If my sweetheart had left Viktorka here that time (if I'd taken his keys from him!), he wouldn't have hit that old lady and wouldn't have fallen into the snares . . . Cut it out! Ugh, now I'm poisoning myself with that dragon's venom.

"You only had to ask; you could have had tea."

"I prefer wine. And I like to walk!"

Hardly! He stood all day on the street and then in the darkroom. At least praise him, if you're not going to pay him what he's worth!

"So far you've done an exceptional job . . ." I let the pictures run beneath my fingers and noticed: after the series of front and side shots of the Major, suddenly a totally unfamiliar face. "Who's this?"

"I just took everyone who went in and out, maybe unnecessarily, but I don't know what you're looking for, so just in case . . ."

"You're a regular Dr. Watson"—I smiled, so he wouldn't regret it—"but these people aren't really . . ." I couldn't find a better way to say it, when suddenly I came across a shot of a woman I knew: of course! His neighbor, dragging a heavy load of groceries. Well, so? What about her? ". . . of interest to me."

Then my heart stopped.

My expression must have betrayed me, because he looked disturbed.

"Is something wrong?"

I couldn't respond. I pressed both palms over my mouth and held them in a cramped grip for the short run to the toilet (my stomach was pumping vomit into it in a frenzy). A torrent burst forth from me, and I was horrified that I was vomiting blood, before a flash of clarity reminded me of the red wine. It and everything else flew into the bowl and all around it.

I was choking, with my head burrowed deep into the bowl so as not to dirty the little room any further than I had already. Alongside my indisposition I was racked by humiliation: this kid would experience, on top of everything else, my most revolting misery. And I already heard a voice.

"Petra! Petra!"

Just like his father not long ago, he opened the door (I hadn't managed to hook it shut), stepped into this wretched scene, and took me by the shoulders.

"Leave me aloooone . . ."

I wailed and water poured into my mouth; my chin hit the bottom of the bowl. He pulled me up by the hair.

"You'll drown!"

He picked me up—the beanpole—as if it were nothing and carried me out. I protested pitifully.

"I have to . . ."

"I'll clean it up later!" Jesus Christ! "Where's your bathroom?" Feebly I nodded my head in the direction. "I'll clean you up!"

With one hand he supported me at the waist like a rag puppet and with the other he gently washed my face, scooped up water in his palm and urged me to rinse out my mouth. Then, as if he lived here, he brought me over to the right bed, propped up my head with a pillow, and cooled my forehead with a wrung-out wet washcloth.

"Shouldn't I call a doctor?"

I was ready for one (even better, a psychiatrist), but not now! Now I had to close my eyes and breathe deeply, so the circulation would return to my brain and it would be able to figure out what my sweetheart had been doing in the Major's building this afternoon.

10

MY execution took place in a crematorium, "for practical reasons!" said the man in robes, the only thing I understood; otherwise they all spoke in an unknown guttural language without vowels, rumbling like beasts of prey—but stronger than the fear of death was my despair at not knowing why I wasn't allowed to remain alive; it must have been a depraved act, which I probably committed in a moment of madness, and I was horrified that they were denying me even the possibility of sincere repentance, meaning I would die unreconciled with Him; when they led me out onto the ceremonial stage, illuminated by floodlights beyond which unseen multitudes breathed excitedly, I realized that my end, too, would be dreadful: bound roughly in a straitjacket, and with a gag in my mouth resembling my grandmother's cushion for darning stockings, I was lifted horizontally upwards, one noose circling my ankles and the other my neck; I longed for it to be over quickly, but the instinct for self-preservation forced my muscles to lock my body into a bridge—when an electric buzz resounded, and from below a man in a black hood ascended to me in a lift cage and placed iron plates one after another on my stomach and breasts, during which his deadpan eyes watched me through two openings in the material; I felt my joints and sinews giving way, the unbearable pain brought tears to my eyes, and through the tears, as if through a magnifying glass, I recognized the executioner as my sweetheart.

I was still crying when it was already long clear to me that I was lying in the safety of my own bed, surrounded by the comforting camaraderie of familiar things—some of which had existed long before I had—and that outside a new May day was in full stride. The sun in the upper right-hand corner of the window announced that it was after eight; I'll be late again! Although . . . isn't it Saturday? I shook off the nightmare that had so upset me (I don't usually sweat, but now my nightshirt stuck to my skin) with its utter strangeness. Except then a fresh memory took the dream's place, and I was appalled. (The only hope: did I dream that, too?)

I jumped up and rushed to inspect the toilet. It was sparkling clean and smelled, as usual, of artificial lemon. The bathroom, too, was immaculate, but then the mirror spoiled my foolish relief: it served up a caricature of me, as if I'd just walked through a hailstorm in my robe (the yellow-green hickey became the least of the flaws in my beauty). Images from yesterday began to return to me and all my other feelings were outstripped by the shame that once again that boy had been witness to my degradation. (At least he cleared out; before I meet him, I have to pull myself back together enough that he'll again think he dreamed it.)

I took off my wet garments, but the hand holding them remained poised over the clothes hamper. Yesterday I'd had on—for the first time this year—a khaki linen summer dress in which I found myself (and wanted to appear to the computer teacher) quite attractive, but at the same time respectable beyond a shadow of a doubt. What end had it met with? This, too, I saw immediately: it was hanging on the nylon cords over the bathtub, washed. Shock! Freeing me from my stained garments, cleaning me thoroughly (now I do remember something of the sort), and dressing me in a clean nightshirt (from the bottom of my linen cupboard!)—only he could have done this! Twice in ten days he'd seen me as the Lord God created me!

In despair I began to long like an addict for a cigarette and coffee, but my freshly tortured digestive system threatened a repeat insurrection. Mindful of my mother's wisdom ("Your stomach will say what suits it today"), I ascertained by questioning it that we'd both be best revived by milk or beer (we'd know before the first swallow), except that for either I'd have to go out, and I didn't feel up to it yet. So probably hot tea, an advance deposit into my emptiness. I headed into the kitchen. V.D. was sitting there, and stuck his head into the lampshade when he politely stood up to greet me.

"Good morning . . ."

"What are you doing here?" I couldn't have asked more stupidly.

"I was waiting . . ."

"All night?"

"I was afraid to leave you here . . ."

"Where did you sleep?"

"First I sat here, but later I took the liberty of stretching out in the other room . . ."

"Did you at least make up the bed? There were fresh sheets there!"

"It wasn't worth it, I was afraid of oversleeping and making you late. I also went shopping." My brain wasn't working.

"How did you get back in?"

"The keys were in the door . . . you're not angry, are you?"

"How could I be?" My stomach growled in need. "What is there to drink here?"

"Milk, pilsner, soda water, mineral water, tomato juice, fruit juice, and cola." I stared. "I don't know your tastes, especially on an empty stomach . . ."

I was amazed how tactfully he described my repulsive episode. Here I remembered the mirror.

"Open me"—now I was absolutely sure—"a bottle of beer, please; I'll take it into the bathroom with me. First I've got to rise reborn from the ruins. Thanks so much."

"Thank you," he said incomprehensibly. (For what?)

I drank the beer construction-worker style, in a few swigs from the bottle, as if I were putting out an internal fire, and my stomach was noticeably gratified. Then I took an especially long time showering, drying off, and doing my hair so I'd have time to concoct an explanation for him (and maybe in general) as to what had caused my collapse. At a loss, I sat on the edge of the tub (the twelve-proof beer had slightly dulled my senses) when all at once I resolved that the greatest respect always accrues to secrets. He has the right to my thanks (which he got!), but nothing more, or else he'll get too big for his britches and I'll never get rid of him.

Swathed in large bath towels (what for? he's already seen what he could, and he was sitting politely in the kitchen), I stopped in my room to put on my traveling outfit. The motorcycle (I'd glimpsed it from the window at the bottom of the street, who else could it belong to?) spoke for jeans, a sweater, and heavy boots. Meanwhile I considered that if I wanted to hold up on it, I couldn't squander my meager strength on haggling over the silverware. So: borrow more, but from whom? (How to recognize a friend in need, if you don't have one in deed?)

The battle between truth and falsehood I found myself in exposed at the same time the extent of my isolation. At the moment in question (Saturday, colleagues and distant relatives at their country houses) I had only one person left, who was absolutely out of consideration, although he was coincidentally sitting in my kitchen.

"Would you please put some water on?" I called through the door.

"It's already boiling!" he announced. "Should I make you some tea?" Why does his prescient obligingness irritate me so?

"That would be wonderful of you." Because it reminds me of someone.

"Better on the weak side, no sugar, all right?" But whom?

"Whatever."

"Besides bread and rolls I also got some ladyfingers . . ." Aha! Mom!

"No, thanks, I don't want anything!" What's this? My stomach vigorously agrees with the idea of ladyfingers!

"You should eat a little something." Because it's humiliating when this particular kid plays mother to me!

"I'll try it." I had no chance against my stomach.

I pulled on a sweater, finished doing my hair, and shellacked it with a strong hair spray (so that it'd stand up to the wind even on the bike). In the meanwhile I figured out (combing is an inspirational activity for me) how to extricate myself instantly from financial distress. The mirror didn't subsequently tell me I was the fairest of them all, but it approved me for a public appearance. In the kitchen the tea was already steaming and a pagoda of ladyfingers was waiting. He sat down (after me) at the unset side of the tablecloth.

"And you?"

"I had a coffee out."

"Why not here?" He didn't want to wake me!

"I didn't want to wake you." I bristled.

"Do you know you're behaving like my mother!"

"No . . ."

"Well, now I'm telling you!"

I hungrily dunked the ladyfinger into my tea and tried, as in childhood, to get the pieces into my mouth before they got soggy and fell off. In the meanwhile he shook his head.

"What's so surprising? Do you know how to eat wet ladyfingers any better?"

"It's not that, but . . . before, you insisted that you could be my mother—and now you're making me into yours."

The telephone saved me from explaining. The only person who came to mind was Gabby, who had probably forgotten that she was supposed to call at noon. Except since the day before yesterday the world had changed, and I wouldn't be able to wait. In addition I didn't have anything to tell her (except the message from her wonderful daddy) and didn't intend to make a fool of myself in front of V.D. on a regular basis.

"Excuse me," I said at the doorway, "it's my daughter calling, she's having some difficulties."

He looked as if he'd probably stuff his ears shut. So he wouldn't have to exert himself, I took the still-ringing apparatus into the bathroom, as I'd always done when I was afraid to wake up Gabby. The cord reached just over the threshold; during every such conversation I promised myself (and immediately thereafter forgot) that I'd finally get it extended to the tub. (My longtime dream: to bathe, smoke, sip an aperitif, and meanwhile gossip on the phone with my beloved.) With my left hand I held the base, with my right I picked up the receiver, and then I froze in this uncomfortable position.

"It's me," said Viktor. "Am I disturbing you?"

"No . . ."

"And am I keeping you?"

"No . . ."

"I'd really love to talk with you . . ." Where is he calling from that he doesn't have to whisper?

"Where are you calling from?"

"From the ministry." Now what should I say?

"On Saturday?"

"It was too painful to whisper again. Can I come over?" My God!

"My daughter's here . . ." The third lie.

"We can have breakfast together!"

"Where?"

"I still only know Café Slavia."

"If it doesn't bother you that I was there not long ago with your . . ."

"If she can get together with you, then why can't I?"

To sit with him in broad daylight in the heart of Prague in public—what would I have given for that a week ago? Now my soul had been emptied (as recently my stomach had been), and the moment in front of the Major's house had made his expressive face alien.

"Don't you want to?" Fear resounded in his voice.

I leaned deep into the dark little room so I could talk louder. (It might occur to him why I was the one who wasn't talking normally.)

"Last time it was you who didn't want to."

"Forgive me! It was a real shock for me. I have to speak with you." Speak! I want to figure out what's going on before I go crazy! "I'll come get you."

"No! I'll take a taxi." A two-wheeled one.

"Fine. I'll go there and just wait; don't hurry, I have time." So many wonderful offers at such an awkward moment . . .

"Fine."

"See you." We said it simultaneously.

In a flash I reworked the schedule. In addition to my state ID I took my passport from the desk and returned to the kitchen. The self-appointed caretaker looked as if he hadn't moved a muscle while I was gone. (Pure onanism that I'd taken this wet blanket for a sex matador!) I cleared the remaining specters of last night into the sink along with the dishes and regained control.

"You'll go ahead and wait with the bike to the right around the corner—even better, go a bit farther along; I'd rather not have the neighbors think I'm taking after my daughter. I'll take care of something at the store and I'll ask you to drop me off at the National Theater. At twelve you'll find me on the same corner and we'll set off for Kladno."

"Yes," he said (almost like *Aye aye, Sir!*) and drew himself up to his full height.

"One second!" My brain was working again and found the connection at the point where it had broken yesterday. "Are those photos in the order you shot them?"

"That would be clear from the negatives."

"Do you have them here?"

"Sure!" He retrieved the roll from his bag.

Lightning-quick I sorted through the pictures. Those of the Major I pushed aside; about a dozen people figured in the rest of them. I chose two unknown men, the neighbor, and Viktor (like in the television detective shows).

"Who did you shoot after our target arrived?"

With a practiced eye he let the edges of the negatives slide between the balls of his fingers, looking at frame after frame against the window.

"Only this one." An unfamiliar face.

"So the rest of them came before him?"

"Well . . . logically, yes." It does make sense!

"And did all of them stay there?" He could have waited at the neighbor's!

"One came out immediately."

"This woman, right?" I covered my tracks.

"No, this one here." He pointed to Viktor.

"Oh . . ." I feigned disappointment. "Well, okay. Do you have everything? I'll look through the peephole and open the door for you;

be quiet as a mouse. There's a horrid gossip next door; she's got takers for her poisons in every regime."

"She was all sweetness and light to me . . ."

"What?"

"She was washing the doorstep and advised me where to go shopping." You were lucky!

Despite this I waited at the window until he'd pushed off the heavy machine and I tried as I left to offer my most nonchalant expression to the neighboring peephole. Before slamming the door I cunningly called inside that I'd be back by evening, and I risked not locking up. (Let her think he was one of Gabby's pretty-boys!)

Fortunately there weren't any customers in the new shop on the corner. The owner recognized me.

"Did you like the wine?" A perfect lead-in.

"Everything from here is good. I used to buy lollipops here at one time. And often begged them off the owner."

"Maybe even from me. I helped out my father here. Except it was a while before I could take over the business."

"Late, but in time." I got to the matter at hand. "Here's my ID with my address, except I need it today; I'll leave you my international passport until Tuesday, all right?" He stared uncomprehendingly at both documents. "I need three hundred crowns for an urgent trip and have no other way of getting it on a Saturday." He noticeably stiffened and I wanted to save him the refusal. "Oh, forget about it, an old-fashioned idea, the world's changed."

"Just a second!" he interrupted me, "Mrs. . . . Mrs. . . . ?"

"Márová . . ."

"Dear Mrs. Márová, I'm not going to take hostages from my customers. Here"—he hit some keys on the state-of-the-art cash register, and when the drawer rolled open, pulled out three green bills—"you go, and I look forward to your continued patronage; within a week you'll find lollipops here, guaranteed."

"May your faith"—I spoke loftily, the way I felt—"in our neighborhood not be soon shaken!"

"If I'm wrong about you, young lady, it's a sign from heaven that I should have stayed retired, the way my wife advised me to, except

I owed my father this satisfaction, and you certainly won't spoil that for me!"

* * *

I stepped into the café with no expectations of approval; I had things to worry about besides displaying how desirable I was. (Anyway, the monstrous helmet I had had to put on, like it or not, had hopelessly ruined my hairdo; V.D. had looked as if he were about to cry, but wouldn't back down.) Viktor was sitting by the window with a panoramic view of the castle; he was, however, watching the entrance, and so he stood up immediately and nodded to me. (With foresight I had directed my chauffeur to come the long way around via Národní, so I could hide behind his tall back.)

"Hi," I said in my most normal tone (practiced en route). "How were things over at our former Big Brothers'?" And caught the scent of his wonderfully bitter aftershave.

"In Moscow?" he asked absentmindedly, evidently concentrating on another subject. "I can sum it up in a sentence: everything there smells like a putsch."

"No! And who . . . What would that mean for us?"

"I'm sure you can imagine." Yes! And that thought alone is enough to drown out our private traumas.

"But their soldiers have almost all left!"

"In '68 they were, too, weren't they? But they came right back."

"The West wouldn't just leave us now!"

"I'm afraid they'd all react just like my dear Canadians undoubtedly would. Sharp protest and then a long wait for the next accident of history."

A languorous waitress appeared; Viktor ordered tea for me (unfortunately no jasmine) and for himself, and some pastries. Behind him the kitsch of the castle floated above the Vltava, this time in the colors of a May morning, rounded off by the lilacs on the island, the gulls and the swans, lazily swimming with the current up to the weir. I could almost believe that this was actually a picture of the modern world that had become accessible for the first time in history. His voice suddenly tore me from this illusion.

"Petra, I owe you a tremendous apology. I love you, believe me!" He didn't even lower his voice and I looked around, frightened, but there was a wall-to-wall barrier of foreigners. "Almost insanely so!" Is this him talking? "It's getting harder and harder for me to hide it, that's what explains my long absences! If Márka weren't so small and Vanesa so vulnerable . . ." Oh, and what about me? "I don't want to belabor the point! I long for you constantly, sometimes I forget myself at meetings, even at home I'm not present in spirit. I'm probably saying it awkwardly, but I'm trying to explain what I felt last time when you believed that man." As if to prevent interruption, he stretched out his arm almost to my mouth. "In your place I wouldn't have reacted differently in those first moments; why should a normal human being consider the possibility that one person would want to destroy another's future with a cynical lie? Except, Petra, that's exactly what it is, and my slamming the door was an expression of despair—that I have no defense against it. Even if I were to arrange a confrontation, he would just repeat it to my face—after all, dissembling was and still is child's play for them—and I'd be the one to turn red and stammer, so long as my nerves didn't fail me any worse than that! Yesterday I was so far gone that . . ." He fell silent.

"That what?"

"Once"—he fixed a sightless gaze on the castle—"you told me about a famous writer who asked his friends how a headache feels, because he personally had never experienced one." Yes, Tolstoy . . . ? "It was the same with me and hatred; fate had spared me. The lustration commission's ultimatum evoked my surprise, and fear, but at the same time the conviction that such an absurd mistake had to be explained, which it indeed was, even before it could start gnawing at me. While your suspicion hit me like a ton of bricks. What followed was the shock of powerlessness. If I'd had a weapon with me I probably would have pulled the trigger. I didn't fall asleep till morning and was awakened by sheer hatred." What a colossal ass I am! "Petra! Do you believe me?" His eyes bored into me.

"How can you even ask?"

"But you believed him, too!"

"I'm ashamed . . ."

"I'm not lecturing you, I'm only pointing out that belief is a deceptive category in a country where a lie proclaimed itself as virtue and millions will testify that for forty years they fought for truth with its help. On Tuesday I ran away like a two-bit thief; you must have thought I was afraid of your questions."

"No! Believe me!"

"Leave belief out of it and ask away; that's why I'm here!"

"I don't have any questions!" Only a request to believe that I believe you!

"Don't worry that I'll take it as mistrust on your part. It'll relieve me if you ask about everything that's bothering you; maybe in the meanwhile we'll figure out what he's after. He must have some reason for doing it; this isn't just ringing the doorbell and running."

The girl arrived with tea and pastries, but had to content herself with my thanks; Viktor didn't tear his eyes from me (and neither of us thought about either the food or the drink).

"So, ask!"

It surprised me that I was having trouble choosing; a slew of questions scrambled to be heard. One had been in my head since Saturday.

"How did the meeting with him go?"

"He started by asking if I could drop him off at a new hotel in Strahov. It was less awkward for me than sitting around somewhere in the car. Then he asked, 'And what can I do for you, Mr. Král?' as if for years we hadn't been on informal terms, but even that I welcomed. To which I said, 'Petra told you.' He says: 'So she must have explained to you how it happened; I apologize belatedly.' Then he was interested in who to write to and where to bring the letter. That's all. Ask on!" I accepted this way of blindly groping for answers.

"You were together for a long time. In the meanwhile Vanesa managed to tell me about her father's adventures."

"Ah, that's also a crazy story! But it's not really that long. On the way back I stopped at the stadiums, near my old dorm. I wanted to collect myself; I hadn't seen Prague from there for years, and the lights had just come on. It couldn't have been more than fifteen minutes with him, all told."

"What else did you talk about?"

"Once we'd quickly disposed of the matter, we both fell silent; it was awkward, but natural under the circumstances. Near the end he was giving me directions, and when he got out, all he said was 'So, on Monday, then.' "

"His most important assertion was that, in your accident before you left, you ran into an old lady. You never told me that."

"First, I was horribly ashamed, and second . . ." He turned his head, but finished his sentence, "after all, nothing happened to her!"

"He had them pretending to you that she was badly injured and threatening you with years in prison."

"Who?"

"Some subordinate of Beneš's. He supposedly got the rundown on the accident and decided to pressure you into collaborating."

"The only ones who spoke with me were the traffic cops. After the collision my fear sobered me up; the fact that I safely drove her to the hospital and turned myself in testifies to it. It made an impression on them; they did make me take a breath test, but during the arraignment they assured me that the old lady didn't have even a scratch. They kept my keys and driver's license, but they themselves called me a taxi."

"Did they call you in again?"

"I went on my own in the morning; I wanted to find out how long I'd be without a license so I could arrange to have my car taken to my mother's in Pardubice." Yes, his mother was forever cropping up; I'd refused once and for all to see her when he told me that he'd given her my poem "I Am Raining" to read, and she had warned him, "That flighty little girl wants to be a tropical storm, but she's more like an April shower." Later it was she who refused to meet, so with our combined might we ripped him apart for all time. "An unfamiliar guy, also in uniform, took my folder—it was on top—and said something like, 'You're lucky, the lady's home and her relatives are quaking in their boots that they let her run out in the street at night, because she's in an advanced stage of senility; that means there's the drunk driving charge left. Do you want to take your driver's test again or pay a thousand-crown fine?' Normally it would have taken my breath away—a third of my monthly pay!—but immediately I realized that under the circumstances I was getting off for almost nothing."

"Weren't you surprised?"

"I saw the light when I brought him the money from the bank and he returned my license and keys without a receipt from the pad. For them it was obviously a run-of-the-mill deal, but for me it was a miracle; I'd already kissed Vienna goodbye." If they hadn't let you go, you never would have left me . . .

"Beneš claimed that his man set you on . . . Oldřich Luna. He was trying to convince me that they were able to"—Be brave!—"nail you to the wall more successfully by playing on your wounded pride."

"In a word: bullshit!" He's getting up! "No, don't worry, my leg just fell asleep."

It was evident that he was as despairing as last time, but this time he was amazingly in control. I could finally give him something to be happy about.

"Paradoxically, it was actually Luna who corroborated your innocence."

"What do you mean?"

"I called him the day before yesterday."

He reacted the way I hadn't wanted. "So you've been looking into it."

I vehemently put it in the correct context. "Of course! To find you an alibi! You got me into your problem, and I thought I still had your mandate!"

"But certainly . . . And what certificate of good conduct did he award me?"

"His friends work in the Interior Ministry. They didn't find anything on you, only on his wife. Who confessed that she put them onto him"—Well! Out with it!—"out of jealousy."

"No!" Now he looked as if he might stand up in his enthusiasm.

"Yes!" I made use of his euphoria for a related question. "You haven't spoken to him?"

"To whom?"

"To Luna. Back then or now."

"I've never had the honor." Time hadn't taken the bitterness.

"Your wife"—Bull's-eye!—"mentioned him as a friend of yours."

"Him?" He was confused, until he remembered. "I was describing for her the situation in Bohemia and as an example from the area of art I took his case, without our involvement in it, of course."

"As if you'd played my part in the episode."

"I quickly got the feeling over there that here I'd always been both you and me at the same time. I think that I told her more stories in which I played your role; in that way you were secretly with me. I already knew that my escape hadn't succeeded; I'd left behind more than I gained."

Although we were practically sitting in a window display, he took my hand with the teaspoon into both of his.

"Petra, please, tell me the truth, why did you never want to marry me?" I shook my head dully. "Why, Petra? Everything would have been different!"

"I was mortally afraid that it would turn out like almost every marriage does. I wanted . . . I was out of my mind! I wanted you always to have to strive for me."

"But you succeeded. I'm after you again."

"And what of it?" I was starting to become slightly hysterical.

"You have me in your power."

"And what's it worth? You don't belong to me!"

"Please, give me just a little time!"

"What are you talking about?"

"You know full well, don't force me to say it." My God, can it be true?

"What's a little time for you?"

"Two years, a year, half, I don't know how to estimate, but I feel our Gordian knot will untie without a sword. Vanesa's still a step shy of maturity, she could well find a more interesting man soon."

"Than you?"

"She knows me completely differently than you do. I think she sees in me a younger edition of her father; it won't satisfy her for long." I couldn't believe my ears.

"What do you mean by that?" I won't spare you this! "Translate that into ordinary language for me, please!"

"I can't sleep with her anymore."

Under the wide windows the Saturday promenade pulsated. The café had filled up; by Murphy's Law there would be a pair of eyes from his circle watching (or foremost: her!). In spite of this he leaned across the table and simultaneously took my hand to kiss it.

"You're my only one! My wife!" The image of Vanesa watching us horrified me.

"Viktor, don't be crazy!" He kept kissing the back of my hand and I couldn't hold myself back. "I love you terribly, too, and for that exact reason I don't want you to get into another mess on my account. Of course I'll wait. However long it takes! And you're my husband, too!"

"May I come by tonight?" It's Saturday; how does he intend to arrange it? And why do I care!

"Yes!"

"From eight to midnight?" Four whole hours!

"Yes, yes! Except I won't be able to buy anything . . ."

"What?"

"For dinner . . ."

"I hunger and thirst only for you." He let go of my hand, glowing. "I almost dropped in on you yesterday, on the way from the airport."

Alarm bells went off in my brain. In my mind's eye a shiny black-and-white photo jumped into view. Everything in me resisted it (his decidedly public confession had raised our relationship to heights I'd never dreamed of), but this question was the key.

"So, why didn't you stop?"

"They were driving me with the prime minister. We're almost neighbors, he wanted to take the shortest route through Motol . . ."

In all probability my face froze over. And in his sudden nervousness he was given away by the way he started to signal the headwaiter (his fingers fluttered over his head as though he were in school). The waiter hurried over in a flash and mutely wondered at the untouched delicacies. I watched, paralyzed, as Viktor carefully put the receipt, the bills, and the change into various compartments of his leather wallet and then buttoned it into the back pocket of his pants. During the lengthy operation he didn't so much as look at me, and inside me the rock of my faith was quietly crumbling.

Why had he lied to me?

And what else had he lied about?

I lacked the strength to stand up, but there was no alternative. I couldn't bear to look at him and hung my head.

"Petra!" I heard, "for the first time just now I didn't tell you the truth."

"What about?"

"If you hadn't asked, I would have kept it under wraps; this way I can't, a single lie between us might destroy everything." Yes, yes! "I went by taxi from the airport to Beneš's." How did he know where . . . ? "The commission gave me a copy of his letter." He reached into the breast pocket of his light jacket and unfolded in front of me a piece of paper; in an upper corner the name and address stood in black on white. "Fortunately he wasn't home."

"Fortunately?"

"I confessed to you how that hatred took root in me; in Moscow it was threatening to tear me apart. I looked at those windbags, who in the sixties just laughed at what happened to us, and was constantly conscious of the fact that he belonged to them. The thought that you'd trust him in the end, because here"—he rapped the letter—"he showed his largesse, was unbearable on the flight back; I was mumbling like a mental case, 'Wickedness must be punished!' The taxi driver had to take me to the office and wait there. I took a gun from the office safe and went to kill him."

"No!"

"Yes. They distributed pistols to us. I never went to the training sessions, but I still know how to use one. If he'd opened the door . . ."

"Jesus Christ!"

"Petra! Do you want some water? You're green!" He looked wildly around for the help.

"No, I don't want anything, it'll pass. Dear God in Heaven"—I clasped my hands together—"thank You that that bum wasn't home, only You have the right to punish!" I was almost shouting, but Prague was undergoing an invasion of cults; they probably took me for a pagan, and no one was the worse for it. "Vít'a, how could you? You would only have harmed yourself. They might have thought you eliminated a witness who wanted to retract a coerced statement!"

He shook his head with a demented expression.

"I would have done it. God knows, I would have done it! But as it happened, after the third ring I went slowly downstairs and outside in the fresh air I already knew I was an idiot . . ."

"Do you still have the gun?"

"This morning I put it away and on Monday I'll return it; I don't want to be tempted!"

"Thank God!"

"But something has to be done! Who knows who else he has on his conscience and in his sights?" I could encourage him.

"There's a promising possibility in the works for catching him in his lie. If it comes off, he'll be left to face his new benefactors as a repulsive lowlife who's ruining their reputation. I'll tell you this evening how my expedition went."

"Your expedition where?"

"Please, hold off for now, I don't want to speak too soon!"

"Could I take you there?" It would be wonderful! But risky!

"Thanks so much, but a colleague from work is dropping me off."

"Fine . . . so, shall we go?"

"You go on ahead!"

"So, this evening?"

"This evening. Cross your fingers for me."

"You're amazing!" He stood up and once again whispered. "I long for you!"

"Me, too!"

"I love you!"

"Me, too!"

Across the empty chair I stared at the picture-postcard castle and tried to imagine that panorama without everything that the hand of man had built there down through all the centuries. That's what my life would be like without him.

A moment later he passed slowly by on the sidewalk under the window, and those few seconds when he looked devotedly into my eyes I will never forget until I die.

❄ ❄ ❄

The trip to Kladno temporarily emptied me of all lofty sentiments; only animal reflexes remained. The short morning leg from Bubeneč to the National Theater had led mainly along a trough of streets; the entrance ramp already should have warned me that a motorcycle is not the most appropriate form of transportation for an (almost-) forty-year-old. At the city limits sign with its slash through the word PRAGUE it occurred to me that I should have gone home for warmer clothing, but time in addition to pride prevented me from returning.

Jolting across the cobblestones of small villages, I was shortly forced to let go of the metal handle and grab hold of the driver. (I'm sorry! I shouted into the wind; V.D. didn't react.) Soon I shamelessly pressed myself against him (only my head in its helmet was warm), unfortunately with the same result as if I were hugging a tree in a storm (my shoulders and sides stuck out against his slender body). He has to know; why doesn't he stop and offer me his jacket, the lout? (Because, silly, you'd never fit into it!)

Love and hate abandoned me; everything was drowned out by the cold and the growing fear that I would fall off like a pear burned in a frost. Ever stronger was the thought of shouting into his ear to stop immediately and then rolling down into the tangle of vegetation in the roadside ditch, which from the saddle looked to me like a warm embrace. However, my vanity proved itself incapable of ceding the high ground to this little boy because of a temporary weakness of the body; at each crisis point it willed *No!* and reanimated my enfeebled muscles for another mile. When they had irreversibly come round to capitulating, the destination sign appeared: KLADNO.

My difficulties at once fell by the wayside. I had to concentrate on a task that seemed hopeless at first glance: to find among dozens of look-alikes a single small house where I had been once before years ago. (It dawned on me that it lay on the connecting road between the bus station and the nearest coal derrick.) First I had to unload my guide. Bravely I let go of his waist and tapped him on the shoulder.

"Find a pub!"

As if in answer to my request we passed one. I collected my strength so I wouldn't stagger as I got off. I wasn't fully successful, but I took advantage of the moment when he was pushing the motorcycle up on its kickstand to climb the steps. He found me in the barroom already at a table, sat down next to me, and put down his bag. (I hadn't even noticed it'd come with him.)

"The wind went right through you, didn't it?" Suddenly you know!

"I'm not made of sugar. I'll have a hot toddy; you, too?" Why is he looking like that; I know he drinks. "Don't you like them?"

"I'm driving you back . . ."

"But not right away. I'll go on from here on my own."

"Don't you need to take pictures?"

"No. I'm sorry, I forgot to tell you you didn't have to schlepp your camera along."

"No problem. Can I help you any other way?"

"By waiting for me. I have no idea when I'll be done."

"No problem." Why does he always repeat the same words? "I'll be here."

"Why hang around here? Go to a movie or something; I don't have to be back in Prague till after seven."

"I'll sit here for a while, just in case you . . . really, it's no problem!" Do what you want, o servile nature!

He had a cola, ugh! The rum in a hot water bath energized my muscles and didn't cloud my mind. I set off along the long, straight road (the lover who was now destroying my sweetheart had led me along here in his embrace), which at the end branched out into the streets of his neighborhood. Memory (and vengefulness?) led me blindly into the middle of the branching; I looked for a rose garden with an arbor for a teensy Snow White along the left side and close to the main street. By the second cross-street a weathered sign on the mailbox confirmed my discovery: BENEŠ–NEDOMIL. I repeated to myself the possible variants from my scenario and rang the bell.

Heaven smiled on my venture. His sister had grayed; only the web of varicose veins on her hands had not paled. She neared the gate, searching my face. I helped her.

"Márová. I was here once with your brother."

"I know. Petra."

As she unlocked the gate she didn't attempt to hide how little my visit pleased her. I wanted to make it easier on her.

"I'm actually looking for you. We could go for a short walk."

"Come on in!"

She turned and led me into a familiar room; my memory registered a single innovation: a gargantuan television (apparently color and of foreign make) was enthroned here. It gave me an easy opening.

"Not much has changed here . . ." An odd noise floated in from somewhere.

"At first glance. My father and mother died, my brother was wounded by a coal combine and didn't survive it. The boys married and moved out." She reeled it off dryly like statistics of equally serious losses. I could hardly offer my condolences.

"You also had a daughter."

"Josefína, yes, fortunately she's filled up our house again; she already has two girls and a little boy." I recognized the noise as a child crying. "Would you like a coffee?"

"Same old java?" For the first time she smiled a bit.

"We could never get used to anything better."

Now I knew what my stomach had been longing for in vain since this morning. As before I followed her into the kitchen unasked, so that an interruption wouldn't extinguish the flame of her good mood. Here there had been more fundamental changes, dominated by the new stove.

"You've made some improvements here."

"Our parents sent them to us from heaven."

"From where . . . ?"

"When Dad died, Mom got confused; she hunted for him endlessly for years. She'd wander in here from the bedroom, out to the garden, into the basement, up to the second floor, into the attic, and back to the bedroom, always in a loop; she'd look around, walk through, and close the door, all without a word. She didn't notice her three grandsons' weddings, or her son's funeral, not even Josef's imprisonment, and we noticed her just as little: when there was time, we'd look her over or feed her and put her back on her circular track. It was only a question of when and where her time would come. It happened on Dad's side of the bed. When we were getting the room ready for the kids, it occurred to Fína's husband to look through the mattress before throwing it out, and he found twenty thousand crowns they'd saved from their pensions in an envelope marked 'For the Kitchen.' Do you take sugar?"

The story was infinitely simpler than Vanesa's, but it made my skin crawl in the same way. (I almost expected a gust of wind as the lost soul passed by me.) Back in the parlor I requested three cubes of sugar (energy for the trip back) and tried my luck.

"Mrs. Nedomilová . . ."

She immediately interrupted: "That's my daughter, by coincidence I married another Beneš from a different family."

"Yes . . ." This paltry mistake threw me off balance. "You're probably wondering why I'm here." What an intelligent introduction!

"Not really. I was expecting you earlier. But better late than never." I gave up on the scenario and played it by ear.

"Are you angry at me?"

"You surprised us." Years ago she'd used the familiar *you* right off the bat; now she was using the formal one. "You had to have known we were welcoming you into our family. We're ordinary people, but we have our standards. It couldn't have escaped you that we accepted you gladly, even though you came from an alien world and it was our Josef at stake. We didn't believe anyone could cure him of his grief over Marie; you managed it and got our respect. And then he had to get over you!"

"He knew that I gave in to my daughter." Why am I defending myself here? "She was at a critical age; she was threatening to run away from home and even worse things. I proposed that we continue the way we were before, but he refused!" It's true, I didn't insist; there was that other problem, too, but he was the one who decided, not I!

Without a word she got up and went into the kitchen, but returned immediately with a third of a coffee cake, a plate, and a knife.

"I forgot. Please help yourself."

I had to get to the heart of the matter. "Mrs. Benešová, do you know where your brother worked?"

"In security."

"State Security!"

"Everyone knew that, at least by the time they locked him up, and also understood why: so the people who wanted a new bloodletting wouldn't have the upper hand."

"Did he confide in you before that?"

"No, but I know him. Don't you believe people you know well?"

"I've probably been warped by the fact that in our circles many people are excellent fakers."

"In ours, too. But each of us has to sense who respects us and to what extent, and whether he would tell a vicious lie." A terribly naïve guide, but let's hold to it for now.

"Do you think your brother has completely stopped respecting me?"

"I wouldn't say that, Mrs. Márová." A noticeable aloofness. "And I definitely don't think he would lie to you."

"Has he spoken to you about our last few meetings?"

"Yes. In public he still keeps quiet, but with me, where it won't get back to them, he talks about everything." She laughed sharply. "I'm sort of his confessional."

"So you know what this is about." She nodded slightly. "He almost ruined a man." Why kiss up to her?

"He explained to you that he hadn't intended to. And he fixed things up."

"He withdrew a false declaration that couldn't hold up, and stepped in with a new one that is no less threatening."

"He did his best to see that an untruth didn't threaten someone's existence. And then he warned you about a deception that someone committed against you."

I wanted to take a drink, to hide my agitation, but I had to abort the attempt; my hands were shaking.

"Except that this someone convincingly denies it and has reliable witnesses!"

"Can someone have witnesses to something he didn't do?" She's as clever as her brother!

"Someone else confessed to it!"

"So why knock yourself out? Supposedly you've known this guy for years; why don't you believe him?"

"Why did your brother even mention it?"

"Apparently he's convinced of it."

"So let him give me convincing proof!"

"Tell him that."

"He wasn't home and . . . I wanted you to persuade him!" I'm saying whatever comes to mind. "Back then I instinctively trusted you most. Yes, I knew this person"—No! I won't say his name aloud!—"long before your brother; I know him like I know myself, but that makes me all the more afraid that he'll lose control of himself. How can he live with an accusation against which there's no defense?"

"Where did he find out about it?"

"I told him."

"But why?" Flabbergasted, I stared at her.

"What do you mean, why . . . ?"

"Why do you torture him if you believe him? Josef didn't intend to make it public."

"And how am I supposed to live with it?"

"So, you do have your doubts about him."

Another StB agent! She could easily be one, too! Had she ever been? That's his expression from yesterday's photo!

"That was the reason, wasn't it?" My nerves finally gave out. "That was the real purpose of his slander! To force me, for the first time ever, not to tell him the truth—and in time, the lie would eat into me, I'd come to believe it and be revolted by him! A little payback for preferring my oddball daughter!"

I hurled the angry words in her face, while she sat immobile with her hands clasped on the table, those hands that recalled a tangle of dark violet snakes, until it hit me that I had botched everything I could. (Renewal of our relationship—see scenario—is excluded; I stood alone against their familial fortress.) In the ensuing silence I noticed the clatter of footsteps on the stairs, and then a young woman stepped into the living room. She'd apparently heard nothing of my outburst; her face reflected surprise at the unfamiliar visitor.

"My daughter," his sister continued in an even tone (yes, she has an abnormal degree of control over herself!), "Fína, you remember Mrs. Márová!"

Her glasses she'd evidently left behind with her childhood and after three births her skinny little frame had matured into a full body; she'd unfortunately loosened her girdle in that small-town way so it filled out her waist into a cylinder. Only her keen glance hadn't changed.

"How could I forget?" Irony? "There's guests for you."

"Spend a few moments with her. Excuse me."

With that she closed the door behind her. (Did she herself need to calm down?) Her daughter applied herself to the task with evident interest.

"How are you doing?" Maybe something can still be saved.

"Much better these days, thanks, like most everybody. And what about you"—I was remembering my fiery speech—"are you a teacher?"

"So far I've been on maternity leave more than in school."

"And did you teach your children that"—How did it go?—"you can live decently off a lie, but only with truth can you have a decent life? Am I saying it right?" She was amazed and warmed to me.

"I even told the examining committee that I intended to say it daily from the lectern. 'That's perfectly fine,' smiled the chairman, 'after all, it's we Communists whom history has proven right.' So I say: 'Right or not, the fact that we're destroying our forests, water, and air is the work of the people who are in charge here.' After a stormy discussion they resolved that a daughter of our mining nobility shouldn't waste away in an elementary school, and they swept me tidily into the education department of the City Council to keep textbook statistics. That's when I acquired both my daughters.

"My dream was realized last January. I couldn't have cared less that I still saw the same sadly familiar faces above me; after all, I could teach according to what I knew was true and right—I thought!" She sneered contemptuously, resembling her mother. "Except pretty soon complaints started raining down: I was from the old order"—she chuckled girlishly—"and was preaching Bolshevik heresies to the children. They called me in and I got a lecture from the very same man who back in his comrade days had chaired my exams. 'You taught the children that between the wars the Communist Party fought against the exploitation of miners; a criminal organization mustn't be praised for the gains it achieved during its earlier, better days!' I reminded him that he'd had a Party ID only a year before, while I never had. An ambulance took him away with a heart ailment, and they trumpeted at me that my meanness toward an old man showed that the blood of secret policemen still flowed in my veins. Your fine democrats, Mrs. Márová"—Why mine?—"instructed their little children to draw red stars on my blackboard daily. In July my husband took pity on me and resolved things the way the Nedomils do; he's from a family of ten. 'When something upset our parents,' he always says, 'they had a child and it made them happy.' So now I'm happy again."

She fell silent and waited for my response.

"We both probably ought to know that it isn't a matter of my democrats or of your Communists, but of people with character or without it."

"I've thought that since I was a kid, but I realized that back then it was you who denied it. You spoke about a Communist mentality"—So she remembers it, too!—"instead of a totalitarian one. And like every herd mentality, it's possible in a democracy, too, when enough of you gather around it."

"Enough of us?"

"I'm still an upstart; in our family education grew on fallow land and still doesn't have roots. I counted on the best figures in the opposition and believed in the millions of Czech intellectuals of all generations, that with their knowledge of history they'd had enough time during that polar night to think up a way not to repeat here what keeps driving people to the barricades again and again. Except it broke, the chance was suddenly here, and what I see is only the repellent other extreme, which already came to a bad end here once this century and'll hit the skids again, in some new revolution"—in her agitation she'd slipped from a careful educator's pronunciation and grammar into the colloquial—"and then in a new dictatorship, because after the Robespierres always come the Napoleons!"

"But I feel the same way!"

"I strongly doubt it." That's already an insult!

"What gives you the right to say that?"

"Your behavior toward Josef." Just what I wanted to hear again!

"What do you know about that?"

"You left him because of your prejudices."

"Mrs. Nedomilová, I appreciate your openness, but even a teacher shouldn't assign grades to a relationship between two people!" He's some kind of god here!

"Except, did you love him or not?"

"Of course. That's why he was probably able to understand that my daughter's ultimatum was just as much of a shock for me."

"How old is she?"

"Seventeen." I took the bait.

"Is that what's still stopping you?" What can I say to that? "You knew him well enough to know he'd never stop waiting. You must have had some idea who those roses were from every year on the anniversary of your breakup." She knows! "Except you simply wrote him off, so he wouldn't spoil your civic profile." Now, this is getting . . . ! "But really, Mrs. Márová, your people are political cross-examiners and inquisitors, too; that's something else we both should know, shouldn't we?" What should I do now? "Back then I liked you right off the bat"—Yes: "You're sensational!"—"you disappointed me all the more later." Get up and leave?

The handle clicked (I hadn't heard the footsteps) and Josef Beneš stepped in, wearing a gray turtleneck, black pants, and white sneakers, masculine and naturally self-assured as in his best years.

"Hi. I heard you were looking for me."

His niece saved me from making an immediate reply. As if she'd been waiting just for him, she stood up and without saying goodbye closed the door behind her. He sat down on the chair his sister had left.

"Is something happening?" Christ, get hold of yourself, Petra!

My silent oath pulled me together instantly. I couldn't sink any lower in my own esteem! I remembered my scenario. (*Scene 4*: Deepen contact so that it will be possible to appeal to his human side. Bingo! I had no other options.)

"I'm at the end of my rope!" Unfortunately true . . .

In our years of acquaintance he'd never experienced me hysterical (while Viktor had countless times!). With him it just didn't work; I perceived in time that he held that feminine weapon in contempt. (The picture of his wife falling to her death swimmingly as if into a pool had fascinated me and kept me in check.) For this reason he now, as I had expected, grasped the exceptional nature of the situation and cast aside his reserve.

"How can I help you, Petra?"

This person certainly still loved me, but in light of his action it was a perverted emotion and could be allowed to become my weapon!

"I feel like I'm caught between the devil and the deep blue sea!" Forgive me, Vít'a . . . "Finally I feel like I understand you, and frankly I believe you"—lie to a liar!—"except Viktor says the exact opposite. For you—please excuse this—lying was a part of your profession and of the courageous game you were playing"—a bit of honey on the tongue will blunt his teeth—"but Viktor turned red whenever he bumped into someone on the tram; for God's sake, Josef"—even his Christian name to further the cause!—"how can I imagine that he's lying to me so coolly? My nerves got the better of me with your sister, for which I'm deeply sorry; after all, you would never have avenged yourself for your spurned affections, and especially not on an innocent person!" Suddenly I was convinced of that, myself. And the darkness was split by a realization like the dazzling ray of light in Gothic paintings. "Please, couldn't your subordinate have done the same thing you did? Pretend a nonexistent contact, so, whatever, what do I know? So he could get a reward, a promotion, or maybe only praise from you! Isn't that entirely possible?"

I was quite amazed how logical it was. (Why didn't it occur to me before?) Both of them could be right, but Josef, one subjective individual, in the muddle of information and disinformation spawned by his dark world of intelligence and counterintelligence, could no longer figure things out reliably for himself! It would be enough if he admitted it, didn't insist on a ruinous assertion lacking the foundation of either proof or memory. And the Major, as he sat there before me, did in fact seem to change into the person to whom I, at one time within these walls, had resolved to join my life. Without knowing (although he surely felt it) he was deciding what path my life with Viktor would now take. If he admitted the explanation that offered itself so plainly, the specter that would lie over us unto death would disappear. God, soften his soul, let him return peace to my sweetheart, I promise You that I'll do my best to see that Viktor doesn't destroy his family's world! (How? Will I continue to bear the burden of a secret love, when I don't have the strength for it anymore?)

"Petra," he said, after what was probably a long time, "you mean more to me than you suspect. From the beginning you've been my barometer." What . . . ? "The representative of the people whom I wanted to serve in this country. The only one who measured up to Marie. Thanks to the two of you, an abstract ideal, which each time can get drowned in blood and shit, became a concrete goal. I'll always be suspect to many people, but"—he smiled with true tenderness, completely unlike yesterday's photo!—"everything I did, I thought of what you would've said about it. You never really left me. When they locked me up, I comforted myself that I'd given you proof of my honesty." I never even knew . . . "I even thought in there that you were praying for me." I didn't even remember . . . "That's how I get along to this day. You're a Christian and with Christianity you offer the people a better alternative." Don't keep me in suspense! "I want to warn you that in and of itself it's no better an alternative than mine was. Beneath your cross—like beneath my star, in its time—go both weak men and liars reincarnated as holy crusaders, where before they went as the vanguard of the working class.

"On your first visit I kept quiet out of fear that you'd suspect me of primitive revenge. But when you told me the second time that I was capable of anything, I decided to set you right where your barometer was wrong. You can think the worst of me, but in spite of the fact that deceit was my working tool, it always served the truth; I never acted against my convictions from my youth onward, and no one will make a socialist of me so long as I live. While your super-democrat Viktor was broken with the help of an ordinary trick, and became a secret collaborator with State Security, whom he set on Luna's and thus on your trail." God, no! "That's why he emigrated.

He returned in the deluded hope, resurrected last year in the press, that the evidence was destroyed in time and the witnesses vanished into thin air. He evidently believed this when I told him in the car that I knew about him. Except: if my best agent hadn't been killed in a car crash, but had cleared out to Russia, your friend would now be an obedient agent of the KGB. So he counts on the fact that it's all water under the bridge, and apparently hopes that I'll remain a gentleman at least out of the fear that you'd start to hate me. And if not, he's counting on his last trump: that his good reputation will take my bad one. I'm sorry, Petra, but I owe you this truth precisely because of my love for you."

I collected the last of my strength.

"Will you tell him this to his face?"

"Certainly. And I'll admire the strength that despair will lend him to resolutely deny it." Will this have no end?

"Give me proof!"

"My subordinate used the nickname Sluníčko—'Sun'—in his contacts with him. And Viktor Král chose—you'll be surprised—the code name Petr. Try it out."

11

Veritas vincit, truth shall prevail! But what is the truth?

One of the two of them is lying! But which one?

With the nail he'd driven into my head it was impossible to think normally. I couldn't face any further questions; we said goodbye lamely (we both behaved as if someone we knew had died) and I left his family's house forever. The women were nowhere to be seen.

At the gate I turned the wrong way and ended up at the coal derrick; it towered threateningly over me as once before. Our scramble under the collapsed rafters of the mine gallery flashed vividly before my eyes, and I shuddered, as if another breakneck crawl into a black grotto awaited me. In spite of the early spring chill, the afternoon May sun ("Sluníčko" . . .) was agreeably warm, but I was hopelessly freezing, buried in a shaft where no one would ever break through to set me free.

I wandered around the neighborhood for some time (I had no reason or desire to orient myself) before I quite unexpectedly found myself in the countryside, if that's what you could call the monotonous flatness that was evidently waiting to be swallowed up by the city: thickly overgrown plots with low sheds and random dump sites ran right up to the fields, while pylons and high-voltage wires crisscrossed the horizon and sky. I was momentarily in no condition to see anyone, least of all V.D.; at random I set off down a path through the fields and tried to put my thoughts in order.

Most of all I longed to crawl under my quilt with some pills and not wake up until at least nine tomorrow morning, so I could resurrect my soul straightaway at Mass. Except at the moment it was too risky to return; I couldn't be sure I'd get home before Viktor arrived, and he might come early. Undoubtedly he'd wait outside for a long time before deciding that my task had delayed me and that I'd get in touch with him on my own. To meet with him before I'd figured out how to extract this nail would mean deliberately plunging him into despair again.

The obduracy with which the Major insisted on his accusation and supported it each time with new shocking details was deadly. I had always subscribed to the ancient truth that besides deceiving, flattering, convincing, and breaking a man, the devil can simply wear him down, too. (To quote Dad, who after the February 1948 putsch found an application to the Communist Party placed on his desk every morning in the teachers' office, and immediately stuffed it in his bag; after a month he signed it, crushed, but in the end he was lucky; as punishment he wasn't accepted.) Although, nail or no nail, I still knew in my heart of hearts who was lying here and why, my faith in the victory of truth also seemed to be failing.

My inability to welcome him as usual and promptly dump the newest crop of rumors on him (because I was afraid of his reaction, and my reaction to it!) warned me that the case had entered a new stage. Although nothing had changed in our relationship's unshakableness and its feeling of destiny, suddenly it had a different effect on me: instead of love, it produced only nervousness and tension. (The devil hasn't confused me; instead he's poisoned me with weariness as I try in vain to trap him in a lie.)

But what to do now, to break out of the devil's circle? Time wound itself into a noose. Today the unpostponable nature of my actions would excuse me; tomorrow I could pretend family business, but a meeting with Viktor was unavoidable by Monday at the latest. By that date the morass had to be cleared away and proof of his innocence brought forth. All of my ideas, however, lost their shape as soon as I tried to formulate them.

An unnaturally large sun on the horizon was swallowed by the smog; in the east night was already falling. I hurried back, grateful to the slowly darkening city—whose ugliness was masked by the gloom—for taking me under its protection. (The primeval fear that wild beasts might attack me drowned out the fear of humans, which these days was much more appropriate.) My guilty conscience toward V.D. also drove me onward, but it let up as soon as I saw him: he sat (faithful doggie) where I had left him.

The only solution was to stretch out our time here inconspicuously; I guessed that Viktor wouldn't wait past ten, to save his precious time for a better occasion. My empty stomach spoke up powerfully; I combined business and pleasure, and invited my chauffeur to dinner. (The menu, written in chalk, intimated home-style cooking and the prices reassured me that full-fledged capitalism hadn't yet reached here.)

I had beef with tomatoes (he did, too!) and made an effort to stretch out the time. I needed, at least for a while, to clear my head of gloomy thoughts, and what other than computers should present itself? Their enthusiastic admirer, surprisingly enough, answered my questions expressionlessly and in staccato syllables, which didn't fit his profile. (Is he bored with me? In a hurry?) I couldn't help remarking on this.

"Is something wrong?"

"What . . . ?"

"All I have to do is look at you!" Something was eating at him; his discontent was impossible to overlook. "Well?"

"Well, nothing . . . I can see you're upset . . ." Once again he was getting on my nerves.

"Is psychiatry another one of your hobbies?"

"All I have to do is look at you, too!" Well, well! The boy wants to play hardball?

"We agreed on certain rules of our . . . cooperation, which you were so keen about!" Don't overdo it, Petra! "Even though I'm understandably grateful to you for your help and participation, the rules haven't changed; please try to understand! All right?"

Instead of answering he drank his soda water, which I'd ordered for him before he could manage to ask for a repulsive cola. He stared at the tablecloth and let me ask again.

"Can you understand?"

"Yes." He raised his head. "But it does make me mad."

"So, then, forget it!"

"I'm mad at myself; I think that's allowed!"

"I don't understand . . ."

"I'm mad that I wasn't able to convince you."

"Of what?"

"That I'm not only your photographer and your driver, but also your ally."

It didn't sound spiteful or hurt so much as it did like a frank assertion, accompanied by a concerned glance, which was quite adult. (Except you're still wet behind the ears, and I have to keep you away from my body; a bit late, but at least . . .)

"Listen to me." No names involved! A first name sounds too trusting, a last name too awkward. "Don't make a big deal out of this. I'll admit that I have certain worries, but it really isn't in your power to do more for me than you've done already. Put it out of your mind; in a while you'll be done with me, on Sunday take a trip somewhere with a girl"—if Gabby were home I'd talk her into it; you'd have a chance with her and she'd be lucky . . . Ugh! Her mother's lover, promiscuity right out of a French film—"and on Monday you'll find me a diligent student." He shot me a glance filled with scorn. "What's wrong?"

"Nothing." Have you hardened your heart? So much the better. It's nine, we can get out of here.

"Forget about it, I'm just tired, it's normal. Better to sleep on it, or take a weekend on it. Check, please!" Even such a down-home dinner cost a hundred crowns; where do people—and there are hordes of them here—get the money? Is poverty really only my own personal problem? "And that's for gas." Do so much as peep and I'll take a bus home, we're through as of tonight!

He didn't peep, but he did surprise me. It seemed he hadn't been idly warming the pub bench; he pulled out a package from underneath it. From the newspaper wrapping emerged a Russian army tunic, epaulettes and all.

"I was looking for something simple to keep you warm on the way back, but the flea market was cleaned out; I took what was left. You'll be a first lieutenant."

One of Gabby's squeezes had dealt in that kind of junk.

"That must have cost a bundle!"

"I'm not selling it to you, though," he said politely. (Or ironically?)

The realization that I would get even colder on the way back robbed me of any desire to play the hero. With the same lack of inhibition I hugged his waist when he pulled his long legs up alongside the machine before smoothly taking off. The cloth of our occupiers seemed like a suit of armor, but, most important, I didn't just flop in the saddle like a dead weight, resisting the law of centrifugal force; instead I leaned bravely into the curves as he did. (At one point I caught myself with the heretical thought that an accident wouldn't be the worst solution . . .)

Sooner than I'd dared hope we'd come to a halt where he'd picked me up that morning, in front of the dark store windows of my grocer and banker. V.D. held the heavy machine with the motor running in silent observation (isn't he deliberately carrying this a bit far?) of my orders. We could have made an exploratory foray down Winter Street—in my new outfit with the helmet, Viktor would never recognize me—but I was ashamed to spy on him. It was much easier to ask V.D. again.

"I'd prefer not to run into the man"—what should I call him?—"who visited that house yesterday and left immediately." He nodded; must have a photographic memory. "He drives a white car, Japanese, big round taillights." Why the high drama? He saw him here, after all! "He's probably parked so he can see the door to the building. Could you take a peek?"

He nodded, waited for me to dismount, and took off, slowly turning the corner, and in the moment after his departure a silence descended. I stepped back into the shadow of the building's double doors, and the sour smell that assailed my nose belonged more to my memories than to the present: I press myself into the corners against the door posts, where the rays of the streetlamp don't reach, to secretly sip a bit of creamily foamy beer from my father's jug. Why do I get so upset at Gábina, anyway, for rolling one joint, when I myself didn't turn into an alcoholic, despite the fact that (at ten!) I was sucking it down so diligently that on the way up the stairs my little legs would (pleasantly) give out under me . . .

The scent wafting from the passageway (or was it only encoded in my nostrils?) awakened in me after almost thirty years the excitement of those first escapes from the world of school, assignments, and chores into a short but intense beguilement where I was visited exclusively by sweet fantasies. (Could it have been in this very spot that the urge to capture life's evanescence in words first hit me? Through beer to poetry . . .)

The truth, of course, is that betrayal saved me from the demon alcohol. Jaroušek Landsman, a year younger than me (my first young buck!) and from the same building, was also sent off regularly to the pub with the family jug; soon we were both sipping on the sly and later hugging each other all over (an expression from my diary) in the alcove. Until, predictably, the custodian from across the street called the Landsmans (most likely Communists, since they had a telephone). Fortunately we were only burying our noses in the foam when the doors of the building flew open. Jaroušek was issued a couple of slaps; his father escorted me ignominiously (by the ear!) home ("Comrades, your daughter is teaching my son to chug beer!"), where I was issued a rare (and moderate) licking and was (woe!) forbidden to get the beer.

However: the time for games and unripe raspberries (to quote Cyrano) was past, and all the little Jarouseks had long since moved away. Even the custodians, not long ago assailed as the extended ears of the regime, were now hailed as the most effective defense against rising crime rates; and I hid myself in the alcove of memory to escape, if only for a while, being shoved down the meat grinder whose gears ground merrily onward. V.D. scared me when, with the motor off, he rolled down the gently sloping street from the other end.

"No one anywhere," he announced tersely.

"Well, thanks." I gave him back his helmet.

"It was nothing." I put out my hand.

"See you Monday in class." I won't be coming anymore!

"I won't be there anymore. I got a friend to replace me."

He slung my helmet by the buttoned strap over his forearm and moved for the starter.

"I hope you're not offended?" That's all I need.

"My father is what he is, but he gave me a few good pieces of advice. Like: Don't force yourself on someone who doesn't want you."

"Who said you were forcing me into anything?" Am I supposed to beg him? "You offered me your help."

"And instead of helping I'm playing 'Go here—don't know where; look for someone—don't know who.' It never occurred to you in your wildest dreams to try asking me for advice, just as an outsider with a fresh perspective." He just won't let up! "So, if it's all right with you, I'd rather stop this altogether."

"As you like!"

Beside myself with rage, I spun on my heel and marched off toward the corner. If he had an ounce of decency he'd immediately ride up and apologize for his unheard-of arrogance! I turned left, and nothing. And as I counted off the sixty remaining steps unconsciously out of habit, my mind took an unexpected turn; it informed me that he was in the right and I was the rude and silly one. (Not grass—an ass has a pen!)

If I needed something as badly as oxygen, then it was an intelligent being to whom I could recount this cheesy detective story (just as Vanesa Králová did with the story of her father) so I could find out how it struck a disinterested party. A brain whose heart wasn't pumping favors toward one party or disgust for the other might uncover connections and explanations that I simply wasn't capable of seeing anymore. (A fresh perspective . . .)

I heard him start the engine (finally!) and slowed down, so I wouldn't have to wait for him awkwardly in front of the house; I dragged my feet and disguised it by looking for my keys in my bag. (Ha! There's a way for him to save face as well: I'm still absentmindedly wearing his uniform!) The sound of the motor said the machine was turning around. Then it quickly faded into the distance. I was stuck in the mess alone.

❄ ❄ ❄

I woke up the way I had fallen asleep: in tears. The night before, when I'd more or less calmed down, unplugged the telephone, and swallowed some pills, I'd decided before going to bed to finish the task I'd left off yesterday. All I had to do was get up on the little table standing by the credenza and open the top doors. After fumbling futilely amidst boxes, crates, and packages with various kinds of junk, I took everything out piece by piece and put it on the floor and the table. The silverware (a dozen knives, forks, tablespoons, and teaspoons), however, was missing, as was its case.

An hour's search conducted in Gábina's room, too (after my parents' death, when the government had divided the oversized apartment, we'd relocated the better pieces of furniture, even into the child's room), brought a shattering realization: a great number of valuable things had vanished. The criminal must have found over time that I was afflicted by blindness, and so helped herself to the things on the shelves as well (a low, oblong Meissen vase that I'd often used for meadow saffrons illicitly picked with my lovely little daughter); with this discovery I finally burst into tears over the crowning fiasco of my life: I had raised a creature so averse to work and so devoid of moral principles that she robbed her own mother!

I awoke on a soaking-wet pillow and kept crying miserably, although now only inside (my tear ducts were salty, but dry). When I pulled myself together and was able to stand up (my coccyx and back were hellishly sore from the motorcycle), I first of all put the nighttime havoc back into order while nostalgically drinking the various juices my one and only supporter had brought me. I covered my ill-treated face with makeup (why should I look like a wreck in Jesus' eyes?) and hurried off to Mass. The only thing that could console me was God's word, and I couldn't expect help until I met with a priest. I resolved to overcome my reflexive dislike of his mannerisms with deep humility. (I can't choose a priest like a barber!)

To avoid noticing the theatricality of his speech, I concentrated so hard on the content of each word that I soon lost track of the meanings of the sentences. I was completely distracted by the relentless gaze of one of the men standing nearby. When I indignantly shot him a withering glance, he greeted me with a deep bow and immediately turned his attention to the preacher. For some time I could only think: who is that? Until I gasped in horror: the Party poet! (What was that stalwart Communist looking for here?)

I had at one time admired his early work. He came from Moravia and in the sixties wrote wonderful poems on the tragic Catholic poets of the fifties sustained by their poetics. At the beginning of the seventies he suddenly belonged (a shock for me!) to the founders of the writers' union, which arrogantly ignored dozens of newly banned authors. Alongside his (nauseating) political propaganda he wrote lyrical poetry that as time went on got more and more sanitized.

He had shown up three years ago in a "poets' " café, where from time to time I would sound out whether my efforts withstood comparison with the work of more established bards. It was obvious what interested him about me (always the same), but I was fired by the chance to tell him without kid gloves what I thought of his poetry, and also of his betrayal. He was evidently hearing this for the first time and reacted unexpectedly: as the level of guilt rose, he fell into the depths of a flagellant's self-torment ("Be abysmally frank with me; I need it!") and I spared him nothing. We drank two more bottles in some bar (that's where my fall began), where he burst into tears and began to recite verses for me that he'd written only for himself.

I don't know what I would have thought of them if I hadn't been tipsy, but they rang with the honest despair of a person who, while too cowardly and selfish to oppose the emperor, was still enough of a Christian (he asserted that it was only fear that stopped his parents from having him christened) not to have completely lost faith in God. Most of all I felt a proud satisfaction at having set him on the path to repentance. I was so intent on this task that when they threw us out—we were the last customers there—I obligingly left with him (with the drunken intention of experiencing some sort of cleansing Te Deum together). Then all of a sudden I was at a hotel.

Too exhausted to take off into the night on my own (where I might have met with other afflictions), I looked on obtusely as he shoved the night watchman a crumpled bill (later it hit me: he was a regular here) and received another bottle along with the key. I can't remember any more than that (although I can imagine), because I'd rather not. (Whenever that memory rears its head, I drive it off with a half-audible *Ugh!*) Of course his Party odes continued to be published. Only once did I read—in our own paper, of all places—some verses of his that described me in embarrassing detail, and in horror I thanked the heavens that he didn't know my full name.

This time, too, my quiet *Ugh!* helped (if I'd been near the entrance I could have defended myself with some holy water), and soon I managed to fully enter into the readings and prayers. By the end of the Mass I had forgotten about him, although he had not forgotten me. He caught me at the sacristy, where I was waiting for the priest —no less affected in the civilian voice with which he begged for my patience—to change vestments. The poet of the old regime had lost so much weight he was nearly transparent (instead it was yesterday's banned poets who were fattening themselves in the upper reaches of government), and hailed me this time in almost a whisper.

"Excuse me . . . aren't you Mrs. Petra?" At least a semblance of formality.

"Yes . . ." No scenes in the House of the Lord, please!

"It must be fate that we're meeting here, and today of all days. After all, it's thanks to you that I'm here."

"Excuse me?"

"Do you remember that night when we . . ." I dropped my misplaced politeness.

"I'd rather not remember it, actually." Maybe I should come back some other time? "And I'd rather you didn't, either." No, the priest is waiting for me already!

"Don't look at it that way! It was you who shook my false security, moreover at a time when people were afraid of me instead. You forced me to return to my own Christian roots."

The praise of my virtues (he was, in the end, a babbling drunkard) grated on me with its servile tone. (He eats humble pie as if it were a Communion wafer!)

"From what I've read by you since then, I don't think it was very effective."

"You mustn't think that! That evening was a turning point for me!" He hung on me imploringly as if my opinion were somehow decisive. "That's why I'm here today, it's the truth!"

"Would you be here if there hadn't been a revolution?"

"I don't know. I can't prove it . . ." At least he admits it. "But I cut my ties with Communism in the most definitive way possible!"

"You gave up your membership card?" These days that was child's play.

"That, too. But most of all, I've been coming here more than a year now for Sunday school. And just today"—his face lit up—"I got the date for my christening. How would you like to be my godmother?"

I saw clearly the dirty beige curtain of the hotel room and almost fainted.

"That's a little rash, isn't it?"

"Don't be afraid! You can test me!"

He implored me like a desperate man before his last make-up exam, and it hit me: I'm supposed to be his fellow soldier in Christ! (He's mastered the process of acquiring favorable references.) The priest appeared and nodded at him personably; evidently they knew each other. (Which of his poetry has he read: pre-regime, pro-regime, or post-regime?) At last I could say goodbye to the poet and go into the sacristy. (Out of sorts: an unfavorable omen for this important conversation.)

He nodded toward the chairs, which were supposed to be modern but were merely atrocious (traces of his taste, or his predecessor's? shame on me: I was never here!), and asked with interest, "So you know our resident poet?" Aha: he's delighted to have a bigwig in his flock!

"A little." The honest truth.

"I mean his work."

"A bit better."

"What do you think of it?" Better to get rid of him altogether!

"That it served a bad end well."

"Yes, that's what he's afraid of, too, as he said when he brought me his collections. It troubles him deeply." Come on! "Did his verses offend you?"

"Very much. At least the profitable ones did."

"Do you know the others, too?"

"A few." Please let him not ask from where . . .

"Did they convince you that he has a better side to him, too?"

"No." Since he asked, let him hear it. "I saw them as a cheap offering to God. A kind of alibi."

"Which would mean that he believed in Him."

"I think he saw God as a potential sugar daddy"—it boiled out of me—"in case he fell from grace. So now he's grabbing onto His coattails!"

"Fallen poets are sort of like fallen angels, aren't they?" Not a bad analogy. "Even they shouldn't be denied salvation, if they desire it."

"Only if the church doesn't offer too easy a refuge. How can others be saved who by the luck of the draw weren't Catholic?"

"They can become Catholic, if they receive the gift of faith."

His logic, in spite of my emotions, stymied me, because it had been mine, too, but those lightning converts simply stuck in my craw.

"Is it true faith? Isn't he looking for a new dogma? A new authority—maybe he can't imagine living without one, because he has no rules inside? And isn't he looking for—forgive the expression—new connections? Which the church offers cheapest? How can you believe a man who wakes up one morning professing what he spent years rejecting?"

"You yourself must know that today even a former leading politician of the regime can find intercessors; aren't there enough of them in the Parliament? The church doesn't intend to be an exception, yet in contrast to others, she doesn't make exceptions, and this proves her righteousness. If our old president Husák asks to be baptized and demonstrates his true repentance, he won't be refused. The sincerity of his conversion is God's to judge."

He got me, but didn't abuse it; he even immediately and unexpectedly apologized.

"I didn't mean to test you. I'm trying—with the help of my parishioners—to draw myself a picture of life here; it's not too familiar to me. Until last spring I worked in the rain forest. I left for Brazil before the Communists came, studied theology in Rio, and preached in Portuguese." So that's why . . . ! "I still have the accent and especially the gestures; my flock there mostly followed the language of my hands. Here I've been trying in vain to hold on to the pulpit, but I still wave my arms and apparently I even sing!"

When after this long digression we finally got around to the matter at hand, it took me by surprise; this morning I hadn't been in any condition to write my usual scenario for such a crucial meeting. But I'd been planning this visit for a long time, and the preceding dispute had emboldened me, so I got right to the point.

"Father, what should a woman like myself do who wishes to join the Holy Orders?"

"Are you married?" He's practical.

"Divorced. He was christened a Catholic, but he refused to have a church wedding."

"I understand. In Brazil, on the other hand, even nonbelievers got married in the church—also for the sake of their jobs." And he knows how things work. "Man is a fragile vessel. Do you have children?"

"A daughter. But my legal responsibilities end this year, and she's been independent for a long time already. Or at least she thinks so."

"I understand. The fundamental assumption is, of course, that you're a practicing Catholic. But otherwise you wouldn't have come up with an idea like this, I guess. When did you last make confession?"

"A week ago, near my office. I haven't made it to confession with you yet . . ." How awkward.

"I've only been here a short time." That's kind of him! I'll make it up! "And how else do you testify to your relationship with God?"

"I often say the rosary. And I read Scripture, when I have time . . ."

"I didn't catch your name . . ."

"Márová."

"Are you considering the veil, Mrs. Márová, so you can spend more time with Him or less time on your own problems?" A hit? A miss? Be frank, Petra!

"I've been considering it since I was a child; the proof is coincidentally in my poems, too, which I started to write when I was a little girl—only for myself, of course—and which I write even today. In addition to that, the orders have started functioning again and my worldly life has ceased to satisfy me."

"Is it for emotional reasons?"

"Not for reasons of love; as far as that goes I've been happy." Say it often enough and you'll believe it. "Since the changes—which I'd always firmly believed in—began, I've expected a return to spirituality and, most of all, an end to the lying. I dread wasting more years in ephemeral arguments and facing superficiality and new deceptions as I grow old. I long to be with Jesus Christ already in this world." Yes, that's it exactly!

"Do you have an example to follow?"

"The blessed Edith Stein."

"So, a Carmelite. With a noteworthy fate. Husserl's assistant, who converted from Judaism and still didn't escape Auschwitz. What drew you to her?"

"I take caution from her observation that being satisfied with yourself as a diligently observant Catholic who votes for the right party is a long way from deciding to lead your whole life as God wills it in childlike simplicity. And I'm chastened by her revelation that the Virgin Mary is the fundamental example of motherhood, and that every mother should transfer the entire richness of her soul to her child like Mary did. In that respect I fall short."

"I see one similarity. Stein entered the order at approximately your age, in the prime of life. It's generally said to be the most difficult sort of transition; when a person is at the peak of his physical strength and has a well-established routine, the first is hard to rein in and the second isn't easy to change. Have you decided firmly on the Carmelites?"

"I feel drawn to them . . ."

"I'll find out for you within a week whom you can consult with for advice. I'd still definitely urge you not to hurry into the novitiate; a woman like you"—What does he mean by that?—"should examine herself carefully to make sure she's not violating her own nature. After all, you can serve Christ in manifold ways. I experienced over there, too"—he nodded his head toward that distant continent—"how badly a believer can hurt himself if he sets his sights insurmountably high."

"What did you mean by 'a woman like you'?"

Just as his mannerisms stopped bothering me (sometimes it's enough just to know the reason), his eyes began to disturb me (they belonged more to a man than to a pastor).

"I don't know you and I'm afraid of superficial judgments, but your severe opinions at the beginning of this consultation testify more clearly to an engagement in civic life than to a need for spirituality." He doesn't pull punches! "Contemplation has to come out of a bipolar desire of the soul and the body. If the soul promises to help discipline the body, it is committing an act of violence. I don't doubt the sincerity of your desire to give yourself to Christ, but Jesus, I'm sure you'll agree with me, isn't an emergency bridegroom."

All the way home I felt ashamed that it took a priest from the primeval forest to show me something so blatantly self-evident (an admirer of Edith Stein should have seen such a humiliation coming). I had appropriated for myself, as the last righteous woman, my privileged right to the cross—as against the right of a sinner, who espied in it his last salvation—and at the same time I had exposed my journey to Christ as a transparent attempt to flee my own responsibilities.

What did my faith amount to, then, when I had never been able to sacrifice anything more for it than the pious intentions I harped on in the rosary? I hadn't delved deeply enough into myself for them to effectively show themselves, not patience or generosity or true self-sacrifice, not to mention the will to self-denial. My Christianity asserted itself and exhausted itself in my ability for self-reflection, but not even in the strongest flash of recognition had I achieved anything more than the Party poet had that long-ago night: to cry over my own weaknesses and comfortably continue to give in to them.

Before I got home, I also realized, however, that in the end even this painful scene had served its purpose. I was imbued with resolution: if I want to attain Christ's kingdom someday (and I do so badly!), all that remains is for me to put my hopelessly tangled life on earth into order straightaway. My first goal was to take Evil by the horns the next day. I had to subordinate everything else to this end: even my dismal failure as a mother and my womanly pride.

I could only manage this task (if at all) with an assistant. My solitude knew only two of them. I could ask the lifeguard Jarek, who had never stopped reminding me of his existence; but how to put the genie back in the bottle later on? So I contritely dialed V.D.'s number, and it hardly rang once when he picked up.

"It's me." Should I use his uniform as an excuse? No! "I want to apologize to you." Better to get it off my chest right away. "I didn't want to drag you into my private affairs, and I didn't realize that I was degrading you to the level of a servant. Will you forgive me?" Don't make me beg!

"Sure . . . I would have apologized first, but I wasn't sure you'd still want to talk to me . . ."

"I'd like to do just that. I'll tell you the whole story; maybe you'll actually catch what I've missed."

"And where?" I'm through with pubs, there are at most a couple of lollipops in the house and there's nothing open today!

"Why not here; that way we can have some peace and quiet."

"I'm on my way." Did he hang up so quickly so I wouldn't change my mind?

After twelve days of unrelenting crises, I saw a ray of hope that from rock bottom, where I had lain at midnight (there was no way to sink any lower), I was beginning little by little to rise upward. Except before I could manage to savor this hope, my stomach heaved (lucky I haven't eaten anything yet today!) so unexpectedly that I didn't make it to the toilet. (The fourth time since Thursday!) I was horrified (stomach cancer?) but when I could breathe and think again, I finally found the time to pull out my calendar. Then I saw black.

My period should have started last Wednesday!

Judging by its regularity, it was clear that I was in a family way.

And my hermetic existence, which since last time had been marred only once, precluded any doubt as to whom I could thank for this blessing.

❄ ❄ ❄

When I regained enough control to dial his number again, a gruff voice answered and I literally shook with the thought that I would be punished with the descendant of a newt. The choices were: not to reveal it, even to the lucky father (gallows humor!), or to let fate take its course.

Choosing the second was an expression of my faith (even though I dared not ask the heavens . . .) that my lateness and indisposition were due to a craziness in the last few days unlike anything I had known since Viktor left me long ago. I forced myself to put off worrying about it until Wednesday, the first time I could get to the doctor's, and to examine my own situation through a special lens emphasizing its bizarreness. (If it were someone else's story, maybe I'd be amused . . .)

Without any idea what an original role he was playing, V.D. had dressed—uncharacteristically for him—in cotton (white pants, white shirt, white blazer, even a white bow tie!), which crowned the absurdity of it: he looked almost like a bridegroom. The first shock, which depressed me the most, was that the potential father (don't wish it on yourself!) was just a tot himself, who undoubtedly understands computers (and thus is also something of a freak) but otherwise has no notion of what to do with his hands and legs. (Jesus Christ, if you join the genetic material of a teenybopper and an old granny, what will it spawn?) His cultivated appearance reassured me a tad.

Of course I hadn't hit on the preposterous idea of telling him about it. Before the examination it wasn't an option, and if this madness did in fact . . . (don't even finish the thought!) a fundamental question would arise: should he even find out about it at all? I could figure how my little world would be shattered by the mere fact that my belly was growing. My imagination failed me, however, when I tried to imagine the reaction when I announced who had bestowed this on me (and hardly by force). It seemed to me that the most socially responsible thing even for that poor little . . . (don't say it!) would be to stay a single mother.

The whole harebrained situation was marked by one notable surprise: even knowing all the possible and impossible turbulences inside me didn't engender as much panic or depression as that which issued endlessly from the case of *Beneš vs. Král*. If this idea had coalesced amidst utter chaos, it couldn't be an accident! And it wouldn't occur to me even in my wildest dreams that I could or would want to reject my destiny!

I ushered him into the uncomfortable kitchen again (why, though? to be as far as possible from the bed? ha ha, too late for that) and forcefully suppressed all thoughts not connected with my tale. His uncharacteristically serious—yes, even adult—behavior obviously reflected the tension of our newly changed relations, as they appeared to him in the aftermath of his rebellion yesterday and my apology today.

"Václav . . . can I call you by your first name?" Immediately I used the formal "you," to set the limits of familiarity. "It wasn't mistrust that kept me from explaining things more thoroughly so much as it was my own sheepishness. It's about two men who . . . were very close to me." Were? Has Viktor died or something? Cards on the table, let him know I'm not available! "One of them still is. Even now I'm going to leave out the personal details, because it might influence you. I need your impartiality, a factual approach to the problem. I'll tell you the sequence of events without commentary—which is what I'd like to hear from you, all right?"

"Yes." With the bow tie he'd stopped saying "Sure."

At that I lit a cigarette and in the following fifteen minutes attempted the impossible: to lay out the history of the past twelve days for him and at the same time of the last twenty years, so he would know everything essential for forming an opinion, and yet nothing that would betray to him the true state (the thirteenth chamber) of my private life. In the course of it I took great pains not to emphasize either revulsion for one of them or sympathy for the other.

I soon couldn't help noticing how the simple fact that I wasn't torturing myself internally, but was trying to name the events out loud, stripped them of their mysteriousness and me of my trauma.

My meetings with Viktor, Vanesa, and the Major marched past me in my own descriptions, as if on a stage; suddenly I was a spectator capable of noticing what had escaped me as a participating character too preoccupied with herself. This remove created an interesting change in perspective, and my curiosity about this intent listener's conclusions grew. I had barely finished my account with both scenes from the day before (it pained me to skip over my farewell with Viktor and our agreement to meet that evening) when he asked me a question off the bat.

"Will you provide me with one more piece of information?"

"What kind . . . ?"

"Unfortunately it's personal. But without it there's no point."

"Go ahead . . ." I don't have to answer.

"The relationship this Canadian has with you"—I hadn't yet revealed his name and "Canadian" rolled more easily off my tongue; it didn't remind me of the real person—"is his primary one. So he says."

"Yes." And I know it!

"Does his wife have any idea?"

"No." And that should be enough.

"So why do you talk about him as if he's some crusader for truth?" What does he want . . . "He must be lying to her up and down. So he knows how."

"Those are two completely different . . ."

"How?" He cut me off! "A lie is a lie. Either you're lying or you're not."

"Now, wait a second; for instance, when you lie to someone who's seriously ill, so he won't suffer needlessly . . ."

"Yes, I know something about that." What could you! "But his wife isn't seriously ill. He's lying to her because he apparently doesn't have the strength to tell her the truth. And he's deceiving you the same way."

"What do you mean?"

"When he says you're number one for him. He'd have to give preference to you."

"He has a small child!" And I acknowledge that!

"You asked me for a factual approach, that's what I'm trying for. I'm not judging this gentleman." That smacks of a Viktorism. "I'm just stating that he knows how to lie thoroughly and believably; otherwise she wouldn't place her trust in you, true?"

"Then I'm as much of a liar as he is, if I accept that!" Deny it, please, if only out of decency . . .

Instead he shrugged perplexedly. I had to shake this accusation.

"Given the situation, it isn't advisable to provoke uncontrollable reactions until the problem is satisfactorily solved."

"And why doesn't he solve it immediately? He's the only one who can and must put his people's life in order." Where does he get all this wisdom from? "Your puzzle doesn't look so mysterious from a distance. The Major's lie seems counterproductive to me, like a badly thrown boomerang. While your friend has every reason to lie." He's like a mule!

"The accusation's been refuted by a witness, the case is officially closed, what should he be afraid of?"

"You, of course. I've only known you for a short time, but I know you wouldn't cover for him. You'd try to convince him that he has to bear the consequences of his failure, wouldn't you? Except that would be the end of his career. And if he decided in favor of his job, he'd lose you." Which is what you're after, you impartial observer! "If you think I'm undermining him for selfish reasons, you've got me wrong again: I'd take his side if I were serving my own interests; at least you'd be grateful to me for it." An unkind cut.

"That's certainly not what I want . . . but you have to admit that these are still only hypotheses. You still know very little—don't take offense—about relationships; I claim that falsehood plays the same role in them as in one's public life." Can I claim that? "And so far nothing rules out the possibility that the Major thought up his saga to get revenge. What I'm looking for is an unshakable proof that one of them is toying with me. You concentrated on the Canadian; I don't want to take his side"—And can I still at all?—"but the other belonged to a totalitarian power until recently. Only he insists it was a scam, proves it with his signature on Charter 77, and then does time for it. Except something there doesn't sit right with me!"

"What?"

I laid out my suspicions for him and was frightened by how little substance they had, once spoken. V.D. was surprisingly fascinated.

"You have the delivery slips?"

"One moment!"

I stubbed out my cigarette (how many does that make?) in the overflowing ashtray and froze: how can I let myself smoke that much when it's possible that . . . ? I swept the bundle of cigarettes and matches off of the table (could it occur to him why? no!), extricated a hidden key, and went to my room to open the single locked drawer in the apartment. (I never would have dreamed that someday I'd need to lock everything away from my own daughter.) Fortunately the slips were still there in my diary from 1988–89.

"Hmm . . ." V.D. studied the date and stamp. "And was it always the same flower shop?"

"Yes. It's near his apartment."

"That would clinch it! I'll go by there first thing tomorrow morning; you call that sculptor, in case he's found anything out. And I'll call your friend." He misread my fear. "He doesn't know me!"

"But why . . . ?" Goosebumps.

He explained it. His proposal had a certain logic to it, except in spite of it everything in me protested. (If I agree, I'm practically announcing my lack of faith in Viktor!)

"I don't like it . . ." But if I don't, I'll never get rid of my doubts!

"Do you have a better idea? If Mr. Major made it up, then your friend will tell me I have the wrong number; how would you react? And it'll be evidence in his favor!" Can't argue with that. "So, should I . . . ?"

I was dying for a cigarette, but my will prevailed (or more likely my superstitious hope that with this belated act of self-denial I'll set something right?) and mainly: I knew that no delay would rescue me from one horrid thought.

"And what if he answers . . ."

The shock continued: he even had that angle covered. And the only possible objection to it was that it didn't set a promising trap for the tempter, only for the temptee. I mentioned this and without hesitation he expanded his plan with an ingenious addition that left nothing to improve on.

"Well?" he repeated. I tried for the last time to buy some time.

"I'd like to sleep on your proposal."

"And when should I call . . ."

The bell interrupted him. Six o'clock, Sunday evening. It had to be him. Wait! Or Gabby, who had once again found her homeland, but for a change had lost her keys. (That disgusting little criminal, my mind fumed—but once she'd been lucky enough to get back, my heart refused to risk not letting her in for the night and thus triggering a new mess for which I'd never forgive myself.) I put my finger to my mouth and employed the same method I'd used in screening her visitors: I slunk over to the peephole.

And spied the face of Vanesa Králová.

It would have been a snap to return noiselessly to the kitchen and wait it out without any signs of life until I spotted her in the ancient mirror on the window (from the stove, both my mother and I had been able to follow periscope-like whether our little girls were actually heading off to school; what a shame that in Gabby's critical years I hadn't been at the stove more often). However: she was the most appropriate ambassador to reassure Viktor that in spite of my absence yesterday nothing was going on and he needn't drop in out of fear. (Oh no! I'm intriguing against him . . .) Swiftly I indicated to my guest not to draw attention to himself, loudly slammed the kitchen door, and opened the one onto the staircase.

She was lightly dressed and carrying a small basket.

"Am I disturbing you?" Just what he says.

"Not at all, come in . . ." So she got in here, after all.

I ushered her directly into my room (fortunately it was clean) and threw myself into the role of a convalescent.

"Would you like some coffee?" No you wouldn't; it'll complicate the situation!

"No, thanks, I really just dropped in for a second."

"Is your daughter in the car?" Stupid question; still, she was surprised.

"Viktor's at home watching her; he has to write a report on his trip to Moscow. He told me that he tried to invite you over yesterday, without any luck; he called you from the office into the night." He really is laying it on a bit thick; after all, they could've seen us! "Today I tried several times myself, and then came over on my own." Maybe he wants things to blow up in his face? "I felt guilty that I might have somehow given you food poisoning."

"You needn't have worried; I got held up outside Prague. And I'm in much better shape now." Although that shape might change soon . . .

Out of habit I offered my guest a chair, and she sat down in the place where I was used to seeing her husband. (Often naked, when I'd have a smoke and he'd sip a soda in minute gulps, blowing on his face . . .) My stomach shuddered, but this time it came unambiguously from my soul, which was fed up with deceptions. It was high time for them to come to an end.

At that moment, on Sunday the twelfth of May, nineteen ninety-one, at seven minutes after six p.m. (the hands of the alarm clock behind her head carved themselves into my brain), I decided irrefutably that I would break up once again and for good with Viktor Král if he couldn't put our life, the life of his people, into order. (To quote the young fellow sitting quiet as a mouse in the kitchen.) For the moment I had to continue the deception. (For the last time!)

"I hope you're not upset, Petra, that I keep disturbing your privacy, but I really do like you; I'm not the least surprised that Vic loved you so much." This is all I need! "And, I mean, he still does: no! I'm not saying that out of jealousy, but as much as I was afraid of you before, now you seem—inasmuch as I know you—to be the fulfillment of my oldest dream: I always longed to have a sister." Oh, please! "Not a brother! A sister, who I could talk about everything with. You're the first person of the female gender"—she smiled almost affectionately—"whom I trust implicitly; I could tell you absolutely everything. I can imagine that you were hardly expecting a Slovak Jew from Canada, who on top of everything else is so much younger, to make a friend of you"—If you only knew what I'm expecting!—"but I'd be glad if you'd occasionally put up with having me around." Except unfortunately you can't be around!

"I'm starting to blush . . ." Nothing cleverer occurred to me.

"I'll stop now; I only wanted you to know that you're dear to both of us." No longer . . . "And that I'd be happy if you'd call me up yourself sometime or even come to visit us." No! Nevermore!

"I'm having problems with my daughter; I'm trying to save my time for her . . ."

"I absolutely don't want to pressure you! And I'll be on my way . . ." She rose, but then sat back down in Viktor's chair. "One more second, I still owe you the end of my father's adventure." Now? "It's short and important.

"After the television program we flew to Europe together; my father advised Simon Wiesenthal in Vienna we were coming, so he could gloat with him over the scalp of Ján Bartolomej Kolodaj. A delightful old man welcomed us; he reminded me more of a jolly grandfather, definitely not the hunter of war criminals who even tracked down Eichmann. My father's videocassette wouldn't work in a European VCR, so he telephoned over to the Canadian embassy, where they had the right kind of machine; everyone bent over backward for our companion. They gave us whiskey there, sat us down in leather armchairs, the film began, and soon Mr. Wiesenthal began to snort approvingly, clapped my father on the back and praised him, until . . . it came to the closing scene. He fell motionless and silent, his eyes glued to the screen. When my father delivered his stirring pronouncement—I'm a Gurfajn from the Jewish street, and the last of that name, since you locked up, starved, and packed my whole family into a cattle car like dumb brutes and sent them off to the gas chambers—I saw Mr. Wiesenthal, although he must have already lived through all of this many times before, sitting quietly as tears rolled down his face. Then Kolodaj started to babble, press himself on my father, and finally even pump his right hand and call out to the camera, roll it, roll it!—when a wail echoed forth. At first I thought that it was still that lunatic Kolodaj, but it was Simon Wiesenthal; he shot out of his chair and shrieked at my father, '*Neiiin! Neiiin!* How can a Jew offer his hand to an enemy of his people!'

"My panicked father was struck dumb; the credits ran past, the man from the embassy turned on the lights, and we all stared in alarm at this famous old man, who was still heaping abuse on my father and shaking him like a tree. Until I got hold of myself, and how cruel it seemed to me; after all, I'd been following my father's unfairly matched struggle since I was a child! I shouted, 'Leave him alone!' And immediately Wiesenthal obeyed, he was so surprised. I heard myself keep shouting, 'My father didn't offer his hand to the enemy; out of habit he took a hand offered to him precisely because he's a human being and not an animal like they are!' Wiesenthal fixed his sad eyes on me and said in a barely audible voice, 'And that is why, little girl, the Kolodajs end up as honorable citizens, and we Jews end up in the ovens!' "

She stood up and suddenly was in a hurry.

"I'm not always this loose-lipped, Petra. I told you this story last week and today so you'd understand what your efforts prevented. There are too many *if*s and"—she finished pell-mell—"I know that there's no comparison, but I must have it in my genes! If it had turned out that Viktor had been a turncoat working for the cops, I couldn't have—and for Márka's sake, too!—even offered him my hand as long as I lived and beyond, let alone . . . That's why I'm eternally grateful that you cleared him of that false accusation. It would have tortured him to death as well."

Her uncompromising stance took my breath away. But the die was cast (for me as well), and I could only pray that he would come through this test cleansed.

And if he didn't?

What does the highest moral principle command me to do? Inform her about it or conceal it? For God's sake, why am I wishing for bad luck? Hope springs eternal!

I accompanied her to the door. On the threshold she remembered.

"Oh, I brought you something . . ." She held out the basket. "Ginger jam, my specialty."

"Thank you . . ." Like an idiot I took the basket, before her expression warned me that she was expecting it back. "One second, I'll be right back . . ."

Any normal woman would have taken it into the kitchen, except hiding in mine was my . . . (this will drive me crazy!) so I took the little glasses one by one from the wicker basket and placed them in the entry hall on the linoleum. (If she was surprised, she didn't show it; maybe she assumed it was an indigenous custom.)

When the sound of her steps placed her on the lower staircase, I went into the kitchen, turned on the light, and was truly horrified: V.D. was slumped in the chair, his head tilted back and his hands at his side, stiff as a corpse, until I finally realized that he'd fallen asleep. First I looked him over, up close and unwatched, to see how the potential father of my belated second child would look. In this all-revealing position he didn't, to my surprise, look awkward; even in his sleeping face a certain spirit was present (and it already had lines indicating the future likeness of a sharply chiseled man). Despite this helpless pose, and his comical get-up with the bow tie, he was no poor little clown (which explained for me once again why I accepted his company after the boat ride).

Once awakened he knew immediately where he was and what was going on, and sleepily apologized, saying he'd been up almost until morning putting together the next three lessons for his replacement; without objecting he allowed himself to be led off to Gabby's room, where he stood, swaying, until I made up the bed. With my assistance (he didn't pay much attention to me) he took off his shoes, shirt, and pants; there he stopped and fell once more into sleep, chastely clothed in his boxer shorts and undershirt.

When I, also worn out, had finished my shortened nightly routine and turned out the light in my room, I was overcome again by the feeling that had entered me at seven minutes after six that evening: that my sixteen years with Viktor Král had irrevocably ended, whether he was guilty or not. It was probably exhaustion (a slender hope still remained that I'd get a good night's sleep and would be the way I'd been before), but my desire to hold out my hand to Vanesa Králová next time without the thought that I was deceiving her (comical: I, not he!) intensified. So, on the same bed where he had embraced me a hundred times in the flesh and a thousand times in memory (oh, this venerable berth is a boat on which I sail up and down the river of my life!), it was his wife who drifted off to sleep with me instead . . .

At midnight my daughter roused me, with her proto-Gypsy or whatever he was looming behind her. In shock—which balanced against my sleepiness—she announced to me that they had found a strange guy in her bed, and what was the deal with him? To that she added, babbling quite hysterically (that ironic, phlegmatic kid) that she'd been worried sick when I hadn't been by the telephone yesterday as we'd agreed, and hadn't answered either that evening or this morning. She'd made Gavros (who? oh, right!) drop his business and bring her back home (apparently in the trunk again, even without her father's advice) from Germany.

I collected myself enough to send Gavros back to wherever home was at the moment, and to express to her my deep distaste for the moral vandalism that she had committed on her home. I then saw her extraordinarily pale and miserable; she swore solemnly that she hadn't sold anything, just pawned things until she'd earn enough (when hell freezes over!) to buy them back, so she wouldn't have to keep bumming money off me. I was no longer the naïf of last week; two men (actually three) had seen to it that I'd hardened considerably.

"Until you're of age I obviously won't throw you out of the house, but you're out of my life until you get a job like a normal person and buy back with your own money—do you understand me?—what you stole, there's no other word for it!"

She swore so imploringly that I almost began to believe her, and, reassured that she'd been spared the worst (the little bitch!), she became curious about why I was pulling out the folding bed, and who was sleeping in her room. At that moment it was as if a dam had burst behind which all my dreams and apprehensions, my joys and frustrations, had accumulated over the years, so that my little one wouldn't catch sight of them and take after her mother's bad example.

"His name is Václav David and he's my lover." She almost shrieked.

"Isn't he kinda young?"

"He's twenty-five and almost two meters tall." She stared at me as if I were mad.

"So you, like, want to go out with him?"

The opportunity had arrived for me to top all her previous provocations in a single blow.

"Yeah. I'm expecting a child with him. So that I'll have one again, see."

12

IF not for the circumstances it would have been a hilarious morning! Although she usually slept till noon, my daughter crawled out from under her quilt at seven-thirty, when she heard the tinkling of our cups and spoons from the kitchen. I heard the water flushing again, and caught her in time to warn her not to breathe a word about my pregnancy. She rolled her eyes in complete confusion.

"You mean, like, he doesn't know?"

"No."

"And why not?"

"Because I don't want him to."

"He's gonna see it!" Such an intelligent observation deserved an equally clever answer.

"When he sees it, then we'll see."

She'd pulled on a quite presentable T-shirt with her jeans (a change had occurred in Munich: in the slogan I LIKE HAVEL the president had been crossed out with a marker and GAVROS written in) and didn't hide the fact that the beanpole in white (even without the bow tie) impressed her. (The feeling didn't seem to be mutual, and I found myself pleased . . .) I maintained my aloofness toward her, so she wouldn't succumb to the illusion that she'd finagled her way out of the doghouse so easily.

"I have a problem," I said to him deliberately in front of her. (Does the girl have any sense of shame at all?) "I'm practically flat broke, and payday is the day after tomorrow. Besides that, I have to return three hundred to the grocer."

"No problem. I'll stop at home for money, and then we'll work it out." Gábina disappeared, one thing taken care of! "I'll make that call from home, too." What call? Oh . . . "Where will I find you this afternoon?"

"At the office. I won't be going to lunch . . ." I was overcome by doubt. "I still don't know if he deserves this. It was a violent system propped up by Russian tanks, stretching people out on the rack who otherwise would have remained decent souls their whole lives!"

"But that way you're already condemning him, Petra. I'm offering him a chance to prove his innocence; according to you he definitely will!" He's right, but . . .

Gabby returned to the kitchen and placed an unfamiliar bank note in front of me.

"What's this?"

"A hundred marks. That's eighteen hundred crowns." I didn't intend to take alms of unknown origin from my guilty daughter.

"Keep it! I was talking last night about money you'd earn honestly." My Lord, is she turning red?

"But I did! Whaddya think of me?" Is she ashamed because of him? "You think I take money from anyone just like that?" Sure: she's ashamed! "I worked my butt off making coffee for them from morning till night; they gave me two hundred, 'cept I used half to buy you those tights, see?"

"What tights?" She began to mumble.

"Youmeanyoudidn'tevennoticeyetthatIhadtoborrowsomeofyourtightsandotherstuffcauseallmyclotheswеredirty . . ."

With her other hand she put a colored shopping bag made of an artificial material on the table; she'd been hiding it behind her back. Václav David watched helplessly, as if this were a foreign-language film flickering before his eyes.

"Well, I actually hadn't had time to notice." Given what else you've ripped off around here! "But we can talk about that this evening, if by some fluke you're home."

"And where else would I be?" No! She's playing the good girl!

"What do I know. Maybe with your Havroš." She would probably have liked to tear the T-shirt off.

"Why?" Maybe so you could rape him again. "He just brought me back and turned right around, he'll be there till Sunday." What? . . . You cut short your week in Germany on my account . . . "So now I'll be home. I gotta find a job, see?" And look here: he couldn't withstand her gaze.

"What're you looking for?"

"Something part-time, you know?" They quite naturally moved to the familiar *you*. "So I could study at the same time." What?

"Sure. Like a janitor."

"Yeah. Or a watchman. Maybe an usher at the movies." This was getting on my nerves.

"You couldn't study there," I snapped.

"Why not?"

"It's dark in the theater." I rose and interrupted the chitchat. "Wash the dishes, okay? And buy butter, milk, eggs, and onions." I put my remaining money on the table, leaving myself only change for the trip.

"ButpleaseMommytakethemoneyfrommeokay!"

She pushed her hundred marks at me and I decided to be magnanimous.

"I'll borrow it until payday. Then you can use it to buy back the first of my things!"

She rolled her eyes at me, imploring me not to make a scene. Our spectator felt ill at ease and squinted at his watch. I released him.

"Don't let us keep you, Václav."

"So what'll it be?" he asked logically.

From time immemorial I've considered myself an optimist (and, what's more, a believer!) who prevents the majority of catastrophes by not even admitting their possibility, and, when they're already in motion, by confronting them with an all-out mobilization of body and soul (like at the dentist's). I convinced myself that it set up a force field that protected me and those dear to me. Since Vanesa's visit that security system had all of a sudden stopped functioning (as if someone had turned off the current).

Up till that moment I had behaved with one-hundred-percent certainty as if Viktor's version were the truth and the Major's assertion a malevolent invention. A couple of Václav David's observations had caused a rift in my firm convictions that grew proportionally with my moral and physical exhaustion. (Today for the first time I felt completely broken from Saturday's ride.) Suddenly I began to consider seriously the possibility that Beneš's accusation would be confirmed and Viktor Král would remain the King of Liars. At first this was accompanied by sympathy (acquired Tuesday on the bench under the chestnut tree as I imagined his conscience's torments); gradually even that grew dim. I was empty and burned out, incapable of feeling sorry for myself, let alone anyone else, whether it was my own daughter or my eternal love.

"Let God's will be done!"

"Excuse me?" said Václav David. I must have whispered it.

"Fate, take your course," I said to him (quoting Nezval, *Farewell with a Handkerchief*); "See you later, I'll be waiting for the news."

I let him leave normally (there was no point playing hide and seek with my neighbor any longer), and felt surprisingly lighthearted. The ball was in motion; I could only be (and of course wanted to be!) pleasantly surprised. (He's getting a chance! I exhorted myself with this alien thought.)

In the bathroom I rapidly put the final touches on my exterior, which I'd brought into a roughly presentable state before waking our houseguest. (Why the effort, when on Friday he saw you drowning in your own vomit?) During my beautification I worried for a change about the creature still hanging around the kitchen.

Why does it upset me so wildly that in a time of wide-open doors she's dropped out of school and prefers to scrub toilets? Yes, I can claim that my stint as a building custodian was only the fault of the times, but hadn't the times helped me to cover up (the way I'm hiding my blemishes now?) my evidently inherited laziness? (My father was a walking dictionary, but he barely finished teacher's college; I found his transcript . . .)

Her stealing, however, pushed the problem to a different, dangerous level, and I was left in the narrow space between a limited acceptance of her life-style and an outright rejection of it. Except: what's completely right or wrong these days? It occurred to me that much (everything?) depended on what sort of example I give her in the most difficult crisis of my own personal life. That gave me courage. I went into the kitchen to say goodbye to her (coolly). The fruit of my loins sat there lost in thought.

"C'mon," she suddenly let slip, "that was a joke, right?"

I played dumb. "What was?"

"Like, that he's your . . ." She couldn't even say it. I began my assault.

"Why do you think that? Do I seem that old to you? Or decrepit? Totally unattractive, or what?"

Her eyes traveled up and down me, until it began to seem she was seeing me for the first time as a woman instead of a mother.

"No . . ." She sounded quite appreciative.

"So, then, why do you say it's a joke?" She was floundering in confusion.

"I dunno . . . but it's, like, you're so formal to each other when you talk!"

"So? Maybe one of these days even you will understand that a set form of behavior isn't just a stupid convention, but an enrichment of the relationship, which raises it to a certain level and gives it a continuing sense of excitement. But first and foremost I hope you'll learn that being a woman doesn't end with marriage or motherhood; actually the farther you go the more interesting it is!" Which momentarily isn't the case with me . . . "That's why men, if they don't stay adolescents, in time begin to notice other endowments besides (for example) our breasts."

"Well okay, but . . . You're really, like . . . and it's his?"

"That's the way it looks at the moment."

"And . . . you wanna keep it?"

I stared at her slack-jawed. She decided that I hadn't understood, and brazenly asked a second time: "You're not gonna have an abortion?"

"Gabby! Now I'm really disappointed in you! I hoped you had at least a speck of Christian principles left. You'd just give up having a child?"

"Well, like, if . . . if I couldn't have one . . ."

"And why should you have to? Just because some little idiot didn't buy condoms? Or because on top of everything else you're too lazy to figure out when he needed to be careful?" If only I'd figured it out . . . "Ugh, Gábina, it's hard enough for me to explain to myself how you could have pawned someone else's property, but that you'd be capable of destroying a life so casually—that I'd never forgive you for!"

Her (most likely feigned) boredom was gone; I'd unexpectedly slipped beyond her grasp. For the first time since puberty she didn't have the upper hand and behaved unsurely. (Could it be respect?) And at the height of my indignation I realized that that miniature thing inside me (whose existence was as of yet not officially confirmed) was changing into a divine surety, which I would give life to (if it existed) even if I died in the process.

I took the bank note (with revulsion, but my daughter was in a vulnerable mood and good will would be rewarded!) and, saying good-bye, set off alone on the last hunt.

Steering clear of the grocer's (I'll go there once I have crowns), I bought tickets for all four legs of my trips with the change I'd collected and on the way cashed in the marks (first time ever) at a government changing office—all expressions of my conviction that only a decent person and an exemplary citizen could lead this final battle with the forces of darkness. I would have corrected my boss's impression, too, except this time he had prolonged his weekend. I could call Oldřich Luna right away.

The secretary apparently was under the impression that I was part of his harem; she connected me immediately.

"Hail Marjoram, o most feline of all my beasts." Above all it was that inane, trendy slang that set him apart from his better, former self. "I am pissed off as all hell!"

"What's happening?"

"Youth down the tubes, revolution up shit's creek, the dean still in America, and you are definitely cheating on me with someone else!"

"Olin, get a grip on yourself!"

"But I have! Since you came I can't sleep from desire; my love, let me mold you one more time and I promise I'll pour you into bronze from head to toe!"

"Big words, but it's all show, no substance; I'll bet you forgot about my request."

"Ha!" He almost broke my eardrum. "Beneš, Josef! Take it as proof that Olin keeps his word and is consumed with love for you."

"What did you find out?"

"What you told me. That Commie really did sign the Charter, and they put him away. When my buddies recently took over the Interior, they said they went looking for him so he could help them figure things out, but he wasn't interested. He retired and they don't know what he's up to now; they're too busy narking on each other, there's no time left for anyone else."

"Olin, seriously, you're a man of your word. Except I need additional information."

"Your wish is my command! The goal is worth the effort!"

"Could you find out if he actually did time?"

"What do you mean?"

"He was one of them!"

"Any of their own who deceived them got flayed alive."

"And couldn't he have gotten flayed just like . . . ?"

"Like what?"

"Like not at all. Just for show."

"Oh, I see . . . They were sure big enough pricks for that! Do you have any proof?" Václav David was checking on that slim chance even as we spoke, without much hope of success.

"No. But most importantly, Olin, I wouldn't want to hurt this person if he was in fact so courageous. You know how these rumors get around." You didn't even stop the rumor about me, and it's that very one that warns me against the deceptiveness of others!

"I know . . ." He must have remembered. "Don't worry, I have a reliable buddy there; I'll entrust it specially to him. So when are you coming? Wait a second, let me look . . . On Wednesday I'll be free at nine, that's the best time, what do you say?"

"Fine." And let's leave it at that for now! "Except I need that information today!" Arrange it; you were one of my thirteen, what else do you want?

"He'll probably be there. Where are you? Give me the number." He got it. "Ciao, love!"

He hung up, and that started my time bomb ticking. To stop torturing myself with ineffectual second-guessing, I threw myself into my work. The tension dispelled my desire to find the customary gem of the day; I corrected ads like a machine would if machines knew how (but only the poor human brain could cope with this soulless drudgery), and watched time drag on where it usually flew by.

First came the conversation I feared most. Therefore I was the best prepared for it.

"It's me," said Viktor and added as always, "am I disturbing you?"

"No."

"And I'm not keeping you?"

"Not at all . . ."

"How are you?" He seems fine. Hasn't he gotten the call yet?

"Fine."

"Hey, how come you're not at home?"

"There's an awful lot to do here."

"Is that your daughter who picked up?"

"Yes, did you talk to her?"

"No, I hung up instead, you know . . ." I know! "But on Saturday I was dying of fright; I waited there until they closed the building."

"I couldn't get away in time." I also know how to lie!

"And . . . ?"

"I'll tell you in person."

"When? I'll make the time whenever you want." So, all of a sudden . . . "Today?"

"No, I promised my daughter."

"Too bad! So, tomorrow! Listen, if she's home, we can go out; there are private hotels now where you can get dinner in the room." I know that from the classifieds. I always thought about you!

"I'd like that . . ." If I weren't a hundred years older than when you kissed my hand on Saturday . . .

"Where and when should I pick you up?"

"Call me tomorrow at this time." If you don't have other worries by then . . .

"Good. So see you. And, Petra . . ."

"Yes?"

"I love you!"

"Me, too," I managed to say.

Then for a long time I leaned on the beveled wall in front of me and swallowed my tears. Had I heard his last confession? (Petra, don't jump to conclusions; he could have been completely innocent the whole time!)

The telephone rang again at one-thirty.

"Ave Maria, ave Marjoram, it's me, your ace detective. Are we still on for Wednesday?"

"For wha . . ." Careful! "Well, it mainly depends on you." So, what's up?

"The sight of your beautiful mountain range takes precedence over everything else. At nine on Wednesday I'll pop open the bubbly and we'll make ourselves a little nirvana just like during those wonderful horrible years."

"Did you find out anything?"

"Yeah. And it's interesting. If unclear."

What he told me shouldn't have surprised me; still, my heart was pounding and I was breathing heavily. (It made sense, too: even a clever fellow can get burned if he makes a small but telling mistake!) If Václav David had been as successful, the Major would be revealed lock, stock, and barrel (and the poisonous gas of his statements would leak out through a hole in his up-till-now-impenetrable armor). As long as Viktor Král successfully passes the test he will soon undergo (now it didn't frighten me anymore), all the remaining inconsistencies will have to be added to the Major's account.

The weight on me was lifted. Immediately thereafter I realized that I was rejoicing, first and foremost, for his wife's sake. And not only because I would be spared an oppressive choice to tell or not to tell (which, given her nature, meant "to be or not to be" for their marriage). Vanesa Králová had expressed yesterday what I had unconsciously known since our first meeting, although she was my rival: that we were kindred souls. As time went on I perceived more and more clearly her absolute devotion to the people and ideas she believed in, a devotion similar to my own. We differed more substantially only in our experience (a point for me), our age (a point for her), and, most important, in that she had remained true to her values.

On Thursday, when she shamed me in her own home with her trusting openness, she had unconsciously held a mirror up to me and my affair (a far more accurate word than "relationship") with her husband. I had seen (only I had still refused to admit it) that my "second life" with Viktor was a fata morgana (most likely a two-sided one), the light of burned-out stars that travels through space, already no more than a memory without substance. We had been seeking in each other (and had appropriately prettied up) the irretrievable time of our youth together, unable (or unwilling?) to come to grips with the present.

Which didn't belong to us! Not because in the meanwhile he had acquired a wife and infant child, but because we had demonstrated our unfitness to love each other and live together in a time that ruined everything except faith and love, which proved to be the true *centrum securitatis*. (Just as Jan Hus, with his almost pathological keenness for heresy and martyrdom, had always been alien to me, so had I loved the early Protestant Jan Ámos Komenský for his guidance from the labyrinth of the world to the paradise of the heart.) Viktor and I hadn't succeeded in finding each other in times that cried out for us to do so (and made it easy); how could we manage it today?

We were faced with warmed-over porridge—at best a series of amatory veterans' evenings, at worst empty sex, changing our fateful tie slowly but surely into banal adultery (burdened with the knowledge that I had far more right to claim its unwitting victim as my astral twin than my ex-husband ever had to make such a statement about her spouse).

No, there was no escaping it. If it is the Major whose parachute doesn't open, I will relish his fall to the bottom (he won't deserve regrets!) and then our last evening as a couple will await me, when I will apologize to my loved one and explain to him why the era of Viktor–Petra has irrevocably ended and that I will never disturb his circles again . . .

At that instant the telephone rang, and out of habit I picked up the receiver quite ordinarily, as if it weren't bringing the piece of news that would decide everything.

"This is David . . ."

"Well, what happened?"

"Where can we meet?"

"Here!" And quickly, let's get it over with!

"I backed out of that course . . ."

"Sure." He's infected me. "So, where?"

"Should I come to your place?"

"I don't want my daughter mixed up in this."

"We can meet at my place . . ." The scene in the bathroom came to mind and black spots began to dance before my eyes.

"Out of the question." Silence. "I don't want to insult you, but I also don't want to risk another meeting with your . . ."

"He's in the hospital. He had an operation." Oh!

"I didn't know . . . and I've been taking up all your time!"

"I went to visit yesterday and today. I can go wherever you want."

"Where are you?"

"Um . . . at home."

"I'll come over. What's the address?" I won't be a priss!

I noted the street and number of the house where I had conceived, grabbed my things, and ran out of the building right into the path of a taxi driver who even had an uncovered meter. ("The sign of a functioning marketplace is when waiters and taxi drivers give their customers a stamped receipt," to quote Professor Viktor Král, in some other century.)

My assistant was waiting on the sidewalk with the key to the elevator, to save me a crown for the phone. As soon as I spotted him I blessed the providence that yesterday had led me to suppress my vanity and my suspicion of this stranger and take him into my confidence. (My God, I keep forgetting that I'm expecting a child with this "stranger"!) My return to the scene of the deed went smoothly; by day the household appeared in a more favorable light—it had definitely been dusted. He led me into the same room, but showed reasonable tact (or brains) in not provoking unfavorable emotions. (I had to search for the bed; in its place stood an honorable dark couch.)

"Would you like some coffee?"

"No, thanks." Only the truth! But I controlled myself. "Tell me first how your father is."

"He's dying." His announcement horrified me.

"What?"

"Yes. A tumor. But he doesn't know. That's why I only go to see him for short periods; otherwise he'd figure out how bad things are." Oh, how well I know it! What can I say? "Please, don't worry yourself over it, Petra. We got lucky at the florist's." He left Viktor till last . . . "The former manager stopped in for a coffee; she recognized Beneš from the picture. He ordered those roses there year after year." We've got him!

"In '88 and '89, too!"

"No. Twice a woman came instead of him."

"Did you show her the picture of the woman from his house?"

"She didn't recognize her. Although she did remember the hands of the woman who came, said they were one big varicose vein."

"The sister! His sister has hands like that . . . so she was covering for him!"

"What did your friend say about him?"

"Three weeks after the trial he left Bory prison near Plzeň by transport, after which, contrary to all the rules, there's no trace of him. After the revolution, though, they give him his release papers, abracadabra! At the prison in Ruzyně near Prague."

"So you were right on target! Congratulations."

"And what is it worth to me, without any proof?"

"You had hopes for his sister in Kladno."

"She began to hate me in the meanwhile, because . . . it doesn't enter into it here. Anyway, the records aren't conclusive; my acquaintance added that they'd deliberately made a mess of things." I took a deep breath. "And what about him?"

"I go back and forth when I try to evaluate the conversation; it often depends on the tone of voice . . ."

"And what . . . ?"

"Don't think I do this all the time . . ."

"What?"

He pointed to a machine I hadn't noticed before: on the small table next to the telephone was a tape recorder connected to it by a cable. He continued his explanation guiltily.

"I recorded him . . ."

"So, play it for me, then!" I momentarily lost my defenses.

He pressed a button and I heard (as if in a radio play) the number being dialed and then a ring, twice, three times, four . . . it clicked and a girlish voice announced: "Council of Ministers."

"Good afternoon," said Václav David. "May I speak with Mr. Král?"

"Which one?"

"Professor Viktor Král."

"I'll connect you."

A rasping noise and then immediately a female baritone.

"Office of the Vice-Chairman."

"Good afternoon, can I speak with Professor Viktor Král?"

"Who's calling, please?" She must have a mustache.

"Tell him it's about a family matter."

"Is it critical? He's in a meeting."

"It's very urgent."

"I'll go get him." And she must like him. "Please hold for a moment!"

The ghostly noises of the overburdened telephone lines whispered from the tape into the following silence. I looked at the tape's producer and met his serious and obviously sympathetic eyes. I anticipated the coming conversation and steeled myself. (My soul coiled up like a hedgehog . . .)

"Hello?" It was him.

"Good afternoon, is this Mr. Král?"

"Yes, who's calling?"

"I apologize for interrupting you, but I have an urgent message for Petr." What will he say?

"But my name is Viktor . . ."

"Sure. You're to pass on greetings to Petr from Mr. Sluníčko and a request to meet with him." Now is when he should hang up!

"Listen"—and I heard fear—"this must be a mistake . . ."

"No!" My partner was suddenly clipping his words brusquely. "And don't even think of hanging up, all right? Mr. Sluníčko will be expecting Petr tomorrow morning, that's Tuesday the fourteenth of May, at seven hundred hours on Petřín Hill in front of the house of mirrors and next to the tower; there's a parking lot just above there. I repeat: in front of the house of mirrors on Petřín, tomorrow morning precisely at seven."

"Please let me explain . . ." His voice sounded like death.

"You can explain it to him. I can also tell you that if you don't come, he'll visit you himself in your office at nine o'clock." Click. The caller broke the connection.

And Václav David didn't lower his eyes. They were brown; what color would his child's be? My brain tried to distract itself, to gain time. There was nothing more to plan.

The game was over. All that remained was to arrange the last scene.

How we would carry it off.

* * *

Amateurism forced us to use bizarre methods, but in Bohemia these had often prevailed over sheer might (witness the wagon barriers of the Hussites, or the way we jangled our keys at the demonstrations two Novembers ago). Václav David took me by my house for my roller skates. (He owned a pair, too). I left my absent Gábina (on the kitchen table was—surprise!—a note that she'd be back at six) a message that I'd have to put off our dinner together until I got back tomorrow. (The thought that I had up and run away might encourage her to behave more responsibly!)

Because I didn't want her to distract me and because our meeting would be so early, I myself suggested that I sleep at Václav's place; I felt confident in him. (And: there's no use crying over spilled milk . . .) I found milk, butter, and eggs in his refrigerator, too, cooked the omelets I'd planned, and after the meal deliberately turned the conversation to his father. (An act of reconciliation and mutual help.)

"Emotionally he's pretty fragile, he never got over my mother leaving him. Also, his work started to disgust him, but he couldn't find the courage to give it up. He was a weakling who dug his own grave out of despair. Do you think I should tell him what his condition is?" The urgency of the question took me by surprise.

"I don't know . . ."

"It's a sure bet he'd be terribly frightened; he's always been afraid of everything: my mother, his bosses, the Russians, but since the revolution mostly of death, day in and day out, in a total panic, and do you know why? You'll never guess: he's afraid he'll end up in hell."

"Is he a believer?"

"The exact opposite."

"Then why is he afraid?"

"He was in the Party apparatus for church matters; he coerced priests into collaborating. It was also the reason my mother gave him the boot. When his own comrades fired him last year, he almost went crazy; he probably got sick as a direct result of it. He started drinking and reading, but guess what he read? All of it was about hell, from Jaromír Erben's fairy tales to brochures from those screwy cults. 'Váša,' he'd say to me like he was out of his mind, 'hell exists; it must exist thanks to people like me.' When you . . . were last here, he'd already been in the otolaryngology ward, but he ran away that evening because they'd put a priest in his room. 'He'll put a curse on me,' he cried to me after you'd left. I took him back the next morning and had a talk with the clergyman, who said he forgave him and gave him his blessing." What a conversion! "Now he's building up my father's will to live, and I'm starting to ask if I have the right to keep his condition secret from him anymore. Maybe he'd want to do something, if he knew . . ." What would I want? I don't know yet. "Truth and falsehood aren't like light and darkness. How do you figure out what's what?"

"You're seeing how right now. I sanctioned lying up to a certain point, and where did it lead? Truth disappeared in it like grass among the weeds. I don't know how it is in the outside world, but here we got used to considering whatever served our purposes to be the truth. Except the convenience we call the 'justifiable lie' definitely ends at the sickbed, and as you yourself know, even there it's a big question mark. In every other case"—I thought of Vanesa—"it covers baser motivations and tries to add a sheen of inevitability to them. When

I jangled my keys on the Letná Fields two years ago and hundreds of thousands of people were singing, 'We have sworn to love each other!' I believed that I was ringing out the liars forever as well. God, it's depressing."

"They'll die off!" he promised me.

"You're naïve." Yes, the father of my child is a babe in arms, a greenhorn, a rookie. "They are legion! Beneš is retired, but Král is at the peak of his powers. And at thirty the lead correspondent of our honored newspaper insists the opposite of what he was preaching two years ago. But even those empty-headed numbskulls seem less dangerous to me than cultured smart-asses who undermine their young democracy with black marketeering and private auctions. The taint must already be directly in our genes." And thus in my embryo, too? "Do you have any tea?" Oh, to return to those jasmine days!

"I'll put it on . . ."

He disappeared. In my field of view sat the small machine where by some mystical process the evidence of betrayal was recorded. I ran through all four of my meetings with Viktor since two Thursdays ago: the situations (I kneel in front of him with his hands on my heart; he drives the two of us in his car; he slams the door of my apartment; he holds my hands in view of all Prague) and the words ("You're my only love"; "My stomach still turns at the thought that this guy pretended to be my friend and didn't tell me he was one of them"; "If Petra Márová decides that Viktor Král is a repulsive stool pigeon, so be it"; "Please, give me time").

No, this kid Václav could be a hundred times a young buck, but he'd seen through Viktor with only my account to help him. So far he's been completely candid and straightforward, and what's more: his whole being testifies to the existence of another sort of person than the kind that so depresses me. He was growing (despite his upbringing, it was safe to say) into an individual (while my tender care had brought forth a clod!) who lacked only what he'd get automatically: ten more years. I tried to imagine him then, and my heart stopped at the thought of what a wonderful guy he'd be. But not for me (a fifty-year-old biddy).

Still, it would be his child, and I would soon have to decide who would become the father: Václav David or Julien Sorel, my fictitious fiancé, who had supposedly traveled here even under the Bolsheviks; therefore (the circumstances, you understand!) I had met with him secretly, and only after the revolution did I dare to wear his (Viktor's . . .) expensive presents in public. The second alternative offered many advantages, especially my freedom. (Julien is either married or will die in an accident!)

The object of my concealed deliberations (which continued mercifully to distract me from far harder ones) entered with a wicker tray that was dominated by a teapot covered with a tea cozy in the shape of a woman in a Russian folk costume. When he'd set out the saucers and cups, he brought forth three cylinders made of black wood with inlaid folk designs of the same provenance. He unscrewed the caps.

"I don't know what kind of tea you like. My father graduated from the Party school in Moscow, and teas were apparently the only delicacy available there; he kept buying them in Prague, too. There's herbal tea, green tea from Armenia, and black Georgian tea pressed into a brick, smell it . . . What's wrong?" My excitement knocked me flat. "Are you feeling . . ."

"No! I'm feeling quite well, because now I think I know where the Major really was! I have to risk it!"

We worked out the supplementary plan (finally directed against the architect of evil!) immediately. Václav David continued to function as a quick and circumspect strategist.

"We can't rule out that they're working together"—this canal is bottomless!—"and have something else up their sleeves."

"Such as?"

"To wear down your nerves."

"But why?"

"Let's take the least-possible scenario; with them it's still a possibility. They need you."

"For what?"

"You're a woman who endears herself to others easily. And you work for the daily paper of a consequential party."

"But only in the classifieds."

"The classifieds have always been the instrument of espionage. You can run an information network through the classified ads." For example: *One-legged man seeks one-legged woman . . .*

"But what network?"

"The famous old StB–KGB one."

"Isn't that a bit passé? The times have changed."

"That's why the network changes, too. The octopus in Moscow hasn't moved, after all, and is obviously working toward the return of the Bolsheviks." ("Everything there smells like a putsch," to quote . . .) "Those inconspicuous Petras who aren't on anyone's list are just what they need."

"They both know me too well to think for even a minute that I'd be amenable to anything of the sort."

"They probably thought that about themselves, too. Until someone broke them. Yes, sure! If you're not mistaken, then they got to Beneš in prison, threatened him with liquidation, and in its place offered him a higher level of collaboration, common practice. And he managed to persuade himself again that this was the best way he could do battle with them and serve the true revolution." It has its logic . . .

"Let's assume they gave in to pressure. How could they pressure me?"

"By saying that you covered for them all those years." He doesn't know what he's saying anymore! "That you'd been their accomplice for a long time already."

"What a wild fantasy!"

"Even the wildest doesn't measure up to theirs. They exploit the fact that we continually underestimate them. You've crossed swords with a treacherous hydra; at least be crafty to the extent permissible!"

So I agreed to a plan by which they could both convict each other, and dialed the Major's number. Václav David turned on the tape recorder at my request, so he could subsequently help me evaluate the conversation.

"This is Beneš," he answered immediately. Before, he just used to say hello!

"It's Petra. Excuse me for disturbing you."

"I was expecting you." Self-confident.

"I used your last piece of information."

"I see . . ." Never asks. Keeps his eyes open.

"I had him invited to a meeting with your dead man." Václav's idea: if they're in cahoots, he knows and can't catch you at your own game.

"Who did the asking?" That's the first thing he's interested in?

"A colleague. He didn't know what it was about."

"Fine! Be careful you don't get yourself known as someone who was involved with that company." Is he threatening me already?

"Thanks for the advice, but I need help."

"Shoot."

He sounded as composed as always, even too much so! The picture of him falling through the air after his wife jumped to mind. Had she flown into nonexistence on purpose, in order to escape him? Or, even more frightening: had he packed her parachute himself, in order to get rid of her, and then not braked when she did? (Then I'm stepping on treacherous ice again for a change.)

"You were willing to confront him."

"And still am, even though I don't expect much from it."

"He was able to hoodwink me successfully; he'll never make it past you!"

"Good!"

"He's supposed to go to the house of mirrors in the morning."

"Where?"

"The house of mirrors, on Petřín."

"It's like something out of James Bond." Go ahead, laugh.

"It was supposed to feel that way." We'll see who laughs best. "Wacky enough so he could refuse if he wasn't Petr and didn't know a Mr. . . ."

"Enough! You don't have to say his name." Yes, he's still in it! "When?"

"At seven. You were always punctual."

"And so I remain."

"He isn't. So it's sufficient if you get there a few minutes early. You can wait behind the house of mirrors; he'll be coming downhill and won't be able to see you. I'll show myself first and at the right moment I'll call you over."

"It's getting more and more like a spy thriller, but why not? Maybe the surprise will help." And if you're working together, how will you surprise me? Fortunately I have secret reinforcements at my disposal! "Is there anything else?"

"Not at the moment."

"Too bad." What did he expect? "So, good night."

"Good night." Should I thank him? No!

Václav stopped the machine, rewound the tape, and we listened to it together. I'd never heard my own voice; now it frightened me: an unfamiliar woman was speaking with the Major in a dark, veiled manner, the kind that, with its ostentatious display of sensuality, always bothered me in other women. I furtively studied the eavesdropper's reaction; he seemed to be listening solely to the content (so he was used to the timbre of the voice). If I sound that way, I mustn't ever play it up even a little bit unless I want to remind people of a streetwalker. (Or, heavens, maybe I always have!)

He stopped at the same places. We worked out a new detailed scenario (with the possible variations). The alarm clock was set for five-thirty, so I could take a proper bath (he had also thoughtfully spruced up the bathroom). However, it was barely past nine, and I can never fall asleep before eleven. I returned to a certain (historical) evening.

"If my memory serves me correctly, last time you invited me over to hear some records. Do you only have that one you played for me?"

"No . . ."

"Would you put one on for me?"

"Sure. Take your pick, I have almost all the greats."

"When I displayed my knowledge of modern music to you, I was wrapping myself in my daughter's mantle. My parents passed on their enthusiasm for the serious music that helped them through difficult times; I never managed (and never wanted) to cross over even to jazz."

"Jazz made the world livable for me. Jazz is my love!" He's got quite a number of them!

"Isn't that what you said about computers?"

"Yes, they won out in the end; it hit me that this world needs something it can count on. Now I only play for fun."

Until now I hadn't connected the old piano in the corner with him.

"So, play me something, if it isn't too late."

"It's fine until ten. Should I tell you something about it?"

"Please, no lessons today. You know how I feel; you can't be feeling much better. Play something appropriate."

He sat down on the round stool lowered to its minimum height, raised the lid, stretched his fingers, and began to play an old-time melody that even I knew (blues for a dark-blue world) and then dove into the variations. I observed his nobly slender hands, then the variously lit windows on the other side of the wide street, offering incomprehensible fragments of actions, and finally the ceiling (we hadn't turned on the lights) on which the reflections of car lights swam like large fish.

The prelude sounded funereal, and reminded me of my first memory (everyone said it was preposterous, but I'm positive): long black banners wafting over my carriage, the hired mourners of the orchestra, and mixing into it (what a counterpoint!) the laughter of my parents. Absolutely impossible, my mother and father insisted later, for an infant to remember how we secretly celebrated Stalin's death.

They even rejected the possibility that as a four-year-old I could have noticed a new hopelessness when their hero Nikita Khrushchev, who had branded the dead man a criminal, ordered the Budapest massacre himself. They admitted, however, that marked by all this they dampened my conscious (already, at fifteen?) explosion of civic pride, when the Prague Spring of 1968 seemed to me to be the final Station of the Cross on the nation's path to freedom. After the tanks arrived, they couldn't get me off the streets for a week. (Until I saw Dubček cry on television and spent the next week in bed with a fever.)

Inside of a year our hero Dubček became a laughingstock when he took the degrading position of envoy to Turkey. Soon afterward (for the first and last time; subsequently I was always afraid of it) I got drenched by a water cannon. I saw it guaranteeing our nation's march toward eternal slavery.

So instead I fell in love (first with Christ, then with my handsome young husband, too), married, got pregnant, gave birth, found my new and fateful love, divorced, loved Viktor and ran from him so he would love me more, raised Gabriela (poorly) and wrote verses (unsuccessfully), earned myself (and my daughter) an honorable living, alone and nearly despairing, and finally even found my civic courage (choosing to vote behind a screen instead of publicly endorsing the Communist slate . . .)—but during all this I became lazy, stunted; I smoked and drank more and more voraciously. Here and there I had affairs (mostly so I wouldn't gain weight), went to confession, but still I was deteriorating spiritually and morally, until the exhilaration of the November 1989 uprising stopped my free-fall.

Without a spark of hope (they were all struck out of me by our repulsive, cowardly lethargy) I set out on the seventh day (when those couple of thousand demonstrators wouldn't keep quiet and there was still no sign of water cannons) for the Letná Fields, and there it happened to me again: amidst a million similarly damaged people I burst into sobs with the new unshakable conviction that Truth Would Truly Prevail. I thought incessantly about Gábina (she rejected politics as crap, and was home sleeping off a party) and repeated to myself like a rosary of repentance, Oh my little girl, forgive me that I haven't prepared you at all for Freedom and Love.

These three fates (T & F & L) within a year and a half had ordained me judge over the two men I'd loved most in life. Even if I couldn't convict them tomorrow morning (I only had a chance with my silly proofs if they confessed voluntarily) they'd already managed to burn each other to ashes, which were now falling from my heart.

Thus my almost forty-year life approaches its end, and as the next one begins I'm expecting a child with this boy harmonizing away for me whom I barely know (every second person—like that waiter—will take him for my son).

I gazed at the ceiling (I'd long since stopped noticing the piano) and imagined that it was a gigantic clean page in my diary where out of habit I wrote a list of my prospects:

Possibility #1. Abortion. (Out of the question: the mortal sin ne plus ultra!)

Possibility #2. Suicide. (Absolutely out of the question: mortal sin squared, a double murder!)

Possibility #3. Convent. (Bursts of laughter: Hello, I'm Márová, I want to be the bride of Christ and I happen to be carrying the seed of the Holy Spirit.)

Possibility #4. Single mother. (And free single woman, who doesn't have to suffer the laughter of simpletons and raise both a son and a husband, although: my poor Gabriela is an exemplary product of this freedom, and only her patron archangel can save her now, if he chases her out of her parasitic paradise and gets her together with a guy like Václav David . . .)

Possibility #5. So, then? (So with him, after all? Horrors . . .)

Here I spotted giant letters on the ceiling.

AND WHY NOT?

For one thing, there clearly isn't a better option, and for another, it's the hand of fate: to reaffirm that I am, and verify who I am. My past has burned away, but the life of the next millennium is stirring within me; doesn't it deserve an unhindered chance?

This outsider, this boy claims (and proves) that he loves me. Why not believe him at least as much as I did those close friends who disappointed me? Why capriciously conceal that he has a part in this growing life; why prevent him from becoming a legitimate parent, and why begrudge this child the right to be someone's?

What am I risking, anyway? That I'll be too old for him in a couple of years? And what if that isn't so? What if I can raise myself to a heightened purpose of body and soul, the kind that doesn't let people grow old, because their springs are so tightly wound? Isn't it worth a try?

And if it doesn't work? If I've overestimated myself, if I can't hold on to him? Then I'll still have a son, a generous reparation after my fiasco with Gabriela.

I'll raise him so that finally, finally he can remake the world in which he grows up in the image of my dreams. I'll certainly teach him two things: not to fear and not to lie.

Yes, I'll reveal it to Václav David, the ally whom I'll drag into battle tomorrow morning—here and now!

Only then did I notice that he'd stopped playing and was sitting (a dark silhouette) motionless at the piano.

"What's up?"

"It's past ten. Can I turn on the light?" (And he immediately politely did so.)

The light changed everything. I left the announcement until next time. He changed the sheets for me, wished me a good night, and at the door added: "I was wrong. You aren't grass. You're more like a snowflake."

"Oh . . . and why?"

"When someone gets too close to you, you melt."

❄ ❄ ❄

I was washing up in the bathroom where twelve days ago a blood-red bite had horrified me. Now I once again saw unblemished skin. (The new, unhealable wound yawned inside me.)

The plan of action looked like this: we'll take up a position far enough in advance for us to observe unobserved the arrival of the secret StB collaborator "Petr." (We expected him through the gates in the fortification wall from the upper parking lot, where he'll leave his car with the large red taillights.) It also wasn't desirable for the Major to discover my assistant ahead of time. We'll have our roller skates strapped on. At the appropriate moment I'll skate at full tilt down the path (in the Soviet jacket and a helmet, so Viktor Král will recognize me only once I'm upon him).

"It's me," I'll say, à la Viktor (if in my agitation I'm up to it), "am I disturbing you?"

No matter how he reacts, I have to make my most essential point: that I wasn't leaving him because of that long-ago moment of weakness (which instead challenged me to overcome it with love), but for the cold-blooded endless lie with which he degraded me into a run-of-the-mill concubine. "Quiet!" I'll interrupt his new sophistries (I no longer expected a confession): "You lied to me from the very first, because you squealed on Luna—and on me, too!—independent of his wife, and you convicted yourself when you told Vanesa about the raid, which like a coward I concealed from you back then so you wouldn't fear for your trip to Vienna—so you could only know about it from them!" A fact that unfortunately had just now hit me.

With that my first speech will end and I'll back up a few meters (o patron Petrus, keep me from falling!) to call over the prosecution's witness, who will be unaware what awaits him next: once he convicts his predecessor it'll be his turn. "You lied when you said you served your sentence at Bory!" He'll have to think I have a highly placed informant (the tea evidence would make him laugh) when I accuse him: "Instead of being in prison you were in Russia! Whether they hid you or kidnapped you, that lie keeps you spinning their webs, and you must have stopped believing long ago that you were still serving your noble ideals.

"The two of you," I'll say to them, if they give me time (the scenario acknowledged that they would try somehow to shut me up), "should be on exhibit in the zoo as exemplary specimens of what our whole nation is composed of. Although you pretend that you're its north and south poles, you turn on the same axis, driven by the same energy of barren selfishness. Your slogans, revolutionary and liberal, are just rags you use to dress up your poor character.

"I don't know why you decided to torture me"—I'd hurl this at the Major—"and I don't understand why you deceived me so unconscionably"—Viktor!—"but you can count on one thing: I won't permit you to darken our door any longer. You"—I'll say to the first one—"think up a good reason why you're retiring from the services of your trusting Austrians, and you"—I'll order the other one—"why, you're returning from the center of a new government to your little students in the other hemisphere, and do it now! Within a week! Or for a change I'll squeal on you!"

At that I'll wave. My second will rush down the steep park path on skates and stop for a couple of moments to shoot a barrage of pictures. I'll push aside the corners of my jacket to reveal a small tape recorder hanging between my breasts (a symbol of the fall which has brought our trio from passionate intimacy to this human Last Judgment).

"So you won't think about cheating!" I'll cry and skate off with my companion down the hill at an insane speed; the dangerous slope down from the park to Újezd Street won't allow me to notice anything for a while besides the interplay of eyes and muscles. I'll coerce some doctor into declaring me sick with something or other for a week thereafter. Then I'll pick up an advance on my paycheck, call my poor alarmed Gábina, so for once she won't worry, and leave my shattered world for wherever my eyes lead me, somewhere I've never been, and therefore where there won't be anything to remind me of anyone, so that I can come to my senses.

Landscapes from calendars flashed colorfully through my mind: Moravian Wallachia, the Low Tatras, somewhere I'll get off the train and hike until my feet give out or the darkness catches up with me. In those parts I sensed there would be a multitude of pious folk (my brothers and sisters!) who wouldn't leave me to the mercy of the night or misfortune. I'll breathe the clean mountain air, eat fresh bread, and drink still-warm milk at old oaken tables, remember the ancient scents that the false prophets of progress have eradicated in the cities.

I'll listen to God and translate his speech for my unborn child, so it accompanies him from the first days of his existence. The Lord is my shepherd, I shall not want!

It was a good plan.

Absolutely none of it came off.

When we circled the park on Václav's motorcycle, the multitude of parked cars surprised us (all with warm hoods, Václav noticed). Despite the early hour (the dew still clung to the stalks and leaves) a tumult of voices and the noise of construction welcomed us at the gate (sawing and nailing predominated). With disbelief we followed the rapid pace (unprecedented in Bohemia) of the helmeted and helmetless workers' movements around the old observation tower and the mirrored labyrinth.

It hadn't occurred to either of us that tomorrow was the opening of the centenary exhibition, which was happening for the third time at this superhuman interval (in fact, it was for the last one, in 1891, that they'd built both these attractions, which time and—most importantly—socialism had gnawed away at). The situation disconcerted me, but Václav saw an advantage in it. ("It's truly an artificial climate; in this commotion you'll feel more sure of yourself!")

We found an excellent vantage point in the bushes, where we could get a swift start down the asphalt path that led to the plateau near the house of mirrors. A sharp, low sun struggled through the still-sparse crowns of the old trees, the birds sang loudly, and the moist soil's pungent breath mingled with the heavy scent of blooming lilacs and the stench of varnish from the rejuvenated tower, a gigantic monument to Czech smallness. (What else could a one-fifth-size copy of the Parisian Eiffel Tower be?) It occurred to me that it was an appropriate backdrop for a personal catastrophe.

It was convenient to persuade myself melodramatically that I had been reprehensibly betrayed by the two men I'd loved (one above all, the other more than the rest). The real issue was my destructive influence on those closest to me, as reflected foremost in the morals of my own daughter. It shook my image of myself, whom events revealed to be the product of a vain and uncritical self-love. In almost forty years I'd succeeded at nothing; on the contrary, all my dreams and goals metamorphosed into caricatures (poet–dilettante, Christian–permanent sinner) or into their opposites (mother and lover inspiring her companions to deceptions and lies).

I realized with certainty that my pregnancy was no unlucky incident (accident), but rather the last chance to partially correct my failures: to instill in a new human being the values I'd (till now falsely) espoused, and thus preserve them for the future world. It only remained to make a rapid determination (in that hour of truth my final decision yesterday seemed yet a further show of strength) whether I'd manage it better alone or with the help of a father so much younger than myself, who could never become an equally mature partner for me (no matter how hard he tried).

He held out his watch to me.

"Could it still be tardiness?"

A quarter after seven. The question tore me from my musings and took me by surprise.

"He always ran late, but today . . . ?"

It should have evoked relief (after all, the simplest explanation was that he was innocent!) that he decided not to come (an unanticipated variant), but instead I started to fear (was I so convinced of his guilt already?) that we'd bungled the whole affair unconscionably (rank amateurs!) and deprived ourselves for good of the advantage of surprise. Because: if the Major was pulling the strings, it was entirely possible that he was lurking behind the house of mirrors together with his first victim in order to pull me into his puppet show. The same thing occurred to Václav.

"I'll head down there. Neither of them knows me; they'll think I'm a worker!"

He didn't wait for my assent; removing his skates, he left them with me and nimbly ran down the steep slope so that the shrubbery would cover him. Immediately he appeared below on the wide path and strolled toward the house of mirrors. The sweater, jeans, and sneakers lent themselves to his disguise; in spite of this he used an age-old ruse: he bent down, threw a short board over his shoulder, and disappeared with it around the right side of the building. After less than a minute he strode out from the left side, put down his burden, dusted off his palms, and sprinted up the hillside to me. I knew the report before he got there.

"No one."

Seven twenty-three. Václav strapped on his skates again and, just to be sure, circled around the upper parking lot and the adjacent areas to check whether we hadn't become observed observers. (Sprinkled sprinklers!) The situation confused us; we were both at a loss for ideas. He walked around the house of mirrors once more after eight to rule out a mix-up in the time.

In the meantime the thought seized me that at the very least one of them would certainly be waiting where I'd logically look for him, and he'd feel safe from my wiles. I shouted toward Václav as he returned: "Quick! We're going to the Major's!"

On the ride over I mustered my strength so I'd be in control of my performance even under the unfavorably changed circumstances. Václav and his camera took up their pretested position (if need be I'll get him out on the terrace!) and with my high level of adrenaline I managed to reach the top floor not even out of breath. I gave the bell a long ring, to add appropriate vigor to my entrance. When I let go of the button a dead silence reigned both in the building and in the apartment.

Annoyance grew into fury, which called for immediate retribution. I'll go get him at his employers'! (There can't be many Austrian general consuls!) I'd already turned toward the stairs when it struck me: how come his neighbor hadn't appeared during such a long alarm? I pressed her bell. The door opened instantly; her eyes betrayed her panic and were red. (She must have been weeping.)

"What do you want?"

She nearly shouted it. I posed her a counterquestion no less loudly.

"Where is he?"

"And who are you?"

"I have an important message for him."

"He left." It sounded vengeful. "Last night."

"Where for?"

"I dunno."

"And when is he coming back?"

"Can't be soon. He had suitcases with him."

"He always told you when he'd be back!"

"This time he slipped out. I didn't know till I saw him getting in a taxi."

"Where could he be going?"

"You can ask someone else."

"Who?"

"One of his bimbos." What . . . ?

"Were there so many?"

"There were more than a few of you!"

I had to defend myself. "I've known him for years . . ."

"Yeah? Then you should have known him better. I don't know what he had you for; I was for shopping, cleaning, and washing." She's crying again! "He probably has a bunch of these places; once a cop, always a cop; we'll never get rid of them, never!"

The tears trickling down her face were the last I saw of her before the closing door loomed in front of me. I returned to my waiting partner with a picture of Josef Beneš as I had never known him.

"Everyone changes," Václav said as he served me herbal tea again in his room to calm me down, "and people like him must have more lives than a cat; why are you taking it so hard?"

Because, I didn't say to him, at one time he gained my favor with a vision of my singular and abiding place in his life. My stomach rocked repeatedly at the thought of him quickly hanging an appropriate portrait from his collection on the wall next to his tragic love, Marie. (Was there ever such a person? And had she ever gone skydiving?) Another part of my consciousness protested: he couldn't have trained his sister and niece to playact, too, so that their convincing performance on Saturday would confirm how irreplaceable I was to him!

Before I'd finished my tea and gathered my strength, Václav had discovered where to find him. The Austrian consul was a native Czech and evidently a charmer; by the sound of it he would have gladly led me himself to the relative I was searching for. (Guile had temporarily become my element; I hoped that its easiness wouldn't taint me.)

The problem was that he didn't know any Josef Beneš.

"And where did you find out that he . . . ?" Václav asked me.

"Well, from him and his neighbor!" He shot me a look of infinite amazement.

It was safe to assume that the Major had had to interrupt yet another game of hide-and-seek because his real employer had ordered him to another task. With the help of Olin's friends, it was certainly possible to uncover his tracks, but I could only offer them this confused story—and nothing more that could induce the Interior (largely overburdened with its own affairs, which the media publicized daily) to take an interest.

Then I remembered the other one. Who would answer the phone: a righteous man, or one too wily to fall into such a simple trap? I was completely confused. Václav was already dialing the Council of Ministers, but twice he got a busy signal. Suddenly I longed to hear Gábina. (She must have been half-dead with worry, and I could put off finding out about Viktor for a couple of minutes.) She picked up immediately. (Was she watching the telephone, poor thing, as longingly as I had so often done?)

"Mommy! You called!"

"Are you okay?"

"What? Yeah. But some lady's been looking for you." Not a word about where the hell am I and if I'm okay; I could learn a lot from her!

"Wait, first tell me how you're doing."

"Great. She kept calling till late last night, then she left a number, said it's urgent."

"Who?"

"Some Vanesa." Oh! "Want the number?"

"I have it."

"Good. So 'bye now."

"Gabby, wait!" A saving idea. "I want to go away for a couple of days; I'd like you to come with me."

"Where?"

"To Moravia or Slovakia, I don't know yet."

"And what's there?"

"We could walk through the hills, talk with people, and mainly" —I suddenly believed this—"we'd be together. Wouldn't it be great?" Say yes!

"Yeah, that'd be fine . . . except . . ."

"What?"

"Like, I have to find a job, see?"

"Don't play games with me; I've been asking you for a year to get a job, it can probably wait a week, don't you think?"

"But, like, Gavros called, see? Said he's coming back today. Ithinkhereallymustmissmesoldon'twanttostandhimup . . ."

"Why are you so hung up on him, out of all your boys? What's so special about him?"

"Well, he's kind of . . ."

"Kind of what?"

"Different, like."

"How is he different?"

"He's so . . . relenting."

"What's that?"

"It's like the opposite of unrelenting, see?"

"Come on, you're not a savage, you finished primary school, can't you express yourself intelligently?" A peculiar neologism . . . "Do you mean he's nice or what?"

"Yeah, something like that."

"But, I mean, he . . . Okay, so it wasn't exactly a rape, but at the least he forced you to sleep with him a couple of minutes after you'd met. In a taxi, no less!"

"Well, yeah," she sighed, as if she were apologizing for some awkward trifle. "I told you already, he wanted to make an impression . . ."

"What kind, could you please tell me?" And what did he take you for?

"Like, that he's a stud. Except he's a totally decent guy and he takes it real hard that everyone thinks he's a Gypsy; they always act like he robbed them. That's why he wants to drive for these firms, see, before he gets his degree."

"He's in college?"

"Not yet, but he wants to be; he's driving while he finishes high school."

It was a useless call.

"So, forget about it."

"You're not angry, are you, Mommy?"

Should I upset the first relationship of hers that—despite its brutal beginning—has developed in a civilized fashion?

"No . . ."

"I'm really glad. Hey, how come you're not going with your guy?"

"Gabby!" I had no choice but to encode it. "Remember what I made you promise . . ." Surprisingly enough, she remembered.

"No sweat, you can count on me, cross my heart and hope to die! So 'bye, and call me, okay? So I won't worry." The world's upside-down.

I told the unsuspecting object of our conversation only that Vanesa Králová had been looking for me since yesterday. He nodded knowingly.

"Sure. She's supposed to apologize for him."

"Why?"

"He's the one playing sick, for a change."

"And what should I tell her?"

"That you'll come visit them. He'll get well quickly enough, so it won't blow up with her around."

While I dialed her number, I remembered Viktor's last glance as he walked beneath the café window. I had read in it a confession of love. Had it been more like a plea for mercy? Will I grant it to him, now that the Major's disappeared? Should he be the only one punished? Let him suggest a worthy method of repentance himself! I wanted to hang up and rethink everything; I was relieved when an unfamiliar voice answered.

"Excuse me, this isn't the Králs', is it?"

"Yes, this is the Král residence. Who's calling?" I was too ashamed to hang up.

"Márová. I was told Mrs. Králová has been trying to reach me . . ." I'll have to work things out with him, anyway.

"One moment, please."

The receiver was put down, steps receded. I shrugged in response to Václav David's querying motion and could think of nothing, nothing at all. The steps grew closer, the receiver was picked up.

"Petra!" It was unmistakably her, but strangely different. "Petra . . ."

"Yes?"

"Did you hear already?" When did she start using the familiar with me?

"What?"

"He's dead!"

13

I EXCHANGED the Russian army tunic for my own sweater. The whole way there (I barely held on to the driver at all, as if even my instinct for self-preservation had withered away) I saw Viktor's face through my half-closed eyes the way it had appeared for years whenever I woke up first. (It had a tense expression, and looked more tired than during the day: "I work hard in my dreams!") Now a wound gaped over his ear from which a thin stream of blood oozed, drawing a red spiderweb on his chalk-white face. ("I took a gun from the office safe and went to kill him . . ." No: he went to kill himself!)

Vanesa was splendidly dressed, coiffed, and made-up—beautiful in a way I'd never seen her before. She led me off to her room. (An older person was busy with the child; V.D. stayed downstairs and at some point slipped away.) Her news was far different from what I'd imagined.

"He'd finished his schedule for the day and as always called me from the office to say he was coming home. When I go back to that conversation now, two things hit me: that he asked so many questions about Márka, as if he weren't going to see her in a little while. And that instead of saying 'Bye!' in English—we never managed to get out of the habit—he said in Czech, 'Farewell.' That was how he ended: 'So I'm on my way; farewell . . .' I'll never hear him again." She recited it with the same detachment as her father's adventure. "Often he got held up as he was leaving, so I didn't worry when he was late. At a quarter after eight, just as I was getting ready to call the receptionist there, I heard the bell instead of the key in the lock. Outside there were two policemen and for a moment in my head I heard an ambulance siren wail. 'Is he wounded?' I gasped, and the older one did something unusual: he put his arm around my shoulders . . .

"According to the witnesses standing on the walkway over the highway, he was driving with his brights on—in spite of the fact that the traffic had died down and it was still light—in the passing lane. Suddenly he swerved and slammed sideways into the pillar; the head-on impact was so strong, they say, that the footbridge shook and one person fell down. The first person to stop was a veterinarian, and he couldn't find a pulse; fortunately Viktor must have been killed instantly. They told me someone had to identify him, and I was vainly calling you, as if you could have brought me back better news. I went to the coroner's and I'm not sorry I did it. Death was also merciful in that it didn't disfigure him; he looked just like when he was sleeping, he used to have an almost tenacious expression." I know! I know . . . "Anyway, because in the meantime they ruled out a heart attack or a stroke, the most likely cause of the accident was falling asleep momentarily at the wheel; the last two weeks, as you know—oh! I'm using the familiar 'you,' excuse me!—were hell on him; sleeping pills had stopped working and, what's more, he had a low tolerance for them. That's about it . . ."

I managed to put words together into coherent sentences.

"Did he write anything? I mean, did he leave a letter or . . . and please, the familiar's fine!"

She stroked my hand.

"Thanks . . . I know what you're getting at; it was my first thought, too; the slander hit him harder than all the previous wounds of his life put together. They were apparently checking into it when they took me over to his office late last night and asked me to look around at home as well. Not a piece of paper anywhere. And, after all, the case was closed, that man finally testified to it yesterday."

"Who . . . ?"

"That Beneš."

"When?"

"While I was still waiting." So, after I spoke to him! "He wanted

Viktor, and later on he also spoke with my neighbor, who stayed here with my daughter." So he already knew yesterday evening! "No, Viktor would never have taken his own life; he loved us too much for that." Yes! He loved you so much that he would scarcely have survived it if you'd refused to give him your hand. "Since yesterday I've been banging it into my head: it was just an accident, and my consolation is that I can raise his beloved Márka to be like him . . ."

"But how will you manage?" I began to worry. "Do you have enough to live on?"

"It's frightful: he took out a huge insurance policy a number of years ago; now I'm financially secure as I wouldn't have been with him until who knows when, if ever." He was afraid of them from the beginning, even there on the other side of the globe! "But Petra, you know that for me, nothing can replace the best man who ever lived . . ."

Finally we both began to cry.

I cried because it would be revealed to me only at the Last Judgment whether a cornered traitor had wreaked punishment on himself, or whether in powerless despair my sweetheart had punished me for my betrayal.

A picture that will never fade: the ice gives way beneath the horrified dog, and in shock he forgets how to swim.

And this time the only person who could save him didn't do so.

Mea culpa!

❄ ❄ ❄

I stayed with Vanesa until the funeral, mourning with her for the most wonderful of men (in doubt, silent death shrouded him in innocence). I accompanied her in the Council of Ministers' car to Pardubice and caught a glimpse (better from afar) of his mother for the first and last time. (A tall, strict, iron-willed woman; what must it have cost him to stay with me all those years against her will! My Pyrrhic victory, because I hadn't known how to appreciate it . . .) On the way back Vanesa hugged me tenaciously; she must have seen in her heart the same image that I had: his face twisting into ruin in the fire when he was cremated. The following day, however, she came out of deep Jewish mourning and with admirable practicality reorganized her life. She decided to return to Canada and apply for Viktor's position at the university.

When we said goodbye, we both cried for the second time with the foreboding that we were evidently parting forever after having barely found each other.

I was firmly resolved to carry out at least the conclusion of my plan, which had disintegrated into a tragedy without a catharsis. My last lie, to my boss, justified my unexcused absence due to the sudden demise of my fiancé Julien in Amiens; at the same time I asked him for an unpaid holiday. I added to this both the money he had lent me from my pay and an announcement that absolutely nothing connected me to the great Anthony Mára. All during my speech his Adam's apple bobbed up and down, but evidently his newfound Christian sympathy triumphed (along with the mature reasoning that in the end I would still be more useful to him than all his punctual slackers).

I obtained the necessary means for my trip by an even more radical method than my daughter had used: at the infamous flea market in the stands of the soccer stadium I got quite a good price for all the beautiful, sinful presents that Viktor had brought me from abroad since last year. As an innocent man he didn't belong to me, and I wanted least of all to attract the attention of other men.

A short visit home yielded extraordinary news: Gábina had cleaned house! I found civilized signs of another person's presence; my daughter was thus momentarily provided for. I packed a couple of easily washable things into my old backpack (before their wedding my parents had taken it on cultural—and most likely romantic?—excursions), and in my hiking boots (I hadn't worn them since I began to wait at home for Viktor's calls) took a test walk to the main train station across the Letná Fields to make sure the backpack wasn't too heavy for me.

The earliest long-distance train was an express to Košice. I bought a ticket to Banská Bystrica (a vision of mountains that had hidden a whole army of partisans during the war, not to mention one woman) and forced myself (maybe he won't be home!) to place a call from a phone booth (maybe it won't work!) to the father of my future son (which was the one thing I no longer had any doubt about). He answered.

"Hi. Am I disturbing you?"

"No . . ." I could hear how upset and on guard he was.

"And am I keeping you?" I froze: I was quoting a dead man.

"Not at all."

"How's your dad?"

"Better."

"Well, that's wonderful!"

"I told him, and he's learning how to die." Oh . . . "He's almost lost his fear."

"Václav, I want to apologize to you once more."

"For what?" He knew full well.

"Suddenly I got the strength to do it. I wasn't even capable of thanking you for your help."

"In what way did I . . ." No going back to that!

"You were a wonderful friend. I don't want to talk about the rest of it. Now or ever again."

"Yes . . ." What is there to add?

"I took a vacation from work."

"You didn't have to do that. I won't be there anymore." Don't draw it out!

"So I wish you success in college."

"Thanks." He behaved worthily; may he stay that way!

"So 'bye."

" 'Bye."

He hung up before I did and thus it was decided: reason won out; my son would be the posthumous child of Julien Sorel.

I wandered from the booth toward the train and sentimentally took in the sounds of the station hall. They transported me back to childhood when here, with this very same backpack, I had set off for my first camp. (Let's confess: the Young Communist Pioneers!) Had that been someone else or had it really been me? And if so, was there anything left in me of that brave schoolgirl (up till then a coddled only child) who at age seven set out on her own with unfamiliar people to an unknown world?

Here I realized what above all linked me with her: like then, I wasn't calling on God today for help when I was cornered (that possibility I discovered only at puberty). In fear I remained standing on the platform: had I lost my faith along with love and truth?

No!

"What wasn't my plan was God's dispensation," a rough quote from "my" Carmelite nun and example, Edith Stein; "coincidence does not exist. The life I am ordained to live has a meaningful coherence, and I can only look forward to the flash of light in which it will one day be revealed to me."

Until that time, however, I alone bear full responsibility for my life.

❄ ❄ ❄

Maybe the wild shaking of the train cars on the battered railway brought it on, but most likely they only hastened it: the splitting headache was merely an overture to pains commensurate with the lateness of my period. I had never before known such suffering, and I believed that my final hour had come. (Was it a miscarriage?)

In Brno I broke off my trip and dragged myself into a waiting room full of lost souls. Surprisingly, two ruined women grasped that I wasn't drunk but in danger of bleeding to death. From their packs they extracted cotton and surprisingly clean towels (later it dawned on me: more than likely stolen). Half-sitting, half-lying, I slumped numbly amidst the drunkards and bums, incapable of movement or speech. I don't know if I fell asleep or lost consciousness. At some point I came to and was missing my pack. I still had my purse (they would have had to cut off the arm the strap was wrapped around), but the money in it was gone (along with my Good Samaritans).

I don't have any idea how I succeeded in wandering over to the stationmaster's, or why he provided me with a replacement ticket at my word (certainly not thanks to my feminine graces; I must have looked like a corpse). I spent the return trip in a swoon and, once back in Prague, it seemed self-evident that instead of going to Bubeneč I should go to her house, where the certainty beckoned that someone would be there to pay the taxi driver and take me in.

When I'd recovered and come to an agreement with Vanesa, I settled my remaining debts (most of all with the grocer, who assured me that this trifling sum was worth more than gold to him). Gábina was all agog, but understanding (and maybe even eager to show me that she wasn't a good-for-nothing). The Greek grandorphan made a convincing impression that he'd take better care of my daughter than her mother had.

I decided not to call my last ally (what luck that I held my tongue). Instead I wrote him a poem. About a snowflake.

I sent it before my departure from the Prague airport on August 21, just as a dangerous coup attempt was foundering in Moscow. In the air I remembered the Major. Would he now learn to smoke fat cigars with his Russian tea? (His most righteous of all revolutions now languished alone in Cuba.)

I flew with my Jewish astral sister across the ocean, so that on the other side of the planet Earth I could help her raise the child of my sweetheart into a person better than either he or I had been.

Whatofit

Whatofit
what's love or hate
friend or foe

Whatofit
if I spin down
or up
where angels go

I drift
unaided
unafraid
of what's below

I am
a snowflake
and thus
I snow

This novel took shape from March 24, 1991, to May 1, 1992, in Vienna, Dachstein, Einbeck, Anacapri, Sázava, and Munich.

HARVEST IN TRANSLATION

Stanislaw Benski	*Missing Pieces*
Umberto Eco	*The Name of the Rose*
Bohumil Hrabal	*Too Loud a Solitude*
Pawel Huelle	*Who Was David Weiser?*
Danilo Kiš	*Garden, Ashes*
Pavel Kohout	*I Am Snowing: The Confessions of a Woman of Prague*
George Konrád	*A Feast in the Garden*
Amos Oz	*Fima* *In the Land of Israel* *A Perfect Peace* *To Know a Woman*
Octavio Paz	*The Other Voice: Essays on Modern Poetry*
José Saramago	*The Gospel According to Jesus Christ* *The Year of the Death of Ricardo Reis*
Luis Sepúlveda	*The Old Man Who Read Love Stories*
A. B. Yehoshua	*A Late Divorce* *The Lover* *Mr. Mani*